W9-BQL-491

LOVER ARISEN

By J. R. Ward

THE BLACK DAGGER BROTHERHOOD SERIES

Dark Lover

Lover Eternal

Lover Awakened

Lover Revealed

Lover Unbound

Lover Enshrined

The Black Dagger Brotherhood:
An Insider's Guide

Lover Avenged

Lover Mine

Lover Unleashed

Lover Reborn

Lover at Last

The King

The Shadows

The Beast

The Chosen

The Thief

The Savior

The Sinner

Lover Unveiled

Lover Arisen

THE BLACK DAGGER LEGACY SERIES

Blood Kiss

Blood Vow

Blood Fury

Blood Truth

THE BLACK DAGGER BROTHERHOOD WORLD

Dearest Ivie

Prisoner of Night

Where Winter Finds You

A Warm Heart in Winter

THE BLACK DAGGER BROTHERHOOD: PRISON CAMP

The Jackal

The Wolf

THE LAIR OF THE WOLVEN SERIES

Claimed

NOVELS OF THE FALLEN ANGELS

Covet

Crave

Envy

Rapture

Possession

Immortal

THE BOURBON KINGS SERIES

The Bourbon Kings

The Angels' Share

Devil's Cut

J.R. WARD

LOVER ARISEN

• THE BLACK DAGGER •
BROTHERHOOD SERIES

GALLERY BOOKS

New York   London   Toronto   Sydney   New Delhi

G

Gallery Books
An Imprint of Simon & Schuster, Inc.
1230 Avenue of the Americas
New York, NY 10020

First Gallery Books hardcover edition April 2022

GALLERY BOOKS and colophon are registered trademarks of Simon & Schuster, Inc.

For information about special discounts for bulk purchases, please contact Simon & Schuster Special Sales at 1-866-506-1949 or business@simonandschuster.com.

The Simon & Schuster Speakers Bureau can bring authors to your live event. For more information or to book an event, contact the Simon & Schuster Speakers Bureau at 1-866-248-3049 or visit our website at www.simonspeakers.com.

Interior design by Davina Mock-Maniscalco

Manufactured in the United States of America

10 9 8 7 6 5 4 3 2 1

Library of Congress Cataloging-in-Publication Data is available.

ISBN 978-1-9821-7999-1
ISBN 978-1-9821-8001-0 (ebook)

To the both of you,
love is all the sweeter for the struggle that is won.

GLOSSARY OF TERMS AND PROPER NOUNS

ahstrux nohtrum (n.) Private guard with license to kill who is granted his or her position by the King.

ahvenge (v.) Act of mortal retribution, carried out typically by a male loved one.

Black Dagger Brotherhood (pr. n.) Highly trained vampire warriors who protect their species against the Lessening Society. As a result of selective breeding within the race, Brothers possess immense physical and mental strength, as well as rapid healing capabilities. They are not siblings for the most part, and are inducted into the Brotherhood upon nomination by the Brothers. Aggressive, self-reliant, and secretive by nature, they are the subjects of legend and objects of reverence within the vampire world. They may be killed only by the most serious of wounds, e.g., a gunshot or stab to the heart, etc.

blood slave (n.) Male or female vampire who has been subjugated to serve the blood needs of another. The practice of keeping blood slaves has been outlawed.

the Chosen (pr. n.) Female vampires who had been bred to serve the Scribe Virgin. In the past, they were spiritually rather than temporally focused, but that changed with the ascendance of the final Primale, who freed them from the Sanctuary. With the Scribe Virgin removing herself from her role, they are completely autonomous and learning to live on earth. They do continue to meet the blood needs of unmated members of the Brotherhood, as well as Brothers who cannot feed from their *shellans* or injured fighters.

chrih (n.) Symbol of honorable death in the Old Language.

cohntehst (n.) Conflict between two males competing for the right to be a female's mate.

Dhunhd (pr. n.) Hell.

doggen (n.) Member of the servant class within the vampire world. *Doggen* have old, conservative traditions about service to their superiors, following a formal code of dress and behavior. They are able to go out during the day, but they age relatively quickly. Life expectancy is approximately five hundred years.

ehros (n.) A Chosen trained in the matter of sexual arts.

exhile dhoble (n.) The evil or cursed twin, the one born second.

the Fade (pr. n.) Non-temporal realm where the dead reunite with their loved ones and pass eternity.

First Family (pr. n.) The King and Queen of the vampires, and any children they may have.

ghardian (n.) Custodian of an individual. There are varying degrees of *ghardians*, with the most powerful being that of a *sehcluded* female.

glymera (n.) The social core of the aristocracy, roughly equivalent to Regency England's *ton*.

hellren (n.) Male vampire who has been mated to a female. Males may take more than one female as mate.

hyslop (n. or v.) Term referring to a lapse in judgment, typically resulting in the compromise of the mechanical operations of a vehicle or otherwise motorized conveyance of some kind. For example, leaving one's keys in one's car as it is parked outside the family home overnight, whereupon said vehicle is stolen.

leahdyre (n.) A person of power and influence.

leelan (adj. or n.) A term of endearment loosely translated as "dearest one."

Lessening Society (pr. n.) Order of slayers convened by the Omega for the purpose of eradicating the vampire species.

lesser (n.) De-souled human who targets vampires for extermination as a member of the Lessening Society. *Lessers* must be stabbed through the chest in order to be killed; otherwise they are ageless. They do not eat or drink and are impotent. Over time, their hair, skin, and irises lose pigmentation until they are blond, blushless, and pale-eyed. They smell like baby powder. Inducted into the society by the Omega, they retain a ceramic jar thereafter into which their heart was placed after it was removed.

lewlhen (n.) Gift.

lheage (n.) A term of respect used by a sexual submissive to refer to their dominant.

Lhenihan (pr. n.) A mythic beast renowned for its sexual prowess. In modern slang, refers to a male of preternatural size and sexual stamina.

lys (n.) Torture tool used to remove the eyes.

mahmen (n.) Mother. Used both as an identifier and a term of affection.

mhis (n.) The masking of a given physical environment; the creation of a field of illusion.

nalla (n., f.) or **nallum** (n., m.) Beloved.

needing period (n.) Female vampire's time of fertility, generally lasting for two days and accompanied by intense sexual cravings. Occurs approximately five years after a female's transition and then once a decade thereafter. All males respond to some degree if they are around a female in her need. It can be a dangerous time, with conflicts and fights breaking out between competing males, particularly if the female is not mated.

newling (n.) A virgin.

the Omega (pr. n.) Malevolent, mystical figure who has targeted the vampires for extinction out of resentment directed toward the Scribe Virgin. Exists in a non-temporal realm and has extensive powers, though not the power of creation. Eradicated.

phearsom (adj.) Term referring to the potency of a male's sexual organs. Literal translation something close to "worthy of entering a female."

Princeps (pr. n.) Highest level of the vampire aristocracy, second only to members of the First Family or the Scribe Virgin's Chosen. Must be born to the title; it may not be conferred.

pyrocant (n.) Refers to a critical weakness in an individual. The weakness can be internal, such as an addiction, or external, such as a lover.

rahlman (n.) Savior.

rythe (n.) Ritual manner of asserting honor granted by one who has offended another. If accepted, the offended chooses a weapon and strikes the offender, who presents him- or herself without defenses.

the Scribe Virgin (pr. n.) Mystical force who previously was counselor to the King as well as the keeper of vampire archives and the dispenser of privileges. Existed in a non-temporal realm and had extensive powers, but has recently stepped down and given her station to another. Capable of a single act of creation, which she expended to bring the vampires into existence.

sehclusion (n.) Status conferred by the King upon a female of the aristocracy as a result of a petition by the female's family. Places the female under the sole direction of her *ghardian*, typically the eldest male in her household. Her *ghardian* then has the legal right to determine all manner of her life, restricting at will any and all interactions she has with the world.

shellan (n.) Female vampire who has been mated to a male. Females generally do not take more than one mate due to the highly territorial nature of bonded males.

symphath (n.) Subspecies within the vampire race characterized by the ability and desire to manipulate emotions in others (for the purposes of an energy exchange), among other traits. Historically, they have been discriminated against and, during certain eras, hunted by vampires. They are near extinction.

talhman (n.) The evil side of an individual. A dark stain on the soul that requires expression if it is not properly expunged.

the Tomb (pr. n.) Sacred vault of the Black Dagger Brotherhood. Used as a ceremonial site as well as a storage facility for the jars of *lessers*. Ceremonies performed there include inductions, funerals, and disciplinary actions against Brothers. No one may enter except for members of the Brotherhood, the Scribe Virgin or her successor, or candidates for induction.

trahyner (n.) Word used between males of mutual respect and affection. Translated loosely as "beloved friend."

transition (n.) Critical moment in a vampire's life when he or she transforms into an adult. Thereafter, he or she must drink the blood of the opposite sex to survive and is unable to withstand sunlight. Occurs generally in the mid-twenties. Some vampires do not survive their transitions, males in particular. Prior to their transitions, vampires are physically weak, sexually unaware and unresponsive, and unable to dematerialize.

vampire (n.) Member of a species separate from that of *Homo sapiens*. Vampires must drink the blood of the opposite sex to survive. Human blood will keep them alive, though the strength does not last long. Following their transitions, which occur in their mid-twenties, they are unable to go out into sunlight and must feed from the vein regularly. Vampires cannot "convert" humans through a bite or transfer of blood, though they are in rare cases able to breed with the other species. Vampires can dematerialize at will, though they must be able to calm themselves and concentrate to do so and may not carry anything heavy with them. They are able to strip the memories of humans, provided such memories are short-term. Some vampires are able to read minds. Life expectancy is upward of a thousand years, or in some cases even longer.

wahlker (n.) An individual who has died and returned to the living from the Fade. They are accorded great respect and are revered for their travails.

whard (n.) Equivalent of a godfather or godmother to an individual.

PROLOGUE

Dhunhd
Four weeks, two days, three hours . . .
. . . and exactly thirteen minutes prior to the Present.

To be immortal was to never know death.

As the Omega, brother of the Scribe Virgin, master of all *lessers*, spectacular purveyor of evil upon the earth, arrived at his lair in *Dhunhd* and became corporeal, the entity reminded himself that he was immortal.

He would not die. Never, ever. No extinction for him.

Fuck the *Dhestroyer* Prophecy.

Stumbling forth, he repeated to himself over and over again that he was going to live forever, and rule in hatred and chaos for an eternity and beyond, because he was energy and energy was not just the basis of the universe, it *was* the universe. Energy did not end, not as long as there were galaxies above the earth, and suns to create light, and planets that do-si-do'd in their orbits. He was infinite, nothing more powerful than he up above on earth, or down below, here in Hell—

Where was he?

The Omega stiffly pivoted and attempted to ascertain his location amid the labyrinth of gray halls. Hadn't they been white once? Or had they been black? As his mind refused to provide him with an orienta-tion and tripped over its own recollections, he was forced to confront all he'd been refusing to see within himself. He was often lost these re-cent nights, even in the alleys of downtown Caldwell, even here in his den where he'd played and fucked and recharged for an eon. And why was he afoot? Ordinarily, he would have simply summoned himself unto where he wanted to be in this, his dominion. Ordinarily . . . he would not have been this depleted.

But he would not die, never, not ever. No extinction for him.

Fuck that prophecy—

Why had he come here?

Ambulating again, in hopes of finding the purpose that had pro-pelled him to this down below, he messy-processed through the corri-dors of his quarters and tried not to relive the past. After all, one only did that if the present was bad and the future offered no prospects for betterment—and such a hopeless place was *not* where he was within his destiny. No, if he currently desired a mental return unto prior events along his timeline, he was merely indulging in pleasant memories, the look back unconnected to his situation—

He was lost again.

Or mayhap that was "still."

All appeared the same, the corridors, the rooms, the torture sta-tions with their chains and their stains, running together and forming a visual one-note that should not have confused him, but did. With his cognition tangling, and a shocking physical frailty gathering momen-tum, the Omega's legs went out from under him and he fell to the hard floor on all fours. The insult to injury was that the pain upon his palms and knees was not sweet. It offered no sexual thrill, and worse, provided no impetus for him to rise and fight further the Black Dagger Brother-hood. The stinging sensations simply . . . aged him.

In a manner that was wholly incompatible with immortality.

Sitting back on his knees, he regarded his filthy robing. The folds had been a brilliant white once, and from beneath them, the dense black of his essence had always spilled. Now, the draping was gray and his aura was as well, gray as the walls around him, the ceiling above, the walls in all directions. With a dull hand, he brushed at the red bloodstains of the four *lessers* he had just indoctrinated, humans no longer, soulless vampire hunters their new lease on life. He told himself that the portion of essence that he had imparted unto them was the reason for his current wilting, but he knew it should not have made any difference. He should have had enough of a reservoir to turn a hundred humans into his servants of evil if he so chose.

In the past, he would have been able to . . . do . . .

His thought became as lost as he was, traveling off route in his mind, diverting from the sad reality that had initiated it as if going into hiding.

In its place? A sinkhole of defeat that drained even more of the evil's strength. For all the centuries he had been at war with his sister's fanged creation, he had always failed to acknowledge that loss for him was a possibility upon the battlefield that his anger and jealousy had conceived. He had recognized only his inevitable triumph over his sister, and he had relished the trophies of the war, those corpses of her birthed species, those vampires she had seen fit to bring into existence because she had been granted a single act of creation. Each death had chipped away at her heart, and the satisfaction he felt with that agony had become the meal he liked best.

It had been such fun, for so long.

Now, however . . . all those to-and-fros seemed like a struggle conducted by another, the victories as unresonant as if they had never occurred. And as he tried to recall the sadistic joy he had once felt, he pictured Butch O'Neal, former human. If the Omega had only known that capturing the Brotherhood's pet would endanger his very existence, he would have avoided that mortal like the . . . well, plague.

Some Trojan horse O'Neal had been. Instead of being a corrupted vessel embraced by those warriors, a weapon of infiltration for the Omega, the sonofabitch had been a tool against the maker who had infected him. The evil had literally engineered his own destruction—and as he considered the manner through which their paths had crossed, he wondered if he could have taken any defense against the *Dhestroyer's* creation. It was as if that human had found him, not the other way around—

"Arrest thee now this wasted reverie," he muttered.

Bracing himself, he forced his torso and his unreliable legs into a concert of movement that returned him to his height. And then he shuffled forth once more.

He was immortal.

He was never going to die, not ever.

He was immortal. He was never going to die . . .

The cadence of the words became the steps he took, a metronome that propelled him even as every extension of leg tired him further. And some time later, mayhap it was the matter of a year, a glint of something bright caught the evil's attention. Stopping himself, he saw that he was upon his private bedding area, and there, across the barren space, a dagger, silver and sharp, stood upon a marble stand, suspended in thin air on its razoring tip.

Yes, he thought. *That is why I have come. I remember now.*

Propelling himself over to the weapon, he willed his robing off—and when he couldn't accomplish even that simple magic trick, he brought trembling hands up to the ties at his throat. It had been so long since he had had to work anything mechanically that he fumbled with the knot he had previously manifested with his mind.

The Omega did not want to dwell upon the inefficiency, the ineffectuality of his ten digits. And in any event, he eventually became naked.

He held out his palm to summon the blade. When the weapon refused to heel, he was forced to reach forth and take the hilt of that which ignored his call. The grip was familiar as he curled his hand around it, but the dagger seemed as heavy as a boulder as he removed it from its invisible buttressing.

Lowering his head, he looked down at his sexual organs. Like every other inch of his "body," they were but an image that functioned, a prosthesis with bodily fluids, a corporeality that suited his purposes when he needed it, and disappeared back into a closet of illusions when he did not.

Using what felt like the last of his strength, he gathered the soft weights of the balls and cock in his palm. He had a thought that they were warm and heavy in combination.

The dagger glinted again as he brought the blade under that which hung from his hips.

"I will not end . . ." he said hoarsely. "I will *never* end."

And yet as he made the pronouncement, he had a thought that it was a lie. Not a vicious one, but a pitiable one.

He did not want to be over. When time had been his to squander, he had wasted it on much that had not mattered, in the manner of a rich male before a marketplace of beautiful things. Now that seconds were precious, he missed the largesse he had once had like a loved one who had departed dearly.

A tear formed in his eye. He would have gone back in time if he could have. But he was too weak. In his arrogance, he had waited too long—

With a savage yank, he cut off the penis and the scrotum, easily slicing through the delicate, sensitive skin. The pain was gasoline in his veins, his heart exploding in his chest, the rapid pump enlivening him, the adrenaline surge giving him a little of that which he needed a deluge of.

As black blood flowed down the insides of his thighs and pooled around his feet, he lifted his palm up to eye level and drew in through his nose. He smelled nothing. Then again, who could smell themselves? Whether perfume or body odor, the nose only knew what was fresh and new, not that in which it had been stewing.

He had been told once he smelled like baby powder. By a human whom he had disemboweled shortly thereafter.

As he recalled his offense, it seemed so childish. But he had had rage to spare back in those days. Now, he had to ration . . .

The thought disintegrated as if to prove the point he could no longer recall desiring to make.

Beneath the organs he had removed from himself, black blood gathered in the cup of his hand and ran a descent down his wrist. He watched it flow, black and slow and lazy, gleaming in the ambient light that had no source.

"My son." He cleared his throat and spoke more loudly. "My son shall recommence and continue if I go no further."

The demand did not effect a damn thing.

"My son shall return now!"

As naught occurred, t'was the same as his cloak not vanishing and the dagger refusing to come unto his palm, the lack of power within him robbing him of his dominion over objects that should have been an easy summon.

Frustration kindled into anger that alit into rage, and he cast the flesh across to the bedding platform in what should have been a throw of strength. When the momentum was little more than a shove at the air, he knew he should never have let his one and only progeny rot as he had. But he had felt disrespected and underappreciated for all he had done for the male, and though the great Blind King of the vampires was named Wrath, the Omega might as well have had that dark emotion as his own middle name.

He had been so vengeful and so petty. A terrible combination.

Now he was here, abruptly old and infirmed, with no one to help him, no son to bear him up, no legacy left within his Lessening Society. He was doomed to be where all of history retreated with enough passage of days and nights: A distant memory that died out when the last of those who knew him went unto their graves.

He had been hubristic about his future. And now . . . it was too late.

In disgust with himself, he was going to turn away and head to the place where he would find one last chance for a rival . . . when he noticed movement upon the bedding platform.

Shuffling forward, he stood over the black bloody mess he had lamely tossed over. The components of what had been his sexual organs were twisting and turning upon themselves, melting, melding . . . reforming. Germinating.

It was a tender mass, however, and he wished he could remain and protect his only begotten. Knowing he had to leave it in such a vulnerable state, the Omega stood over his progeny and played witness to the mass doubling in size, and then incrementally coalescing into an infant: Arms and legs, chubby and uncoordinated, sprouted from the trunk, as the head also emerged. Movement unrelated to the gestation was next, the limbs beginning to flex and churn.

Underneath the veil of black blood, the skin was white and matte, like bone.

"My son," he whispered.

If the evil had been capable of love, he knew that the feeling so many lived and died for was what was coursing through him the now, the strange, unfamiliar weight behind his breast forging a connection with the burgeoning young that was nothing logical, everything instinctual.

And indeed, though he resented it, he knew that the sensation was in fact love because he had felt it for one other. His sister, however, the so-called great Virgin Scribe, had always been too busy for him, too concerned with her single act of creation, to pay any attention to the brother who had followed her everywhere when they had first been called into existence by the Creator. Her negligence had been the seat of his hatred for the vampires.

So petty. So childish.

"I must needs go." He brushed his hands over eyes that watered. "You shall survive. With or without me. You've done it once before."

Though he wanted to stay, he had to get into the Brotherhood's most sacred place, to those jars the fighters had collected over the course of the war. In them, though dried and in some cases ancient, were the hearts that had pumped his blood through the bodies of his inductees, trophies for the Brothers as dead vampires had been his trophies against the Scribe Virgin. If he could consume those repositories, he could fuel himself by accessing the residue of his essence left in those chambers. Yes, it would be only scraps, but there was volume. Hundreds and hundreds and hundreds of cardiac muscles would be available to him, and even morsels could fill one up if there were enough upon the plate.

He was also certain where they were located. The Creator had been forced, out of fairness, to allow the Omega one advantage to cure an act of overreaching by the Scribe Virgin.

So no, he would not die, never, not ever. No extinction for him.

Fuck that prophecy.

But just in case? His son would live on after him—and as he had to force himself to go, and as he worried over what would happen to the young if he did not survive, there was an irony. The Omega's need to ensure the continuation of a part of himself, of a fraction of who and what he was?

It was the one and only thing he had ever had in common with mortals.

Now he understood why humans cherished their children.

And vampires, too.

CHAPTER ONE

Present Day
267 Primrose Court
Caldwell, New York

No, not this one. This one is not for you."

As Detective Treyvon Abscott stepped in the path of Detective Erika Saunders, she stopped. Then again, that was what you did when you hit a brick wall. Her partner was a former college football player, an honorably discharged Marine, and at least four inches taller and seventy pounds heavier than she was. But even with all that going for him, he still braced his weight and put both palms out in front of himself, as if he were protecting his end zone against the likes of a Mack truck.

"Dispatch sent me here." Erika crossed her arms over her chest. "So I know you're not standing in my way right now. You're just really not."

Behind her colleague, a run-of-the mill two-story house with an attached two-car garage was strobe-lit in blue, the flashing lights of the squad cars parked in front of the driveway reflecting off the storm windows, turning a family's home into a disco ball of tragedy.

"I don't care what dispatch said." Trey's voice was quiet, but I'm-not-fucking-around deep. "I told you on the phone. I got this on my own."

Erika frowned. "FYI, your detective of the month award could get revoked for this kind of scene hoarding—"

"Go home, Erika. I'm telling you, as a friend—"

"Of course, I"—she indicated herself —"have never gotten a collegial award. You want to know why?"

"Wait, what?" her partner said. Like she was speaking a different language.

She dodged around him and spoke over her shoulder as he stumbled over his own feet to turn around. "I'm not a good listener and I don't like people in my way. That's why I never get awards."

Marching up the walkway, she heard cursing in her wake, but Trey was going to have to get over himself—and she was surprised by the territoriality. Usually, the two of them got along great. They'd been assigned together since January, after his first partner, Jose de la Cruz, retired following a long and distinguished career. She had no idea what kind of hair Trey had across his ass about this particular—

"Hey, Andy," she said to the uniformed cop at the door.

—scene, but she wasn't going to worry about it.

"Detective." The uniformed officer shifted to the side so she could pass. "You need booties?"

"Got 'em." As she slipped a set on over her street shoes, she noted that the hedges around the entrance were all trimmed and a little Easter flag was pastel'ing itself on a pole off to the left. "Thanks."

The second she entered a shallow foyer, she smelled both vanilla-scented candles and fresh blood—and her brain went to a hypothetical episode of *Cupcake Wars* where one of the contestants got their hand stuck in a mixer.

Care for some plasma with your Victoria sponge?

Wait, that would be *The Great British Bake Off*, wouldn't it.

While her brain played chew toy with all kinds of stupid connections, she let it warm itself up and glanced to the right. The disrupted living room was what she expected in terms of furnishings and decor. Everything was solidly middle class, especially all the framed pictures of two parents and a daughter in the bookshelves, everybody aging up through the years, the kid getting taller and more mature, the parents getting grayer and thicker around the middle.

Those photographs were her first clue as to why Trey had tried to put his foot down.

Well actually . . . there had been a couple of others when she'd been getting basic details from dispatch.

Ignoring the alarm bells that started to ring in her head, she stepped around a broken lamp. In spite of all the homey-homey, the place looked like a bar fight had gone down in front of the electric fireplace: The flowered couch was out of alignment and its cushions scattered on the rug, one armchair was knocked over, and the cheap glass coffee table was shattered.

There was blood splatter on the gray walls and the low-nap carpet.

The facedown body in the center of the sixteen-by-twelve-foot room was that of an older white male, the bald spot on the back of the head identifying him as the father according to one of the candids taken at a field hockey game. He had one arm up, the other down by his side, and his clothes were vaguely office, a button-down shirt, it looked like, tucked into polyester-blend slacks. No belt. Shoes were still on.

Two long steps brought her in close, and her knees popped as she dropped onto her haunches. The knife sticking out of his back had done quite a bit of work before before being left deep inside his rib cage: There were a good four to five other stab wounds, going by the holes in the shirt and the bloodstains on the cotton fabric.

As she took a deep breath, she had a thought that half the oxygen in Caldwell had mysteriously disappeared.

"Erika."

Her name was said with an exhaustion she was familiar with. She'd heard that special brand of tired in a lot of people's voices when they were trying to talk sense into her.

"Frenzied attack." She indicated the pattern of stabbings, even though it wasn't like there was any confusion about what she was addressing. "By someone strong. While this victim was trying to run away after they'd scuffled."

Erika rose up and went farther into the house. As she passed through an archway that opened into a kitchen, she was careful not to step on any bloodstains. The second body was faceup on the wood laminate flooring in front of the stove, the wife and mother sprawled in a pool of her own blood. The victim had extensive head and neck trauma, her facial features totally unidentifiable, the bones all broken, the flesh pulverized. So much blood covered the front of her that it was hard to make out the pattern on her t-shirt, but the leggings had to be LuLaRoe, given the garish repeat of peaches against a bright blue background.

Above her on the cooktop, a glass-lidded saucepan full of what appeared to be homemade Bolognese had boiled over, a black-and-brown halo of the stuff toasted around the heating element's coil. Behind it, a big pot filled with only two inches of water sat on the largest of the burners, and next to the mess, on the counter, an unopened box of generic-brand spaghetti was beside a cutting board that had half a diced onion on it.

The woman had had no clue as she'd chopped the onion, browned the beef, and filled the boiling pot that it was the last meal she'd ever cook for her family.

Bile rose into the back of Erika's throat as she glanced across at the open cellar door, the stairwell lit by an overhead feature mounted to the side wall.

"The killer had two weapons," she said to no one in particular. Mostly so she could get her goiter to calm down. "The knife used on the father and a hammer used here. Or maybe it was a crowbar."

"Hammer," Trey interjected grimly. "It's upstairs in the hall."

"She started the water boiling." Erika went over to the basement steps and breathed in deep. "Then she went down there to the washing machine—which explains the vanilla fragrance. It's not scented candles. It's Suavitel laundry detergent. My college roommate, Alejandra, used it all the time."

"Erika—"

"She hears the commotion upstairs. Runs up to see what's going on. By the time she's on this floor, her husband is dead or in the process of dying and the killer is on her with that hammer." Erika met Trey's dark eyes. "There was no damage on the front door so the father let the killer in. Do we have a Ring?"

"No."

"Where are the other two bodies—upstairs?"

Trey nodded. "But listen, Erika, you don't need to go—"

"You're on my last nerve saying my name like that. Anytime you want to cut out the pity, I'm ready to be treated like the adult I am instead of the child I was."

She went back out through the living room and took the carpeted steps to the second floor. As soon as she got to the top landing, all she had to do was look down the dim, narrow hallway. At the far end, in a bedroom that was the color of Pepto-Bismol, two bodies were in full view, one on the bed, the other propped up against the wall on the floor.

Erika blinked. Blinked again.

And then she couldn't move any part of herself. She wasn't even breathing.

"Let's go back downstairs," Trey said softly, right by her ear.

When her colleague took her arm, she pulled free of the compassion and went forward. She stopped when she got to the open doorway. The body on the bed was half naked, a t-shirt shoved up above her pink-and-white bra, her black Lululemon leggings yanked down and hanging off of one foot. She had dark hair, just like both her parents, and it was long and pretty, curling at the ends. In her right hand . . . was a gun. A nine millimeter.

For some reason, the pink polish on the fingernails on the grip stood out. There were no chips in the finish, and as Erika glanced over at the cluttered top of the dresser, there was a little bottle of OPI in the exact shade. The girl had probably done them earlier in the day, or at least very recently.

Right next to the nail polish on the bureau was a framed picture. The girl who was now dead was standing next to a young man who was a good head taller than she was. She was looking into the camera with a wide smile. He was looking at her.

Erika's eyes shifted over to the second body. The teenage boy in the photo was propped up against the pink wall, his legs straight out in front of him like he was a scarecrow that had fallen off its pole-mount. He had the muscularity of an athlete, with broad shoulders and a thick neck, and he was handsome in the way of a quintessential jock, square-jawed with deep-set eyes. There was a big patch of blood on the front of his Lincoln H.S. Football shirt and some splatter up his throat as well as under his chin. His hands were stained red, likely from when he'd killed the mother by beating her face in with the hammer.

His jeans were open at the fly.

Focusing on the gunshot wound, she noticed a second one, lower down, just under the diaphragm.

You got him twice in the torso, Erika thought numbly. *Attagirl.*

As she took a step forward, she noticed that the door to the room was busted in. Between one blink and the next, she heard the pounding, the crying, the screaming, as he'd broken the thing down after the daughter had locked herself inside, after her parents were murdered right under her—

Erika covered her ears as they began to ring.

"It's fine," she mumbled as Trey stepped in front of her again. "I'm fine."

"I'll walk you out."

"The hell you will."

Leaning to the side, Erika looked at the girl's face. She was staring at the ceiling, the makeup around her now-vacant eyes smudged, the sooty rivers down her cheeks and smeared lipstick making a clown mask out of what had no doubt been very expertly applied, given the amount of brushes and compacts on that dresser top.

There was one other mark on her visage, but it wasn't from MAC or NARS or whatever. The bullet hole at her temple was a circular penetration, and the entry wound was relatively neat, just some powder residue around a small pink-and-red extrusion of flesh. It was what was on the other side of her skull that was more gruesome, the bone, blood, and brain matter splattering across her pink duvet.

"He came with three weapons," Erika heard herself say. "The knife, the hammer . . . and this gun."

Had she gotten the nine millimeter away from him as he'd attacked her? Yes, that was how it had to have gone down. He had broken in here after he'd killed both her parents, and he'd gotten on her . . . and she'd somehow disarmed him . . . maybe because she'd pretended to go along with the sex?

She must have listened to the slaughter downstairs, heard her parents' panic and pain. At least one of the pair of them, probably both, had no doubt yelled up at her to lock herself in and call for help—

"The parents don't know yet," Trey said. "His, I mean. We just sent a squad car over to the address."

"Who found them all?" she asked roughly.

"We did. She called nine-one-one before she shot herself."

Erika's eyes quickly scanned the bed—there it was. A cell phone was on the bloodstained duvet cover, right by her.

The girl had held on to the nine millimeter, but not the phone.

"The operator who took the call heard the gun go off." Trey went over and knelt by the boy's body. "The girl was crying so hard, she could barely speak. But she managed to give his name, and tell the operator that he'd broken in and killed her parents. Then she provided her own address and . . . pulled the trigger a third time."

"But it wasn't her fault," Erika whispered as she leaned across the bed to meet that vacant stare. "It wasn't your fault, sweetheart. I promise you."

As her voice broke, she cleared her throat. And cleared it again.

Without conscious thought, her hand went to a spot below her left collarbone. Through her jacket, she couldn't feel the scars, but they were there.

Surrounded by the black-hole stillness of death, Erika's own past came on her like a mugger, stealing reality from her, sucking her back to the one night she never wanted to relive and always did. Always. She had fought back, too, during the worst moments of her family's life. And God knew, there had been so many times in the last fourteen years that she had wished she had killed herself—or could.

Trying to control the urge to vomit, she listened to a surge of voices down below by the front door. Some more people were entering the scene. No doubt the photographer. Maybe it was CSI already.

Erika looked at her partner, focusing on him properly for the first time. As always, Trey was military-trim in his trademark CPD fleece, his fade sharp as always, his clean-shaven jaw the kind of thing Superman would have envied. As he stared back at her, his dark eyes were hooded and his lips drawn tight.

"It's okay," Erika said. "I can handle this. But I appreciate you . . . you know, looking out for me."

"If you want to go, no one will blame you."

She looked back down to the bed, to the beautiful young girl whose life had been cut so short. All those family photographs in the living room? All those pictures that had been consciously and carefully taken to record her growing up with her loving parents?

No more pictures. Of any of them—

Out in the stairwell, steps creaked as someone ascended.

Actually, that wasn't correct, Erika thought. There would be one more set of images, taken by somebody trained in forensics, to record the way they had all died.

"I can handle this," Erika said to her partner.

And also to herself.

She didn't believe the words at all.

CHAPTER TWO

2464 Crandall Avenue
Approx. 7.2 miles away

o! No, no, I don't want this, I don't want you! Stop—
Balthazar, son of Hanst, woke up shouting and shoving
hands off his leather-clad hips. As he beat at his privates, he
exploded up to his feet and tried to get away from the demon who was
on him, all around him, inside of him. Banging into something hard—a
tree?—he ricocheted into thin air, tripped, fell.

Landed in something soggy.

As he planked himself on his palms and the tips of his shitkickers, a
nose-ringing combination of soot, toxic chemicals, and wet dirt drilled
into his sinuses. The stench was what orientated him: He was at the
site of the house fire where Sahvage and Mae had both almost lost their
lives.

With desperation and a good dose of numb stupidity, he looked
around his shoulder at the ruins of what had been a nice little ranch
house. The cremated remains of the structure were bathed in shades
of gray and pale blue, the ash-coated fragments of beams and boards,

Sheetrock and plywood, furniture and belongings, nothing that could ever be put back together and made usable again. The blaze had been so intense that there was even scorching over the property line, the fences and houses to the left, right, and rear all airbrushed with soot.

The neighbors were going to have a helluva Windex bill, but at least they had something still to clean.

Crab-walking over to a drier patch of toasted grass, he rose to his full height and brushed off his leathers. Given all the shit that was going on, worrying about whether he had ash on his knees was ridiculous. Then again, the list of things he could control was a short one, and in life, you had to take what you were given.

Sometimes this was only keeping your pants clean. And of course, what he really wanted was to keep them on when he was asleep.

"Fuck. *Fuck.*"

Balz glanced back at the charred maple he'd run into and deconstructed his nap time. After he'd stalked through the rubble and come up with nothing, he'd copped a squat at the base of the tree to consider all his no-go. That split-second time-out was all it had taken. Sleep had claimed him with such force and stealth, he couldn't remember fighting the tackle of it, and that was all the demon needed. His lack of consciousness was Devina's open door and she never failed to take advantage of the invitation he never offered.

He needed that goddamn Book of spells. If he wanted to lose the demon, he was going to have to find the thing and use it.

Reassessing the debris field, he wondered if he should walk it once more. Then again, why would anything with pages and a cover survive this kind of heat?

Because the Book wasn't just a book. That was why.

And to think that at one point, he'd had the stinking, repulsive weight in his hands, felt that human-skin binding, held the heft of the parchment pages—and he'd let it go.

"Lassiter . . . you fucking asshole."

The fallen angel had told him there was another way to get Devina evicted from his mental. So at the moment it had really counted, during that tug-o'-war with Sahvage, Balz had gone the *Frozen* route and let it go. But since then, he'd thought better of the angel's solution. True love wasn't going to save him—

An image of a human woman in a navy-blue suit barged in and pulled a chair up to his mind's eye.

Abruptly, all he could see was her looking at him over the gun she was pointing at him. Her eyes had been sharp, her brows locked into a stop-right-there-asshole glare, her stance like something out of an action movie. Funny, he remembered every one of her particulars, and not just because he was a thief and she was a cop and never the twain shall meet. To say nothing of the species divide.

No, he remembered her like she was something he had been searching for in all the homes he'd ever broken into, and all the gems he'd taken, and all the money he'd stashed in his pockets.

"But you're not saving me, woman," he said to the moonlit night, the ashes around him, the shithole situation he was in.

True love didn't exist, for one thing. That shit was just a Disney delusion, peddled to humans for profit. For another, the fallen angel might well have tossed the romance angle out because he'd just finished a Sandra Bullock marathon and *While You Were Sleeping* was on auto-loop in his poindexter brain.

One thing that was real fucking clear? Thanks to Lassiter's piss-poor advice, Balz was now out of options, stalked in his sleep by a sex harpy, and half insane from lack of REM.

As he checked to see if his fly was still buttoned, a wave of nausea spiked and he was glad he hadn't eaten anything. The feel of that demon straddling his hips, while she stared down at him with glittering black eyes full of jealous hatred—

How dare you, you bastard. And she's just a human.

The demon's voice came to him clear as a bell, and as the words translated into proper meaning, Balz felt the blood drain from his head. Glancing over to the tree again, he wondered if he was dubbing that jealousy in out of paranoia or whether it was something that had actually been said to him just now.

Had Devina found out about . . .

He told himself to get a grip. There was nothing to find out about that human detective and him. For fuck's sake, he'd crossed paths with her for a split second, when she'd walked in on him and Sahvage playing mine-all-mine over the Book at that collector's crib. And she didn't even remember they'd ever met because he'd been careful to scrub her memories.

There was nothing for Devina to get bent over. Nothing at all—

Yeah, except for your preoccupation with the woman, you sad-sack, his inner ass-kicker pointed out. *And just now you fell asleep for the first time since you've seen her. You think your demon night rider ain't going to know you want to do more than polish that detective's badge and gun?*

With a curse, he let his head drop back on his spine.

"Not her," he growled. "You're not going to fuck with her—"

The demon's voice interrupted him, sure as if she were standing right behind him: *I don't like competition even if it's beneath me.*

Balz palmed one of his forties and swung around, pointing the muzzle at—

A whole lot of thin air. And yet he spoke up like his enemy was corporeal and within earshot: "She's not fucking competition—she's not anything! What the fuck are you talking about?"

As his yell echoed off a charred fence line, he could swear he heard feminine laughter coming back at him on the wind, mocking him. But if this was really happening, if the demon was making a target out of that innocent human woman, Devina was going to get a nasty surprise. It was one thing for him to be used as unwilling gym equipment. Another entirely if some bystander who had nothing to do with any of this was put in the crosshairs.

"She's not anything, damn you," he snapped, like the syllables were rocks to be thrown. "She's nothing!"

Keeping his gun out, Balz stomped his way through the site again, kicking at burned beams and twisted metal with his shitkickers, determined to find the one thing that could save him. With any luck, there was more in the Book than just how to de-demon a person. Maybe there was a spell to get rid of Devina altogether.

When he came up all U2 again—still not finding what he was looking for—he stopped at what had to have been the garage, given the concrete slab that was under his boots. Rubbing his eyes, rubbing his hair, rubbing his face, he wanted to light the place on fire all over again. Instead, he mined what he could recall of the story Sahvage had laid out: Mae had taken the Book home here to resurrect her dead brother. Devina had shown up. Shit had gone down . . . and when it was all over, the Book and the demon had been destroyed, and Sahvage had saved Mae's life thanks to a little tricksy-tricksy the guy's first cousin had pulled centuries before. Everything tied up in a nice, if slightly ashy, bow.

Except Sahvage had to be wrong. The Book couldn't be gone. It was part of the demon or the demon was part of it, and Balz knew firsthand that Devina was still around—

Do you know what I do with competition? More of that silky, evil voice entered his head. *I eliminate it.*

All at once, rage like Balz had never known seized him.

"Two can play at the elimination game," he gritted.

Bringing up his gun, he measured the contours of it in the moonlight, the blue-black metal of its barrel and body gleaming like a gemstone.

Fine, he thought as he put the weapon up to his own temple. *No Book?*

And Lassiter talking shit about happily ever afters while Devina was busy drawing fresh battle lines around a woman who had nothing to do with this?

He'd take care of things on his own. All he needed was a really big nap. A dirt nap. Like, lights out permanently. Relief, finally—

Something came around the corner of a garage two houses down and he quick-shifted the muzzle in that direction. But it was just a human male, going by the scent—and the guy was hardly being any kind of aggressor. He was carrying a recycling bin out to the curb, grunting noises percolating from his mouth like the empty plastic bottles plus the weight of their bright yellow holder was more than his honed-by-a-desk-job bod could handle. When he got to his mailbox, he dropped the load and a clatter rang out.

As he pivoted around to return to his cozy Colonial, he looked up—and froze.

The expression on his middle-aged puss was a cross between total confusion and utter terror. Which was how Balz realized that between the unobstructed moon and the security lights around the neighborhood, there was enough illumination for even human eyes to get a bead on some guy dressed head to foot in leather with a gun to his head.

Jesus, Pops, why'd you have to ruin the moment, he thought. *And this is not for you.*

The next bullet in the chamber had Balz's name on it, not Harry McHappyHusbandandFather over there with his recycling and his sciatica and his two weeks of vacation a year.

The human took a step back. And another. And then he was high-tailing it for base like he was being chased, his Hanes undershirt and those Lands' End plaid PJ bottoms as aerodynamic as the extra thirty-five pounds around his middle. A second later there was the clap of a door slamming, and Balz could just imagine the fever-pitch locking, the fumble for the cell phone, the 911-there's-a-serial-killer-in-the-yard-of-that-ranch-that-burned-down call.

"Sonofabitch," Balz muttered as he reholstered his gun under his left arm.

Can't a vampire just shoot himself in peace for once? Fucking humans everywhere.

The obvious logic that perhaps said vampire should pick a better, more private place, like an empty city park or a tenement, was not something Balz was going to spend a lot of time on. And meanwhile, upstairs in Papa Panicker's house, a light came on behind pulled drapes. Great, the wife had heard the commotion. They probably had a couple of kids, and Balz wondered whether Joey and Joanna and Jay-jay were being gathered up to Mama's bosom and rushed into a closet—

And then he had another problem.

"I know you're there," he muttered as he closed his eyes and wondered how much more goat fuck could fit into one night.

There was some mushy tracking in off to the side, footfalls coming closer—and hey, at least it wasn't a demon, although he couldn't say he was excited to see his little visitor.

Fine, his big-ass, whiny, assassin cousin visitor.

Syphon was a highly trained, heavily muscled, green-and-black-haired sonofabitch dressed in black leather, too, and the thief in Balz—which was fifty-one percent of him, the other forty-nine percent evidently being a frickin' demon—appreciated how quietly the bastard moved in spite of his size. The fighter was also a looker, which kind of made a guy envious from time to time. With his streaked hair shellacked back from his high forehead, his blue eyes were the focal point of all his wow-that's-handsome . . . and his pupils were dilated thanks to the moonlight.

And also probably emotion, not that Balz had the energy to worry about the Dr. Phil stuff.

"What is up with you and the Dippity-do now?" he said to his cousin's hairline.

The male ran a palm over his comb-job. "It's a look."

"Yeah, like Dieter from Sprockets."

"Mike Myers is a god."

"I'm more a Ted Lasso man myself. But tomato, tomahto."

They both went quiet. And all Balz could think was that at least his cousin hadn't showed up when the gun had been out.

"Balz, you're killing me."

Those brilliant blue eyes were locked on the house next door like the bastard had X-ray vision and was checking out the leftovers in the fridge. In reality, he had always hated making eye contact whenever things got confrontational. It was a trait that had always made Balz wonder. Did the guy not know he killed people for a living? If you could sight the center of a chest and hit that target, why couldn't you look a person in the eye when you were in an argument?

Then again, maybe it wasn't such a bad thing.

Taking a leaf out of that book, Balz went back to staring at ashes. "Killing you? How. It's not like I have a gun to your head."

Har-har, he thought.

"You can't keep avoiding home, Balz. It's been three days. You need to come back to the Brotherhood mansion and sleep, for godsakes, not waste your time poking around out here."

Didn't we just do this, he thought as he sucked back his anger.

Trying to keep a level tone, he pushed a hand inside his jacket to take out another of V's hand-rolleds. "I told you over the phone yesterday, the demon and that Book are both still alive. I can feel it." *I can hear her,* he tacked on to himself. "I respect the hell out of Sahvage, but he's wrong about them being consumed in this fire—and if the Brothers are making decisions based on that dangerous misinformation, we're all fucked."

"Everyone's still out in the field. Wrath's not changing the patrols—and we're not finding anything dangerous. So what decisions do you think are being made badly?"

As Balz came up empty-handed from the cigarette hunt, he couldn't believe he'd smoked everything V had given him already. *Shit.* And had it really been three nights and days?

It felt like a lifetime.

"I don't have the energy to do this," he muttered.

"Because you aren't sleeping."

"Thank you, WebMD."

Syphon cursed. "See? The right clapback is 'thank you, Dr. Obvious,' given that I'm not on the Internet. Jesus, you're a shadow of your former self."

"And you're making this differential diagnosis based on an insult?"

"Just come home. Please."

As his cousin said the P-word, there was a hopelessness to the tone that was totally out of character for the guy. Syphon was a ridiculously nitpicky sonofabitch—although if your job was to drill things with little bitty bullets from a tremendous distance, you better have an instinct and an eye for perfection as well as an obsessive drive to rectify all kinds of micro-mistakes.

The fighter did not lower his standards, did not bend to any kind of battle stress, and never got tired or admitted defeat.

Except, apparently, in this situation.

"I gotta go." Balz tried the pockets in his leathers, even though he always kept his hand-rolleds in his jacket. But like he expected V's nicotine sticks to sprout like mushrooms on his ass? "I just . . . gotta go."

"Where? Seriously. Where are you going?"

"I'm already in Hell," Balz replied grimly. "The precise location of my body is irrelevant."

With that, he took off, dematerializing into the cold, damp spring air. The only thing he knew for sure was that he had to stay awake. As long as he had even the thinnest grasp of consciousness, the demon couldn't get at him, at least not fully.

What he needed was some wakey-wakey that was more reliable than his will alone.

Time to go downtown.

CHAPTER THREE

Caldwell Insurance Building
13th and Trade Streets

As the demon Devina sat in her secret basement lair, surrounded by her clothing collection and all her precious shoes and accessories, she was feeling pretty fucking premenstrual: She was irritated to the point of wanting a shotgun, seriously considering cracking open a pint of Häagen-Dazs chocolate chocolate chip, and she might—*might*—be getting teary. The only thing she had going for her was that she wasn't bloated.

Then again, when you could conjure up your body at will, you didn't have to worry about water retention.

She wasn't about to get her period, though.

That goddamn fucker, Balthazar. That cheating fool.

And oh, he'd been sneaky, too, hiding that human woman in the way-back of his mental meat locker while he deliberately stayed awake.

After a good couple of days of not being able to get to him, she'd been so damned excited when he'd slipped up and fallen asleep by that house fire smudge-fest in the 'burbs. All she'd needed was a momentary departure of his conscious mind and she'd jumped at the chance to take him on her terms again.

Say what you would about the vampire, but dayum. He had a magic wand between his legs, he really did.

Except the second she'd gotten her hands on him, literally, she'd received a nasty surprise from his memory banks, sure as if he were a house-trained dog who'd left a pile of shit on the living room rug. A woman, a human woman, with an average face and a suit that was right out of T.J. Maxx, was on his mind.

Unbelievable. Even though Devina was the fuck of the century, once again, some idiot with a cock was looking in an opposite direction when they should have been seeing her, and her alone.

And this wasn't the only time she'd been jilted. Jim Heron, her one true love, hadn't wanted her—had chosen a pasty-faced virgin over her, for fuck's sake. Then Butch, the Black Dagger Brother, had likewise passed because he was married. Mated. Whatever. And sure there were other fish in the sea, but as for all the other humans in Caldwell? They were easy marks for her and therefore uninteresting except for a now-and-then orgasm on her part.

Maybe a murder if she was bored and felt like playing.

Well, and she had been making entrées out of some of their hearts.

"Fat lot that's gotten me."

As her temper—which was on a hair trigger on a good night—started to boil over, she went on a stomp up and down the racks and racks of haute couture fashion she had collected over the years. Even though the silks and satins, velvets and brocades, were usually enough to buoy even her worst mood, none of it helped.

All she wanted to do was wreck something.

That was the thought that went through her mind as she came up to her Birkin display. And of course, something already had been wrecked there, hadn't it.

"Thank you, Mae," she snapped.

Struggling to control herself, she focused on her babies, her favorites among favorites, her prides and joys. The gold-leafed table supporting the Hermès purses was a good eight feet long and six feet wide, and on it were more than a dozen Birkins in different sizes, colors, and skins, all arranged on Lucite stands that ascended in height, forming a veritable Mont Blanc of beauties. She had lisse porosus crocodile in rose tyrien, and black matte niloticus croc, and Horseshoes that were combinations of rouge casaque and black, as well as ètoupe and gold, and white and gris. There were also four ostriches, two lizards, and a Touch.

The only thing she refused to have were the 25s. Too small. She liked the 30s and the 35s.

"You would never forsake me," she whispered to them as if they were good little children. "You are always here for me."

Yeah, assuming no one came in like a serial killer and brutally dismembered somebody in her collection.

The demon needed to brace herself before she could bear to look at the top of the display, at the highest Lucite stand . . . at the crucifix on her altar to the atelier's very best creation.

"Oh, God . . ." She clutched the center of her chest as the pain hit as fresh as it had when she'd found the bag destroyed. "Oh . . ."

For the last three nights, she had not been able to bear the sight of the burned Birkin corpse. But she hadn't been able to get rid of it, either.

Then again, the Himalayan crocodile with the diamond hardware was the rarest and most spectacular of all the world's handbags—and even more valuable because she had the matching diamond bangle. With a central snowy-white skin that faded on both sides to browns, grays, and a sprinkling of blacks, not only was the masterpiece a shining beacon in her collection, it was the very finest testimony to the fact that the best things in life were *not* actually free.

Andthensomevampirebitchhadlitthethingonfire.

How the *fuck* did anybody do that? If the stupid cunt had been so desperate to try to get out by triggering the fire alarm, she could have lit up a Balmain jacket. A Chanel suit. An Escada gown. But nooooooo, out of all the racks of clothes, and the shoes and boots, and the other, hello, *regular* boring flammable shit like sheets, pillows, the fucking Saks catalog, for fuck's sake—that female had had to pick the Himalayan. With the diamond hardware. And the matching bangle.

That waste of skin had picked the most expensive, most rare, and most desirable purse to try to get out of this parallel dimension.

It was almost like she'd known what she was doing. Which she had not.

Torching that stupid little ranch in retaliation hadn't gone nearly far enough. And then the vampire had managed to waltz away with her immortal fucking mate, all in love and happily ever after and crap.

Who knew Sahvage had been immortal? It was like finding out a housewife could bench-press a car.

And when all was said and done, what did Devina get? Not true love, yeah, not at all on that, but rather a toasted-beyond-recognition Birkin, and now PMS—without the period.

Looking down at the floor between her Louboutins, Devina wondered if maybe she needed to put the bag's remains to rest. Considering the way the night was going, what with her frustratingly sleepless vampire lover betraying her with thoughts about a human, how could she feel worse? And hadn't her therapist said something about part of mourning being a gradual confrontation of loss? Like you bit off the death in pieces, working through your *horror d'oeuvres* in degrees?

God . . . the Birkin had been so perfect.

At least the diamonds still sparkled.

As she took the burned carcass off of its stand, she cradled the remains to her heart and closed her eyes. Tears started coming and she pictured that human therapist, the one who had always worn earth tones that had blended her into her brown sofa.

Feel your feelings, Devina. That's all you have to do.

"I'm trying . . ."

That Balz thing had cut really deep, the idea that the guy she was fucking was actually into someone else such a goddamn stinger. She definitely could not feel worse than she did right now.

When she was ready, she conjured a child-size coffin out of thin air and willed open the lid. The glossy white-and-cream box with its tufted satin interior seemed like a fitting reliquary for the cream-and-brown-and-gray color scheme of the Himalayan.

With resignation, she placed the Birkin onto the cushioned interior, setting its handles on the little tufted pillow. As tears blurred her eyes, she ran her manicured fingertips over the pattern of scales where things were not burned and she tried to shut out the campfire smell. She could still remember what it had looked like as she had first seen it in the private room at the mothership at Rue du Faubourg Saint-Honoré, so fresh, so clean, that fragrance of the crocodile hide rising up as she had held it as if it were holy.

Because it had been. Because it still was, no matter its marring.

With trembling hands, she closed the lid. Then she rested her palms on the lacquered contours of the top and bowed her head. Breathing shallowly through her mouth, she told herself that she could get a new one.

But this one had been *hers*.

As the grief became unbearable, she willed the remains away, sending them down to the Well of Souls. For a split second, she remembered that that vampire Throe was still there on her worktable, and then that thought went right out of her mind.

The silence surrounding her registered as total isolation, sure as if the humanity had been wiped off the earth along with every animal, insect, reptile, and fish. She felt alone, like she was no longer even tethered to the blue-and-green planet she had for eons called home, but rather lost in a galaxy, floating through space, cold and useless, passing by uncaring planets and suns that had no time for her.

The thought that she was, in fact, not by herself snapped her back to reality.

She glared over her shoulder at her roommate. "But you're going to change all this. Aren't you?"

When there was no response, she embarked on a walk across the vast open space—only to pause by a rack of formal gowns to check herself in a full-length mirror. Her long brunette hair was a cascade of waves over her bare shoulders, and the bustier she had cinched on her waist made her tits look incredible. The leather pencil slacks were as always a nice touch, but she wasn't sure she liked all the black. It was a bit of a dour one-note.

Tilting her head, she willed the shrink-wrap outfit blood red.

"And people say perfection can't be improved."

Resuming her strut, she clip, clip, clip'd across the bare concrete floor. When she got to the far corner of the lair, she stopped in front of a municipal-parks-and-recreation trash receptacle, the kind that could be found all around downtown Caldwell, the kind that people threw nasty trash out in, like half-eaten sandwiches, the last inch of coffee that was cold, dog shit in bags.

Used condoms and needles.

Okay, maybe those last two mostly ended up tossed to the ground, but surely there were some prostitutes, some johns, some casual vein fuckers who were tidy.

"Enough with the bullshit," she said. "It's time for you to give me what I'm owed. I've been fucking patient, but that is so over right now."

She wasn't talking to the bin.

She was talking to the piece of shit sitting on top of the goddamn bin's square lid. "You owe me, and you know what I want. So get to it."

Crossing her arms over her breasts, she stared down at the closed cover of the Book. Bound in human flesh—or maybe it was vampire skin or that of a demon, who the hell knew—the ancient tome of spells had body odor like roadkill, pages that could say something or nothing at all depending on its mood, and a checkered history of compliance.

"We had an agreement," she reminded the thing. "You give me my one true love, a male who will love every single part of me, the whole me, for eternity—and I rescue you from the ashes of that house fire." When there was no response, she pushed at her gorgeous hair and tried not to show how much this game was getting under her skin. "Might I remind you that without me, you'd be on your way to the dump right now, which is more than you deserve—"

A soft, rhythmic noise rose up from between its hump-ugly covers, the sound so quiet that Devina had to lean in to figure out what the part purr, part snuffle was.

Oh, hell *no.* "Do *not* pretend to be sleeping. Don't even *try* that bullshit with me." As the Book just continued to snooze, she stamped her stillie. "Goddamn it, self-care doesn't apply to you—you're an eternity old, not a millennial. And P.S., in an earlier life you were probably a Publishers Clearing House fucking mailer, so don't get it twisted and pull this attitude."

The top cover popped up a little and the pages ruffled like it was repositioning itself on a Tempur-Pedic mattress. Then the snoring got louder.

"Wake up!"

With a swipe of her hand, she cast the Book to the floor—then sent it for a big ol' ping-pong ride off the walls of her lair, the pages flapping, the front and back covers flying, more of that horrible smell wafting around. She would have torn it apart, lit it on fire, drowned it in her claw-foot tub . . .

But she needed the thing. Especially after this Balthazar shit.

And it *knew* that.

Pinning the recalcitrant volume against one of the stout, graceless columns that held the ceiling up, she marched over to her perfume tray, grabbed a bottle of Coco Noir, and stiletto'd back. Holding the Chanel bottle over the rancid stench, the atomizer made little *shcht, shcht, shcht's* as she pumped it with her forefinger—

The sneeze was loud and strong enough so the front cover almost opened wide. And then the Book's pages let out a couple of coughs.

"You fucking stink. And I hope you're allergic."

The Book coughed one more time. Then it blew its cover wide, stood all of its folios straight out of its spine, and—

Phhhhhhhhhttttttttttttttttttttthhhhhhhhhhhhhhhhhhhhpppppppppppppppp.

The raspberry was drawn out for so long, and at such volume, only someone who didn't require an air supply to make such a noise could have pulled it off.

Something, rather.

"Fuck you," she snarled. "You're going to keep the bargain with me or you're going to learn the real meaning of print-is-dead, you useless, motherfucking, ungrateful, piece of shit, ass-biting, no good . . ."

She kept up with the ranting, hitting her stride and throwing in some Urban Dictionary just to get the vernacular going, the vile syllables tearing out of her blood red lips, her anger resplendent, her body humming with rage. She was so pissed off, the air around her warped and racks of clothes and bureaus all around her rattled. As the perfume bottle shattered in her hand, the sting of the alcohol sizzled into the cuts, the resulting wetness part blood, part fragrance, not that she gave a crap—

Not that the Book gave a shit.

At some point, the pragmatic disinterest of the tome registered, and what do you know. All that advice about not giving drama more air to feed off of was right. The frustration eating Devina alive gradually drained out of her veins, and all that was left was the hollow realization that for all her glorious temper tantrum, she remained alone in a space crowded with things.

As her voice dried up and she stood there panting, the dripping from her hand was like a snare drum as it hit the concrete floor.

"You're going to give me what I want," she said weakly.

More snoring was the only response she got. Then again, the damn thing knew that everything she said was just a threat.

Gripping the cover with both her hands, she yanked at it and got nowhere: Even when she threw her caboose out and pulled with everything she was worth, the thing remained stuck to the concrete column. She gave up when sweat bloomed across her forehead and her décolleté.

She was not going to cry in front of the fucking Book.

That was not going to be part of this shit show.

Not tonight.

"Fine, I don't have to sit around and be ignored by you," she said in what was absolutely not a *Fatal Attraction* voice. "I can leave here. You, on the other hand, are going nowhere fast without any legs. Enjoy your night."

Fluffing her hair, she pivoted and stalked over to the door. As she got to the reinforced steel panel, she passed right through the seam in the space/time continuum that insulated her private quarters from all kinds of things that went bump in the night and lame in the day.

As she re-formed on the sidewalks of downtown Caldwell, she sealed up the cuts in her palm and smoothed the contours of the bustier. The night was laid out before her, all twinkling lights and possibilities for distraction, the clubs open and full, humans everywhere, in their cars, in their homes, in their party places.

She'd find something to amuse herself with.

No . . . really. She would.

As a soul-sucking wave of I-don't-wanna nearly swamped her, she was reminded of another thing the therapist had shared with her: Unfortunately, everywhere she went . . . there she was. So she took with her her jealousy over Balthazar, and her frustration with the Book, and, worst of all, the dogging, nagging fear that, for however powerful and immortal she was, she might possibly be alone for the rest of her unnatural life.

Which would mean that she really was as awful and unlovable as she suspected she was.

For all the busyness of this city, for all the things that she owned and cherished, for all her strength and resolve . . . true love was as ever nowhere to be found for her.

CHAPTER FOUR

As it turned out . . . no, Erika couldn't handle it.

Sitting at her desk in the Bull Pen, a.k.a. the Caldwell Police Department's homicide division, she was having a hard time believing that she had left a murder scene. Voluntarily. And not because she had somewhere she desperately needed to go.

Like an emergency room for an arterial bleed.

Trey had been right with all his warnings, and she knew she should be grateful that he'd tried to look out for her. Instead, she was annoyed with everything. It felt like a theater light was trained on her fragile parts, and everybody, from the patrol officers who'd stepped out of her way as she'd run for the bathroom to the CSI people she'd mumbled to as she'd left the house to Trey who'd seemed like he was thinking of following her back to headquarters, was seeing way too much of her behind-the-scenes.

That was the problem with being the only survivor of a family massacre that had been so awful, it had been national news, so gruesome that there had been renewed coverage on its ten-year anniversary, so true-crime-discussion worthy it had its own hashtag. With something as high profile as the #SaundersTragedy on your existential résumé, you wore that proverbial name tag for the rest of your life, particularly if you'd insisted on living in the town where it had happened and decided to become a homicide detective.

Then again, when your boyfriend killed your parents, your brother, and very nearly yourself, and then slashed his own wrists and shot himself in the head to die in a pool of his own blood, people were kind of curious about the whole thing. Especially when there was no obvious "why" behind it all.

Here was the thing. On the whole, other people's demons were better hidden than hers. Secret vices, shameful pasts, actions that made somebody ache with regret in the dark? Most of that crap was on the down low for the folks you stood in line with at Starbucks, got stuck in traffic behind, worked around, walked past. Maybe if they drank too much you guessed something was up for them. Or if they banged too many people, did drugs hard-core, or gambled their way to bankruptcy, there was a tip-off for the peanut gallery at large—although even with those obvious markers, rarely did third parties get details. Her worst life events, on the other hand, were public knowledge, just an Internet search away if anyone needed a refresher on the fact pattern. Hell, not only was there a Wikipedia page that had recently been updated with all those "decade later" reports, but there were a good dozen or so amateur podcasts and YouTube videos about that night.

At this point, she was just praying no one made a Netflix documentary about it all. The last thing she wanted when she was busy not sleeping was to find herself and her family on the "Trending Now" lineup. And the reality that so many strangers had seen the dead bodies and mortal wounds of her mother and her father and her brother made her nauseated all over again every time she thought about it—

Erika pushed her chair back and yanked the wastepaper basket out from under her desk. As she tucked her ponytail into her suit collar and leaned over, she remembered doing the same thing at the Primrose house.

When she'd gotten overwhelmed in the doorway of that pink bedroom, she'd tried to make it downstairs and outside for some fresh air before she threw up. Halfway to the first floor, it had been clear that she wouldn't make it, so she'd rerouted herself into the powder room off the kitchen. As she'd fallen onto her knees in front of the bowl, she'd discovered that the family had one of those floor mats that went around the base of the toilet. It had been pale blue to coordinate with the wallpaper, and part of a matched set that included a little rug in front of the pedestal sink.

While she'd wondered why anybody would insulate the soles of their shoes, given that it was unlikely there would be bare feet in that particular loo, her knees had been grateful as she'd vomited up bile.

"Shit . . ." she groaned aloud.

Trying to get out of her past, she straightened, kicked the wastebasket back into place, and decided that at least she knew she wasn't pregnant. You had to have sex for that—you know, sometime in the last year, year and a half.

Or had it been more like two for her?

Whatever, like she had time or the inclination to worry about her nonexistent love life.

Focusing on the glowing computer screen in front of her, she was a little surprised to find an open email window front and center. Nobody was in the To: part and the Subject: was likewise vacant. She sure could have used a clue as to what she'd been on the verge of composing. Putting her fingertips on her keyboard, like that would jump-start her brain, she waited for it all to come back to her.

Blink. Blink. *Blink* . . .

Well, this was getting her nowhere except maybe an early-onset Alzheimer's diagnosis, and no, that wasn't a facetious hypothetical.

In her experience, people who had had near-death experiences or lived through violent tragedy went one of two ways. They either became fearless, and coasted on a Death Pass card that made them feel as if the biggest worry of mortals no longer applied to them . . . or they became hypochondriacal shut-ins who were paranoid that every hangnail was an amputation in disguise, each cold was viral pneumonia, and all the normal aches, pains, and forgetfulnesses of daily existence were cancer, cancer, more cancer, and/or dementia.

She was the latter.

"But I'm fine," she said as she looked around numbly.

Throughout homicide's open floor plan, the cubicles of her fellow detectives as well as those of the shared administrative support staff were unoccupied, all kinds of office chairs pushed out from under after her colleagues had stood up hours ago to go home for the night. Here and there, a blazer or a coat was draped over the short-stack walls of the workstations, and there were plenty of travel mugs, notepads, files, and pens scattered around any flat surface that presented a set-down opportunity. Although most of the monitors had been turned off, there were a couple that had been left on, CPD badge icons floating as screensavers over the CPD-branded network sign-in page.

As her nose tickled and she sneezed, she brought up the crook of her elbow to cover her mouth and nose.

"Excuse me," she said to all the absolutely nobody.

Putting her hand to the side, she palmed up her coffee cup—and the good news was that the java was so cold, so bitter, so nasty, that the taste of it re-grounded her.

Grimacing, she put the mug back down.

Trey was right. She shouldn't have gone into that scene. She'd known from the dispatch call that the victims were an older couple, their teenage daughter, as well as an unrelated teenage male—and that there were no signs of a home invasion. She'd *known* what all that meant. But she'd refused to get real with herself because she'd been pushing through fear and sadness and anger for so long, she didn't know how to turn the perseverance off. Didn't even know when she was doing it.

Frustrated and edgy, she checked her cell phone to make sure that it was still working, had the ringer on, and was getting adequate service.

As she set the unit faceup, she refused to wish for another new case to come in tonight. It was hard to believe in karma after what had happened to her and her own family, but on the outside chance that the what-goes-around-comes-around stuff was real, she was not going to hope for somebody else to get murdered tonight in Caldwell. She was, however, willing to pray that if anyone did because that was their destiny, she hoped like hell dispatch would call her again. And hey, she *was* the backup detective on duty—which was why she'd been pulled into that scene at the Primrose house even though Trey had been put in charge.

She just wanted to prove that she could do her job right, after undermining her reputation as a hard-ass cold fish in front of so many colleagues by bolting off in her unmarked like she had. After she'd thrown up in the victims' downstairs bathroom.

"Damn it," she said as she put her hand on her mouse.

Signing in to the case board, which listed the active investigations and provided status updates as well as links to filed reports, she checked all twelve ongoings. She and Trey were leading several of them, including the one on Primrose that involved the Landreys, Peter, 48, and Michelle, 43, and their daughter, Stacie, 16, and their murderer, Thomas Klein, a.k.a. T. J., 15, a state-ranked wrestler for Lincoln High School.

So he was a jock, just as she'd assumed. And she was going to be right about everything else, too.

Struggling to stay inside her own skin, she would have taken a cigarette break, if she'd smoked, or had a glass of wine, if she'd been off the clock. Instead, after considering all her options, she gave in to a secret vice she'd recently been indulging, one that was every bit as unprofessional as her cracking open a bottle of Chablis right on her desk.

Within seconds, as if her mouse knew the way to the file, a video was up on her screen. Before she hit play, she had a thought that she shouldn't go down this rabbit hole again—

Yeah, that hesitation didn't last longer than a heartbeat. And this was going to be better than sitting here doing nothing but wondering why she couldn't remember what email she'd been thinking of sending. Plus it was related to work . . . right?

Hitting the play button on the footage, she leaned closer and settled in at the same time . . . and there it was, an interior shot of a filthy trailer, the furniture ratty and stained, all kinds of clothes and drug paraphernalia everywhere, a bar-sized sink full of crusty dishes by an equally cluttered counter.

Directly across the way from the camera, a door was loose in its hinges and she stroked her throat as she re-memorized every detail about it, from the scratches around the knob to the bend in the metal panel itself.

God, she'd watched the file so many times, she could count down the cue for the mouse to scamper across the cloudy windowsill over the sink.

"Three . . . two . . . one—"

There it was. And there it went.

Just before that door opened, Erika felt her breath get tight, but it wasn't because she was back standing over the body of a sixteen-year-old girl who had killed herself. No, this constriction was more like Storytown-rollercoaster-excitement, that special, tingling sense of awakening you got when a thrill was about to hit you in the right spot—

And there he was.

The man who pulled open the trailer's busted door was not what belonged in a drug dealer's crack den. He was powerfully built, rather than wasted by narcotics use, and his black clothes were clean and well-fitting. He was also the complete opposite of strung out and half crazed. His affect was one of total control, like he owned the place—or at the very least was utterly unconcerned with whatever was going to go down or whoever might ride up on him.

The latent dominance was sexy as hell.

"Yeah, and he's a criminal," she muttered.

Tilting even farther forward, she focused on his face—and not because she was trying to ID him from some previous case. In fact, they had nothing on him at all. The department's facial recognition software hadn't yielded anything out of any database, and nobody had made him, either. So no, she stared at him not to place him . . . but because he was just way too handsome to be a felon, his features sharp, his eyes deeply set and very intelligent, his lips . . .

She stopped that line of thinking, right there. And refused to look into why she would ever assess a suspect's mouth like it was something that might go on naked skin.

Her naked skin.

Yeah, no-go on that. She was not living a Jackie Collins novel, for godsakes.

"I've lost my mind."

Shoving herself back in her chair, she let the video continue and absently reached for the mug again, but she caught herself before she took another try of the crankcase oil in there.

Boy, the way that man moved. His body was so fluid, it made her think of a predator.

Oh, wait, he was about to look into the camera—yup.

"There you are," she murmured as the suspect stared right where the camera had been hidden.

He knew he was being recorded, and he didn't give a shit. And the other thing that didn't seem to bother him? The dead guy on the couch. Although the lens angle cut off any visuals for the footage's viewer, Erika had both been to the scene and gone through all the photographs from it: The body of the drug dealer who owned the trailer was sitting upright on the sofa, the back of his skull blown out all over the wall behind him.

And yet this man in black didn't seem affected in the slightest by what all that looked like, smelled like. He might as well have been checking out a parked car as he glanced at the sofa.

So actually, in spite of how in shape and attractive he was, he did in fact belong *exactly* where he was. A civilian, unrelated to the drug trade in Caldwell and all the brutality that went along with it, would have illustrated some kind of shock, dismay—flat-out horror, given how grue-some the scene had been.

Not this guy. Just another day at the office for him.

As Erika shook her head, she got ready for what was coming next. After he glanced around at the squalor, and murmured to himself as if he disapproved of the mess, his left hand moved forward ahead of his body—and that was the first time the sizable black box he was holding showed. With a lean forward, he put the thing down among the bongs, crack pipes, and measuring scales on the coffee table, and then he picked a supermarket plastic bag off the carpet. After a quick inspection of the contents, he took some money out of it and spoke to the dead body.

Then he left in no particular hurry.

That was it. That was the footage.

Erika hit replay. And as she did, she heard a woman's voice in her head: *That's him. The man from my dreams.*

As she rewatched the footage, the soundtrack of those two sen-tences was as familiar as the movie's visuals were, and the simple declar-ative statements—made by the widow of a murder victim whose watches were in the black box the man had left in exchange for some-thing in a Hannaford bag—was as close to an ID as they had.

Which was to say, they had no leads at all on him.

Mrs. Herbert Cambourg, of the vivid dreams, couldn't go any fur-ther than that. She had no recollection of ever meeting the man in per-son, and yet she was completely certain that she had dreamed about him.

She even seemed a little obsessed with the guy.

Not that Erika could relate.

At all.

And there was something else that was weird. As Erika considered when she'd shown this trailer footage to Mrs. Cambourg, and taken that specific and yet ambiguous statement from the woman, she could re-member everything about arriving at the top floor of the triplex pent-house at the Commodore and watching this file with the young and beautiful widow. She could picture the sitting area they'd gone over to, and Keri Cambourg's long blond-streaked hair and black turtleneck with leggings. She could also recall with perfect detail the sparkly diamond necklace Mrs. Cambourg had been wearing, even though the woman had been casually dressed and it was hardly a glamour gig for a homicide detective to show up and want to talk to you about your murdered husband.

Then again, Herbert Cambourg had somehow been torn in two like something out of *Game of Thrones*. So it had seemed like common decency to cut the woman a little slack when it came to anything making any sense.

It was right as they'd been talking about the mysterious man from the trailer footage that things got strange. Just as Keri Cambourg had let fly with the man-in-her-dreams statement, a security alarm had gone off down below on the triplex's first floor, where the collections of odd objects and eerie books were . . . where the murder had happened.

As a shiver went through her, Erika closed her eyes and pictured the next sequence of interactions with precision, slowing it all down: In her mind's eye, she saw herself stand up, and watched, sure as if she were viewing footage from a security camera, as she told the woman to lock herself in the panic room. Then, to reassure Keri Cambourg, she explained that it was probably just someone from the CPD who had failed to call in their on-scene.

After that, Erika had descended the curving staircase alone, passing by all the modern art on the walls, arriving at the first floor and . . .

She was back upstairs with the widow, telling Mrs. Cambourg everything was fine, that it was a false alarm, that no one was down there.

After which Erika had left.

Rubbing her eyes, she reviewed it all again: Watching the footage from the trailer with the widow. The alarm and the stay-here-I'll-go-check. Then the descent—

Back up with the widow. Then leaving.

The sequence of events was just like the footage playing again on her computer screen, something she knew each second of, something that, no matter how hard she mentally probed, did not change. And her conclusion at this moment was as rock solid as it had been the first time she'd come to the realization.

There was a black hole in her memory.

Sure as if her recollections were a tape that had had part of its recording spliced out . . . no matter how hard she concentrated, she couldn't remember actually walking around the first floor and checking that nobody was—

As a sharp pain pegged her over the left eye, she groaned, but she was not surprised. For reasons that made no sense, the sudden spiking headache happened every time she tried to break through the amnesia. And yet she couldn't resist trying to pull something, anything, out of the void. But wasn't that the definition of insanity? Doing the same thing over and over again, and expecting a different result?

On that note, she fired up the video for a third time, sat back, and watched the mouse run across the windowsill, and the man enter the trailer, and . . .

Even though she was getting nowhere, she reminded herself it was better than going home alone.

Too many demons waiting for her there.

CHAPTER FIVE

The Black Dagger Brotherhood Mansion

As Vishous, son of the Bloodletter, stood with his shitkick-ers planted on the mosaic depiction of an apple tree in full bloom, the Bastard who was in front of him in the mansion's grand foyer looked like shit on a Triscuit. Which was not only an *hors d'oeuvre* even Rhage wouldn't *amuse* his *bouche* with, but a very real commentary on what under better circumstances was a male with a lot going for him in the Cary Grant department. Syphon, son of some other guy-who-had-been-good-with-a-rifle, had dark circles under his baby blues, and lids that were half-mast and sinking, and hollows in his cheeks.

And the streaked-back hair thing he'd been rocking on and off for the past month was just reinforcing the facial wreckage, making him look like the "before" in a skin-care ad.

"Anyway, that's it," the male was saying. "Oh, and he's out of your smokes, assuming my cousin wasn't patting around all his pockets look-ing for change. Now if you'll excuse me, I have got to get a kombucha tea and some kale chips—"

V caught the Bastard's arm. "Hold up, what was that? I didn't follow."

Syphon looked confused. Then clearly assumed he'd mumbled his report.

"My cousin, Balthazar," he said on slow-repeat, "the one who's been missing? I just found him at Mae's burned-up house lot. He still believes the demon and the Book have not been destroyed—"

"Yeah, yeah, I got all that shit. And the hand-rolleds request. But kombucha? Why are you drinking that shit without an axe over your head. Have you never heard of Grey Goose—fuck it, Budweiser? Hell, tap water? Jesus."

The Bastard blinked like his brain was having trouble downshifting from his current Crisis of Demon-ish Derivation to the Whole-Foods-gastronomic virtue signaling that seemed to be his voice box's favorite octave. "I—it's healthy. Why wouldn't I eat healthy?"

"You eat fucking sad."

"My body is my temple."

"Then why are you feeding it compost. You need to have a Twinkie and lighten up, true?"

Syphon made a dismissive noise—which was as close to "fuck" as he ever got outside of the field, the exhale containing some combination of syllables that equated to "fudge" or "feronica" or "fizzle."

Kinda like kombucha or kale was a cousin of anything actually edible.

And what the fuck was a feronica, anyway?

"It's harmonica with an *f*," Syphon said with an arched brow.

Oh, V'd spoken that out loud. "Okay, Ben Stein, you realize that don't make no sense. In spite of your everybody-knows-that tone, which I'd take offense at except for the fact that you've clearly had a crap night and I'm feeling sorry for you—'feronica' is not a real word."

"Yeah, well, 'true' isn't a question mark, either."

V took a pause. Because he'd been working on his temper lately. "Don't make me slap the stupid out of you."

"Lately, I feel like stupid is all I've got. At least I'm giving you a big target."

Syphon, the heartbroken assassin, turned away and started hoofing it for the pantry entrance to the kitchen.

Just as he rounded the base of the grand staircase, V said, "Sy."

The Bastard glanced back. "What."

"I believe him. Balthazar. If he says we still got problems, I take him at his word, and I'll make sure I'm not the only one who does. If the Book and that demon are still around, we'll take care of them."

Syphon's heavy shoulders slumped. "I can't decide what's worse. The idea my cousin's gone mad . . . or that the enemy that attacked me in that stairwell at the psychic's is inside of him."

"We can fight anything. Together."

"Can we?"

Leaving that rhetorical hanging, the fighter ducked his head and kept going, disappearing through the door into the pantry and his holier-than-thou diet.

"Motherfucker," V muttered as he looked up at the ceiling.

Three stories above him, the mural of warriors on great steeds was baroque as hell, the charging movements, fierce expressions, and bulging muscles of the males and stallions all exaggerated, the colors bold, the shadowing strong.

For some reason, anytime he'd ever glanced at the artwork, he'd dubbed in debates of grave nature:

You're wrong, Andy! the guy on the black horse screamed. *You reseed lawns in October, not April!*

Fuck you, Stewart! The dry season, coupled with the colder nights, won't support root growth!

That's why you need in-ground irrigation and proper fertilization, you twat!

sounds of thundering hooves, battle cries, and clashing swords ensue

Vishous re-leveled his head. Last week Andrew and Stu-Stu had gotten into it over which Paul brother was worse, Logan or Jake. At least both sides had won in that dated argument.

You know what you have to do, V thought as he looked toward the billiards room.

Funny, he'd rather try to quit smoking.

And as he started for the archway into pool table land, he realized he'd been avoiding going in there for . . . well, at least forty-eight hours. He, too, had sensed that Devina was still on the planet, and that meant that the Book couldn't be completely written off. But he'd been determined to give the universe a chance to provide him with another option for getting a confirmation on the pair's status. Any other option.

Big fat punch in the nad on that.

As a tide of exasperation crested, V shitkickered into the one place he really didn't want to go—which, considering there was an open-late Hobby Lobby eight point four miles away from his precise location, was really saying something.

Pausing just inside the wood-paneled room, he forefingered his back pocket, took out a hand-rolled, and lit up. It was on the exhale, as he started by his preferred pool table, that he noticed the TV was off.

Had there been a fuse blown? Was the cable/Internet out?

And . . . wait, what? Why was the couch empty, nobody with assless chaps long-legging it in front of a *Golden Girls* marathon over there.

Just to be sure he wasn't missing anything, V went around to close-inspect the sofa. There was no depression on the cushions and the throw pillows were plumped and arranged nicely in the corners created by the arms. So nope, even if the angel had gone invisi to avoid interacting, and was somehow able to tolerate his own company without benefit of the distraction of Netflix or Hulu or the Cartoon Network, his weight would have registered.

Plus come on, there was *no* way the screen would be dark. Lassiter ran on two sources of energy: Sunlight and anything with Bea Arthur in it.

"Where are you, angel," V muttered.

As he tried to remember the when/where of seeing the guy last . . . it was more like, where had the disco ball been? V hadn't been viscerally irritated for . . . well, shit, the respite had been at least a long weekend's worth of time.

And to think he hadn't recognized the non-noyance for the staycation that it was. Pity.

"Sire? May I help you?"

V glanced away from the unused remote. Fritz, butler extraordinaire, had materialized in the billiards room archway, sure as if the ancient *doggen* had an antenna out for anybody in the mansion who had even a passing need he could assist. In his penguin suit, and with that old, wrinkly face, the head of household staff was a fixture that, if V had been the sentimental type—which he was not—he might well have felt a little apple pie warmth in his chest for.

Okay, fine. Maybe he had some affection for the old guy. But like any sociopath wouldn't catch a case of the fuzzies when faced with all that earnest?

Not that V was a sociopath. Not really, at any rate.

Fine, he was mostly not sociopathic. Especially when he wasn't around fallen angels—

"Sire?"

"Hey, my man." V cleared his throat and focused. "Have you seen Lassiter anywhere around?"

"No, Sire." The *doggen* bowed low. "Neither inside nor on the grounds. May I summon him for you?"

By like, what, hanging that remote off the second story balcony and humming a few bars of "Thank You for Being a Friend"?

"Nah, I'll find him. Thanks."

"May I get you anything?"

Talk about your loaded questions. "I'm good. I appreciate it, though."

The butler bowed again, so deeply, his jowls nearly Swiffer'd the floor. "Please let me know if there is aught I may do for you, Sire."

After the *doggen* left, V considered whether to make himself a Goose, but he passed on that idea. He was off rotation, but you never knew, and the night was young in a way that inevitably would mean good news was *not* coming. So instead of sucking back some liquid sanity, he smoked the hand-rolled down. Then he flicked the stub into the cold fireplace, closed his eyes, cursed three times . . .

And just like Dorothy with her ruby fucking shoes, he was up, up, and away, traveling in a scatter of molecules to the Other Side, to the Scribe Virgin's Sanctuary, to the place from which his *mahmen* had run her little cult of personality for eons.

As he re-formed up on the perpetually green lawn, he wanted to avoid thoughts of the one who had given birth to him, so he got his walk on and tried to view all the white marble, Greco-Roman architecture as a disinterested third party might: From the bathing temple to the treasury to the library, the last time there had been so many columns in one place had been Seti I's hypostyle hall at Karnak.

Yes, it was true, he'd been watching ancient Egyptian documentaries lately.

Anyway, all the buildings he passed by were empty, and it was with no small amount of satisfaction that he took note of the persistent vacancy. Ever since Phury had become the Primale and freed the Chosen from their servitude, the Sanctuary had been a ghost town—and good for those females. They were out living now, not tied to the black robes of his *mahmen*.

They had left even before the Scribe Virgin had. So maybe this ghost town thing was part of the reason she had quit her job and given the reins of the race's existential shit over to the David Lee Roth of fallen angels.

Thanks, Mom.

On that note, there was one place up here that was inhabited—or rather, that had better fucking be. The Scribe Virgin's private quarters had a new tenant, and that must be where Lassiter was.

Vishous stopped as he came up to the wall around his *mahmen's* courtyard, and it took him a couple of deep breaths before he could enter. When he finally stepped inside, the twinkling sounds of the fountain should have been a peaceful concert of water droplets falling into a marble basin. Instead, it was like fingernails on a blackboard. A human two-year-old screaming after they were denied a cookie. A wounded badger.

Who knew that the only thing harder than having the Scribe Virgin around . . . was not having her around—

Jesus, that was Lassiter, too. That was exactly how he felt about Lassiter.

No wonder his *mahmen* had picked the guy to be her replacement. The pair of them were lockstep right from the jump of the new era.

Yay, he thought as he stared at the magical fountain.

Like everything in the Sanctuary, the damn thing ran itself, no electricity or cleaning required, the specially charged H_2O originating from no discernible source, every gallon forever sparkling fresh. The whole of the refuge was like that, self-perpetuating in its perfection: The illusion of all these temples, like the Augusta-fairway-worthy grass and the stupid Easter-ish tulips and the milky-white illumination that made everything seem to have an Instagram filter on it was an eternal kind of thing.

And no doubt exactly how it had been the moment the Scribe Virgin had *I-Dream-of-Jeannie'd* it all.

Well, not exactly. Phury had added the color. Before him, it had been shades of white.

And Lassiter? He'd made his own special contribution to the place.

"Where are you, angel," V said as he pointedly ignored the tree he had once packed with songbirds.

When there was no answer, he crossed into the colonnade. The doors to the inner space were closed and he had a thought that, all of his black-wax, BDSM extremism aside . . . he might not want to know what was going on behind any of this Privacy-please.

"Lassiter," he snapped. "You know I'm here. Stop playing hard to get."

As he took out another hand-rolled and lit up, the smoke left his mouth in a rush. Just as he was about to do something really aggressive—like curse and stomp his fucking shitkicker—a set of double doors opened like Miss America was going to stiletto out in her pageant wear.

What was on the other side was about as far from evening gown elegant as you could get. Unlike the rest of the Sanctuary, there was nothing ocularly peaceful about Lassiter's crib. And P.S., Spencer's at the Aviation Mall ca. 1982 was missing their supply of black-light'able zebra print. Probably half of their poster selection, too.

"Where have you been?" V said as he regarded the Technicolor bedding platform.

Lassiter, the fallen angel, successor to the Scribe Virgin's authority, possessor of powers that could barely be comprehended, was lying back against a stack of hot-pink satin pillows, his Fabio-worthy blond-and-black hair flowing everywhere, his bare chest rising and falling evenly. His long legs were k'd out, the leggings done half and half with black and turquoise this time. No shoes, no socks.

Because why not flash your ugly flappers for all the world to see.

Oh, and he'd painted his toenails coral. How cute.

"Hello?" V prompted. "Do I have to toss a hand grenade at you?"

Please let me toss one at you? he dubbed in.

Annnnnnnd that was when he noticed the book that was propped up on the angel's ripped abs.

"Who the fuck is René Brown?" V demanded.

Lassiter lowered the spine, his odd-colored eyes lifting from whatever paragraph he'd been Gorilla-glued to. "Oh, hey. Wassup—and it's *Brené.*"

"What the hell are you doing with that baloney." V nodded at *Atlas of the Heart.* "Sorry, I mean, *bre*-loney."

"I'm transforming my life."

V indicated the zebra print on the walls, the throw rug that should have been thrown out, the sheets that were a spicy cheetah print. "FYI, I'd start with a dumpster, not the library, if you're looking to fix anything."

"I have to learn how to be the best me I can." Lassiter flipped through the pages. "You know, go from a zero to a hero. Get my potential to become my reality. Be a looker not a hooker—wait, that came out wrong."

"Did it, really?"

Abruptly, the angel's eyes narrowed, like he'd picked up on a spill on V's muscle shirt or something. Glancing down, V brushed at his pecs.

"What the hell are you looking at."

Lassiter shook his head. "I'm sorry, I can't."

"Can't do what?" There was a pause. And then V caught the drift of the fallen angel catching his drift. "Bullshit, you can't."

"No, I really can't interfere in all this stuff with the Book. Your *mahmen* overstepped in the game back in March, and you know where that got us with all those *lesser* hearts down the throat of the Omega, the Brotherhood nearly getting slaughtered in that alley thanks to the evil's recharge—"

"I don't want to think about that."

"Well, you better if you're going to get fluffy at me for not playing Dungeon Master to the Black Dagger Brotherhood's benefit. I would if I could, but I can't. The repercussions are going to hurt you all more than the situation as it stands now—"

"You've helped before. And FYI, I'm not getting 'fluffy.'"

"Do you need a time-out in the ball again?"

V bared his fangs and hissed as he relived being stuck in that invisible prison—and Lassiter dribbling him, for fuck's sake. "No, I don't need a time-out in the—oh, fuck off."

Lassiter put both his hands up, all whoa-Nelly. "You just look a little worked up, s'all."

On the verge of losing his shit, V paced around so he didn't prove the point. Then he decided to be the bigger vampire.

"Look, I'm not asking for you to destroy either one of them for us. I just want some information."

"Knowledge is power. It's more than the *Schoolhouse Rock!* intro." Lassiter re-propped the book on his pelvic playing field. "Now, if you'll excuse me, I'm on a journey to self-discovery."

V walked across to the eyesore of a bed and stood over those naked-ass, nail-polished feet. For a brief moment, he remembered when he'd been the most cool-headed in the Brotherhood, the icy intellectual, the laser-sighted truth layer. Lately, the stressors had been coming at him so hard and fast, he'd turned into a Flamin' Hot Cheeto.

Maybe he should be Brenéing his Brown.

But more than that . . . he needed Lassiter's help. The whole Brotherhood needed the angel's help.

"Francis Bacon said knowledge is power first." He kept his voice low, level. "And all we want to know is whether the demon is gone. That's it. We just want to confirm our target."

Crossing his arms over his chest, there was a long period of silence—and V did not move. V wasn't going to fucking move. Even if this took an eternity, he wasn't budging one goddamn inch until he got what he came for. The Brotherhood, the Bastards, and the other fighters in the mansion were a powerful pack. But their numbers were not infinite. At any given time, there were threats from humans who might expose the species, the ever-present challenge of what remained of the *glymera*, and then a civilian population who wanted, and needed to be able, to see their King in person.

If resources were going to be diverted, it could not be on a wild-goose chase.

It just couldn't.

Lassiter put his hardcover down for a second time and looked to the double doors V had come through—like he was considering using them himself. Or ruing the fact that he had opened them.

"I thought this was only about the Book," the angel murmured.

"They're a BOGO and you know it."

Lassiter shook his head, for once losing his playful resistor act and getting dead frickin' serious. "You're rolling dice that may fall on your head, V. I know that you and I don't see eye to eye, but I want you to listen to my warning here."

"I'm willing to take that chance."

"Why don't you assume that she's still here and call it a night?"

"Is that your final answer?"

"It's not an answer. It's just advice."

V stared at the angel and stayed quiet. After what felt like an hour, a soft, warm breeze wound its way around his ankles. And then the whole room they were in started to rotate, the garish horror of the animal prints smudging as the spinning increased in velocity, the multiple patterns blending into a swirl that began to fade away, like a fog was encroaching— or more accurately, the private quarters were disintegrating.

As everything disassembled into ether, V glanced down at his shit-kickers and found that he was floating.

"Now can you tell me," he said to the angel who was up on his feet and levitating as well.

"A fundamental can never be destroyed." Lassiter's long hair was teased in the wind that carried no sound. "It can be transferred into other forms, but it cannot be destroyed. There is no entropy with an immortal like Devina."

V frowned. "What about the Omega? He was destroyed."

"No, you shifted his energy to another plane. Butch delivered his essence to you, and you were the portal to that other dimension, but nothing died or disappeared. He's just no longer here with us."

A tingle went down V's spine and sizzled his remaining testicle. "So the Omega is still around?"

"No, I told you, he's on another plane. The Creator has many of them. The 'reality' we all are in at the moment is merely one."

"Can the Omega get back here?"

"Maybe. Maybe not."

A sense that time was of the essence made V not ask for even the

Cliffs Notes on all that. "The demon isn't gone then, as the result of that house fire. She's still with us, true?"

"Flames aren't going to do anything but inconvenience her. The Book's the same. That's all I can say, though." Lassiter lifted his finger. "No, there's something else."

V leaned forward. "What. Tell me."

The angel glanced around the milky white that surrounded them, and it struck V that this landscape—wherever it was—was made of the same components as the sky over the Other Side. Then he forgot about all that. The angel's face was drawn in such tense lines that for a second, V did not envy the guy—and not just because Lassiter was an idiot a lot of the time—

"Betty White."

V popped his eyebrows and closed his lids at the same time. "I'm sorry?"

"I had a crush on Betty White, not Bea Arthur. It's a world of difference."

Shaking his head, V couldn't believe in the middle of everything, this was the point Lassiter had to elaborate on. "Listen, my guy, once you're in Geritol territory, I'm not sure there are many degrees of separation."

"And before you go, one other thing."

"Rue McClanahan I can kind of see—"

"Do not open it."

" 'Scuse me."

"The Book. It's a portal. When the spells on its pages are used, they open up cracks in the separation between planes. Some of what's in it is nothing more than party tricks, but other incantations can change the course of destiny. In either case, every time it's used, the boundary that protects our reality is weakened. You think the Omega is bad? Wait'll you see what it's like when you have to deal with the toxic waste of an entire other world on top of what's on your plate now."

Great. Christmas in April.

As V stroked his goatee and did some real Armageddon math, he was aware the angel had just confirmed that the Book was still kicking around, too. Nice.

"I'll tell everybody to leave it closed."

"Especially you." As V's brows arched, Lassiter demonstrated opening and closing with his palms. "The Book interacts with whoever is handling it. We do not want your power amplifying its own. You're liable to blow a hole in the space/time continuum. Stay the *fuck* away from that thing, Vishous. I'm telling you. We do not want those kinds of consequences."

V rubbed his hair. "Okay. Important tip."

"You better believe it. Now, you and I? We didn't have this conversation."

There was a tremendous *whoosh*, and then the private quarters rematerialized.

As V's body weaved from reorientation, he felt tired to the point of death. "No offense," he muttered, "I've wanted to forget most of our little chats. So yeah, keeping quiet on this one won't be a problem."

Walking away to the double doors, which had opened again, he stopped in the jambs and stared across the white marble courtyard at the fountain.

"Thanks, angel," he murmured.

"You're welcome, vampire."

CHAPTER SIX

As it turned out, Balz didn't make it down to the bridges where the friendly neighborhood drug dealers were. He'd planned to go do a deal for some powdered energy to keep himself awake, but a sidetrack happened—and no matter how much he'd tried to get to goal, he couldn't seem to reroute.

Which, given that his measure of bright-idea was securing a controlled substance, really said something about where he was and what he was doing.

On the where-he-was front, he was sitting on the roof of the security kiosk in the Caldwell Police Department's mostly empty administration parking lot. And as for what he was doing?

He was being pathetic. That's what he was doing.

Stretching his lower body out of its cross-legged position, the metal roof under his ass had no give in it at all and he grunted as his weight transferred from cheek to cheek. The good news was that there was a chill in the April air so shit back there was numb as a box of rocks. Provided he didn't move it.

After settling into a halfway comfortable lean-back, his eyes drifted up the flank of the building once again. The structure was low and long, and as adorned as a pizza box, the rows upon rows of windows inset into the brick without any kind of flourish. Ah, yes, municipal architecture from the sixties, when four corners and a roof that didn't cave in were considered a stylistic trend.

Then again, that decade had coughed up macramé, bell bottoms, and lava lamps. So it could be worse.

There had to be a good seventy-five to eighty offices in the sizable expanse and almost all of them were dark. Not every one, though. On the second floor, over on the left, there was an entire bank of glowing glass rectangles.

And that was why he was here. He'd checked in on a lark . . . and found what he shouldn't have been looking for.

The detective he should *not* be getting anywhere near—in person or mentally—was sitting at her desk and staring at her computer screen like it held the answers to every question she had ever had—or at the very least this month's Powerball numbers. God, he would have given his eyeteeth to know what was holding her attention like that. Given her job, he had a feeling it was nothing good.

Saunders was her last name, Erika, her first. He'd learned both when he'd had to scrub her memories.

He'd learned a few other things about her, not that he'd been prying. She was unmated, or unmarried, as her people called it, and she lived alone. She also had no family, and he knew the terrible reason why, the horror . . . the tragedy.

God, he didn't want her involved in all his shit with that demon.

"How can I protect you," he said into the wind, "when you can't even know me."

As if she could hear him, Erika sat back in her chair and let her head fall free on her neck. With his keen eyesight, he could tell she was murmuring something to herself. Then she re-leveled things . . . and reached forward to her computer monitor. Brushing the screen, her fingertips lingered on whatever was on there.

Even though he could only see her profile, the yearning on her face was clear. Then she jerked as if she were snapping out of a trance.

Fuck, she had a lover.

Although Balz had never considered himself a ladies' male, he'd been with enough females and women over the centuries to recognize that particular kind of distraction.

Well, he was just going to have to kill the guy. It was really that simple—

"You are *not* going to murder anybody," he snapped. Except then he had to do some editing. "You're not going to murder her man."

Fine. Just a little castration. Snip, snip, over the shoulder—

"You're not doing that either, idiot."

With a wince, he realized that he was arguing with himself. Thank God no one was around to—

"Here, I made these for you."

Balz shifted so quick, he nearly fell off the side of the kiosk—and talk about a hi-how're-ya. Standing over him, tall as a tree, broad as a mountain, dressed in black leather, was the only male on the planet he had any interest in seeing.

Vishous.

"Thank fuck," Balz muttered as he kept himself from broken-egging his butt chips on the pavement below. "Even though you snuck up on me like a ghost."

"You want me to announce myself with a bullhorn while you're camping out in front of the police?" The Brother lowered himself onto his haunches and extended his palm. "I heard you need more of these. And you mind telling me what you aren't doing? I'm not going to comment on the idiot part."

The orderly little stack of hand-rolleds being offered was *exactly* what he needed.

"You're going for sainthood, you know that?" Balz said as he took the largesse.

"Not hardly. You still have that lighter I gave you?"

By way of answer, Balz outed the Bic that the Brother had lent him and flicked his thumb at the same time he put one of the cigs between his lips. Then he offered the Brother his own creations.

"And you're a gentlemale," V murmured as he accepted it.

Balz lit his own. Lit the Brother's. Put what remained of the stash away inside his leather jacket.

"So I'm guessing you ran into my cousin."

V nodded. "We crossed paths."

When the Brother didn't move on to another subject, Balz felt his exhaustion get heavier by about seven hundred thousand tons.

Shaking his head, he said, "No, I'm not going back—"

"Good. I'm glad that's what you're not doing."

Balz blinked. "Excuse me?"

"I don't want you at the mansion, not right now. And I know where you've been staying during the day. I've asked Fritz to kit your flop out a little more properly so when you're there, you're more comfortable."

"Thanks, but I don't need anything."

"I didn't ask whether you did. Besides, you want to tell Fritz he can't make up a bed?"

Balz conceded that one. Then he frowned. "How did you know where to find me—"

V waved his Samsung cell phone. "Like you have to ask, true?"

"Oh. Right." Balz took another drag and looked over his shoulder casually, making it like he wasn't checking on the human woman in that window. "I'm not too bright right now."

"You're smarter than you think. And you're doing the right thing."

"I'm curious, why do you believe me?" He picked a loose flake of tobacco off his lower lip. "No one else does."

"A hunch—that happens to have a pair of wings and a sun fetish.

Also really bad taste in pretty much everything. But you don't know anything about that. I just want you to have confidence that it's all going to be handled."

How, he wondered.

"Will the others believe you?"

"I'll make sure of it."

Balz stared down at the hand-rolled in between his fore- and middle fingers. "Thanks."

"So why are you sitting here?" V indicated the lot with his gloved hand. "You think that demon doesn't want to get arrested or some shit? Important tip, human police don't mean anything to her."

"Oh, yeah, no. I mean, no particular reason."

He was very careful to lock eyes with the tip of the cigarette. And ignore the soft chuckle that came back at him, said sound suggesting that the Brother had taken one look at the woman spotlit in that row of windows and guessed precisely why no-particular-reason meant this very specific kiosk.

"I'm not talking about it," Balz muttered.

"You're right to stay away from her, too."

Fuck you, Vishous. Even though the guy was spot-on and then some.

The Brother rotated his right shoulder like it was stiff, his black leather jacket creaking. "I want you to call me if you need anything, 'kay? In the meantime, I'm going to find out what we can do for you. The Scribe Virgin's library on the Other Side has all kinds of information in it, and there's no way that demon doesn't have a weakness. We're going to find it, and exploit it without using the Book—"

"Vishous."

The Brother frowned and tilted his head, the tattoos at his temple highlighted by illumination from the security lights. "Funny tone in your voice there, Bastard."

Balz stood up and stared at his detective—not that she was his. When he finally spoke, his words were slow and steady. "If we can't get the demon out, I want you to take care of the problem." He glanced over at V. "And don't pretend you're missing my drift. If something . . . needs to be done, I want you to put a bullet in my head. Don't let my cousins or Xcor be the one. I don't want them having to live with that kind of thing on their conscience for the rest of their lives. For you, there's enough distance so it'll just be another shit job you got stuck with, instead of something that eats you alive."

"Don't have much faith, do you."

"Life has trained me to be realistic. So promise me, here and now. You'll do what has to be done. You're the only one who'll walk away clean. And if I do it, no Fade, right?"

"Not to throw a wrench in your grave, but your death might not be your salvation. It might keep you with that demon forever, a little commitment ceremony that has no divorce court, feel me?"

Balz closed his eyes. "Fuck."

"Give me some time." There was a pause. "And yeah, if there's no other way . . . I'll take care of you."

The Brother extended his dagger hand, and as they shook, Balz nearly cursed in relief. A moment later, V dematerialized into thin air, nothing remaining of him but the exhale of smoke that left his lips and drifted off.

Left to his own devices again, Balz smoked his cigarette down to his fingertips and enjoyed the view of the human woman, soaking in the planes and angles of her profile and the way her hair was so sensibly pulled back and her frown of concentration as she checked her phone as if she were expecting a text or a call.

There were probably no more than fifty yards between them, as the crow flew. And considering he could dematerialize through glass, even if it was perma-thamed—

Thermopaned, he corrected.

"What am I doing here," he muttered. Other than increasing the likelihood of Devina finding the woman.

In which case, the Brotherhood wasn't going to have to worry about what to do with that demon. Balz was going to drag her to *Dhunhd* his damned self.

Dropping the stub of the hand-rolled on the tin roof, he crushed the last little bit of the Turkish tobacco with the treads of his shit-kicker. Then he stared at the woman in the window for a moment longer.

He could be by her side in the blink of an eye. He could calm her down by controlling her fight-or-flight response. He could insert into her brain things that were true about him: He wasn't going to hurt her. He didn't want to scare her. He only wanted to protect her.

"Yeah, and then what. You going to take her out to dinner?"

Well, there was that 24-hour diner that had the good pie . . .

Balz stayed a little longer, playing out a fantasy that involved the kind of insanity that he was embarrassed to admit to himself. He was no prince, and paying for some woman's dinner and holding some doors open for her was not going to turn this thief into anything charming. Besides, he came with one hell of a caboose, at least until V figured out how to file eviction papers with the Department of Good-bye Demons.

But God, he hated to leave the woman. He really did. And it wasn't all about the protection thing.

He just liked looking at her. She calmed him down, focused him, made him stop chasing the inanimate objects of other people.

Closing his eyes, he took a couple of deep breaths and willed himself to dematerialize to the closest bridge. When nothing happened, he tried again. And a third time.

Great. All this shit was turning him into a pedestrian.

With a mutter, he jump-of-shame'd it off the kiosk's roof and landed on the pavement with a clap of his boots. After a jack-up of his leathers, he got to hoofing it—and chilled his bad mood by pointing out that at least she didn't have to know he was skulking off like his Kia Soul had run out of gas.

Not that there was anything wrong with a Soul.

As he went along, passing by dark office buildings, restaurants that were closing up, and ghost town surface lots and parking garages, he couldn't remember the last time he'd walked anywhere, except for when he was on rotation and patrolling the field.

On that note, he wasn't sure when he was going to be back at work.

His real life seemed a thousand miles away. Maybe that was why the fifty yards between him and that woman had struck him as a painfully close divide he desperately wanted to cross.

After a number of blocks, he caught sight of the first of the bridges, the span lit up with multicolored lights, the four lanes lightly traveled on account of the late hour. As he closed in, he made quick work of the sidewalk, pulling a *Saturday Night Fever* without the platform shoes. Or John Travolta's dance moves.

Also no Bee Gees soundtrack, although, yes, he would like to stay alive, thank you very much.

When he arrived at the bridge, he went around the base of an on-ramp and entered an underworld that had its own rules. The stink of the place instantly registered, the combination of river mud, burning trash, and human waste burrowing into his sinuses. He was too tired to sneeze as he checked out the shadowed, littered landscape for things that went bump in the night.

No threats anywhere, but that didn't mean there was nobody around. A couple dozen humans in ragged clothes were shuffling between tents and cardboard pallets, and little groups of like individuals circled around trash can fires. Lit joints, cigarettes, and liquor bottles were out in the open; the meth and crack pipes were generally kept hidden.

Putting his hands in his pockets, he strode forward with a lowered head and eyes that tracked everything. The man he'd come to see was nearly a quarter mile away, stationed all the way across at the brick wall boundary created by the start of the warehouse district. On the approach, the dealer didn't look Balz's way, but his hand ducked inside his bomber jacket. With his hoodie up and the darkness surrounding him, he was a sentient shadow in gray clothes.

Or he better be. Drug dealers didn't last long in Caldwell if they weren't halfway decent in the noggin department.

"I want something," Balz said by way of introduction.

"I don't know you."

"I'm looking for a bump."

The dealer glanced left. Glanced right. What little of his hair showed was dark, clean, and gelled, and his beard was trimmed tight. That bomber jacket of his was battered, but in a store-bought way, not from the authentic wear-and-tear that came from being homeless. He even had fresh kicks on, those sneakers the only thing on him that was white.

Not that great an idea if he were trying to stay hidden in the darkness.

Also not so hot in a bad part of town.

So clearly he was armed.

"I don't have anything. Sorry."

Balz casually put a hand out. "I got three hundred."

There was a pause. Then a pair of heavy-lidded eyes shifted in his direction. As they swept up and down his full height, it was like getting scanned at an airport, a beam penetrating through Balz's outer layers and skin to the bone structure underneath. The dealer wasn't looking for metal in the form of weapons. No doubt he knew Balz was carrying. Nah, he was looking for a badge—and naturally, he was going to miss the real story.

The vampire shit probably wouldn't have been relevant to him, however. Long as the cash was good.

"Nice jacket," the dealer said. "Better'n mine."

"I didn't know we were competing."

"Nice boots."

"Yeah, well, I don't covet your Nikes." Balz looked to where a couple of hard-luck humans were walking away. "So are you helping me out or am I going somewhere—"

As he turned his head back, he got a gun in his face.

"Gimme your money and your coat."

Balz let out a curse. All he needed was a little cocaine—okay, fine, an 8 ball. And instead, he was going to have to dance with this fucker.

"You do not want to do this," he told the guy.

"Fuck you. Gimme your money and that jacket."

"I'll give you one chance to lower your weapon."

As Balz drawled out the words, he was so tired of the whole world, especially as he had no faith that the reasonable advice he was offering would be taken—

The muzzle pushed into his nose, shoving it off-center, and a whiff of gunpowder cut through the bridge funk. "I'll kill you right where you stand."

As an undercurrent of Taco Bell registered—because clearly the guy had just had a Doritos Locos combo meal—Balz stared into the eyes that were only about eighteen inches from his own. FFS, if he hadn't fallen asleep at the house site, he wouldn't be here. Hell, if he hadn't been electrocuted on the side of the Brotherhood mansion back in December, and provided the demon with the keys to his existential Airbnb, he wouldn't be here.

Or maybe this had been his fate all along.

"I'll pull this fucking trig—"

Annnnd that was as far as Mr. Nine Millimeter who didn't wash his hands after eating got with the yapping. Balz entered the man's mind, intending to accomplish with mental manipulation that which conversation was failing at: A quick reholster, a completed transaction, both going about their merry ways. That shit got sidelined quick, though.

The guy had had a busy night, and not when it came to the drug trade.

"You miserable asshole," Balz growled. "Why the fuck you do that to her, huh? Pretending you're the big man? Connie didn't cheat. She's never cheated and you know it. You frickin' *know* this."

"Wha . . ." Under the lip of his hoodie, the dealer's face paled. "What you talking about?"

"You went too far tonight. You took it *way* too fucking far."

The man's fresh, brutal memories of what he had done back at the apartment he shared with a woman he regularly abused were close to the surface of his consciousness, but as Balz followed them back in time, they went deep. Years deep. And there were so many women. So many . . . girls.

"You sonofabitch . . ." Balz let his voice drift because he didn't know enough pejoratives to cover the depravity. "You don't need to be here. Nope. I think you're done, pal."

Balz took a step back and narrowed his eyes. "And you don't deserve jail. You need to go to Hell."

As the dealer's arm began to move, and the muzzle of that gun started to swing around to face himself, the man tried to fight against the override of his control panel. The pungent scent of terror-sweat bloomed and his entire body shook, but there was nothing he could do to stop what was happening against his will.

It was just like all those women had been when the fucker had been beating them . . . and doing so much worse.

"Say goodnight, motherfucker."

Balz willed that gun up so it was pointed at the dealer's own temple. And then he made the guy pull the trigger.

The pop of discharge echoed and no doubt created attention, but Balz knew two things: One, people under the bridge did not get involved in other folks' drama as a rule; and two, if there was an onlooker or an interloper who was inclined to get involved, he could handle them no problem.

The body collapsed to the ground, landing like a side of beef. And while muscles randomly twitched in the arms and legs, and the smell of urine wafted up, Balz kicked the torso over so that things were faceup.

The subpar bomber jacket was partially open, and inside, he found all kinds of white-powdered goodies. As he peeled the dead—well, dying—dealer like a grape, he was jealous of the lights-out.

And prayed V would keep his promise.

Tucking the cocaine into his own jacket, Balz wanted to curse a blue streak. But he didn't have the energy.

Especially because he was now sucked into drama that was not his own.

CHAPTER SEVEN

*I*n the dream, Erika was back in the triplex at the Commodore, descending the curving staircase, passing by the modern artwork while an alarm went off down below. From her shoes on the fine carpeted steps to the gardenia-scented air to the up-high view over the Hudson, everything was both crystal clear and also foggy, the details as familiar as her drive to work and yet disorientating, too.

Except this isn't a dream, *she thought to herself.*

At the bottom of the stairs, she paused and looked across a sitting area that belonged in a hotel lobby, everything so anonymously perfect. On the far side of the silk chairs and sofa, there was a high-ceilinged hallway off of which were many dark rooms.

That was where she had to go, where the collections of strange and somewhat disturbing objects were . . . where Herbert Cambourg, owner of the penthouse, collector of the Victorian surgical instruments and the bat skeletons and the books about death and black magic, had been nearly torn in half by forces that could not be explained.

Kind of made someone wonder if his explorations of the dark side . . . had made something reach back at him.

As soon as she entered the corridor, the other rooms disappeared from her periphery, fading away unevenly as if they were being manually erased. Dim lighting was her beacon, but she would have known her destination even in the pitch dark.

She was being called . . .

And then she was at the threshold of the room that held all the books. Bracing herself before she looked up, she took a deep breath—because she knew what was coming.

Erika's exhale was sharp as she lifted her eyes: There he was, the man she could not find during the day, whose presence she could not forget at night.

"It's you," she said roughly. Which was what she always said to him. "And this actually happened, didn't it. This is not a dream."

Wincing, she put a hand to her head, but that was what she always did. And so was her wondering why she could only see him like this, when she was sleeping. Then she forgot all of that and properly focused on the man. He was not alone, but the guy standing next to him didn't register. All she saw was the tall figure dressed in black, his eyes locked on her, his body poised and muscled. He was . . . incredibly beautiful, even though she knew he was dangerous.

And she didn't need to count all those weapons on him to come to that conclusion.

"What did you do to me?" she asked. "Why can't I remember you when I'm awake?"

His lips moved, as if he were answering her, but she couldn't hear: Even though the alarm's staccato beeping was loud, and her own voice was in her ears, his words couldn't cross the short distance between them.

"You did something to my mind," she accused him. "What was it—"

The man looked away from her, to the guy who was with him. Now both of their lips were moving, their expressions changing, becoming aggressive. As she studied the profile that haunted her, she told herself that this time would be different, this time, when she woke up, she would remember him properly and be able to do something about it.

What that was . . . she didn't know.

The man looked back at her and he seemed sad in a remote kind of way. As his lips moved, she leaned in, trying to hear him—and then she realized . . . he wasn't talking to her. He was still talking to his partner in crime, even though he was focused on her.

She had a moment of confusion, and then she thought, Oh, right. This was how it went.

This dream somehow inserted herself into the memory she couldn't access when she was awake: Everything that he did or said had actually happened. Everything she did was just her trying to get through to a recording in her mind.

And now he was staring at her silently, and she knew what was coming. There was no time left before he took from her what she was chasing.

"I'm going to find you," she vowed. "I don't care what I have to do—"

The man frowned, and then he jerked forward and put both of his hands up to his throat, his mouth dropping open. As his face reddened and he gagged, Erika reached for him.

No, no, this wasn't right, *she thought.* This was not how the dream went.

"What's wrong—"

His retching became so violent that his head jerked back and forth, and then he bent over at his hips, throwing out one of his hands blindly.

Just as she was about to grab hold of his arm to help steady him, his eyes locked on her. "Run! Ruuuuuuuuuuun—she's going to get you—"

His words cut off as his voice strangled into a clicking, like he was trying to speak but there was no air in his lungs or what air there was couldn't get through a constriction. And then something . . . came out of him.

It was like a curl of black smoke, but it was more than that. A chill shot down Erika's spine and she felt an instant revulsion, as if she were confronted by something festering, something . . . rotten.

Something evil—

◆   ◆   ◆

Erika came awake on a scream, the horror-movie sound effect rever-
berating around the empty walls of her bedroom. To keep herself from
waking up the other half of her townhouse—hell, the whole city—she
clapped a palm over her mouth. Then she threw off the covers and sat
up on her knees. Even though there was nothing in front of her, she
reached forward into the thin air with her free hand.

As if she could touch the man—

A sudden sharp pain in her head made her squeeze her eyes shut,
but she fought the discomfort. If she could just stay with the memory a
little longer, she was so close . . . so close to seeing . . .

Seeing what? She knew she had dreamed of the triplex at the Commodore again, of going down to that first floor where the books were.
She had no other details, though—other than a yearning to return to
where she'd been in her mind, a striking conviction that someone who
was in deadly trouble needed her help, that she had to defend and protect somebody from—

Evil.

As her head pounded to the beat of her heart, her eyes went to the
glow from her open bathroom door. A persistent disorientation made
her question her location, even as she got a good look at her sink and
her toothbrush and the Post-it note on her mirror that read "Dental
Floss" in her messy handwriting—

The sound was subtle, but in the dim silence, she caught it even over
the roar in her ears. Holding her breath, she listened.

There it was again. A creak.

Outside her room on the stairs.

Snapping her hand to her bedside table, she whipped open the
drawer and grabbed her nine millimeter. On her feet, she took the safety
off and led with the muzzle. Her bare feet made no sound over the wall-
to-wall carpeting as she toe-heel'd to the closed door. Back-flatting by
the jamb, she held her breath for a second time—

Creeeeak.

No pets. No boyfriend. No family outside of the cemetery.

No keys hidden on her stoop in a flower pot, and her partner, Trey, would have called first before letting himself in.

No alarm going off, and she'd set it as soon as she'd come in like she always did.

Since joining homicide, she'd helped put all kinds of drug dealers, mobsters, and sociopathic monsters behind bars. But she'd never been afraid. She'd already lived through a home invasion where everyone was supposed to die. She'd never worried about a second.

Until . . . now.

Something was wrong in the townhouse. Something was . . . very wrong inside—

Some*one*, she corrected. There was no reason to get all metaphysical about this.

Still, the overhang of that disturbing dream was making her paranoid, her mind skipping around subjects that didn't bear thinking about. Not in the real world at least.

"I am armed," she said in a loud voice. "And I have called for backup."

Creeeeeaaaaaak.

Prepared to defend herself, she watched as her left hand gripped the doorknob—and abruptly she wondered what the hell she was doing. She hadn't called anyone for backup, and there was a window by her bed that opened out to the garage roof. She should leave that way, drop down onto the lawn, and go to her neighbor across the street who was a fireman. If the person inside her townhouse had managed to get past her alarm, they were a professional hired to kill her and they were not going to want to run the risk of getting the attention of people who lived on the street.

So why would she risk confronting the intruder alone, even if she had a gun?

Because she didn't run, that was why.

Three, two, one—

Erika yanked open the door, jumped free of the jambs, and pointed her gun directly in front of her, at the stairwell.

Which shouldn't have been dark.

The light fixture over the staircase, which she always left on, was off for some reason, so there was nothing but a dense void in front of her—and down below, she should have been able to catch the glow from the porch fixture. It was off as well.

Nothing but shadows.

Her breath was loud. Her heart thundered.

Something in her dream had been as black as the void in front of her. Something . . . that had curled out of the mouth of—

Creeeeeeaaaaaaaaaaaak.

"Get out of my house!" she yelled as she slapped for the light switch.

When she flipped it, nothing happened. No illumination. A brief recap of locking herself into her room and taking the window escape to the garage occurred to her. It didn't last. As if she were compelled by a force outside of herself, she went forward, even as her legs began to tremble.

"When I find you," she called out as she looked down into what felt like the pit of Hell, "I'm not arresting you. I'm shooting you in the chest."

Holding her position, her eyes finally adjusted enough so that a gray glow from the slot windows on either side of her front door pulled free of all the unseeable.

Tap.

"I have a gun," she said hoarsely. "I have . . . a gun."

Tap. Tap.

The repetitive sound was soft, softer than the creaking had been; it was barely audible.

Erika swallowed through a dry throat and extended her bare foot over the first step of the stairwell. Even though she knew that her weight would be caught, she felt as though she were tilting into oblivion, initiating a free fall she wouldn't be able to pull herself back from, plunging into a descent that would end in something far, far worse than broken bones and torn veins and . . .

Tap. Tap. Tap.

. . . a pool of her blood beneath her dead body.

The ball of her foot landed on cold wood and she wanted to grip the banister, but she needed her gun controlled as she took another step down. And another. Her hands were shaking so badly—maybe that was her whole body, especially as the hair on the back of her neck stood straight up, and everything felt icy, her skin prickling.

Tap.Tap.Tap.

She was halfway down when she recognized what the sound was. It was a finger, softly hitting on a window—

The shadow that crossed the foyer at the foot of the stairwell was quick as a blink, obvious as a scream.

The sudden rage that gripped her was the kind of thing she'd have to figure out later. The moment it hit, she gave in to the wave of aggression: Against everything rational, she pile-drove the rest of the way down, her feet thundering over the remaining steps. Leaping off the end, she landed with a thud, her gun pointed in the direction the intruder had gone, through the archway into her little living room.

Dear God, what was that smell? Like . . . spoiled meat.

All of a sudden, the temperature dropped so far that her breath became clouds in front of her face.

Creeeeeeeeaaaaaaaak.

Her eyes shifted to the front door, where a mirror hung by the exit so you could check your makeup as you left. The smooth glass reflected her own image back at her . . . as well as that of the darkened kitchen in the rear of the townhouse.

There was someone in there.

No, it was more like something. *Something* was there—

The shadow rushed up on her from behind, coming from out of nowhere.

As Erika was punched in the back, she screamed and turned and pulled the trigger, bullets discharging in a fat circle, shattering the mirror, hitting the door, penetrating one of the side windows, before passing through an indescribably evil entity—

◆   ◆   ◆

Erika shouted and put her hands up to her face, shielding herself from attack as her recoil took her backwards. Set into a free fall, she had a brief, confusing impression of her work computer screen and then she was ass-over-tea-kettling it and landing faceup on a crash—

In the aisle between cubicle rows? At homicide?

For a couple of dragging breaths, she stayed where she was, wondering if she were still dreaming, if she was going to "wake up" another time. Or two. Or twelve.

When nothing happened and nothing changed, she patted the carpet with her palms. She was too shaken to look around properly, too confused as to whether she was awake or not, but she better get over all that quick. As fear shimmied over her skin, she turned her head and went eye to eye with the wastepaper basket under her desk. The Post-its she'd wadded up earlier and thrown badly in a series of near-misses were a little halo of yellow and blue on the carpet.

Did that little detail mean she wasn't dreaming anymore? Or was her subconscious just getting the minutiae right like a good film editor?

Sitting up slowly, she took her hair out of the band she always had it in. Then she ran her fingers through the waves and resecured things.

Like maybe she could pull herself together that way.

A quick check of her watch informed her that, at least in theory, she had been asleep at her desk for a couple of hours: It was just past two a.m. At some point, she must have put her head down, and then . . .

The dream. The one she'd been having lately, the hazy details of which haunted her during the day. And after that a second nightmare where she'd been hunted in her house by something she didn't believe in.

The only true evil was human. She'd learned that at age sixteen.

Demons didn't exist in the real world.

As she finally looked around, she got scared for a different reason . . .

How did she know any of this was real?

In a desperate attempt to ground herself, her eyes skipped over the empty office chairs, the buff-colored felt walls of the cubicles, the darkened computer monitors, the silent telephones. As she closed her mouth and started breathing through her nose, she smelled the chemical fragrance of the shampoo they regularly scrubbed the carpet with—and remembered commenting to Trey that licorice had been a weird choice for the scent.

It was like they'd used Dr Pepper as a cleaner.

Getting to her feet, she turned in a slow circle as she righted her jacket, her blouse, her slacks. Oh, look, she'd blown out of one of her shoes—and as she reached down to grab it, she had to ignore how badly her hand was shaking.

Everything looked too normal, was too quiet, and there were shadows everywhere, thrown off of file cabinets and lurking under chairs and desks, each one of them like what had attacked her in her house.

In the nightmare she'd just had, rather. Unless she was still dreaming—

The door to the Bull Pen was thrown open behind her, and she whirled around, her gun up and pointed at the invasion before she could think anything through.

"Put your hands up! I'm armed!"

"What the hell!"

As the shout back echoed around the empty division, the uniformed cleaning woman splayed her arms out and hit the floor facedown so hard she bounced.

"*Shit,*" Erika barked as she swung her muzzle away to the ceiling.

For a split second, she held her position.

On the far side of the woman, the door was propped open by a cart of supplies, and out in the hall, there was a bright wash of fluorescent ceiling lights and yellow walls and that laminate flooring that had been installed a year ago.

No shadows.

"You think I'm a robber?" the cleaning woman muttered as she turned her head to the side. "Like anybody would come to police head-quarters to steal something?"

Erika put her weapon back in its holster—then again, bullets only worked against living things, and what she was scared of, what had been so close to her when she'd been asleep . . . wasn't alive.

It just wasn't.

Rushing over, she helped the woman up to her feet. As she recognized the maintenance worker, she studied every detail about her, from the way her gray hair was pulled back with barrettes to the pores of her face and the wrinkles around her watery blue eyes.

She was real, Erika told herself.

"I'm so sorry, and I'll be reporting the incident to my superior," she said. "I just thought—well, it doesn't matter what I thought."

The woman brushed off the front of her dark green uniform, passing a hand over a stitched-on name tag that read "Brenda." "I got clearance to be here, you know. I got a pass card. You've seen me before. You always work late."

"Yeah, I'm really sorry. There's no excuse. I just—you surprised me."

Brenda patted at her hair, pushing it back into place. "Well, you deal with frickin' dead people all the time. Guess I can't blame you for being jumpy. And don't worry about telling your boss. I don't want to waste a lot of time talking about something that doesn't matter."

"It's a departmental requirement."

"Whatever, you do you. I gotta get back to work."

The woman gave a nod, like things were done as far as she was concerned, even though she'd just had a loaded gun pointed at her. And then with a pragmatism that came from either her age or the kind of life she'd lived, she pushed her cart over to the twin bathroom entrances. Popping open a tripod caution tent, she put the orange warning in front of the men's room, and disappeared inside.

Okay, surely, if this were a nightmare, sinks would not be getting cleaned—

The sound of her cell phone going off on her desk snapped Erika's head around. Instead of lunging for it, she let the thing ring a second time, and when she picked the iPhone up, she turned the screen over slowly.

You know, in case a demon was calling or something.

Nope. Dispatch.

She took a deep breath. "Saunders." Then she tried to focus on what was being said to her. "Ah, no, no, I left the scene at Primrose so I'll take it. No reason to wake up Creason—you already did? Okay, fine. Where's the body again?" A quick glance to the right gave her pause as she wondered whether a coat across the aisle had moved. "Another one under the bridge, huh. Do we have patrol there? Good. Tell them I'll be there in five—what? No, I'm at headquarters. Ah, no, I didn't go home."

As she ended the call, she measured all the shadows on the carpet, on the walls, by the filing cabinets. Over at the bathrooms, there was a muffled singing coming through the closed door, the cleaning woman—Brenda—running through some kind of song that Erika didn't recognize. Or maybe it was no song at all.

The strange tune was like something you could open an episode of *American Horror Story* with.

Grabbing her bag, Erika headed out, still unsure of what kind of reality she was in.

The sense that evil lurked everywhere persisted.

Or stalked her, was more like it.

CHAPTER EIGHT

I know him."

As Erika made the ID down by the bridge, she was kneeling beside the cooling body of a man who appeared to have shot himself in the head. The entrance wound was on the right temple, and the gun was still gripped in his hand.

Twice in one night, she thought as she noted the bomber jacket, the hoodie, the dark clothes and the bright white sneakers. But no pink nail polish this time.

"Who is he?" Detective Kip Creason asked.

She glanced up at her colleague. Kip was a lean man who always wore skinny cut slacks and bow ties. He and his husband were just back from their honeymoon, and she had a passing envy at his tan and the natural sun-streaks in his dark-blond hair. Kip was born and bred in California, and coming to Caldie hadn't changed the fact that he always looked better, more rested, and happier than everybody else did. Even down here by the river, after two a.m., he was fresh as a daisy. And didn't that make her feel older. More tired. More crazy.

"Christopher Ernest Olyn." Erika refocused on the body. "He's got a long rap sheet for drugs and assault, and he brushed up with homicide for the first time about six months ago. Remember the case? He almost beat his girlfriend to death—we were sure she was going to die as soon as she was taken off life support. She survived, but refused to testify, and there were no witnesses. The DA had to drop the case, but Olyn was ready if it went forward. He lawyered up with some big-time, mob-connected criminal attorney from Manhattan."

"I remember, yes. You really were good with the victim. She trusted you."

Erika stood back up. "I'm worried he finally killed her tonight—and then came down here, unable to live with himself. They had a really toxic, codependent relationship. We need to do a welfare check on her."

"You should go over and do that. If anyone else in uniform or with a badge shows up at her place, I'll bet she won't answer her door. I can handle things here."

Looking around, Erika took some quick mental pictures of the scene. The body was at the far edge of what was considered "under the bridge," lying at the base of an old brick wall that encircled one of the original Caldwell warehouses.

"We're not going to have any witnesses," she murmured.

"No," Kip agreed as he pulled his fitted peacoat closer across his chest. "Nobody will have seen a thing."

No one was around to even be interviewed. The population who lived in and among the forest of concrete pylons had emptied out, the burning drums of trash casting flickering orange light over the littered, vacant acreage.

"Erika? Are you all right?"

She shook herself back to attention and smiled at her sun-streaked colleague. "Fine, thanks. And absolutely I'll do the welfare check. They were living over on Market, assuming they haven't moved. I can confirm with the probation database."

Getting out her cell phone, she signed in to the CPD system and ran a search under the name of Constance Ritcher. Street name had been Candy. She'd had some prostitution convictions on her record, but no drugs, nothing violent.

Erika could still remember what the emaciated woman had looked like hooked up to a ventilator in the ICU over at St. Francis.

"Yup, she's still on Market." She put her phone away, and took note of the uniforms who were bringing over a privacy screen. "It won't take me long."

"As I said, I'll take care of things here."

She nodded and murmured a few more things to Kip, not that she was tracking—and then she was walking to her car, stepping over brown-paper-bag-wrapped bottles and twisted-up cloth wads that could have been towels, shirts, sweaters. As she came up to her un-marked and unlocked it with her remote, the sense that she was being watched brought her head around.

Reaching up to the nape of her neck, she rubbed at the tingling sen-sation and then she looked back at the scene, which was only about fifty feet away. In the lee of the brick wall, the uniformed officers were un-folding the screen and Kip was kneeling where she had just been, talking into his phone, recording notes.

As a breeze came off the river, she smelled shore funk and dirt and the greasy smoke of trash burning in those steel drums.

Everything was right about this . . . just like back at headquarters. And yet her instincts were telling her—

Out of the corner of her eye, she caught sight of something red, and she pivoted quick. Then she frowned and wondered if she was seeing right. The flash of one-of-these-things-does-not-belong was actually a woman, and she was leaning against one of the bridge supports, looking as out of place as a cultivated rose in the middle of a landfill. With long, wavy brunette hair and a breathtakingly beautiful face, she was wearing nothing but Christmas-red skintight leggings and a matching bustier, seemingly impervious to the cold.

The scent of a grapey perfume drifted into Erika's nose.

Poison by Dior, she thought. God, she hadn't thought of that oldie-but-goodie since college, when she and her friends had bought designer perfumes on the cheap from CVS's locked case of rejects, resales, and fakes.

"Erika? You forget something?"

Erika jumped and glanced back at the scene. Kip had risen to his feet and was staring over as if he were thinking about doing a welfare check of his own. While he fiddled with the navy-blue-and-gold bow tie that peeked out under his peacoat's lapels, she realized he was wearing the same expression Trey had had back at Primrose—after she'd emerged from the Landreys' bathroom.

"Yup, just great," she called back to her colleague.

Opening the driver's side door, she dumped herself behind the wheel and immediately locked the unmarked. As she started the engine, she looked back to where the brunette had been leaning against the bridge pylon.

The woman was gone.

As if she had never existed.

Erika squeezed her eyes shut. The sense that the world around her wasn't as solid as it had seemed made her want to tear up. Made her want to sob. Especially as she had a feeling she was going to find another dead body when she got over to that address on Market.

But instead of losing it, she put her car in drive and hit the gas.

◆   ◆   ◆

Over by the bridge's support, the demon Devina made herself invisible not because she couldn't handle that cop. Detective. Whatever the fuck the woman was.

Nah, she poof'd out because she was looking to have some fun with this. God knew there was nothing much else happening in her life, and as she felt herself once again falling into the sulk that had dogged her for the last couple of months, she had to do something to cheer herself up.

Driving Balthazar's woman insane was going to be a little pet project.

Unless that fucking Book gets off its ass, she thought as an utterly uninspiring American sedan drove off. *Why did it have to be such a little bitch?*

That piece of shit collection of parchment had given so much to so many as it had come down through the millennia: Death to enemies, riches to the greedy, sickness as an act of vengeance, lovers back where they belonged. Always on its terms, though.

That last one was the problem, of course. The thing was like a gun with an opinion about its targets.

"What the hell do I have to do to get what I deserve—"

Not much really. Just jump in front of a train.

Gritting her teeth, Devina pivoted around to the disembodied voice—and got an eyeful of somebody who, under different circumstances, would totally have been worth a fuck or two.

Lassiter, the fallen angel, was standing in the cold wind just as she was, half naked and unaffected by the outside temperature. With his muscular torso bare except for all his gold chains, and his blond-and-black hair blowing around his handsome face, he was like Magic Mike without a stage. And of course, those beautiful gossamer wings rising up on both sides of him were a nice touch, too.

They were a deliberate reminder that she was dealing with somebody out of this world, and not just because he was so fuckable.

All things considered . . . she wanted to scream at him.

Instead, she smiled and then nodded toward the crime scene. "Come to save the soul of some poor wretch? Isn't that how the song goes? I think you're a little late, going by the lack of an ambulance. Nothing to revive, Lassiter."

Actually, I've come to see you.

Devina flushed and felt the need to plump her already luscious hair. As she gave in to the impulse and brought some of the waves over one shoulder, she ran her eyes all the way down the angel's body. In those leggings he insisted on wearing, his thigh muscles were nice and obvious in all their corded strength, and what was between them, that bulge, was downright impressive.

Why had she never considered him before, she wondered.

"What exactly are you looking for, angel. And FYI, I'm not sure you're my type."

This was a lie, of course. He absolutely was her type. He would hate fucking her, and getting him to compromise his principles would be a very good time. And then there'd be the orgasms.

Well, what do you know. The night was looking up.

I think you and I need to have a little discussion about property lines and boundaries.

Devina frowned. "I beg your pardon."

You heard me. I want you out of Balthazar. You're trespassing and you know it.

Oh, she thought. *That.*

"It's more of a time-share, really." She smiled and wondered what it would feel like to have him on top of her. "And my sex life is none of your business, is it."

I'm not asking you. I'm telling you. Get out of Balthazar.

"Nope. Sorry." She shrugged and then ran her fingertips from her collarbone to her sternum, lingering on the bustier's contouring of her cleavage. "And not to go five-year-old on this, but you can't make me. I'm also pretty sure the Creator is going to have an opinion about you getting overly involved. Isn't that a thing? I think it is, what with your new promotion and all."

This is just between you and me. You've got a million other people in this city to play with. You can have another.

"I don't want another." She leaned forward toward the male. "And you're not very bright, angel. I want him even more now that you have an opinion about my little infestation."

All at once, the air between them changed, the charge of heat so intense, it came at her in a warping, nuclear rush that pushed her back against a concrete support and held her in place. As she fought to get free, she didn't really want the liberation. The power wielded on her made her nipples tighten and her thighs loosen.

"I didn't know you had it in you," she moaned as she arched into the pain, knowing that the bustier wasn't going to be able to keep things decent given how full her breasts were in the cups.

Lassiter stalked up to her, his iridescent wings unfurling fully over those strong shoulders, his body a thing of both beauty and vengeance. In the wind coming off the river, his blond-and-black hair pulled back off his face, and the gold chains around his neck, his wrists, and his waist gleamed like they were alive.

"Careful . . . angel." She smiled even as she began to pant from the suffocation. "You started . . . this about boundaries. Now you're . . . treading on mine."

Get out of Balthazar, Lassiter snarled without moving his luscious lips. *Leave the male alone.*

Devina shifted her eyes over to the crime scene, where humans both uniformed and plainclothed milled around doing their duty for one of their dead, totally oblivious to the fact that no more than two hundred yards away, a pair of elementals were in a dogfight over the soul of a vampire.

The demon started to laugh, although the sound was ugly because she couldn't breathe.

"I . . . will . . . tell . . ." She hauled in some air and met Lassiter's strange, odd-color eyes with her own. ". . . the Creator."

After a glare session that would have melted paint off a wall—assuming the angel's temper didn't blow the whole house down—the ace in her pocket worked. The heat and the pressure were sucked back in a retraction, and then he dropped the psychic connection bullshit.

His voice had more depth than when it had been willed into her head. "Go to Him. Tell Him everything. You entered Balthazar's soul without permission when he was in the transition between life and death. You're in the wrong. You stepped over the line and you're going to have to explain yourself if you bring me to His attention."

Devina swept her hands up from her waist and tugged the bustier into place, her breasts aching in their whalebone cage. "How do you know I wasn't invited by Balthazar?"

"Because he wants you the fuck out of him."

"Lovers' spat, and yet you're treating it like domestic violence."

"Get out of him."

With an arched brow, Devina smoothed her hair and then once again ran her fingertips over her cleavage. As she imagined the angel's mouth on her breasts, his tongue licking at her nipples, she was aware of a stinging need inside of her.

"You want me to leave that vampire alone?" She straightened off the pylon and took three steps forward, closing the distance between their bodies. "That's what you want?"

God, the angel smelled incredible. Like fresh air and sunshine, even though the two of them were standing in the middle of a debris field of filth and human waste and river mud.

When she went to put her hand on his chest, he slapped a hold on her wrist. "Yes, demon. That's what I want."

Devina focused on the angel's mouth and then licked her lips. "Fine. But you have to give me something I want."

"I don't have to give you shit—"

"Yes, you do. You're stuck because you have no leverage. You see, if you try to turn me in with the Creator, you're also going to have to explain yourself. And you can't compel me, only He can. So you need to give me something and I'll bet if you think really hard . . ." She bit her lower lip with her sharp, white teeth. Then hissed a little as she slipped her free hand inside the cup of her bustier. "I think you'll figure out what it is."

Lassiter's gleaming stare narrowed. "I'm not fucking you."

With a quick yank, she ripped her arm out of his hold. "Then I have no incentive to leave Balthazar and we have nothing to discuss. Have a good night, angel."

Blowing Lassiter a kiss, she took off.

And she was smiling as she ghosted out.

CHAPTER NINE

Over on Market Street, about fifteen blocks away from the bridge, Erika's unmarked rolled to a stop in front of a graffiti-covered walk-up that was battened down like its inhabitants expected a siege. The windows on all four levels were boarded over with plywood, and makeshift bars were screwed in on top of those sheets. The inset entry door was a solid steel panel that was totally at odds with the old brick building, and she half expected to see a sentry patrolling the rooftop.

As she got out, she glanced across the four lanes of no-traffic. Back about ten years ago, this end of Market had all kinds of local restaurants, hair salons, and tattoo parlors. It hadn't been ritzy, but there had been plenty of going concerns. Now, the businesses had been deserted and the residences were either defended like this one or taken over by squatters after being condemned by the city.

Closing her door and locking everything, she went around the back of her vehicle and hopped up onto the sidewalk. With a dodge to the left, she squeezed by a rubbish bin that was bolted into the concrete. The thing was overflowing, the ring of litter around its base making her think of the wastepaper basket under her desk with all of her near-miss Post-it notes.

There were five cracked steps up to that steel door, and it went without saying that there wasn't an intercom system she could buzz the third floor on—

As she gave the heavy panel a test-tug, she was surprised to find the thing loose in its reinforced jambs.

"Hello?" she called into the dim interior.

Stepping inside, she wrinkled her nose. They'd been cooking meth here—and recently. The chemicals in the air made her eyes water and her throat instantly irritated. Coughing into her elbow, she undid the buttons on both her coat and her blazer so she had access to her service weapon.

Just in case the chefs were still on duty.

The building's layout was as she'd remembered, the stairwell on the right against the wall, the apartment doors on the left, one per floor. She thought about announcing herself, but she wasn't here to make arrests.

The steps creaked as she went up, and every time they did, she looked behind herself. Shadows. So many shadows.

"Get a grip," she said under her breath.

Up on the third floor, she paused—and then broke away from the staircase to go to the sole door on the little hallway. The thing had hunks out of its boards, like somebody had gone after it with a hammer, and most of its paint—red, it seemed—had flaked off, the wood underneath stained with dirt and filth from decades of no cleaning and lots of hard living.

"Connie?" she said as she went to knock. "It's me, Erika . . ."

The door opened a crack as her knuckles made contact, and unlike everything else in the building, the hinges were silent, having been oiled. The smell that was released was bad . . . but it didn't carry with it that telltale death stench. There was garbage, yes, but no rotting human remains.

Fresh kills didn't smell like that, though.

"Connie?" Adding some more volume, she called out, "Connie, it's me, Erika."

Out of habit, she did some quick math on whether she had probable cause to enter the premises, but then again, if anything had happened to the woman, Olyn was by far the most likely aggressor and it wasn't like they could prosecute Olyn from the grave.

"I'm just here to check on you, Connie . . ." she said.

The living area was cluttered with weeks-old pizza boxes, empty two-liter Mountain Dew bottles, and dirty clothes. A faded sofa was off-kilter, its front right foot busted, and a chipped coffee table was splintered down the middle, yet pushed together. Like whoever had broken it had tried to put it to rights.

Most likely, Olyn had slammed something into it, and Connie had been the fixer. Which was the bandwidth of their relationship, as far as Erika had seen.

"Connie?"

A filthy kitchen was next in the lineup of the long and narrow apartment, and it was clear things had degenerated in the three months since Erika had paid her last visit. Underfoot, plastic food containers crackled and crunched, and the smell was like a restaurant dumpster on a hot August night: With the windows all boarded up and the radiators pumping out heat, the flat was an incubator for spoiled meat, milk, cheese, and whatever else.

The far side of the kitchen put her by the bathroom, and as she leaned into the cramped space, she checked the tub, which was stained but not with blood, as well the shower stall, which was the same.

It was as she went farther down the hall toward the bedroom that she caught the undercurrent in the air.

Beneath the garbage stink . . . there was blood.

For the second time in one evening, she had to brace herself before entering a stranger's sleeping space, and as she pushed open the half-closed door, she—

Erika froze. Caught her breath. Then threw a hand out for something, anything, to keep her on her feet.

"It's . . . *you*," she breathed.

◆   ◆   ◆

At the sound of the female voice, Balz looked up from his kneeling position by a dead woman on a bare floor mattress. When he saw who was standing in between the jambs of the victim's room, he couldn't believe what he was seeing.

Then again, that made two of them. His homicide detective—*not* that she was his—seemed equally poleaxed at his presence, the pair of them locking eyes and sharing a common astonishment.

She recovered first, shaking her head like she was trying to rattle loose some rationality in the middle of something that made no sense to her. "What are you doing here?"

And then she was groaning and putting a hand to her temple. The obvious pain she felt made him wince in sympathy, and God, he hated that he had stolen anything from her.

Kind of ironic for a thief, he thought.

"Hi," he said softly. "It's good to see you again—and no, I didn't kill her. I came to see if I could help."

As Erika Saunders looked down and opened her mouth, he didn't really want to hear how there was no way she'd believe a piece of shit like him. But that wasn't what came out at him.

"Oh, Connie," she whispered in a sad way. "Shit."

The woman he had watched at her desk earlier in the night entered the squalid bedroom on feet that were silent and careful. When she got to the mattress, she, too, kneeled down, one hand coming up to hold her chin, the other resting on her knee.

Her hazel eyes roamed around the bloody remains, seeing everything he had—and maybe more because this was her profession.

"I don't think she suffered much," he said dully. "That puncture through the heart . . . it happened fast."

"Actually, she suffered mostly by being alive. Oh . . . Connie."

The hand that was on her chin moved down to below her collarbone and she seemed to massage an ache there.

He wanted to tell her that the knife was in the kitchen, in the sink, where that piece of shit down by the bridge had gone to wash the blood off his hands. Balz also wanted to tell her that he was sorry the woman had died, even though he hadn't known her. And that he was sorry this was obviously so hard to see.

Then again, it was a dead human, and Erika clearly had a heart. How could it not be hard?

As a period of quiet stillness seemed to permeate the whole building, he had to look away because he felt as though he were intruding on a private moment. Unfortunately, the body was the only other thing to really look at, and he saw what he had walked in on with fresh eyes: The victim was lying faceup, in the position that Balz had found her in. She was wearing blue jeans that had rips in both knees, a t-shirt that seemed way too thin for the season, and nothing on her feet. Her blond hair, which had a brassy tone to the frizzy ends and two inches of dark regrowth, was matted with blood that had darkened from bright crimson to black. The face was so bruised and swollen, the features were unclear, and the mortal wound, that penetration in the center of the chest, had bled so extensively that half of the mattress underneath was showing the stain.

"Why did you come here?"

At the sound of the brisk voice, his head came up, and as he met those hazel eyes again, it was clear his detective's professional composure was back in place. No more sadness in her eyes or her expression; she was all business.

"Do you know them?" she prompted. "Connie and her boyfriend."

"In a way."

"And what way is that?"

God . . . even though this was definitely not the place, and completely not the time, he wanted her—and part of the attraction was the power in her. There was no come-hither bullshit, no flirtatious eyelash batting or that awful pet-the-hair-and-preen stuff. Nope, this woman was like a water cannon, hitting him with the force of her intelligence, her try-me-if-you-dare, her confidence. And what do you know, she blew him out of his boots.

"So how do you know them?" she repeated.

Yup, she was going to make him answer that—and his explanation, that he'd read a man's mind and saw that he'd hurt his girlfriend, was not going to make her happy. Oh, and then there was the fun fact that he had cocaine in his jacket, unregistered guns under both arms, and a matched set of steel poke-and-tickles strapped to his chest.

But hey, as penetrating as that stare of hers was, at least he knew it didn't detect metal. Important tip.

"From the street," he said. "That's how."

When she rose to her full height, he did the same—and she had to tilt her head up to look at his face. "You're a hard man to find, you know that."

She mostly kept the grimace of pain to herself, and he wished he could tell her to please, *please*, stop probing those memories he'd buried.

"If I'd known you were looking for me," he said, "I'd have made myself easier to locate."

She blinked at that. "Do you mind telling me your name?"

"Balthazar, no last name. I'm like Cher. Madonna. Bono. Guess those references date me, huh."

"Will you come down to the station and answer . . ."

Her voice drifted off, and for an egotistical split second, he entertained the fantasy that she was so captivated by him, she'd literally lost the ability to speak. But then a trembling came over her, her hands shaking so badly that she raised them in confusion and alarm. With a stumble backward, she arched as if she couldn't control her balance—

Balz jumped over the body and caught her just as the whites of her eyes flashed and she went limp. "Erika? Erika—"

With an abruptness that made no sense, her face turned to his, and that sightless stare met his own as if she could see him.

In a guttural, unreal voice, she said, "You are in danger. I need to save you."

CHAPTER TEN

Rural Route 149

Nate, adopted son of the Black Dagger Brother Murhder, was desperate . . . just really, really fucking desperate . . . for his best friend, Shuli, to finally stop talking about—

"—and then she took my shirt off. Listen, naked is all well and good, but I didn't give a crap about my top half. I wanted the pants gone. But it was like she read my mind. All of a sudden, I feel her hands on my belt buckle and—"

"That's enough," Nate cut in with a wince. "I'm good with the details stopping here. I'm *so* totally good with closing the curtain now."

Shuli looked over from the driver's seat of his white-on-white Tesla like someone had insulted his taste in cars. The male was an aristocrat all the way, diamond studs the size of bowling balls in his earlobes, some kind of big, heavy rose-gold watch on his wrist, the air of someone who had gotten what he wanted all his life as golden a halo as anybody could get. And yet in spite of all that, he wasn't a bad guy.

"But the details are the best part," he said. "Besides, don't you want to know what it's like before you and your female bang—"

"Whoa. Hold up." Nate put both his palms out. "There is no me and any female. And if I wanted to go the porn route, it's not going to be hearing a blow-by-blow about you and some human woman you picked up in a club two nights ago—"

"There was only one blow, actually. The other three times were straight sex."

Closing his eyes, Nate wanted to plug his ears. "Like I was saying—"

"I'm going to pay her back for that, though—"

"Stop."

"Fiiiiinnnnne. But I knew she was going to call me. I *knew* it."

"Why, because you slipped her a hundy along with your number?"

"No, it's 'cuz I'm fucking hot."

Nate rubbed his aching eyes. "You know, the only thing worse than you talking about your sex life, is you talking about how much you love yourself."

"Okay. So how much do you love me?" As a death-glare came his way, Shuli shrugged. "What. You wanted to change the subject."

The pair of them had just left a job site in a part of town where the houses were huge, the lots were measured in acres not feet, and the garages had spaces for four cars at least. The owner was finishing his basement by putting in a workout room, a sauna, and a movie theater, and the both of them had been called in to help with the drywall. Nate was the only one who'd been on time. When Shuli had finally arrived, he'd smelled like perfume and been wearing a wrinkled silk shirt and a set of slacks that should have had a belt, but did not. His hair had likewise been a mess—and, not that anybody had needed the confirmation, the hickey on the side of his throat had neon-lighted the virgin-no-longer vibe he was clearly dying to talk about.

"Anyway." Shuli put his directional signal on. "It was phenomenal. Like I said, we did it three times, and the last one was up against the door as I was leaving."

"I wouldn't think that was possible."

"Standing up is absolutely a position. A good one, too."

"No, I don't get how you were doing it as you were leaving—watch out for the deer."

"Huh?" Shuli cursed as he swerved away from a doe at the side of the country road. "And don't be pandemic."

"Pedantic."

"That, too."

Fortunately, Shuli went quiet at that point, although the way he kept running his hand around the top curve of the steering wheel suggested he was in his mind where he'd been told his mouth couldn't go.

Nate looked away from the stroking and stared out of his window. The landscape was all fields now, and as they passed by a rickety split-rail fence and then a stone wall, a kindling in his gut made him adjust himself in his seat. The closer they got to Luchas House, the more he fidgeted, and he supposed the one good thing about Shuli finally having sex for the first time was that the guy was too busy reliving his orgasmic glory to notice how itchy Nate was getting.

"At least we have tomorrow off," Shuli announced.

"Do we?"

"It's Saturday. And we're going out, remember?"

"Oh, right."

Why hadn't he just dematerialized out here on his own?

Well, he answered himself, because then it was way too obvious. If Shuli was wingman'ing it, he had some kind of cover.

Granted, it was cover of the ridden-hard-put-up-wet variety.

"And here we are," Shuli said as he turned into the gravel drive.

Down at the end of the lane, a farmhouse with a wraparound porch had loads of lights on in its interior, and as the illumination spilled out onto the still-brown lawn, Nate decided that the place looked like a spaceship that had just landed, but come in peace. With a tree in the side yard and a meadow out behind, it was a really special spot—and not for the first time, he could see exactly what the Brother Qhuinn had loved at the setting.

Luchas House was named after the fighter's brother, and was part of the race's social services program, offering a haven for youth who needed shelter, resources, help. Unlike Safe Place, which was reserved for females and their young, males were allowed into the facility, both as residents and as guests. Which was a good thing for Nate.

With a desperation he didn't want to admit to himself, his eyes shot to the second floor on the left. The windows of that particular bedroom were dark, and he had a moment of panic.

But surely if she had left . . . she would have said something?

Taking a deep breath, he brushed at the front of his SUNY Caldwell sweatshirt. There were some paint streaks on the bottom and he pulled the hem up and took a whiff. Great. Cologne by Benjamin Moore.

He had to take these opportunities when he could, though.

The second the Tesla stopped by the walkway to the front door, all Nate wanted to do was break out of the car and bull-rush the entry, knocking the barrier down so that he could race up the stairs and check to make sure she hadn't—

"Listen," Shuli said in his best I'm-two-months-older-than-you voice, "tomorrow night's going to be good for you, and I'll make sure it's chill. We'll go to this new place, Dandelion. You'll love it, and you don't have to stay forever if you don't want. You can just have a drink and see what happens."

"I don't know." Nate popped the door handle. "It's not something I'm really interested in. Besides, I'm guessing you're going to be busy getting busy."

Shuli threw out a hand and caught Nate's upper arm. "It's way better than . . . you know."

"Better than what?"

"Coming out here every chance you get."

Nate froze for a second. He thought he'd been smoother than that, and if Shuli had noticed—as self-absorbed as the guy was—who else knew he was kind of stalking the house?

Pulling out of a tailspin, he said, "What are you talking about. I've been here twice since we finished working on the garage, including right now."

"And those were the two chances you had."

Nate took his arm back. "I just need to get my sweatshirt."

"Oh, really? The one that's exactly like what you have on? And is worth twenty bucks, tops? Look, I don't care about what you pretense to the rest of the world, but between you and me, we should be honest."

"Pretend," Nate muttered as he got out of the car.

Caught up in a surge of nervous, he closed the passenger-side door and forgot about Shuli, the guy's big, fat, hairy opinion, and all the clubs that were, or ever had been, in Caldwell. Striding up to the front door, he tugged at his paint-smudged sweatshirt, stamped his work boots to get any mud off of them—and would have run a hand through his dark hair if Shuli hadn't been riding up on his ass.

The door opened before he could knock.

"Good timing, dawn is close." The social worker smiled as she stepped back. "Your sweatshirt's in the kitchen."

The female was just what you'd expect someone in her line of work to be, motherly, kind, soft-spoken. Shoot . . . what was her name? He'd been told a couple of times, but he always forgot it. He did remember her blue jeans, though. Wrangler. Not a brand he was familiar with—but like he knew anything about clothes?

"Thank you so much . . ." He returned her smile as he came inside—and hoped she didn't catch his forgetfulness. "Oh, wow, smell the chocolate chip cookies."

"They're right out of the oven," she said. "Every night, just like clock-work."

As Nate walked through the living area, he could hear footsteps up on the second floor. They were heavy. A male's.

"Has someone else moved in?" While he frowned at the ceiling, he reminded himself it wasn't his house—and then straightened a throw pillow on a couch and tried to be casual about it. "Sounds like you have another resident."

"We have a new one, yes." The social worker went ahead into the gray-and-white kitchen and stopped at the inset desk by the eating table. "Here it is."

His sweatshirt had never been treated so well. The thing was folded neatly, and as he took it, he could smell fabric softener.

"Thanks." He glanced over to the stove, at the lines of cookies cooling on racks. "You know, those Toll Houses look great."

"Help yourself." The female headed over to the cupboard and took out a plate. "I always make a full batch even though there's just three of us here. Old habits, you know. From Safe Place. Milk?"

"I'd love some. Shuli would, too."

"Have a seat and I'll wait on you guys."

Pointedly ignoring his buddy's double take, Nate pulled out one of the chairs and sat down at the table. Like the rest of the house, everything in the kitchen was neat as a pin, the stainless steel stovetop sparkling, the sink free of dirty dishes, the granite counters clear except for the cooling cookies.

So yeah, nothing he could volunteer to fix or tidy up or help with.

"Actually," Shuli said with a gleam in his eye, "I am feeling a little peckish. I've been working out."

"Oh?" The social worker—God, what was her name?—put the plate she'd layered with Toll Houses on the table and turned away for glasses. "Where have you been exercising? And what kind of stuff are you doing?"

Nate narrowed his stare at Shuli, the universal signal for "don't you fucking dare bring up your fucking." Shuli made googly eyes in return, but at least he didn't go there.

"We have a home gym," was all he said as he took a cookie and bit off half of it.

Home gym, Nate's ass. Shuli's mansion had a D1 football team's worth of equipment and floor space. He got points for not bragging, though.

"These are amazing," Nate said as he tried one of the cookies. "No nuts."

"Just like you," Shuli whispered.

Nate flipped the guy off on the side, then he leaned out and tried to see through to the back hall. You know, just in case somebody had walked in from the garage. Even though no doors had opened and closed.

"That's really convenient." The social worker put a milk carton back into the fridge. "We'd love to add one off the garage here, but we don't have the funding quite yet."

Crap, what were they talking about again, Nate thought as he glanced into the living room.

"Exercise can really help with mood and feelings of mastery," the social worker continued. "It's an important component to health and recovery—"

"Gym," Nate blurted.

The female laughed. "Yes, I wish we had a—"

"We'llbuilditforyou." As her brows went up and she stopped in mid-delivery of the glasses of milk, Nate forced himself to slow down. "We can totally build one here for you." He nodded at Shuli. "He was just saying the other day that he wanted to do something charitable for the community with his allowance."

"I was?" Shuli said around a bite.

"And he and I'll do the construction work for free."

"We will?"

Nate shot his buddy another look. "Our foreman, Heff, can draw up the plans and give us a deal on the supplies with his contractor's discount. We can work here on our off days."

The social worker put a hand to the base of her throat and her eyes shimmered with gratitude. "You guys . . . that would be so kind. But are you sure?"

Nate nodded as if they'd sealed the deal with a blood pact. "It's our pleasure."

"It is?" Shuli muttered.

◆   ◆   ◆

Out behind the farmhouse that smelled like chocolate chip cookies, Rahvyn walked through the meadow, the grasses and wild flowers yet to kindle, the acreage still scruffy and barren of life from winter's cold embrace. As she zeroed in on the far-off wood line, she thought of her arrival in this place and time. Her trajectory had been off. She had had to visit a few other finite folios before she'd gotten it right.

Halting, she let her head fall back and looked at the galaxy above. The fact that she was where she was . . . she knew it was a miracle, an exception to the order of natural things, and she should have appreciated the rare power she possessed as the boon it was. Instead, she felt empty. Lost. Alone.

Then again, this was a whole new world, and not just because she was no longer in what people in the here and now called the "Old Country." Old Country indeed. Back where she was from, there had been nothing old about it. It had just been where all vampires had lived.

Centuries had passed, however, and therefore perspectives had changed. Unless one had hopped across all the years as opposed to plodding through them.

Time, as it turned out, was not linear in the strict sense of the word. It was more like a book full of short stories, all of the moments simultaneously re-readable, relivable, existing in paralleled perpetuity because they were bound together. Mortals, like readers, passed through each proverbial page of their tale, the letters, the spaces, the punctuation being the years, the decades, the life they lived.

None of them had any idea that it was all predestined. Even their free-will choices were a given—because their fates were on an endless loop, nothing finishing, just infinitely restarting, ever new, ever old.

The trick was, once you started your story, you couldn't not finish it. And you had no choice but to read and no conscious memory of what you had been through before.

It was vital that mortals did not know the truth of time. If they did . . . they could jump into the stories of others and influence things they were not supposed to—and like a third party editing something that had already been published, that was a mess the original author did not care for.

Rahvyn re-leveled her head. As she regarded the meadow, she felt herself get sucked back in time, although not metaphysically. With her memories coming to the forefront, she was transported to another field, one that had been in the "Old Country." And there, beside her, was her cousin, Sahvage, yelling at her, his face twisted into rage. He was screaming at her to go as the guards approached—but she would not leave him . . . and then the arrows came . . . and he was killed in front of her.

After that, other things happened, violent things, things that changed her, but in a necessary way. The pain she endured had given her the power to bring Sahvage back—and then she had had to leave him. He had seen inside her the change. He had also seen what she had done to the aristocrat who had taken her so violently. She had thusly come here, to this point in time and this location, to find him once more. She had hated to force Sahvage to suffer with not knowing what her fate had been, but she knew he needed centuries to evolve from what he had seen her do.

And now they were here, in Caldwell, the two of them once more together. He had even found a mate, which was such a blessing.

He did not look at Rahvyn the same way, however. How could he.

Thoughts of the little cottage they had once shared, back when she had been an orphan and he had been her *whard*, had her glancing at the farmhouse where she had been staying. The females there had been so kind to her, so gentle.

If they knew she had skinned alive a male and impaled him through his anus on a pole, right over the entry to his castle, would they continue to be as compassionate? She did not think so. And yes, it had been centuries ago for their timeline, but that murder, and all the others that evening, had been so violent, she did not believe the traditional passage of years mediated them at all.

Which was, of course, why her cousin treated her differently.

Lifting her hands, she stared down at them, expecting to see blood dripping off her fingers and gleaming red in the moonlight. For her, the carnage had been mere nights ago. Her body was still sore from how the aristocrat had used her.

He had deserved everything that had come unto him. She regretted nothing. She did have a secret now, though, and a side to her that no one knew about.

No, that was not true. Sahvage suspected it, and that was why he looked at her the way he now did. The young that he had been so carefully protecting . . . had turned out to be something he feared.

"I do not belong," she whispered into the night. "Here or anywhere."

Some kind of movement pulled her out of her internal trap, and as she focused properly, she realized she had pivoted to fully face the farmhouse.

In the windows of the kitchen, there was a gather of three, two males and a female. They were sitting at the table, a piece of paper between them, some kind of sketching going on.

The dark-haired male in the sweatshirt captured and held her attention, and as if he sensed her regard even through the distance that separated him, he looked up and stared out at her.

With the lights on as they were for Nate, he could not in fact see her.

It was best that things stayed that way for her sake.

But mostly for his.

CHAPTER ELEVEN

Erika regained consciousness to find herself lying with her head cradled in the crook of a strong arm and one of her hands clasped in a warm, firm grip. As her eyes fluttered open like she was a damn Victorian, she was confused by the stained ceiling overhead, and what was that delicious smell—

She sat up in a rush. The sight of Connie's body, laid out on a bare mattress, brought it all back.

Wrenching around, she looked into the face . . . of the man she had been trying to find, who she just *knew* she had seen properly in her dreams. But the recognition of him was as far as she got. The moment his features registered, her thoughts began to spin and the buzzing that had knocked her out returned. Aware that she was likely to pass out again, she grabbed hold of his leather jacket and jerked their heads together.

Except before she could demand to know what he was doing to her, he said roughly, "How do you know."

It wasn't a question, more a declaration. What was he talking about?

Whatever. That wasn't what was important.

"You've done something to my memory," she groaned through the pain between her temples. "You need to stop it—"

He grabbed her in return and gave her a shake. "How do you know!"

"Let my mind go!"

Their faces were so close, she could see the flecks in his irises, and for no good reason at all, she decided his cologne was the best thing that had ever been in her nose—not that that was in any way helpful or appropriate.

Breathing through the headache, willing herself to stay conscious, she said hoarsely, "I know you've taken something from my memories. You have to give it back. Whatever you've done is making my mind unstable and causing me to question my sanity. Please. Give it back."

She was talking fast, slurring her words, careening through the begging request, but it was the best she could do. Her thoughts were loose in a way that scared her and made forming cogent statements nearly impossible.

"You don't have to save me," he said roughly.

Save . . . *him*, she thought.

Yes . . . in the dream she'd just had back at headquarters. The black smoke that had come out of him. And then the second nightmare, with the shadow in her house—

"How do you know what was in my dream?" she whispered, aware that she was standing on the precipice of mystery, of another reality.

"I don't. Those were the words you were saying as you passed out." Then he cursed. "You've been dreaming of me?"

"Yes, and it's always the same." The headache got worse as she tried to access the recollection, but she forced herself to keep going. "I can't . . . I can't remember the specifics. It's not with me when I'm awake, but when I'm asleep, I see you. And I know . . ." All at once, she felt a terrible dread. "There's something coming after you, isn't there."

The man in black leather eased his hold on her arms. "No, there isn't."

When he didn't go any further, she had the sense she wasn't going to get anywhere pushing him on that front.

"Give me back my memories," she demanded.

On some level, she couldn't believe she was talking like this, especially because she didn't believe in hypnosis or mind control or any of that kind of crap. But he wasn't disagreeing with her, was he? If anything, he was looking guilty.

"You know what you've done to me is wrong," she said.

"It's to protect you," he shot back. "You have no idea what I am."

"Yes, I do. You're a thief." He winced at that, so she went harder, probing his weakness, her mind becoming a little clearer as she went on, more grounded. "You're a thief and a violent criminal. I've seen you on a hidden camera bringing the watches of a murder victim to the trailer of a known trafficker in stolen goods—who happened to be dead on his couch as you walked in. He'd been shot in the head, but you barely noticed. It didn't bother you in the slightest. You just took some money and left."

"How do you know the watches were stolen?"

Were they really doing this next to Connie's body? she thought numbly. But like she was going to get another chance? If he took off, she knew she was never going to see him again. Their intersection right now was a one in a million stroke of luck.

Unless he killed her. Then it was not so lucky at all.

And she should probably care a little bit more about the danger she was in, being alone with a man like him.

"So you don't deny you were there in that trailer?" she said. "With the watches?"

"I have to go—"

As he started to move away, she jerked him back with a yank on his leather jacket. "You stole from me. From my mind. I want what's mine back—I don't know how you did it, and I don't care about that. *Give me my memories.*"

Strong as he was, it was no problem to disengage from her and get to his feet. Staring down at her, his face was remote. "I don't want you involved in any of this."

"It's too fucking late for that, isn't it."

"Exactly what kind of danger do you think I'm in."

"Stop deflecting—"

"What kind of danger!" His words were harsh and loud, and they echoed around the barren, dirty room and the body that lay on the mattress beside them. "*How do you know.*"

Erika looked at Connie's remains and her heart ached. There was always death in Caldwell, but tonight the Grim Reaper seemed to be everywhere. And the idea this man, with his criminalities, was in trouble was not a news flash. The problem was . . . the danger was not from his life on the street. It was from that shadow from her nightmare. She just knew it.

"My dream changed," she answered roughly. "I fell asleep at my desk tonight, and I know I had it again . . . but something was different. Different in a bad way. If you give me back my memories, I'll probably be able to tell you."

She couldn't believe what she was saying. She couldn't believe any of this.

Because it was as if there were two parts of Caldwell, the obvious and the hidden, and these moments with him now were causing her to straddle a divide she sensed she wasn't even supposed to know about.

"You can't save me." He shook his head as he spoke, his eyes seeming to drink every detail of her in. "And this whole fucking mess is a rabbit hole you shouldn't go down."

Erika thought back to when she'd woken up at her desk in a free fall to the floor. There had been two dreams, the recurring one at the triplex, and a new one that had scared her . . . where had she been in the nightmare? Where had she . . .

"Down my stairs," she blurted. "I was at my house. The lights were all off. I was going down my stairs to my front door. I looked into the mirror there—a shadow. It was a shadow that came after me—and it was a shadow that came out of you."

The rush of clarity ushered in a return of the headache, but she didn't care. It was a relief to be able to remember something, anything— even as the hairs on the back of her neck stood up and a shiver went through her body. And it was weird. Getting chased in a nightmare by some kind of darkness was pretty standard spooky-subconscious crap, yet she knew down deep that whatever it had been . . .

Was *real*.

She pegged the suspect in the eye with a hard stare. "You don't want me to save you? Fine. Just don't leave me in a position where I can't protect myself. That thing is in my *house*."

◆   ◆   ◆

Note to self: *Shit can always get more complicated.*

As Balz stood over his detective—not that she was his—he knew he shouldn't be where he was. Vampires and humans did not mix—more to the point, they *shouldn't* mix. But after he'd gotten into the brain of that asshole down by the bridge, there was no way he was going to let some poor woman bleed out if he could help it.

And the dealer had left the woman alive.

The moment Balz had come in through the front door of the apartment, he had followed the copper scent here to the bedroom—and as soon as it was obvious things were too late, he'd intended to leave immediately.

Something had made that impossible.

Guess his destiny had known his detective was going to show up.

And now here he was, in even deeper.

"Fuck." Balz looked around the squalid room. "Mother . . . fucker."

When his eyeballs provided him with absolutely no quick-fixes whatsoever—but like, what, this sad scene was a Kmart for solutions?— he refocused on Erika. She was staring at the body, the stillness in her a clear indication she was going through so many mentals. A lot of which were his fault.

"I never believed in the list," she said absently, as if she were talking to herself. "Never did . . . but I think I do now."

"What list."

It was a long minute before she glanced back at him, and again, he had the sense she was speaking her private thoughts out loud: "Everyone who joins homicide, sooner or later, sees the list." Her eyes traveled up and down his body, like she was recording every detail about him. Just as he'd done to her. "It's not merely cold case files, it's totally unexplained cold cases, and they go back a hundred years or more. Bodies with black blood in their veins that later disappear from the morgue. Autopsies that show physical anomalies that no coroner has documented before. Remote sites where ritual murder has clearly taken place, but there are no human or animal remains. Missing persons reports and homicide cases that are 'solved,' except no one can figure out exactly how or why."

There was a pause. "Then there are murder victims who were skinned alive or had organs removed without any instrument markings on their bodies . . . victims like Herbert Cambourg, whose watches you turned in to that dead black market dealer. Cambourg's torso had been split up the middle." She shook her head and looked back at the dead human woman. "But something tells me you know this."

When he didn't respond, she smiled in a hard way. "Do you have any idea how many detectives get MRIs because they have persistent headaches and are convinced they have a brain tumor? But it's never that. And there's nothing wrong with my mind, is there."

Balz took a deep breath. "No, I'm afraid there isn't."

"I can't believe I'm talking like this."

"You can trust me."

She laughed in a harsh rush. "Spare me that line, okay? Especially when we're both next to a woman you probably killed."

"She was dead when I got here." When Erika went to counter that, he cut in, "Your forensics guys will prove it wasn't me."

"Will they?" Her eyes returned to his, and they narrowed. "Or are you just going to make me and everyone else in the department believe that? How the hell do you manipulate people's minds? It's some *Scooby-Doo* stuff, for sure."

"I love that cartoon," he said remotely.

"Me, too." She rubbed her forehead and seemed to exhale in defeat. "Except the monsters aren't real in Cabot Cove. I'm beginning to believe they're real in Caldwell, though."

"Cabot Cove is *Murder, She Wrote*."

"Oh, sorry," she murmured with exhaustion. "I didn't mean to Jessica Fletcher this situation."

" 'S okay. I like that show as well."

She took a deep breath and seemed to be unaware of what she was saying, her words coming out in a jumble. "I binge-watched the first five seasons in February when I had the flu. I don't like it from then on because of the other detectives that got brought in."

"Agreed. Plus the computer instead of the typewriter in the opening, toward the end of the series."

"I was downright offended."

And people say vampires and humans had nothing in common, he thought grimly.

God, if only he could keep talking to her like this. About nothing special or stressful. He loved the sound of her voice.

But of course, that wasn't their reality.

"I'm going to call this scene in," she said. "And I'm not going to stop looking for you. Sooner or later, I'm going to find you and figure this whole thing out. If you have any decency at all, you'll make that easier rather than harder on me—because, quite frankly, I've been way past my limit for years now. But that's not your problem, is it."

"I can save us both. You aren't going to have to defend yourself."

"You're speaking to a woman who lives alone and puts murderers behind bars. I always have to defend myself." She threw up her hands. "And if you'd let me know what the hell we're talking about, that would be just *great*."

In the silence that followed, he reflected how, lately, his life had been one bad decision after bad-luck-kick-in-the-nuts after another. So of course, he had to open his piehole.

"You're right, Herbert Cambourg wasn't killed by a human," Balz heard himself say. "And you're right. That shadow in your dream is very, very real."

"So what is it?" she asked in a reedy voice.

"It's evil. Pure evil."

"What's going on here in Caldwell? What's behind the curtain? You've got to tell me."

"The less you know, the better. But I am going to protect you." He put his palm up to her again. "Yes, I know I'm a low-life criminal, a thief, a killer, all that bullshit. But when I tell you I'm not going to let anything happen to you, I mean it."

"I'm not going to remember this, am I." She shook her head. "I've tripped and fallen into another world, haven't I. And you're going to fix it so I stay in mine."

She had an odd look on her face, as if she had tried to reconcile two mutual exclusives, and when that had proven impossible, had resigned herself to a dual reality that was at once against everything she believed . . . and the only explanation there was.

Balz had an absurd impulse to reach out and touch her in some way, give her shoulder a reassuring squeeze, brush her face with his fingertips.

"I'm sorry," he said as he kept his hands to himself.

"Please . . . please, don't erase me again." When her voice cracked, she cleared her throat—and God, those eyes of hers were cutting right into his soul. "All I have in this world is my mind and you're ruining it."

"Not by choice." Shit, he couldn't bear this. "Erika . . . I won't let you get in the middle of all this."

No, he was just going to bring Devina right to her front door, if he didn't leave right now. Jesus, the demon had been in her dream already . . .

Balz took a step back. And another one. "You can't remember me. It puts you in danger."

"No, please—"

He hated the vacant look on her face as he went into her mind and started editing himself out of her. Again.

She was right. He was doing damage, and though he had harmed many, many things in the course of his life of fighting, hurting her was wrecking him.

But what choice did he have. She had to stay far away from him, both in her mind and physically, while he got Devina out of himself.

And then killed that fucking demon.

Funny, he had been pissed when it had just been about him. Pulling this woman into it? Devina had made a big fucking mistake.

He was incandescent with rage—and if history had proven anything, he was a very, very bad enemy to have.

"I won't see you again, Erika," he said softly. "And even though you won't remember me . . . I will never forget you."

CHAPTER TWELVE

L ate the following afternoon, as the light started to fade quick
    thanks to some heavy cloud cover, Erika got in her unmarked
    and headed for the exit of the CPD headquarters parking lot.
After she swiped her card at the kiosk and the gate lifted, she was careful to check both ways before pulling into traffic, and when she hit the
gas, she didn't hit that pedal very hard at all.

As she negotiated her way into the stream of traffic, she could remember reading a study that had assessed the reaction times of tired
drivers. The conclusion was that those who were drowsy were just as
impaired and dangerous as drunks or those under the influence. It made
sense and so she was super careful, all ten-and-two'ing the wheel while
she peered over the dash like a little old lady, the other vehicles around
her a dodgeball game she just wanted to survive.

It had been yet another really, really long night.

God, Connie.

While Kip had processed the suicide down by the river, Erika had
handled the sad scene at that walk-up on Market—

Her perennial headache, which had mercifully backgrounded it-self for the afternoon, took a sharp step forward, like a security guard getting ready to deal with a trespasser. Jesus, it was like any time she thought about walking into Connie's, the thing came back—

"Damn it."

The pain across her frontal lobe rocketed to abscessed-tooth lev-els, and she had to pull out of any thoughts involving her arrival at that apartment. But it was strange. If she remembered anything after she got there, the headache went away: She could dwell all she liked on calling in the body, taking preliminary photographs with her phone, and wait-ing for the crime scene processing unit to get there. And then leaving the scene was okay, too: Going back down to the bridge, meeting with Kip for an update on that case, staying there until ten in the morning . . . none of that made her head pound.

As she came up to a red light, she threw out a hand for her bag. The Motrin bottle she had been hitting hard since around four a.m. was right in reach. Maybe she should just make things even easier and Vel-cro the thing to her palm.

Or her forehead.

Shaking out two more pills, she swallowed them dry—or tried to. She was gagging and coughing and thinking about brain tumors when the light turned green.

Driving on, she thought of all those other detectives who complained about migraines, aneurysms, strokes. It was almost a rite of passage in homicide for someone to insist that their doctor order an MRI—

"Ow," she muttered as things started to pound again.

Fighting through the pain, she got stuck at the next intersection—and reminded herself things could be worse. With the way the pedestri-ans on the crosswalk were hunkering down against the wind, you'd have sworn it was January, not April.

Ah, spring in Caldwell. The only thing warmer was a meat locker, the only thing less gusty, a turbine.

As she watched the people trudge by, she found herself sinking into sadness, sure as if she were missing somebody. The sensation at her sternum made no sense, and yet she couldn't shake the idea that she had left someone behind.

Ghosts following her even before the sun went down.

About ten minutes later, she pulled up in front of the Commodore. By the grace of God, she managed to find an open parking spot—and when she went to put money in the meter, there were twenty-eight minutes remaining on the thing.

"Maybe my luck is changing," she murmured as she stared up the flank of the high-rise.

The Commodore was luxury living at its finest, at least according to its fancy new trademark. The building had previously been all condos, but a management company had bought out most of the lower floor units to take advantage of short-term stays. Functioning now as part hotel, part residence, it had gotten a major facelift.

Walking over to the entrance, she pushed her way into the marble lobby and instantly smelled a pungent fragrance, something that was a combination of astringent and rose petals.

Guess the spa they'd added was up and running.

There was a concierge at the front desk, and as she flashed her badge, he didn't even ask who she was on-site to see. He just nodded her through like he didn't want any more trouble in the building—and really didn't want a detective loitering around, chatting it up.

Given that she had been here a lot lately, on account of two very messy homicides, the Commodore's corporate overlords were no doubt getting antsy. Murder houses were great for road traffic, foot traffic, and the month of October. They were *not* great for the renters and owners of expensive urban real estate.

The elevator took her up to the first floor of the penthouse triplex— and as soon as she stepped out into the hall, her footfalls faltered.

Something had happened here . . . something involving—

Her thoughts fragmented as her headache got worse, sure as if the agony was determined to redirect her or lay her out flat on the carpet if necessary—and she was sick of it. Tomorrow morning first thing, she was calling her doctor and getting a referral to a neurologist. She couldn't keep going like this. The headaches were constant, and though she could swear she'd found a pattern to it all, the idea that what she was thinking about was the driver was just nuts.

It was also not a medical diagnosis.

Pushing through the discomfort, she went down the hallway's runner and stopped at an ornate door that was marked with a little brass plate that read: "Mr. and Mrs. Herbert C. Cambourg."

Before Erika could ring the bell, the entrance to the triplex opened. The tall, thin woman on the other side had long, blond-streaked hair that was straight as a ruler, a face as smooth and lovely as a Renaissance marble bust, and a body that was right out of the Kate Moss tradition of models. As a chaser to all that, her dark blue pencil jeans and high-collared blouse were tailor-fit to her—and definitely cost more than Erika's monthly mortgage payment.

Then again, Mr. Cambourg had had good taste in art, whether it was inanimate or the living-and-breathing variety.

On the other hand, the objects he wanted to collect was a different matter.

"I saw you on the security camera," Keri Cambourg explained. "And as I said, you never have to apologize. Anytime you want to come here, you're welcome."

"I wish I had some news about your case." Erika stepped inside the long, formal corridor. "I do want to assure you that we're going to find the person who killed your husband."

Keri closed them in and then leaned back against the paneled door. "I'm not sure you will, and I don't mean any disrespect. Nothing about this has made any sense to me."

"I'm not giving up."

"I'm not sure I care anymore." The widow crossed her arms around herself. Looked away. Looked back. "I guess that sounds bad."

"People grieve in different ways. There is no right or wrong—"

"I've had three women come here in the last two days. Three of them. They walked past the concierge downstairs—and do you want to know why? My husband has another unit in this building, and the concierge knew them all. They've been rotating through, evidently." As Erika cursed under her breath, the widow shook her head. "I knew that Herb . . . well, I wasn't oblivious to what he was doing on his business trips. He never threw it in my face, however—or that's what I thought. In reality, he was just a better liar than I could have guessed. Another apartment . . . downstairs, in this very building. Can you believe it? The lawyer broke the news to me today."

"Oh, Keri."

"His lovers . . ." Keri ran a hand through her silken hair. "Those women are asking about his will. They want to know what they've been left. The lawyer wouldn't talk to them so they came here to me. *Three* of them."

"I'm so sorry."

"I thought that it would be over with him gone. The humiliation, I mean." As Keri's head lowered, that hair fell forward in a wave that shimmered. "But he's found a way to make me feel inadequate even after he's dead. It's a gift, really. So no, I don't particularly care who killed him anymore, as long as I'm not in danger."

Why did rich men have such a lock on being douchebags, Erika wondered. Fucking masters of the universe attitude.

Abruptly, Keri straightened her shoulders, straightened herself. "But enough about my problems. That's what my therapist is for, right? Now, tell me, what did you need?"

"I, ah . . . are you sure now is a good time?"

"It's not going to get any better, I'm afraid."

After a moment, Erika nodded down the hallway. "Well, I'd like to see the book room again. If you don't mind?"

"Sure." The woman's hands went to the base of her throat and ran back and forth between her collarbones over the blouse's high neck. "You know, I haven't been down there since . . ."

As her voice dried out and her fingertips probed at something under her shirt, Erika had a feeling the woman was wearing that diamond necklace again, the one she'd had on when she'd viewed the footage from that trailer, the one Erika had remarked on just before the alarm had been triggered and she'd gone to investigate and—

With a groan, she rubbed her head. "Would you prefer I go in there alone?"

"No, I think it's time. And I'm glad you're here when I finally go . . . into that room. You give me courage."

Keri took the lead, her high heels clipping delicately on the parquet flooring, the blunt cut ends of her hair swinging back and forth over her narrow waist. After passing through an arch, she led the way into a rabbit warren of rooms that were like drawers in a dresser, each separate and discrete space holding a curated subsection of Mr. Cambourg's collection.

"I'm selling all of this crap," Keri said, her hand lifting in a dismissive wave as they passed by taxidermied rats, possums, and raccoons. "I've always hated it. I don't get why he was into such gruesome, ugly things."

The next room was full of antique clamps and probes and other kinds of medical equipment—and Erika totally agreed. Herbie had been into some weird stuff, for sure.

Ah, yes, here were all the bat skeletons.

Keri slowed down as she came to the entrance of a room full of old, leather-bound books. "Here . . . it is. You can go all the way in, if you'd like. I think this is as far as I'm going to get."

As the woman took a step back, Erika gave her shoulder a little squeeze, and then went inside. Immediately, she caught a whiff of bleach, and the fact the swimming pool smell didn't carry suggested that, as in museums, each space had its own system to control temperature and humidity. And you'd want to watch both in here. All around the walls, shelves filled with Lucite stands supported ancient texts, medieval manuscripts, and first editions of God only knew what.

She didn't have to be able to translate the titles to guess that they all covered dark subject matters. It wasn't like Herb was going to deviate from his Wes Craven theme just for this part of his hoarding.

Although he certainly wasn't buying anything anymore.

Across the way, the rigid order of the displays was not just disturbed but destroyed, a whole section of shelves broken off from the wall, their bracket supports bent if they were still screwed in, the polished wood planes gone. In the center of the crash zone, there was a dent in the Sheetrock—as if a grown man had been thrown against it all—and beneath that impact, there was a stain on the parquet floor and chips out of its high-polish varnish.

"I had the professional cleaners in," Keri said in a remote way, as if she were holding herself together. "The company you suggested. They got rid of everything, and they were super nice, too."

"They're very good in a difficult situation."

Between one blink and the next, Erika saw the body sprawled there, the blood everywhere, the torso split from the juncture of the thighs all the way up to the base of the throat, as if Herbert Cambourg had had his ankles pulled apart with violent force—

Hissing at a renewed hit of pain across her forehead, she turned to an empty floor-mounted display unit.

"Keri, what was here again?" she groaned. "I'm sorry, I feel like I've asked that before."

"Oh, God. I hated that thing. It smelled like rotten meat and gave me the creeps. I'm glad it was stolen."

"What kind of book was it?" Erika rubbed one temple. "And I could swear we've already been through this."

"We have, but it's okay." The woman took a cell phone out of her back pocket and started going through images on the screen. "I don't know what the title was, but he sent me pictures of the thing when he bought it. He was so proud of the acquisition. I remember, he came home with it acting drunk, except he hadn't been drinking. He was literally that excited—oh. Here it is."

With a sound of disgust, Keri turned the cell around.

Erika went over. "May I?"

With a nod, Keri gave the phone up, and Erika's breath stopped in her throat as she expanded the photograph. The lighting wasn't great, and there was a faint blur to the thing, as if the hand of the person who'd snapped the image had been shaking a little. It was impossible to get a sense of scale, and she couldn't read any printing on the mottled leather cover.

But an instinctual revulsion made Erika more than ready to give the phone back.

"It smelled *so* bad when he brought it in," Keri muttered. "Herb was obsessed, though. It was his new baby. I mean, he always got worked up about what he collected, but that book was over the top. I couldn't stand to touch it. He couldn't seem to stop running his hands over it."

Erika glanced at the security camera mounted up in the corner. The night of the murder, all monitoring systems in the penthouse had mysteriously gone on the fritz.

So they had nothing about who killed Herb and took his book—

"Did he tell you anything about it?" Erika grimaced and rubbed one of her eyebrows. "Like where it had come from?"

"I never paid attention to any of that stuff." Keri shrugged. "Herb bought a lot of things, and I didn't care about any of them. Neither did he, after a while. It was the same with our marriage, too, as it turned out."

As the woman's hand went to the base of her throat again, Erika thought about the last time she had come here to speak to her.

"May I ask you something else?"

"Anything, Detective."

"Do you remember that dream you told me about?"

"Which dream—oh, you mean the one with the man from the video with the watches?" The flush that hit Keri's face made her glow like she was facing a romantic sunset. Then she seemed to pull herself out of a very private reverie. "No, I haven't. But I . . . every time I go to sleep, I hope he'll come back to me—hey, are you okay? Erika!"

CHAPTER THIRTEEN

Annnnnnnnnnnnnnnd there she was.

As Nate opened the front door to Luchas House, he had a roll of plans under his arm, a very pissy Shuli on his ass, and a fragile hope he would cross paths with the female he had really come to see . . . and yes, *yes*, Rahvyn was sitting on the sofa in the living room. She had her legs tucked under her, a copy of the *Caldwell Courier Journal* in her hands, and the second he walked in, she lowered the newspaper and looked across at him.

Like maybe she had been waiting for him to come.

She was tired, he thought as he cleared his throat and tried to remember how to talk.

"Hi. I mean, hello—hi."

"Hello," she said softly.

Her smile was hesitant, as if she weren't sure about her reception—and she was always like that with everybody, not just him. He'd never understood why, and he worried over the reasons. She might have been the first cousin of a member of the Black Dagger Brotherhood . . . but there were shadows behind her eyes. Deep, dark shadows.

"How are you, Nate?" she asked as she sat up and pulled at the thick black sweater she had on.

Even though he wanted to reply, he could only look at her. Her silver hair was long and shiny in contrast to the hand-knit cabling, and her jeans were dark and fresh, her face free of makeup. She looked utterly perfect to him. Painfully so.

And yes, he could have listened to her say his name for the rest of his life and still not gotten enough of the sound. Maybe it was her accent. All of her words, not just the proper nouns, were tinted by what others said were "Old Country" vowels. To the point where some of the older females who worked at Safe Place got a nostalgic look on their faces whenever Rahvyn spoke—which was rarely and always quietly.

Say something, idiot, he prompted himself.

"We're building a gym." He put the roll of blue construction plans forward like it was an all-access pass to the house. "I'm here to drop these off so everyone can check them out. If they're approved, we can start tomorrow."

She smiled more widely. "Oh, that's wonderful. Hello, Shuli."

"I'm paying for it," the other guy muttered.

"And helping with the building." Nate looked through into the kitchen and didn't see anybody—which was great. Maybe he would have to wait. "It's the least we can do to help here."

Rahvyn put her palms out. "Well, if you need another set of hands—"

"Yes, yes, we do. Great, that's just great."

As Nate rushed in with the yes-please-thank-you on that, he tried to plaster some nonchalant on his face. Otherwise, he was liable to look like he'd won the lottery: If she was volunteering, not only could he spend time with her, but she had to be staying. Right?

Wouldn't that be awesome.

"Are you going to leave the plans?" Rahvyn asked. "Because there is a staff meeting going on downstairs and I do not believe anyone is going to be available for a while."

"You know, I think I'll wait."

"They just began. But I can tell them you were here?"

Trying to be casual, and not a heartbroken loser, he shrugged. "Oh, okay, I guess I can leave them on the kitchen table—"

"Thank God, we can go to the club," Shuli said under his breath. "We'll come back at the end of the night."

"Club?" Rahvyn looked at Shuli. "As in a private organization you belong to?"

"It's a place to go where there's music and dancing."

The male made a show of tucking yet another silk shirt into the waistband of his pressed slacks. Shuli had two uniforms: the Izod-polo-and-khaki-shorts look, which he wore to work or when he was kicking around his parents' mansion, or this smooth, sexy, urban stuff that some of the guys on-site last night had called Bradtastic. Whatever that meant—

"May I come with you?"

Wait, what? "Ah . . ." Nate tried to picture Rahvyn in the same space with a shitload of drunken, drugged-up humans. "I'm not sure whether it's your scene or not."

Translation: *That is definitely not your scene.*

With a sharp pivot, Shuli turned his back to Rahvyn and bugged out his eyeballs, all what-are-you-doing-my-guy.

Nate pushed him aside. "It can be kind of rowdy. You know, loud. 'Cuz there'll be a lot of people there—and they won't always be like us, if you get what I mean."

"I am not afraid of humans." She folded the paper and put it on the coffee table; then got to her feet. "And I should like to get out and see a little of the world. I am feeling trapped here."

Clapping his palms together, Shuli looked like he would have spiked a football if he'd had one. "Great, let's go. I have my car."

As the male headed for the exit, Nate rubbed his jaw, a ball of not-a-great-idea churning in his gut.

"Shall we?" Rahvyn said.

"I'll take care of you," he mumbled. "Don't worry."

"Oh, I am not worried about my safety." She smiled at him shyly. "But I appreciate your concern."

Well . . . if that didn't make a male feel ten feet taller, he thought as he went into the kitchen and put the plans on the table.

But this was still not a great idea.

"So where is this 'club,'" Rahvyn asked as he returned to the living room.

"Downtown, and Shuli does have his Tesla tonight." Because it was hard to pick up humans with only thin air as transport. "Unless you'd like to dematerialize?"

"Tesla? You mean that electric car I have seen on the television? I have never been in one before."

"They're the best," Shuli announced from over by the door. "You're not going to believe how smooth they are. You'll never go back."

"I have never been in any car, actually."

As Shuli looked surprised, Nate felt the same way. And yet when he'd gotten free of that lab he'd been held in, cars had been a revelation for him as well. God, he really wanted to know her full backstory—and feared it, too.

"Would you like to ride in one tonight?" Nate asked. "It's your choice."

Rahvyn leaned a little closer to him so she could see through a window out to the driveway—and she smelled so amazing, all clean laundry, soap, and shampoo. He wished he knew the brands she used, but it would be way stalkerish to ask, and way too pathetic to buy the stuff just to have it in his own home—

As her hair slipped off her shoulder, he wanted to touch the white fall of waves. Run his fingers through the strands. Feel it . . . on his naked chest . . .

"Yes, please, I would like to ride in it," Rahvyn said. "As long as you shall be with me."

◆   ◆   ◆

Darkness was a vampire's freedom.

As Balz dematerialized away from his mountain hideaway and headed for Trade Street, he was in a rush, and not just because he had the afterburn of what felt like a kilo of cocaine still racing through his veins. It turned out, if you did enough blow, that whole thirty-to-forty-minute buzz routine skated into a perpetual high. Of course, your bonus prize was a scrambled brain and a body that might as well have been hooked up to a car battery for all the spasms and twitching.

Frankly, it was a miracle he could concentrate well enough to ghost out. Then again, saving Erika's life was one fuck of a motivator.

When he re-formed, it was downtown, and as he checked the address he was looking for on his phone, a pedestrian walked right into him. Rearing back, he went for one of his daggers—

"Oh, sorry, mate," the guy said in a British accent. "Wasn't watching where I was going."

The human held up his own phone by way of explanation, and then went back to texting and walking.

"Fuck," Balz muttered as he looked down at his shitkickers.

In all his distraction, he'd re-formed in the middle of the sidewalk, no more than six feet away from a streetlight. So, yeah, if Mr. Downton Abbey had been paying attention, the poor bastard would have gotten one helluva hi-how're-ya.

"Fucking concentrate."

It was a multi-f-bomb kind of night.

The block he was on was two down from where he'd intended to be, so he got his hoof-it on, striding over the concrete pavers, kicking a crumpled McDonald's bag out of his way, checking behind himself. Across the street. And in the dark windows of the rundown shops he was going by.

Not a great part of town, he thought. But when he'd Googled what he'd been looking for, this was the only one that came up.

The Bloody Bookshoppe, 8999 Trade Street.

There'd been a telephone number, but all he'd cared about were the hours of operation. Eight p.m. close was a winner for him.

And check it, they were keeping their promise to their customers. As he came up to the tiny storefront, light the color of a urine sample glowed in windows that were so dirty, it was like they had privacy curtains drawn. The door was inset and structural soundness was the only thing it had going in its favor, the dark paint thick and cracked, its chicken wire window hanging by a thread in its glazing.

When he gripped the knob, he wasn't surprised something registered as sticky, and he thought of Syphon. His cousin hated sticky anything, unless it involved cinnamon rolls—which he refused to put into his body temple now that he was a food martyr.

As a corollary, his least favorite word was "moist."

Pushing his way inside, Balz wiped his hand on the ass of his leathers as a little bell tinkled overhead. The smell was dust, mothballs, and atomized age, and talk about hoarding tendencies. The place was crammed with overstuffed, floor-to-ceiling bookcases, little handwritten tabs Scotch-taped to each shelf, the printing so wobbly, there was no telling what the labels said. A quick look around, and it was clear there was no rational plan to the aisles, to any of it, really, the layout obviously an iterative kind of thing, grown over time as the owner had continued buying, but not kept up with the selling side of the business.

"Welcome," said an elderly voice from the back. "Come on in."

And you don't even know that you're talking to Dracula, Balz said to himself.

It was always funny when humans tripped over their own fake mythology about vampires.

Moving in between the stacks, Balz had to turn sideways to accommodate his shoulders, and under the treads of his shitkickers, the floorboards creaked like there were no joists or supports under them. As his nose tickled, he sucked back a sneeze. After the amount of cocaine he'd done during the day, his septum couldn't take any more deviation without blowing apart like a Christmas popper.

He was going to need a different upper, but that was a problem he had at least ten hours left to solve.

First things first.

As he rounded a particularly wide shelf that housed a matched set of black-and-gold volumes that seemed to number in the hundreds, he—

Froze.

Blinked a couple of times.

Couldn't understand what he was seeing.

Against all reason and probability, it appeared as if Detective Erika Saunders of the Caldwell Police Department was standing at the checkout counter of the bookstore, talking to a man who was old enough to be considered a fossil. She was focused on the shop owner, but Balz would recognize that profile anywhere—and now she was turning her head to him.

As they locked eyes, she paled. Then she put her hand out to steady herself, patting around a pile of books on the counter, looking for purchase—and not the cash-in-exchange kind. She seemed like she was going to have another seizure.

On the far side of the old-fashioned cash register, the elderly man tilted his head, his loose skin shifting to one side as his features found a new equilibrium.

"Oh, you are friends, I see," he murmured in that quavering voice. "How nice."

"What are you doing here?" Erika asked.

"I'm looking for a book," Balz replied. And wasn't it a relief to be honest with her about something, anything.

"So is she." The shop owner smiled and tugged at the sleeve of his patched-up cardigan with an arthritic claw. "Perhaps you are looking for the same book?"

Some instinct had Balz checking out the old guy again and all he got was the impression of tufted white hair growing from the eyebrows, the sideburns, the ears—then again, given the clutter of the shop, he wouldn't have expected a fade and a set of manscaped arches and lobes on its owner. And how the poor guy managed to sell anything to anyone was a mystery. There were books all over the counter, and even more books in the back, an open door that led into a dim storeroom revealing stalagmites of tomes sprouting from the floor and heading for the ceiling.

"Allow me to answer your question, young lady." The man smiled at Erika, his watery eyes as focused as Mr. Magoo without his Coke-bottle specs. "The book you speak of, the one I sold to Mr. Herbert Cambourg, came to me by chance. My best finds are always by luck, as if there is a channel of good fortune that brings them to me. In the case of Mr. Cambourg's purchase, a man simply walked in off the street with the volume. He had no idea what he was holding in his hands and told me so quite plainly. He wanted a hundred dollars for it. I gave him the money without hesitation. I knew before even opening the cover that it was very old, very rare."

There was a pause, as if Erika was hoping Balz would leave. Then she cleared her throat. "Did the man say where he got it from?"

"He told me he'd found the book in an alley, as if someone had thrown it away. Can you imagine?" The old man glanced at Balz. "Is this the reason you have come as well? The book you were looking for?"

As Balz's instincts prickled, he looked past the shop owner again, to the darkened storage room.

"I'm afraid it's rather a mess back there." The old guy turned away from the register and creaked over to shut the door. "I'm going to get to cleaning it, however. Very soon."

As the shop owner returned, he linked his gnarled fingers and leaned into the chipped counter. At his elbow, a series of handwritten receipts had been stabbed onto a nail stand, and given the fine coating of dust over the flimsy slips, it seemed like they were a record from a year ago. A decade ago.

"What was the title," Balz asked in a low voice. "Of this book."

"It did not have one."

"So what was the content?"

"It was in a language I do not speak."

"But you paid a hundred dollars for the thing."

The shop owner smiled, revealing a broken picket fence of stained teeth. "The inking was quite extraordinary."

Erika spoke up. "All right, thanks for the—"

"You couldn't read a single page," Balz cut in, "but you knew to call a collector of gothic and ghoulish shit to buy it?"

"Why, yes." The old man smiled again, as casual as anything in spite of the curse word used in his presence. "As soon as I held it in my hands, I knew it was perfect for Mr. Cambourg's collection."

With a frown, Erika stepped between the pair of them and put one of her arms out. Like she could sense the aggression. "That's all I wanted to know—"

Balz took out his gun and pointed it over her shoulder at the old man's head. "You're full of shit."

"What the *hell* are you doing," she demanded.

As Erika tried to grab his arm, Balz shuffled her around behind him and held her in place. "We're leaving—"

"I'm not going anywhere with you! What the—"

"Back in my day," the shop owner said in a clipped voice, "men knew how to control their women. And people were not rude."

That was when the shadow came out of nowhere. The damn thing popped up from the floor, or maybe it came around one of the shelves—but like that mattered? As Erika continued yelling at him and yanking at his hold on her, Balz swung his gun to the right. The entity was the size of a fighter, broad in the shoulders, narrow at the waist, thick in the leg, but it had no facial features and no true corporeality. Translucent, but capable of wielding weapons and throwing punches, Balz didn't need to stare into any kind of eyes to know it was soulless, dangerous, and out for blood.

Without hesitation, he pulled the trigger three times in a row. The shadow was hit once, twice, three times in the chest, its dark cloud-body taking the bullets as if it were solid, an unholy screeching exploding into the air as it was driven back.

Except that retreat wasn't going to last, even with the special ammo he had. To truly eliminate the thing, he was going to have to pump it full of lead, and he had something else he needed to worry about first.

Then again, two birds with one stone.

Two evils with one trigger.

Balz pointed his weapon at the old man—

And blew the bastard's head clean off.

CHAPTER FOURTEEN

Everything went into slow motion as the suspect Erika had been looking for, and not able to forget, and feeling really bizarre about, started shooting into the shelves of dusty books. Three discharges popped off, one after the other, at a victim she couldn't see because he was holding her in place against his bulk.

And then he swung his gun back around at the shopkeeper.

And pulled the trigger.

As Erika shouted, the old man was blown off his feet, his hands breaking free of their grip on the counter, his arms flopping wide open as he stumbled and fell to the floor. For a split second, shock rendered her utterly frozen—but she got over that quick. A heartbeat later, she unholstered her service weapon and jammed her muzzle into the man's side.

"Drop your weapon!" Her voice was loud as she yelled up at him. "Drop your fucking weapon!"

"Stay behind me," he hollered back, his free arm flailing around, batting at her. "Stay back!"

"I will shoot you—"

"Do you want to die!"

As he twisted to the side to glare at her, she—

Stopped moving. Stopped breathing.

Across the shop, about twenty feet away . . . silhouetted against a stack of books . . . something was rising off the floor. For a split second, she thought it was a man and that what she was seeing was the shadow he was throwing. But then she realized there was no man.

It was just a shadow.

As her blood ran cold, she steadied herself on the suspect's strong arm. "What . . . the hell . . . is that."

And yet she knew: It was what had been in her dream. A shadow that was so much more, and so very evil.

The suspect squared off at . . . whatever the hell it was. "Fuck you! *Fuck you!*"

He opened fire at the thing, emptying a clip's worth of bullets into what she had been attacked by in her nightmare. With every impact, there was more of that high-pitched, scream-like sound she'd assumed was a person in pain. With every wounding, parts of the entity billowed out in response, the shape shifting like water.

Even as Erika witnessed this with her own eyes, her mind refused to process what she was looking at—except then everything clicked. This had to be another nightmare. She was asleep again, probably at her desk in the Bull Pen, her subconscious coughing out more of this crap—no doubt because she had been to see Keri Cambourg, and they had stood in her husband's book collection room, and they had talked about the ancient, ugly tome that had disappeared. And then right after Erika had almost had another seizure, just as she'd headed for the triplex's door, Keri had remembered the name of the bookstore. After which, she had gotten in her car and driven over . . .

Oh, God, maybe this was actually happening.

Stopping her thoughts, she pointed her own muzzle at the shadow, and as the suspect in front of her took out another gun from somewhere, she started to shoot.

'Cuz if this was just a dream, it wouldn't matter. And holy hell, if this was actually for real? She needed to defend herself, defend him.

Pop, pop, poppoppop—

Just as she was coming to her sixth discharge, as the suspect began pulling his trigger once again, she heard a female voice in her ear. "That's my pet you're fucking with."

The words were so unexpected, so calm and measured, so out of place in all the high-pitched shrieking from that entity, that Erika yanked her head around to see who was—

It was the brunette. From down by the river.

But instead of her clothes being red and skintight . . . she was wearing the old man's cardigan.

"You are really underwhelming in person," the woman drawled through the noise, in a way that couldn't be explained. Unless she was implanting her words directly into Erika's mind. "And you're coming with me."

Before Erika could respond—or fight back—a crushing weight bore down on both her chest and her back. It was as if she were pinned between two walls, and her body went limp under the pressure. As her gun dropped to the floor, she strained against suffocation and pain, tried to fight the compression, groaned to get the suspect's attention.

"Yeah, you're not going to get anywhere with that."

As the suspect switched to a set of long knives and attacked with the twin blades flashing, Erika went into a tilt, her stiffened body drawn backward by some invisible force as if she were on a dolly. While her vision phased in and out, she caught sight of the cash register and the back of the checkout counter, and then she was sucked into the darkened storage room—

Down on the concrete floor, by a pile of books that had been knocked over, the body of an old man was lying faceup on the floor, the eyes open and seeing nothing. Blood had pooled under his head, and going by the pasty white skin tone, he had been dead for at least an hour or two. He was wearing . . . the exact same cardigan as . . .

"Oh, shit," the female voice said, "do I still have that mothball sweater on—ah, much better."

A clipping sound, of high heels on the bare floor, circled behind Erika, and then the door started to close, seemingly on its own. She got a last look at the suspect out on the far side of the counter. He was fighting with a ferocity that only came with serious training and experience, those silver-bladed daggers flashing as he battled the shadow. And in response, the thing, whatever it was . . . was slapping back at him with these arm-like extensions, and when there was contact, the man hissed and reared back as if hurt—

The storeroom's door slammed shut, cutting off Erika's view.

"I hate when you look at him like that," the woman's voice said. "It makes me want to kill you right now."

✦   ✦   ✦

Even though Balz was fully engaged with the shadow, he was aware of when Erika stopped shooting from behind him. As he transitioned from his gun to his daggers, he prayed that she'd gone the self-protection route and run out the back of the shop—

"You *fucker*," he growled as the shadow nailed him another good one in the shoulder.

Doubling down on his slasher routine, he leaned into the fight, the blades of his steel weapons flashing in the low light, slicing through the shadow's punch-like offensive. Whenever he came into contact with the entity's form, the thing screeched and shifted away—but it always returned. Two magazines' worth of bullets, and now this up-close-and-personal, and the bastard was showing no signs of slowing down.

Balz was getting into trouble as he was forced into a retreat that took him up against the counter where the cash register was. Along with a horrible burnt fish stench, he could smell his own blood, and he was sweating more than he should have under his leather jacket, his body like a car engine overheating on a hill, smoke pouring out from under its hood. He was not going to make it through this alone, but how was he going to get a break to call in for help—

Clink!

As the heel of his shitkicker hit something that answered back with a metal note, he glanced down.

A fire extinguisher. Where the hell had that come from—

Use it.

As a third-party voice entered his head, he didn't waste any time wondering where the hell the advice came from. He grip-switched his dominant hand, releasing the hilt and grasping the point of the dagger between his thumb and first two fingers—then he threw the weapon end over end at the "head" of the shadow.

Perishable skills that were all nice and pruned and fucking tended-to meant that even if you were a coked-out, self-induced-insomnia train wreck, when you absolutely needed to hit a target in the middle of a fight you damn well could: The dagger went right into the head-like top of the shadow, and as the entity let out a roar of pain, Balz pulled a power-squat, palmed the extinguisher, and reholstered his remaining dagger. Yanking out the pin on the handle, he pulled the hose off the side and pointed the nozzle forward. As his opponent righted itself, he discharged the chemical cloud at the thing—

The sound was like a semi-trailer truck braking on hot concrete, the ear-splitting soprano-scream so loud, Balz froze, sure as if he'd suffered a blow to his head. Fortunately, his hand stayed in squeeze-mode, and within seconds, he couldn't see anything as the fog filled the shop.

And then he realized all he was hearing was the hissing of the extinguisher. No more screaming. Backing off the handle, he stopped the stream, but remained braced as he wheezed in the white cloud of chemicals swirling around the stacks of old books. As it dissipated, it revealed . . .

The shadow was gone.

"Erika!"

Conventional fighting and survival rules would have him popping two new magazines into the butts of his autoloaders, calling for backup, and doing a quick search of the aisles to clear the shop. Instead, he kept the extinguisher with him and jumped over the counter. Landing on the far side, the "old man" he'd shot was nowhere to be found. Big surprise— and there was a quick shot of satisfaction that the demon had had to clothe herself not only in that Mr. Rogers's cardigan, but in the loosey-goosey skin of the elderly human.

"*Erika!*"

There was no way she'd gone out the front.

Balz bum-rushed the closed door of the cluttered storeroom, and as he ripped it open, he saw the body of the actual shop owner on the floor. A pool of blood had emanated from his head, and something had been dragged through the congealing plasma, leaving a trail, as if from the heel of a boot or shoe.

"Erika . . ."

As true terror gripped him, he let go of the extinguisher's nozzle and went for his shoulder communicator—

Fuck. He hadn't put it on because he wasn't on rotation.

He took out his cell phone. His hand was shaking so badly that it was hard to get the thing to work. A voice command. He needed to do a—

"Call Vishous," he ordered.

Under any other circumstances, he would have hit up Xcor, the head of the Band of Bastards. And if he had the chance for a second ring-a-ding-ding, that male was up next. But this was not a *lesser* he was dealing with. This demon was something else—

"Why, thank you."

Balz jerked his head up.

Devina was standing in front of a leaning tower of plastic bins, the look on her beautiful, evil face like that of someone about to buy a new car: delight, excitement, and a good dose of self-satisfaction. In her black skinny jeans and a skintight black turtleneck, her body's curves were set off to perfection.

And left him completely cold.

"I dressed up for you, by the way." She swept a hand over her hip. "Do I look like a thief? Well, except for the footwear. But honestly, those soft-soled shoes you wear when you steal shit are not my thing—"

"Where is she," Balz said in a low growl.

"Where is who?"

"Hey, Bastard," came V's voice out of the speaker. "What's doing?"

Keeping his eyes on his enemy, Balz lifted the phone closer to his mouth. "I have the demon right in front of me. I need you here right now."

"You bought Marlboros?" Vishous cursed. "I can't believe you're slumming like that—"

"What?"

"—after my shit. Listen, I'll bring you some more. I'm going into a meeting with Wrath and the brothers. Soon as I'm out, I'll hook you, true?"

Balz raised his voice. "I need you! You know where I am downtown! I have her in front of me—"

"Sure, I can do food—"

"I don't need food!"

"Meeting's starting. See you soon."

As the connection was cut, the demon smiled. "He seems like a real prince of a guy. And it's Uber Eats just with fangs, right? How chef's kiss perfect."

Ignoring her lip-press/finger-flare, Balz stepped over the body of the shopkeeper. "Where is she."

"The only female you need to be looking for is me."

"Fuck you."

"That's the plan."

With a perfectly steady hand, Balz palmed his remaining dagger. "I'm never fucking you again."

He put the blade right to his own throat, and pressed the sharp edge in over his jugular. Following a bloom of pain, he smelled more of his own blood and became aware that his shoulder was killing him.

"Never again," he repeated.

The demon narrowed her gleaming black eyes. "You're not going to do it. All it gets you is Hell for eternity and me left alone with your little friend. Not that I won't enjoy my time with your girl."

"She has a protector stronger than me."

"Does she." Devina waved her fingers beside her face and went ooooooooooo. "I'm *so* scared."

"You should be. Lassiter will take care of her—"

"You think he'll waste time on a human? Fine, so where is he right now?" Her tone was bored. "Will you just stop. You're not going to kill yourself. Don't you know you shouldn't bluff with something like me—"

"I'm not bluffing. She's an innocent, and if you hurt her because of me, she becomes one of his own." Devina's stare narrowed and he nodded. "I kill myself and she's free for two reasons. No more ties to me and no way you're going to get at her."

"I thought you said she didn't mean anything to you." Devina cocked an eyebrow. "Or did you think I couldn't hear you then?"

"Have fun with that fallen angel."

As he tightened his grip on the hilt, Devina said quickly, "You'll end up in Hell. No Fade if you do it."

"I don't care if I'm in *Dhunhd* forever if it saves her."

With that, he pulled the blade over his throat, slicing his vein right open. The river of blood was immediate, and the gurgling as he tried to breathe through the flood made it hard to talk.

Nearly impossible.

And still, he managed, "Never . . . again."

CHAPTER FIFTEEN

Sitting across from Butch—on a silk sofa that belonged in a museum with a "Do Not Sit" sign on it—Vishous was trying to concentrate on what was being said in the great Blind King's study. The Brotherhood, the Bastards, and all the fighters were crammed into the frilly room, looking like a military squadron that had been rerouted into Versailles.

The French furniture and the pale blue walls went with all the gunmetal and the leather like a lace hankie wrapped around a grenade.

But like he gave a crap about decorations.

"—destroyed," Sahvage was saying. "And the Book, too. Why are we still talking about this?"

V checked his phone, then put it facedown on his thigh. "Because our boy Balthazar is feeling that demon—and he's seeing her."

"In his dreams," Sahvage countered through the SRO of warriors. "And I'm not disrespecting the Bastard. It's just I was there in that fire. I saw what I saw. Both were ashed."

Sahvage was a big boy, even when he was standing next to a brother like Murhder. With his dark hair cut short and the five o'clock shadow, he was exactly what he looked like: A highly intelligent, very aggressive killer, who was willing to lay down his life for his mate, his King, and everybody else in the room.

Speaking of kings, the leader of the species was parked on the far side of a carved desk that was the PB to the J for the enormous carved-ass palace he was sitting on. Both had been his sire's, just like his name, just like his son's name. That long black hair falling from a widow's peak was also inherited, but his short temper and his potty mouth? That was a no. By accounts, his father had been a gentlemale. Wrath, on the other hand, was . . . aptly named.

Then again, as far as V was concerned, they didn't need a king with manners. They needed one with balls.

"I believe him," V announced to the crowd. "And we have to take him seriously. You think he's avoiding his home here on a goddamn whim?"

To say nothing of the ask he'd laid down the night before. Not that V was about to put that out to the group.

Conversation sprang up from all corners, and Wrath sat back, his black wraparounds as much of a mask as his tight expression was. When the voices got even louder, the King reached to the side, gathered up George, his service dog, and put the golden retriever in his lap. George hated conflict. So he spent a lot of time cozied up to his master.

And this dissension wasn't going to last long. The King was going to once again order everyone to make like the Book and Devina were out and about somewhere in Caldie. It was the only way to proceed, and though Sahvage still maintained his position was correct, the brother was going to come around quick. It cost nothing to be cautious and assume the worst—although Wrath wasn't going to put his shitkicker down right away. He knew the kind of males he was dealing with. They needed to blow off some steam, not that anybody was disagreeing with what Balz had reported.

V frowned and checked his phone. Then he leaned into his room-mate and whispered, "I'll be right back."

Butch tilted in as well and kept his voice down, not that anybody was going to hear them over the booming back-and-forths. "Where are you going?"

"Smokes."

"Can you bring some Mr & Mrs back with you?"

"If Fritz catches me with a silver tray and a glass of that new bour-bon you like, I'm a dead male."

"You can outrun him, you know. Especially for the black label."

"Not without killing him from a heart attack. And how'd that go over in this household, true?"

Leaving that hell-no where it landed, V got to his feet and weeded his way to the door—and as he came up to Xcor, he tugged the male's arm. The Bastard didn't ask any questions; he just followed the way out into the hall.

As V shut the double doors and leaned back against them, he looked at his phone once more. Then he stared across the second story landing with its gold balustrade and its blood red runner. When he looked to the right, the Hall of Statues was where it had been last night, and down by the entry into the servants' wing, he could hear two female *doggen* speaking in low tones about the schedule for bedsheet changing. To the left was the second-story sitting room, and beyond that, the east wing that had been opened to accommodate the Band of Bastards moving in.

When he went to look at his phone for a third time, he shook his head. "I just spoke with Balz."

The head of the Bastards nodded once. Xcor was broader than all the others, and with his deformed upper lip, he looked like a bare-knuckle street fighter. He wasn't crude, though. Mated of the Chosen Layla, adopted sire to Lyric and Rhamp, he was a good guy to have at your six. In your house. Guarding your King. Your *shellan*.

"And," the male prompted.

"He wanted cigarettes and food."

"Okay."

Vishous glanced at his phone and couldn't figure out what the fuck his problem was. "I told him after the meeting, I'd roll him some and hook him up with the calories."

"Yeah?"

"Yeah."

"Good." Xcor crossed his arms over the steel daggers that were holstered, handles down, onto his thick chest. "He will not speak to me. I call, he never returns it."

When the urge to check his frickin' Samsung hit again, V shoved the thing in his ass pocket. Then he gave his hands something to do by lighting up a hand-rolled. As he exhaled, he thought about the conversation he'd had with Balz out behind the Caldwell Police Department's headquarters.

"What are you leaving out?" Xcor demanded. "You tell me the now. He is mine."

The Bastard had plenty of Old Country in his accent on a good night. Tonight? His words were almost a language other than English.

"Last evening," V said, "he made me swear I'd kill him if the shit with Devina came down to it." As Xcor's face hardened, V shrugged. "He doesn't want to saddle you with the deed. And you need to chill. I know he's serious, but we can get that demon. I know we can."

Xcor broke away and paced over to the head of the grand staircase. As he stared down the red-carpeted steps to the foyer below, he looked like he wanted to throttle the other Bastard with his bare hands. He also appeared devastated in the manner of someone whose best friend was dying.

It was a hot minute before he came back. When he did, there was no expression on his face at all. He was showing absolutely nothing.

But his words were rough: "He has broken my heart."

V put up his gloved palm. "Look, I'm sorry I had to shit on your parade, but I need to know. Does he cycle, or something? Like, go through periods of depression and mania?"

"Never. He is steady. Always."

V stroked his goatee and shook his head. "I don't get it. Just now he called me, talking about nicotine and a meal. In the middle of everything that's going on. Like nothing's wrong."

"Maybe he got some sleep, finally," Xcor muttered. "Either way, if he was serious about what he asked you to do, we need to help him in any way we can, whether or not the Book still exists."

"Agreed." V narrowed his eyes. "You have to know, though, I gave him my word."

Xcor's upper lip peeled off his fangs. "You have a choice."

"Not when I give my word, I don't." V pointed the lit tip of his hand-rolled at the Bastard. "I don't want us as enemies if it comes down to it. If he kills himself, there's no Fade, and he knows this. And I'm not in a big hurry to put him in his grave, are we clear. I'm telling you this ahead of time so that you and I are on the same page. You got a problem with it? Then let's you and me fuck that demon to the wall."

There was a period of silence, and the tense quiet went on for so long, V wondered whether or not they were going to have an issue right here, right now.

"The one you really have to worry about," Xcor said grimly, "is Syn."

♦   ♦   ♦

In the dim and dusty storage room at the bookshop, Erika was blacking out from lack of oxygen. The inexplicable, invisible constriction on her body was so great, so unrelenting, that she couldn't inflate her lungs properly and the shallow panting she could draw in wasn't enough to keep her going. And shockingly, life-threatening hypoxia wasn't her main problem.

"He's mine," the brunette said into her face, "until I'm bored with him. And in any event, our relationship's got shit-all to do with you—"

The door broke open and the suspect filled the jambs, the light from behind turning him into a shadow with substance—as opposed to . . . whatever had been out there.

"Where is she," he demanded.

I'm here, Erika answered. *I'm right here . . .*

She was yelling at him. At least she thought she was. But it was as if the suspect couldn't see her, hear her. In desperation, she screamed as loud as she could. And screamed again. As sweat beaded on her forehead and ran down into the collar of her coat, she had to give up because remaining partially conscious was more important than repeating her vocal failure.

Meanwhile, the man came forward, stopping underneath a light bulb that hung from the ceiling on a rusted chain.

Under the harsh lighting, his face looked barbaric with rage, the hollows under his cheekbones, the cut of his jaw, the slash of his brows, the very depiction of wrath and vengeance, his anger so great it was tangible—

"I'm *never* fucking you again."

The words were spoken with hatred in every syllable, and as the brunette stamped a stiletto in response, Erika tried to focus. Looking down at her chest, as if that would help, she saw absolutely nothing. No chains of steel, no bands, no compression. Yet the breathlessness and suffocation, the tilt to her body as if it were suspended in midair at an angle, were all very real.

With her mind trying to reconcile the inexplicable, she had a thought that either none of this was happening . . . or the world she had always known was a lie: The thin veil between nightmare and consciousness had been blurred to such an extent that she was beginning to believe in things that made no sense—

Was he taking out a knife?

As her vision went on the fritz, she blinked things back into focus. Surely he wasn't putting it against his—

"You're not going to kill yourself," the brunette snapped. "You shouldn't bluff with something like me."

"I'm not bluffing. And I don't care if I end up in *Dhunhd* forever if it saves her."

With a savage yank of his arm, the man sliced open his own throat, blood geysering out of his vein. As Erika screamed again and still made no sound, he spoke in a horrific gurgle.

"*Never again.*"

The man went down on his knees, that illumination from over his head casting him in a theatrical light, the terrifying red rush pouring over his black leather jacket and covering what appeared to be a weapons holster. He did not raise his hands to try to stop the flow, he did not fight the effect of a critical hole in his windpipe. He just stared in utter fury at a spot up and over to the left of Erika.

She yelled again, feeling the stretch of her mouth, the burn in her throat. Nothing came out—and all the while, the sound of him breathing through the blood, the most terrible thing she had ever heard, seemed to be loud enough for the whole world to hear—

"You've *got* to be kidding me." The brunette's voice was merely annoyed. Like people killing themselves in front of her was at least a monthly, if not weekly, inconvenience. "I mean really. You're just going to see me in Hell."

As the man bled out, his face paled to the point of fresh white wall paint, his skin becoming matte in a way Erika knew she was going to never forget. Then he fell forward and landed on the floor in a clang of metal from the weapons on him hitting all that dirty concrete.

God . . . the copper in the air—

The brunette passed through Erika's field of vision, those stilettos clipping along until she stood over the man. A pool of blood was forming fast around his head, and she extended one of her shapely legs, cocked her fancy shoe, and drew the fine point tip of her heel through it in some kind of pattern.

Erika's eyes strained to track what she was doing.

Devina

"Well, shit," the brunette muttered as she finished what clearly was her name. "You were a really good lay."

Then her head flipped up and she looked toward the storeroom's open door. "Oh, come *on*."

In spite of Erika's delirium, she saw what had gotten the brunette's attention: A light had gathered out in the shop proper, at first little more than a pinpoint, now becoming bright as a car beam . . . and continuing to intensify until it was the kind of floodlight you'd find at an airport or running up the side of a skyscraper.

The brunette put her hands on her hips and stamped one foot again, a splash of the man's blood landing on her pant leg.

And then something close to a miracle happened.

The illumination somehow entered the storage room, as if it were a sentient being moving at will. And instantly, Erika felt an easing of her discomfort, her fear, her sense of impending doom. A split second later, she knew why. The glow coalesced into a figure that was at first made only of the light, but then solidified into something that appeared to be living and breathing, a man with blond-and-black hair that was down below his shoulders . . . who had eyes that were as compelling as a rainbow, as full of vengeance as a crusader's.

"Oh, and now you're going to do what you accused me of doing." The brunette jabbed a manicured finger at the apparition. "You're interfering, you're over the line—blah, blah, blah. The Creator's going to have a goddamn opinion about you playing the resuscitation card here, unless you just showed up to watch him die."

There was a petulance to her now, like a kid threatening to tattletale because someone ate Play-Doh in the back of a classroom.

"You save him, and you and I are even," she announced. "I may have trespassed, but you're stealing from fate if you intercede now—oh, and if you let him live? I'm not leaving him. There's still only one way I'll go, and you know what it is, angel. He gets his freedom if I get what I want from you. So be a savior, or don't. I don't give a fuck."

With that . . . the brunette disappeared.

Right into thin air.

Closing her eyes, Erika moaned and prayed for an end to the pain she was in, the confusion, the conviction that she was in a different world altogether . . . even as she was ostensibly in Caldwell—

Instantly, the pressure on her chest disappeared. Between one heartbeat and the next, the squeeze was just gone, and she fell to the floor, landing on her back, her head smacking into the concrete and stunning her. But now was not the time for that. The ragged inhale she took was loud in her ears. She grabbed another. And another.

That was when she realized the gurgling had stopped.

Rolling onto her side, she reached a hand out for the man, and opened her mouth to say his name. But she didn't know what it was—

She was not alone.

Turning her head, she looked at the figure who had come through the doorway in the form of illumination. She should have been afraid. She wasn't—and not because she was confused.

When the entity just stood there, staring at her, she refocused on the man who had cut himself. As a feeling of helplessness choked her, she stretched even farther to reach the suspect, not that she could save him. Nothing short of blood transfusions and an operating room could—

"Save . . . him . . ." she whispered as she looked back up to the mysterious man. "Please."

The man looked over his shoulder as if he were checking to see if the coast was clear. Then he stared off at something that was beyond her, maybe to a back door.

As he seemed suspended by his inner thoughts, she knew he was their only hope. She was losing strength fast, and she was worried she was going to pass out. And the suspect—well, it was probably already too late. But she couldn't not beg.

"Please . . ."

Later, she could wonder why she was so determined to rescue a suspect. Then again, he had come in here to help her.

Abruptly, the glow returned. An outline of light appeared around the man with the long blond-and-black hair, and its magical warmth reverberated outward from him, engulfing her, calming her, healing her pain and easing the burn in her lungs.

The man came forward and knelt down beside her—and that was when she recognized the sensation on her face, her body: Sunshine. She felt as though she were lying out on a towel, at the Million Dollar Beach at the base of Lake George, the late August sun shining down on her, getting into her bones as a breeze coming from the water kept her from overheating.

Rays of heavenly grace.

Is this Jesus? Erika wondered.

No, came an answer in her mind.

A hand extended toward her, and she had a thought that he was out of luck if he wanted to help her to her feet. As much as his presence seemed to magically improve how she felt, she was empty of energy, incapable of moving.

"I can't . . ." Except then Erika frowned.

In the seat of his palm, a ball of light formed and hovered. And while she tried to comprehend what she was looking at, the man reached out and brushed her face. His touch was not sexual in any way, but it traveled through her bones, registering all over her as warmth.

As kindness and compassion.

Gently, he took her limp hand and turned it over. Placing the orb in her palm, he rose up to his full height again.

Erika gazed upon the energy source with wonder and awe. Then she lifted her heavy head and met his oddly colored eyes.

The man nodded over to the suspect.

After that, he took a step back and disappeared just as the brunette had: One moment he was there, the next . . . he was just gone.

With a moan, Erika held the ball of energy up to where he had been, like it was something that could bring him back. Then she refocused on the suspect.

He had disappeared. It was too late.

And what was she holding anyway?

That rumination was momentary. Even as she questioned what she was doing, she rolled over onto her stomach and started to drag herself over to the man she had been searching for, the man who, as with Keri Cambourg, had been in her dreams.

The man who had sacrificed himself to save her.

Snippets of what had been said between him and the brunette floated around her mind. None of it made any sense and she didn't even attempt to sort things out. Trying to pull herself over the concrete with only one hand and her feet to push was all she could handle at the moment.

When she got to the man, she was breathing hard and getting dizzy. She didn't know what she was supposed to do—

No, she did.

Erika pushed her palm with the glow under his throat, where the injury was. As she felt the warmth of his blood, she closed her eyes.

"Please . . . don't die," she prayed.

CHAPTER SIXTEEN

The "what" was less important than the "why."

That was what one of the TED Talks had said. Or maybe it had been a book? YouTube video? Certainly an Insta post from that CarpeDaDayum account.

As Lassiter stood outside the Bloody Bookshoppe, he looked up at the sky and breathed in deep. When all he could smell was frying food from across the street, and then a bunch of uninspiring clouds drifted across the face of a wan moon, he put his hands in the pockets of his Mark Rober sweatpants and started walking.

He didn't know where he was going until he got there.

And then when the destination presented itself, his location struck him as inevitable.

Maybe all that should be in some human's book. If he'd learned anything over the last couple of days of relentless self-improvement, it was that *Homo sapiens* could elevate almost any banal statement of the obvious to a self-referential mood-cue for profundity.

He'd read that in an article, too.

Tilting his head back, he read the sign over the entrance of the club: Dandelion. The place was painted a spring green, from the roofline down to the sidewalk, and the trippy music that atmosphere'd out of its block-long expanse was all syntho stuff, not a conventional instrument anywhere near the beats.

"Are you coming or are you going?"

At the stiff demand, Lassiter glanced to the front door. A bearded human male with a man-bun and some swallow tattoos was looking like bouncing anything out of the establishment that weighed over a hundred and twenty pounds was going to be a problem. Maybe he was banking on his librarian-like stare of disapproval to corral the drunken and disorderly.

Yeah, good luck with that, buddy.

Although maybe the guy was just cranky about his uniform. In keeping with the weed theme, the powers that were had made him wear a bright green t-shirt and brown pants. He looked like he had on a bad Halloween costume and was going as sod.

"Hello." He waved a hand in Lassiter's face. "Anybody in there. You can't loiter here. You'll fuck my wait line."

A quick glance to the left, and either Lassiter was missing a lineup of humans, or this green-and-brown goaltender of absolutely nothing was flexing for shits and giggles.

"There's a female inside," Lassiter heard himself explain, "that I want to see, but I shouldn't. Nothing good's going to come out of it. I should leave her alone."

Man Bun did a double take for show, like he thought the world was an Instagram story. "Do I look like your therapist? What are you doing. Or am I calling for backup."

"Who am I bothering out here?" Lassiter indicated his feet. "This is public property, right? Maintained by the city, not you."

The guy stepped right up and jutted his chin out, in a move that he clearly thought would work for him. Too bad there was a big rate limiter to all that aggression: The guy worked at a club named after a weed and was wearing brown pants.

As Lassiter remembered with fondness the opening scene of the first Deadpool movie, Man Bun arched every brow he had and then some.

"Are we having a problem?"

Lassiter shook his head. "No."

"Then move along or get in line."

Shifting his eyes over the guy's shoulder, Lassiter took note that there were no windows to look in, and he tried to imagine what Rahvyn was doing inside. Who she was with. Whether she was dancing.

None of this was his business. But he couldn't help himself, and the fact that he had his ass in a crack over a female who should, and had to, remain a stranger, made him move quickly from mild annoyance to downright pissed off when it came to the human in front of him.

"—calling the cops. Right now—"

Lassiter locked eyes with the guy . . . and suddenly, shit wasn't funny for either one of them. The human stopped in mid-sentence with his mouth open, and although it was probably because something was showing in Lassiter's face that was terrifying, the fallen angel side of things wasn't going to worry about it.

He'd suddenly had it with everything and everybody, from Balz and Devina's drama, to that human woman back at the bookshop, to this hipster right here, with his little seat of influence that he was deter-mined to wield over a sonofabitch who was in love with someone he—

Oh . . . shit, Lassiter thought. He wasn't in love with Rahvyn. He didn't even know her.

Then again, wasn't that how bonding worked?

"It's okay, my dude," the bouncer backstroked with a stammer. "Like whatever—"

"No," Lassiter snapped. "It's not whatever. And I'm not your dude."

When the human tried to take a step back, Lassiter mentally held the bouncer right where he was, and as he began to tremble, the tables-turned power trip did what nothing else could. It brought Lassiter some relief, a cooling to his impotent rage, a focal point to release his tension.

Killing this random man, out here on the street, in the world of humans who were so much less than Lassiter was, who weren't on his level in any way, who were like ants under his feet . . . was the only thing that felt right in what seemed like forever.

The itch scratched. The burn extinguished. The ache gone.

For only a moment, sure. But like he fucking cared about duration. A moment was enough—

"Say goodnight, you sanctimonious asshole," Lassiter growled. "See you on the morning news."

◆　◆　◆

Back in the bookshop's storage room, Erika had to lay her head down on her outstretched arm. As she did, she realized she was lying in a pool of the suspect's blood, and she had a thought that this vantage point, of a floor, of the kind of puddle she was in, of the body beside her . . . was a version of what many of her homicide victims saw right before their ends. It was what her father, her mother, and her brother had seen.

The girl in the pink bedroom. The man down by the river, too.

With her eyes fluttering and her heart beating in an irregular rhythm, her fear ebbed and was replaced with a helpless sadness that seeped into her marrow. For so long, she had been fighting to find answers in the aftermath of violent death, but she had never thought about this moment here . . . this acceptance . . . that came when a person was about to die. And knew it.

It was shockingly peaceful.

Just before she passed out, she looked at her hand under the open wound. The glow of light in her palm was diminishing, fading away like an old-fashioned kerosene lantern when you turned the—

Thump. Thump. Thump . . .

Footsteps. Heavy ones.

Out in the shop.

Within a brief flare of energy, she tried to retract her arm and get to her service weapon. But then she couldn't remember where it was. Had she dropped it? She didn't know, couldn't guess. What did it matter, though. She didn't have the strength to point it at anyone.

Anything, that was.

The sounds of someone walking on the old floorboards got louder, and then it became obvious that there were two people out there among the shelves and the books. And she'd have had to be a different person, who'd had a different life, to believe that whoever it was was good news for her and the suspect—

The door to the storeroom reopened, the light from over the register streaming in on a slice that widened until it hit her face. As she blinked blindly, she heard a curse and then all kinds of illumination flared from what seemed like all directions. Someone had turned a ceiling fixture on.

Two men came in, and her first thought was that they were dressed in black leather, just like the suspect. The one on the left had a goatee and tattoos on his temple. The other was stockier, with a distorted upper lip. Both stopped and stared down at her as if they couldn't understand what they were seeing.

"Help him," she said in a guttural voice. "Save him . . ."

The one with the goatee turned his head to his shoulder and triggered a communicator. His voice was too quiet for her to hear what he was saying—but she prayed it was nine-one-one. The other man approached her and knelt down slowly, as if he were afraid of spooking her.

"Female, worry not. We shall take care of you both."

His eyes bored in her own, and the steady confidence he projected made her vision go blurry with tears of relief.

"I'm trying to save him . . . he cut himself. With . . ."

His eyes left hers and locked on what had to be his colleague, his friend, his brother? When his lids closed briefly, it was as if he couldn't hold in the pain he was feeling. And then he was leaning over her and laying his broad hand on his friend's shoulder. The man started talking, but she didn't understand the words, the language one that seemed to have words in common with both French and German.

She didn't need a translation to know that he was rocked to his core.

"I tried," she mumbled lamely, "to save him."

"Female," he said, "he's still alive. He's still breathing."

"He is?"

The man nodded and then seemed confused. "Your hand . . . has stopped the bleeding somehow."

"Not my hand." When he frowned, she looked at where her palm was still pressed to the knife wound. "The light. The glow. It was . . . the glow. He's alive?"

His brows got tighter, but then the man with the goatee ended whatever communication he'd initiated and spoke loudly.

"T minus five minutes. Manny's not far."

And then they were staring at her, like she was a stray at the side of the road and they were trying to decide if they had enough room in the back of their car.

"Don't take my memories," she blurted. "I don't . . . understand any of this, just please. My mind can't take any more amnesia."

"We're bringing you with us," the stockier of the pair said. "Don't worry."

"Motherfucker," the one with the goatee muttered.

"She's his female," came the counter. "She has to come."

Abruptly, she heard the suspect's voice in her head: *I don't care if I end up in* Dhunhd *forever if it saves her.*

Annnnnnnnnnnd that was the last conscious thought she had. As she took one last look at the injured man, and tried to see if he was drawing breath—or if maybe his friend was just wishful-thinking on that—she wondered if she hadn't imagined the ball of light.

I'm his? she thought as she gave up fighting the darkness that rose to claim her.

CHAPTER SEVENTEEN

Lassiter rode the evil rush of holding the human's life in his hands—right up until the moment someone came out of the club. He almost didn't look over, but at the last minute, he glanced in the direction of the figure who emerged from the confines of the computer-generated music and the drunken crowd. It was a woman, and her hand went to her hair and lifted its weight up off her neck as if she were hot.

It was not who he had come here to find.

Species divide aside, this woman had dark hair, not silver, and she was wearing a short skirt that he couldn't picture on Rahvyn. Still, as she noticed him and the bouncer, he transposed onto her the features he had in his mind every waking moment.

As she narrowed her eyes, it was Rahvyn looking at him with suspicion. Like she knew something was wrong.

"Is everything okay here?" the woman asked.

Her words were a devastating condemnation of his actions. His lack of self-control. His absence of perspective, compassion, and connection.

It was as if that demon had possessed him even as she didn't enter him.

Lassiter released his casting over the bouncer, and then, because he couldn't bear even a hypothetical Rahvyn having caught him about to do something unforgivable, he went into the woman's mind and sent her right back into the club with no memory of what she had inadvertently walked in on.

Yet closing off her mental storage unit did nothing to reverse time and reengineer his intent. Reprogram his response—

"Am I okay?"

The bouncer in the grass-green shirt and the shit-brown pants was bringing his hands to either side of his face, going Kevin McCallister in a cautious way, as if he weren't sure whether his head wasn't going to pop off his spine, like, well, a dandelion.

"I don't know . . . if I'm okay," he said hoarsely.

Closing his eyes, Lassiter had the urge to run out in front of a car. It wouldn't kill him, but maybe if he broke a couple of bones, got a concussion, and bled out a little, he might be able to atone for what he had almost done.

"You're all right, Pete," he muttered.

"Oh." The guy shook his head. "Hey, how do you know my name?"

"I know everything." And he wished he fucking didn't sometimes. "Your father is Ted. Your mother is Marilyn. They almost got a divorce last year. Your sister married an asshole—she's pregnant, by the way, and not sure how she feels about it. Your car needs to go back to Midas. They put in the wrong kind of oil, but you're probably not going to do anything about it because you can be a lazy sod—no offense to your uniform. And yes, your girlfriend likes that kid you went to high school with, but she hasn't cheated on you and she's not going to. If you didn't get so extra with the jealousy, you two could be really happy together, but like the oil, I don't think you're going to work on that, either. Oh, and your roommate used the rent money to buy seven hundred dollars of hash this afternoon. He's not going to share any of it with you. If I were you, I'd sign up for extra shifts."

Peter Phillip Markson, who had gone as Poopson in elementary because he'd had diarrhea at school once—and didn't that seem like a predicator for this job's uniform—blinked like he was fact-checking the run and shocked to find that it was all correct. And Lassiter could have gone on with how Pete had lost his virginity at sixteen in the back of his first cousin's car with his first cousin's best friend, and then continued with the bout of mono he'd shared with five other members of his frat because he was always drinking out of soda cans whether they were his or not. And also mentioned the STD he'd gotten last summer. But really, that would just be showing off, wouldn't it.

"Jesus . . . Christ."

"Yeah, still not me." Lassiter glanced at the club. "Look, can you just chill with the attitude out here? You're not exactly protecting the Presidential motorcade."

And it had almost gotten you killed.

"That's what Franny says," Pete mumbled.

"You should listen to her."

"Thanks . . . ?"

With a nod, Lassiter turned away and just started walking. He didn't care where he was going, as long as the inevitability rule didn't pivot him back around and replant him on the threshold of the club again—

As he came up to the end of the block, he stopped at the curb even though the pedestrian signal was counting down to a light change so he should have hurried across the intersection while he could.

He pivoted and raised his voice. "Check your watch, Pete."

Pete, who was still looking stunned, did as he was told. "It's eight-twenty. Well, two. Eight twenty-two?"

There was a pause. And then Lassiter said, slowly and clearly, "In thirty-two minutes, a car is going to come around this corner." He pointed to his feet to emphasize the location. "There are going to be two guys in hoodies in the front seat. As soon as you see it, I want you to hit the concrete and stay there. Cover your head and do not look up. Let it pass you by and take off. It's not you they're after, but bullets don't use discretion when they're flying through the open air."

"Wh . . . at?"

"You heard me. Thirty-two minutes from now. Thirty-one, actually."

Lassiter resumed his ambling, aimless stride, stepping off the curb and heading into the intersection even though the pedestrian warning system was beeping like it was about to explode.

But that was the thing with free will.

You were free to make bad decisions.

And better ones.

◆   ◆   ◆

"This makes no goddamn sense."

As V made his pronouncement over the roar of a powerful engine, his brother-in-law, Dr. Manny Manello, was leaning across the treatment table in the back of the mobile surgical unit, examining a six-inch-long horizontal throat wound that had somehow magically healed up.

Like the anatomy had knit itself back together, *sui generis*.

The evac from the bookstore had been quick. V and Xcor had extracted Balz from the grimy storeroom, hand-and-footing the fighter out the back and into this operating room on wheels. As Manny had hooked up the monitoring equipment to their comrade, and Xcor had hopped behind the wheel, V had gone back and picked the human woman up.

He wasn't sure he agreed with Xcor on the whole she's-his bullshit, but he wanted answers and she had seen what had gone down in there.

Before taking off, he'd also assessed an elderly human who was clearly dead; then he'd killed the lights and locked up. There'd be time to return and retrieve weapons and clean the scene before the human police were called. There were bigger-and-betters to worry about at the moment.

"I can't disagree with you," Manny muttered as the RV went over some kind of pothole and they swayed to catch their balance like something out of a *Star Trek* episode. "I mean, you vampires are good at the self-repair, but nothing like this."

In spite of the fact that Balz had been lying facedown in twelve quarts of his own plasma, all the skin, the veins underneath, the tendons and ligaments were sealed up. Which wasn't to say that there hadn't been a hell of an owie there. The red line of the injury was very evident, the slice a clean and deep one given the amount of blood loss.

"We've got to get him fed," Manny said as he took out his cell phone. "His blood pressure is for shit, and he's tachycardic. Oxygen stats are in the basement. He's out of the woods by inches, not feet, and if he stays where he is much longer, he's going to have brain damage."

As some other obstacle in the road was run over, V had to catch his balance a second time, throwing out a hand to a grip that was bolted on the ceiling. The second he was steady, his eyes went back to Balz's naked body. They'd cut off his leathers, in search of other wounds to explain the bleeding. But except for some lashing burns on his arms and abdomen, a handful of contusions consistent with having been in a close-contact fight, and a couple of cuts worthy of Band-Aids, there was nothing obviously wrong with the fighter.

That mysterious throat injury was what had caused him to bleed out.

"How are we?" Xcor called back from the driver's seat.

"We're arranging for a Chosen," V answered.

"Good. We're pulling into the garage now."

More lurching, the IV bag swinging on its pole, Balz's body lolling in its restraints on the table. V glanced over to the shallow bench he'd put the human woman on. He'd strapped her into the seat, and she was clearly not too with it, her head jerking up like the rough ride had roused her out of a coma.

He remembered how he'd found her, lying on the concrete beside Balz, her hand palm-up under the front of the Bastard's throat. Right where that red flush was.

As if her touch alone had buttoned things back together.

Not possible.

Humans were a lot of things—bad drivers, nosy, dangerous because so many of them were stupid and there were too many of them on the planet—but they were not able to reconnect veins and arteries, and close the wound of what might as well have been a surgical cut all the way through Balz's esophagus.

So what the fuck happened back there? he thought as he focused on that right palm of hers.

"He slit his own throat."

The softly spoken words were rough, like the woman's own throat was having trouble, and V shifted his stare to her face. She was almost as pale as Balz was, and even with her being fully dressed, he could tell she was going to have her own set of black-and-blues: She had scuffs on her pants, her shoes, the jacket she was wearing.

While the surgical unit came to a halt and the engine was cut, she pushed herself up a little higher on the bench; as she grimaced and pulled at the seat belt that crossed her chest, it was impossible to tell exactly what part of her body was hurting. Maybe all of it.

"I'm sorry," V said. "What was that?"

Even though he'd heard her just fine. He wanted her to repeat the words, though, to make sure she knew what the hell was coming out of her mouth.

"He took out a knife, put it to his throat . . ." Her breath hitched, but then she overrode the constriction with such force, it was obvious she had experience reining in fear. "He cut his own throat."

Up in the driver's seat, Xcor's head whipped around. "What."

"Guess he decided to save me the job," V muttered.

"Chosen's on the way," Manny cut in.

The woman then became the focus for all three of them.

As if she knew what they wanted from her, she said in a surprisingly steady voice, "I went to the shop to see if I could get more information on a book that was stolen from a crime scene. He was there." She nodded at Balz. "We were talking to the owner of the place—or what I thought was the owner."

She stopped dead there. And as the silence continued for a minute, V knew her human brain was trying to make sense of things that she'd seen and heard that did not fit in with her species' version of what was real.

"This shadow appeared," she said eventually. "I don't know where it came from, I don't know what it was . . . and he started shooting at it. Then he shot the old man behind the cash register in the face. But it wasn't an old man. It was a woman—look, I know this all sounds crazy."

"Keep going," Xcor said gently.

"The woman got ahold of me somehow. Without touching me. I don't know what she did, but I couldn't breathe, I had no control over myself and she was taking me with her—but then he . . ." The human swallowed hard. "He came after me, to save me. He confronted her, and that was when he put the knife to his throat. He told her . . ."

"What did he tell her," V prompted.

"That he wasn't . . . sleeping with her anymore." As V cursed, the woman looked up, her eyes imploring him, but about what, he wasn't sure. "They were arguing, it was hard for me to follow. And he told her he was going to kill himself to save me. That someone . . . Lassiter? . . . was going to protect me. After that, he . . ." She put her hands to her face, covering her eyes like she wished she couldn't re-see it all. "He sliced his own throat open."

"What did the female look like?" V asked as Xcor started to say a prayer in the Old Language.

"She was beautiful. With long brunette hair. She somehow managed to—I know this sounds crazy, but she killed the shop owner, I know she did. He was on the floor, dead, in the storeroom. And then . . . she *became* him for a while." The woman rubbed her forehead. "You have to believe me—"

"We do," V said. "Every word."

Lowering her arms, her bloodshot eyes lifted to meet his again. "I feel so insane."

"What happened next." He asked this even though he knew exactly where they were heading—and at least everything was making sense now, even if she was confused as hell. "Tell me what happened next."

"There was . . . a light, out in the main part of the shop. It came into the storeroom and then a man was there—I was blacking out at that point, but I can picture him in my mind clear as day. He glowed . . . like an angel, he glowed. He and the brunette argued and she left. Then he took my hand and gave me this ball of . . . energy." She looked down at her palm. "Just holding it made my whole body feel better. He left, too, and I wasn't sure what I was supposed to do, but then I crawled over and I put it . . . to where the bleeding was."

"That explains the healing," Manny said in a quiet way.

Closing her eyes, she exhaled with defeat. "I'm trying to make sense of this all, and the thing is, I dreamed about a shadow last night. Just like the one I saw in the bookshop, that he fought. I keep thinking I'm going to wake up. But I'm not going to, am I?"

"You don't have to worry about any of this." V made a move to get a hand-rolled out of his leather jacket, but there was no smoking in the surgical unit—and definitely not when there was pure oxygen being pumped into a Bastard. "Not any of it. It's not about you."

Those exhausted eyes met his own. "Are you going to take my memories like he did? Because he has. I know he has."

"What did you say your name is?"

"I didn't. But that doesn't matter, does it. Who are you?" She moved her hand around. "What is this? Where am I."

"Caldwell, New York," Vishous murmured. "Where do you think."

That stare of hers moved to Manny. Then to Xcor. Finally, it settled on Balz as he lay on the table. Slowly, she shook her head.

"This is not my Caldwell." Her face became a mask of composure, like she was trying to accept some really bad news. "It's yours, isn't it."

CHAPTER EIGHTEEN

Inside the club named after a weed with a cheerful sunny thatch roof upon its stem, Rahvyn ducked her eyes as another round of pink lights spun around the open area of the meadow-themed establishment. When she had first arrived, she had been a bit taken by the decor. Flowers were everywhere, hanging from the ceiling, arranged in vases mounted on the walls—depicted in framed photographs and amateur art down a serving area that was so long, she could not see the terminus of it. But then she realized the blooms were silk, the leaves plastic, and in spite of the large footprint of the building, things were very, very crowded.

Another problem for her was the noise level. Music with a fast beat and a thumping lower percussion sent shock waves through the hot air. The scents were equally overwhelming. So many humans, their colognes and perfumes not the least of it. The sexual pheromones were choking her, and it was no mystery why there was so much arousal.

The dancing was body-to-body.

So it was hard to know where to train one's eyes.

Dearest Virgin Scribe, she was getting to the point where she couldn't breathe—

"Weca nlea veanyt imey ouwa nt."

"I'm sorry?" She turned to Nate. "What did you—"

"We can leave anytime you want," he said more loudly.

The only saving grace to this whole experiment in exploration was that Nate seemed just as awkward as she was. His friend, Shuli, on the other hand, was fitting right in. From the moment they'd arrived nearly an hour ago, the male had been buying drinks that smelled as pungent as the mead had back in the Old Country. He purchased them for himself as well as for others, not that he appeared to know the humans. There were many introductions.

Verily, he was very interested in meeting new friends.

Particularly of the female variety—

"How we doing, kids!"

Shuli came up from behind in a rush of two-handed fruity drinks. As he threw his arms around her and Nate, frothy yellow liquid splashed out onto the floor.

"Isn't this fucking great!" He curled his arm around Nate's neck and took a drink from one of the glasses. "I love it!"

The male was speaking with great volume, but she had the sense it was not to be heard over the music, but rather his vibrating excitement. His eyes were not even upon her or Nate. They were trained on the dance floor, on the human women whose stares sought his own.

"Berightback!"

Extricating his draping holds, he bounded into the crowd, holding the drinks up as prizes to capture—whilst she suspected he himself was also up for grabs.

Literally.

"I believe I would like to leave," she said, mostly to herself.

"Then let's go."

Rahvyn looked over at Nate and thought perhaps she should pretend to have misspoken. Alas, she could not lie like that. "Thank you."

He nodded, and then indicated the way forward—which to her seemed no way forward at all. There were so many humans, both static and moving, everyone bumping into each other. As an abrupt suffocation o'ertook her, she faltered, unable to follow him.

"Let me help you."

As Nate's words barely registered, she felt a warm, firm hand envelop her own, and then he was drawing her through the humans, leading the way with his far larger body, people moving to accommodate him because of his size even as he was not being aggressive.

Breaking through the worst of the crowding, they approached the door they had come in through, and she paused to look over her shoulder.

" 'Tis a shame, really. I liked the flowers very much."

With that pronouncement, she went to resume her departure—

Nate was staring down at her with a fixation she recognized. It was that which Shuli had just shown the women before him.

It was also that which the aristocrat had demonstrated. Right before he—

Memories of what had happened in that bedding chamber caused her heart to seize up and she gasped, releasing Nate's palm and putting her hand to the base of her throat. Not that that relieved anything.

"We'll be outside in a second," he said tightly.

As Nate turned away from her, she had a sudden instinct to pull him back and apologize. Instead, she let him go through the door first. There would be a better time—and a quieter place—to explain later.

Well, tell him that her withdrawal was no fault of his own.

The instant she stepped out, the cold, clear air hit her flushed cheeks and the perspiration on her brow. Whilst her pores tightened, the tingling was a refreshing relief.

"Oh, no," she said, glancing back. "What about Shuli?"

Nate shrugged. "I'll text him and tell him we're taking his car. He gave me his keys earlier and he's already too drunk to drive. With any luck, he'll be sober enough before dawn to demater—"

A loud growling sound brought both of their heads around to the intersection of roading beside the club. A vehicle was coming about the corner with such speed that its tires squealed, its shiny black body and darkened windows like a harbinger of evil.

"Get down!" someone said.

Surprised by the commentary, Rahvyn glanced to her right. The human man who had granted them access unto the club's building dropped to the honed stone underfoot, laying himself out facedown.

"Sire?" she inquired as she reached out to him. "Are you ill—"

Over the roar of the car's engine, three sharp sounds rang out, one after another, *choo, choo, choo.* This was followed by a loud shout, and she looked up. At the opposite end of the building, a human male in a dark coat, who seemed to have come around that other corner, covered his head and stumbled back. After finding his footing, he dove for cover as the black car increased its velocity upon the straightaway, the shooter ducking down behind a blackened window that was rising.

"Rahvyn?"

As Nate said her name, she patted at the human who was on the ground. "Sire? Are you okay? Nate, we best call for help. He is not responding—"

"Rahvyn . . ."

"We need to get aid." She twisted around. "What is the number they call—"

Nate was standing over her with the strangest expression on his face. "Help."

"Yes, we need to get some . . ."

His hands were trembling as they went to the hem of his sweatshirt. When he lifted the bottom up, she frowned. There was a red dot on the white t-shirt underneath.

The dot was getting bigger. Fast.

"Nate?"

He fell to the ground upon his knees, the sweatshirt still wadded up in his hands. His eyes clung to hers, fear dilating his pupils.

"Rahvyn," he whispered.

She screamed, even as she abruptly could not hear anything. And as he slumped to the side, she lunged for him. She got there too late to keep him from landing hard, landing as if he were lifeless.

"No!" she yelled. "*No!*"

CHAPTER NINETEEN

The landscape Balz found himself in was desolate as far as his eyes could see, nothing but obsidian sand beneath his feet and black clouds roiling overhead. As red lightning licked the underside of the sky's thick cover, a strange, troubling wind blew in from the horizon, ruffling his hair.

"So Lover Boy is back, I see."

Balz closed his eyes at the sound of the demon's voice, but if he wanted to shut the sight of Devina out, it wasn't going to help. He saw everything just the same whether his lids were up or down—and that was when he knew he was inside his mind. And he wasn't the only one who was there.

Devina stepped in front of him. She was wearing a long white dress that was like a waterfall, and in the odd wind, her brunette hair seethed around her shoulders in a way that reminded him of snakes.

"I've been waiting for you." She laid her red-tipped fingers on his bare chest as if she were claiming him. "I've missed you."

He looked down and saw that he was completely naked.

"And I know you've missed me."

Something hit his back lightly. A drop of rain. And then there was another drop. And another. A stream of them now.

Blood was falling from the black clouds and landing on his skin, and he watched as if from a great distance as his torso began to stripe with red. The sanguine wash stung wherever it came into contact, and he had a thought that it was like her red nails had scratched him all over.

"Kiss me," the demon demanded.

The rain did not touch her. It was as if there were an invisible umbrella above her, the discharge from the storm diverting from her head and that white dress.

A wedding dress, he realized. Like the human women wore at their altar.

"*Kiss me.*"

Leaning into him, the demon tilted her head back and parted her lips. From under a veil of heavy eyelashes, her black eyes glowed with a heat that made his stomach churn. She was ugly in a way that defied the eye. She was evil in a way that decried the soul.

When he didn't respond, she lifted a brow.

"Playing hard to get?" Her husky laugh was an auditory caress. "That's not your style, even though you hate me. Like I've always said, one of my favorite things about fucking you is the way your body betrays your mind and your heart. It's a beautiful sacrifice of principles, especially when you come inside of me."

With that terrible smile, she sank slowly to her knees, the bright white gown pooling on top of the red puddles that were forming on the black ground, the satin skirt floating on top of the blood.

"Fine, I'll take care of things." Staring up at him, she slipped her hands over the curves of his hip bones. "I like this view. And so do you."

She licked her bright red lips, her pink tongue taking its time with the route.

Fuck that, Balz did not enjoy the view. He hated the view, especially as she opened her mouth.

His cock was flaccid as she sucked it down, and the warmth, the slickness, the pull, made tears come to his eyes. He did not want this. He never had.

As she retracted her lips, his stomach rolled and he turned his face to the blood rain, closing his eyes and feeling the tip-taps on his cheeks, his nose, his chin.

Down at his hips, she put more work in, more with the suction, faster with the back and forth. The even edge of her teeth, as they scraped over the ridge of his head, was a clear warning to him. But he didn't care if she bit the goddamn thing off.

Pain now. She was roughing him up.

And then she gripped his balls and twisted.

Balz locked his molars and held in the pain, his hands tightening into fists at his side—

The demon stopped. "What the hell is wrong with you."

Leveling his head, blood dripped into his eyes. "I do not want you."

As he spoke, the rain got into his mouth and he tasted dark wine. And when he swallowed properly, a trail of heat, of strength, sizzled down his throat and bloomed in his gut.

"You don't get it," she snapped. "It doesn't matter whether you want me or not."

The demon punched at his pelvis in frustration. Then she shoved herself back, planting her palms in the puddles that did not touch her.

"You're still mine." She glared up at him. "Your little trick with that knife—it didn't change anything."

So he was dead? he thought. *This was* Dhunhd?

As he glanced around at the harsh emptiness, he thought of Erika Saunders, the homicide detective he had met by chance and remembered like she was his destiny.

This is worth it, if she's safe now.

Even if he had to spend eternity fighting off the demon.

Lightning flashed again, bathing Devina in red, the shadows thrown by her features, her body, moving even as she did not, little pockets of her defenders flaring in case they were needed. And when the storm's crimson show faded, she was untouched once again, a lie in virginal white.

"I can see you anytime I want," she drawled. "And I will be with you, anytime I want."

She didn't so much get up as materialize into a standing position, and gone was the white wedding gown. She was in black now, with a blouse that was low-cut enough to show her dot of a belly button as well as the swells of her breasts.

Devina stepped into him, pushing herself against his chest. "Anytime."

Lifting his hands, he cupped either side of her cleavage and pushed things together. As he stared down at her assets, he watched the rain flow off the top of his head and well up in the basin of flesh.

When there was enough pooled there, he lowered his head. The demon let out a moan, as if she were expecting him to caress and pleasure her. Instead, he drank from what had gathered.

He was going to need all his strength to blow this bitch out of the water.

"Fucking vampires," she muttered. "Can't you just have a steak."

◆   ◆   ◆

Inside a garage that had a cathedral ceiling, more floor space than a tennis court, and no windows, Erika stood next to the tall man with the goatee. They were at the back of the RV unit, which had been parked butt in to a concrete wall that was painted matte black. The rest of the well-lit interior was steel plating, everything reinforced with beams and rivets to the point where she would have called it a bunker if it had been wartime.

She glanced at Goatee and decided he fit in perfectly with the hardcore facility. So did the others. In fact all of these men dressed and acted as if they were at war. With what, though. Those shadows? That . . . woman?

Was there a secret arm of the U.S. government that fought against the things that she'd seen with her own two eyes and still didn't believe? As she contemplated the possibilities, the fact that she was so calm meant she was probably in shock—as in the clinical kind that involved your blood pressure and your heart rate.

Meanwhile, Goatee was enjoying another smoke, and not with any kind of frenzy. He was slow and steady on the chain of hand-rolleds he kept taking out of his leather jacket. As he went through each length, he reminded her of someone waiting in line, just hanging out in neutral because of a delay he refused to be frustrated by. And even though normally she hated the smell of cigarettes, whatever he was exhaling was not offensive in the slightest. It was kind of nice, actually—although she couldn't say the same about his company. If his affect were an aftershave, it would have been called *Le Disapproval*.

Then again, maybe he just had resting bitch face.

"You remind me of my grandfather," she said as her eyes made yet another circle around the garage's spit-and-polish interior.

Over on the left, there was a little grouping of mismatched, frat house furniture, the armchairs and folding card table both out of place with the high-tech RV and all the reinforcements and completely in keeping with the idea that these men cooled their jets here.

"Do I," the guy said.

His response wasn't phrased as a question, and she wasn't surprised that he didn't seem to care one way or the other about her granddad or whether she filled him in on the particulars of any resemblance between one Archibald Saunders (deceased) and himself. The lack of interest struck her as refreshing. Too many people had been way too frickin' curious about her for way too long.

"He smoked a pipe. It was fragrant, like whatever is rolled up in those things."

"Turkish tobacco is the best."

"Hmm. Go figure."

How long had they been out here? It was hard to know. She'd been given an examination and then provided fluids by mouth—otherwise known as a high-test Coke served in its ice-cold red can—and when it had become obvious that she could stand on her own and was fairly steady, Goatee had escorted her out the back of the surgical unit. A moment later, someone she hadn't been able to catch a glimpse of had entered the garage through a side door and gotten in the vehicle's front passenger side.

The perfume of fresh flowers had suggested it was a woman. Maybe a nurse?

"You cold?" Goatee asked.

"No, why do you ask?"

"You just shivered."

"Did I?"

What do you know, she didn't care if she were cold. And she wasn't sure she actually was.

"What are you going to do with me?" she asked.

"Nothing."

Erika glanced over. God, he was big, and all the black leather made him seem even larger. He also had some of the strangest eyes she had ever seen, icy white irises surrounded by a navy-blue rim. The pupils in the center were black as the pits of hell.

She thought of the suspect lying on that examination table, nothing but a blue surgical sheet covering his lower body. She remembered him standing up against the brunette, and saying things about a place called *Dhunhd.*

"I want to see him before I go." Or before they killed her? "The man in there."

When there wasn't a reply, she was acutely aware that she had no gun on her or within reach. And the fact that she couldn't remember whether hers had been taken from her or lost along the way was nothing she could get too worked up about. Too many other problems were ahead of worrying about where her service weapon was.

At this point, she could only pray that she'd live long enough to have to make a report on it.

Man, she was breaking all kinds of protocols recently, between what had happened with that environmental services woman last night and now her empty holster. Her badge was gone, too. When she'd gone to pat for it at the clip on her belt, she hadn't found it, and given that the CPD shield wouldn't have fallen out, she had a feeling they'd taken it and knew she was a cop.

Staring down the flank of the RV, she wondered whether she was ever going to be on the far side of those garage doors. Alive, that was. And as she confronted the idea that she wasn't going to walk out of this situation, but rather be carried out, she thought . . .

Well, she was worried she'd forgotten to turn off her coffeepot when she'd poured herself a traveler at two p.m. that afternoon to go back into the Bull Pen.

Okay, that was ridiculous. She'd seen a man fight a shadow and try to murder himself, had people *poof!*'ing in and out of sight right in front of her, held a glowing orb in her hand . . . and was currently standing next to someone—something?—who had Grim Reaper stamped all over his bad ass, and she was worried about a fire hazard?

Look at her, being all civil servant. Even when she was on the verge of being killed.

"I told you, nothing."

She glanced over at Goatee. "I'm sorry?"

"We're going to do 'nothing' to you, and that includes killing you."

If his words were any drier, they'd come with tumbleweeds.

Erika wanted to curse at the guy, but she didn't have the energy. "So you're just going to take my memories and leave me at the side of the road with a headache that dogs me and the sense that I'm being stalked—while those shadow things that attacked him come after me and I have no way of protecting myself because I don't know what the hell is going on."

He looked over at her, his half-mast eyes making her think of a Siberian husky. Who bit, didn't bark. "We're going to leave you at home, not on the side of a road."

Down at the front of the RV, the passenger door opened and closed, and then on the far side of the mobile unit, two sets of footsteps walked the length of the bunker and went out some exit.

"He wants to see her."

Leaning out the passenger door, the guy in surgical scrubs motioned to her—and when Goatee opened his mouth, he put up his palm.

"Doctor's orders."

"I'm over this security risk."

"He's alive and asking for her. And you like shooting things. So what's your problem."

There was some muttering, but Erika ignored it—and so did the doctor with the orders. Heading over to the RV, she was offered a hand up, and she took it—because she was beyond caring about trying to appear tough.

The interior of the cockpit was like the garage itself, neat and clean, and a panel had been pulled aside to reveal the treatment area.

The patient was still lying where he had been, on that stainless steel table, the sheet draped over his lower body. As if he sensed her presence, his head turned and he looked at her—

With a desperation that she did not understand, he reached out . . . and Erika did not even try to hold herself back from him. For reasons she would worry about later, she threw herself across his bare chest and held on to him.

"I thought you were dead," she said through tears she couldn't stop.

"So did I," he replied hoarsely.

As his heavy arms wrapped around her and held her tightly, she took the first deep breath in what felt like a year.

Or maybe an entire decade.

CHAPTER TWENTY

To Balz, it was the most natural thing in the world to hug this human woman so close. Even though he was weak in his body, his soul was rock solid and that was where the strength to raise his arms came from. This moment, this vital, transcendent moment, was what he'd fantasized about since he'd first seen her.

And what he'd sacrifice the Fade for if it saved her.

"Are you okay," he croaked.

When she shook her head, he hated what she had seen him do . . . what she had heard Devina say.

"I don't know what happened back there," she whispered. "What you were fighting . . . what you did . . ."

Her lips were moving against his shoulder, and her scent was in his nose, and her voice was all he could hear—and the combination of all that was a short-out he didn't want to fight. He'd rather stay where he was, submerged in so much of her.

But he didn't want to leave her question high and dry, and she deserved an honest answer. Not that he had a good one.

"I'm so sorry," he said in a thin voice.

Her head lifted and he got to look into her hazel eyes properly. Her hair was a mess, all kinds of flyaways framing her face, and she had a scrape on her cheek that made him want to call Manny over and schedule her OR time.

Even though the thing probably just needed a Band-Aid.

"Hi," he whispered like a lameass.

Erika brushed her own hair back. Then she opened her mouth and her tense expression made him think she was going to say something briskly. But then she closed her lips and went quiet.

It was a while before she spoke again. Which was fine. He was content to memorize her up close. She had what looked like a chicken pox scar off to the side of one eyebrow, and half of her upper lip was a little higher on the left side. She had a mole on her cheek, right in the place that Marilyn Monroe used to draw one on. And no contacts. Her eyesight was evidently 20/20 without correction.

Made sense to him. She was perfect, after all.

"You came back there," she said roughly, "to save me."

"You're damn right I did."

Her lids closed briefly. "I don't know from what, though. And the weird thing is, I'm not sure it matters."

"It doesn't."

When she looked at him again, there was a reserve to her, and he knew where she'd gone. "I'm sorry you had to see me do that," he said before she could comment.

"I'm sorry you felt like that was what you had to do."

Her eyes drifted down to the front of his throat. Then she flushed and straightened. After a moment, she grimaced and rubbed her temple.

Crap. She was poking that memory patch again. "Erika . . ."

"How do you know my name?" With an abrupt shift, her eyes left his and traveled around the inside of the mobile OR. He was willing to bet she didn't see much of the medical equipment. "But this was not our first meeting, was it. Did you ever introduce yourself to me before?"

There was sadness in the words, and a helplessness, too. Both ate him alive.

"Don't lie to me," she murmured. "Not after a night like tonight. After everything we went through, I've earned the truth, don't you think."

"Balthazar. That's my name."

Her eyes came back and her head tilted a little as she regarded him. "It suits you."

"You've made my night. Unless that's not a compliment."

Her smile was pretty much the best thing he had ever seen, but he wasn't surprised it didn't last very long.

"How many times?" When he frowned in confusion, she cleared her throat. "How many times have you introduced yourself to me."

Fuck. "Only once."

"And how many times have we met."

Well, if you count my fantasies . . . "Twice."

And even though it was causing so many problems for her, he just wanted to do more scrubbing. He wanted to sanitize what she knew of him until to her, he was just a regular male—

Vampire.

"Christ," he muttered. Like she was going to be happy to learn what he was?

"He told me that wasn't who he was."

Balz stared at her for a moment. Then sat up on his elbows. "Who said that to you?"

"It was . . . I don't know what he was. There was a light around him, and he . . . he gave me this energy." She held her palm out. "I put it to your throat. That's why—it wasn't me who saved you. It was him."

"Lassiter," Balz breathed.

"The brunette told him . . ." Erika shrugged. "Something about him knowing what he had to do to get her out of you? What did she mean?"

A beeping sound started up in the front of the RV, and he knew

what that meant. It was the all-hands-on-deck alarm of the Brotherhood. Someone was injured, seriously.

Someone else, that was.

"What's that?" Erika asked.

Twisting around, Balz tried to get a bead on the alert as Manny
jumped behind the wheel and grabbed his phone from somewhere. As
the guy put it up to his ear, it was impossible to get a read on his face,
and instinctively, Balz reached up to his own shoulder, like his communicator was mounted there on his jacket—except he was naked, but for
the sheet.

And shit, everything hurt as soon as he moved quick.

While he groaned and collapsed on the examination table, Erika
looked like she was about to call for medical reinforcements—but she
didn't have to. Manny jumped into the back.

"We've got a medical emergency. I gotta go now. You're stable
enough for the time being, and if you can wait here—"

"I'm okay. I'm good." Balz sat all the way up, gritting his teeth as
lashes of pain flared across his chest, down his back, through his thighs.
"Who is it? Who's down—"

Vishous ripped open the RV's rear double doors. "We gotta go—"

"Help me out the back?" Balz said to Erika. Even though he wanted
to ask questions. But that would just slow things down.

Erika got right on it, grabbing him under the armpit as he put his
feet down and tried to set his weight on them. When he nearly fell over,
she locked a hold on his waist—and the fact that the sheet dropped to
the floor of the treatment area didn't seem to bother her.

It kind of bothered him.

Okay, fine, her gasping and saying something like, "Gee, I didn't
know they came that big" was probably not reasonable under the circumstances. But now he was worried she wasn't impressed at all.

Or hadn't even noticed that he was a male?

Ah, yes, the penis ego was fragile, wasn't it.

With his marching band of dick insecurity following, he shuffled to the drop-off at the rear bumper, and at that point, V briefly took over from Erika, lifting Balz up and out, transferring him to the garage floor like a piece of luggage. Erika came right back against him to hold him up—and even though he hated how weak he was, he did not mind being so close to her.

As the RV's engine came alive and one of the garage bays started to open, the sweet scent of diesel made him sneeze and the two of them backed out of the way.

"Who is it?" he called out as V hopped up into the OR compartment.

"You know where the weapons are." V started closing the doors. "We'll be back as soon as we can—"

"*Who is it.*"

"Not any of us."

And then the Brother tossed out the sheet. *Slam!* went the panels, and then the massive, lumbering RV took off into the night.

Watching at the red glow of the brake lights make a right-hand turn, Balz remembered when the Black Dagger Brotherhood and the Band of Bastards had been mortal enemies. Funny, how time changed things. "Us" was now all of them.

Maybe it was just a civilian who needed help getting to Havers's hidden medical facility.

The garage door automatically began to lower itself, cutting off the city sounds and the stink of the river shore. As it bumped back into place, Balz had one and only one thought—and it wasn't something that reflected well on his character, given everything that was going on. He should be concerned with things stuff like safety . . . and that demon.

Instead, it was all about Erika.

Finally, he was alone with her.

✦   ✦   ✦

Naked.

Really naked.

As Erika held on to Balthazar's waist, she was acutely aware that her hand was on a whole lot of bare skin. And given everything else that was . . . well, hanging around, so to speak . . . she supposed she should have been more embarrassed. There was a lot of him—and private parts aside, it wasn't because he had a beer gut.

Oh, no, Balthazar was all muscle. All. Muscle.

And that was a great name, truly.

"Can you help me over there?"

When she couldn't immediately find her voice, she was glad when he pointed to the mismatched set of armchairs and the card table that was—

"Is that a charcuterie board?" she asked as she noticed a cheese and cracker display that was right out of *Gourmet* magazine.

When had that magically appeared?

"Fritz," he replied.

As they began a hobble over to the sitting area, she muttered, "Is that 'yes' in a foreign language I'm not familiar with?"

"It's a butler."

Erika lost the rhythm of their stilted walk. "Butler? As in the Windsor Castle kind of thing?"

"You got it. Penguin suit and perfect timing, there's no one else like him. He must have delivered it while—well, when some extra help came in."

"Yeah, I would have noticed it before."

There were so many more questions to be asked, but as she glanced at his white-as-an-envelope face, she knew that he was hurting badly and trying to cover it up.

"Almost there," she murmured.

The armchairs were mismatched in terms of color, but equally f-ugly, their patterns floral and bright, yet blessedly faded. Totally man cave decor—which made sense. Did she think there was a knitting circle hanging out in this fortified-but-not-like-kids'-cereal bolt-hole?

"You're going to have to help me sit," the man said. *Balthazar* said.

"Sure. Just lean on—"

"Here, I think I can—"

Crash! He landed like something that had been thrown down a flight of stairs, the chair screeching back, his arms flopping on the—well, arms. And then his head dropped onto his collarbones like he was exhausted—

"Shit, I'm naked."

He slapped his hands over his private area and blushed like he'd never been unclothed in the presence of anything remotely female before. And what were the chances of that.

"Here." She doubled back and picked the sheet up off the cold concrete floor. "This'll work."

As she came over, she kept her eyes up and focused on the garage door that had just shut, and he took the lead on the awkward handoff. While he covered his lap, she parked herself next door, in the armchair that was the color of an eggplant and had little paisleys all over it.

"I think Prince left this here a decade ago," she murmured.

He chuckled a little. "You want to eat?"

"I'm not hungry."

Still, she helped herself to a slice of what looked like brie and some kind of whole-grained cracker. As she bit down, her stomach woke up.

"Oh, my God. Wait, I think I'm starved."

"Help yourself. I think there's wine here in this cooler—"

"No wine," she said as she chewed. "I'll never get out of this chair."

He whispered something under his breath, something like, "That would be okay with me."

And that's when things got really weird. Which considering what she'd seen earlier in the night was saying something.

But the thing was, as she nibbled, and tried not to enjoy the view of his pecs and his shoulders, and those arms, and that stomach—

"What was the question?" she blurted.

"I wasn't aware I'd asked one." He smiled a little. "How's the cheese going down?"

"Amazing."

"I like watching you eat," he said with a sigh. When she froze and glanced at him, he looked away. "Sorry."

"No, it's okay."

Because suddenly things felt like a date to her, too. Which, yes, was weirder than the glowing guy, and that brunette, and the shadow—

"Your burns," she said, "or whatever they are, it's like they're healing in front of my very eyes."

He lifted an elbow and rolled his forearm over. The raised welt on the underside was red as a strawberry and looked like the cable in a cable-knit sweater. But both the swelling and the discoloration were decreasing as she stared at his injuries.

"You really got hurt from fighting that thing," she murmured.

"Nah, I'm good."

Maybe this was better, she thought. As much as her brain struggled to think about what had happened, maybe it was better to remind herself why they were sitting together. Because this was not a swipe-right-meet-up situation, fantastic cheese board aside.

"I am a thief," he said absently as he glanced down at a similar wound across his chest. "You're right about that."

Yup, this is good, she emphasized. Even though she hated the reminder that he was a criminal. A suspect, actually, in one of her very own open cases.

"So you did steal those watches from the triplex." She pushed the board away, no longer feeling the food. "From Herb Cambourg."

"Yes, and I'm not sorry."

Erika cocked an eyebrow. "Well, if you had a problem with your conscience, you wouldn't be stealing in the first place, would you."

"That's one way of looking at it."

When he went quiet, she shook her head. "Can we please stop bullshitting now? I'm exhausted and confused, and there's no reason for you to go through some big confessional if I'm not going to remember it. That's like hanging up the phone before leaving a message. Or erasing the message." She went back to rubbing her temples. "I don't know what the hell I'm saying. I have no business making metaphors."

"Technically, I think the first one was a simile."

Erika looked over at him. "I really want to tell you to fuck off right now."

"I don't blame you."

"Strunk and White have no place in this garage."

"Strunk and who?" He waved a hand. "Wait, I know that. From a clue in the *New York Times* crossword puzzle last week."

"Thursday."

"Yeah, that's the one." He smiled a little. "Do you do it, too?"

"I usually crap out on Thursdays. It gets too hard for me past that."

"I have to do it in pencil. My cousin does them all in pen and is a pain in the ass about it. We have twelve issues of the *Times* delivered every morning because it's the only way no one gets hurt at First Meal."

Her brows arched. "You live with a dozen of your family?"

"They're not all blood relatives."

"Are you in the mafia or something?"

"No."

She focused on his throat. The line that was there was fading just as fast as the burns, and as she witnessed even more of the swelling disappear . . . she had a thought that he was different than her, and not just because he was a man.

Or . . . masculine.

And when she spoke, she surprised herself: "I haven't been this scared since the night of June twenty-fourth, fourteen years ago."

"Oh, God, Erika, I'm really sorry—"

When he reached for her hand, she moved it away. "You've got to stop apologizing. What you need to do instead is whatever it is up here . . ." She motioned around the top of her skull. "And then send me back home. I'll clean up the pieces somehow, God knows I've done it be-fore. Besides, if one of those shadows comes after me?" She shook her head. "I'm dead whether I know they exist or not."

She could not believe she was being so calm. But what choice did she have.

"I want to protect you."

Erika looked over at him—and did not mean to do a stem-to-stern on the guy. But for one, she was remembering him fighting with that shadow-whatever, and as someone who had been trained in self-defense, it was obvious he had skills. For another . . .

Well, the view was goddamn spectacular. From the pads of those pecs to the curls of his biceps to that eight-pack he was sporting like he did ten thousand sit-ups before he had a protein bar with his egg whites in the morning—

"I know you want to keep me safe," she said in a low tone. "Thank you for that. Seriously. But the sad truth about life is that sometimes we can't always get what we want. And hey, I've been fighting for a really long time with things that aren't actually in front of me. Who knows . . . maybe I'll win against a shadow."

It was a stupid thing to say. Even more stupid to think it could be true. She had seen what that attack had done against a man like this one, and he had seventy-five pounds of muscle on her. At least.

"Just take my memories again," she told him, "and let me go live my life, however it turns out."

He was quiet for a very long time. Quiet for an eternity.

And she just sat there. Like a bump on a log, her father would have said.

"Learned helplessness," she murmured.

Balthazar jerked to attention. "Sorry?"

"I was a psych major in college. Learned helplessness is a maladap-tive behavior pattern where someone feels like there's no cause and ef-fect to their actions. It leads to a collapse in problem-solving strategies and generalized apathy." She held up her forefinger. "What's interesting in my case here is not that I can't see the cause and effect, it's more like I don't know what behavior is actually mine or what kind of a world I live in. Anyway, that's why I'm a zombie—and it's too bad I can't rewrite my final paper on this whole thing."

"Rolling Stones," he blurted.

"What?"

"The song. I couldn't remember the song."

Are we having the same conversation? she wondered.

"You can't . . . always get . . . what you waaannnt." He cleared his throat and sang a little more loudly. "You can't always geeeeet what you wannnnt."

When he stopped there, she said, "Wow. You . . ."

"Can't sing at all."

"Yeah, I mean really. It's—"

"Bad. Real bad. Couldn't-hold-a-tune-in-a-basket bad. Alley-cat bad. A step down from tone-deaf."

Erika started to smile. Then she laughed. "I'm no opera singer, either."

"I promise never to do it again."

"No, you don't have to." She shrugged. "It's kind of nice to think that not everything about your body is perfect."

His eyes shot to hers, and she flushed as she looked away.

And that was when everything changed between them. Sure, they were both sitting where they had been, and he was still getting over—God, slitting his own throat—and she was in another kind of recovery. But suddenly there was a charge in the air.

That had nothing to do with fear.

Maybe she should have stuck with the cheese-eating, date side of things. Because this sexual charge right here? It had nuclear one-night stand written all over it, and given that she had clearly lost her mind . . . she couldn't think why such a thing was a terrible idea.

Erika glanced back and met that hooded, hot stare of his.

"You know what the last part of the song was?" Balthazar asked in a deep voice.

"Song?" she parroted as she focused on his lips.

He leaned into her, all bare muscle and that amazing cologne that suddenly flared in the air, like he'd magically reapplied some. "The last part of the chorus to that song. 'But if you try sometimes, you just might find . . .'"

Don't do it, the reasonable part of her demanded. Like if she filled in the blank, she was not only acknowledging whatever was flaring between them, she was saying "yes" to a question he hadn't even asked—

"You get what you need," she finished breathlessly.

CHAPTER TWENTY-ONE

Nate's parents came running down a long, white corridor in a dishevel of arms and legs, a flapping of jackets, a flurry of panic. They were holding each other's hands as if their grips were all that would keep them from being carried out by a vicious tide, and with their eyes wide and their mouths open like they were screaming, they were the very picture of terror.

Rahvyn had not been introduced to either one of them. But in these circumstances, it was obvious who they were.

From her perspective, sitting on the hard tiled floor with her legs tucked under her, she stared up at them as they raced by. They didn't look at her. They didn't even seem to see her. They had one and only one priority—and yet she wanted to jump up and embrace them. And tell them she was sorry and that somehow this was all her fault.

Maybe if she hadn't tried to help the human on the ground?

Maybe if . . .

Shuffling her sore body around, she brought her knees up and rested her cheek on the bony apex of her legs. The destination for Nate's parents was the patient room down at the far end of the hall. Outside of the closed door, a gathering of members of the Black Dagger Brotherhood was a fierce knot of well-armed worry. She did not know all of them, but she recognized the Brother Rhage, who had blond hair and eyes that were very blue, and the Brother Butch, who was dressed in a formal fashion, rather than in togs of war. There were a couple of others . . . and also her first cousin, Sahvage.

As the frantic male and female disappeared into Nate's treatment room, Sahvage glanced back at her and she replayed the trip here to this subterranean healing facility, remembering the moment she had looked up to see Nate lifting his sweatshirt . . . and then him falling to the ground . . . and finally her shouting and lunging onto him.

The man by the door to the club of Dandelion, who had gone prone, whom she had thought had been injured, had wanted to get involved. She had frozen him where he was and put a patch on his recollections—and then she had seen a car go by. And another. Across the street, there had been several humans paused in their tracks, their bodies leaning forward as if they were imminently going to fall into a race-across.

That was when she had stopped it all.

Everything in Caldwell.

All humans, all vampires, all rodents and snakes. The cars, and the trucks, the bicycles, all braked. No more smoke rising from chimneys nor water swirling into drains. No gasping, no cursing, no whispers for to strain.

Stopped.

Except for Nate and herself. And others that she extracted from the tableau as she required.

With hands that shook, she had rifled through his pockets, found his cellular device, and put its screen close to his face. When the recognition succeeded, she had gone into the favorites in his contacts, grateful that he had taught her how to use the unit. The first call she had made had been to his adopted father, Murhder. When that had gone to a recorded voice-over, she had tried his mother. Also a recording.

The third one had been Shuli. Again with a recording.

All the while, Nate had been gasping for breath. And then he had stopped gasping.

Blessedly, the fourth number had been answered, an elderly, solicitous voice announcing with good cheer the name Fritz Perlmutter.

She had no idea who the male was, but within five minutes of the call, a tremendous-sized healing vehicle, like a mercy ship on wheels, had pulled up.

A human wearing loose blue clothing and the Brother Vishous had jumped out of the back with a pallet and removed Nate from the scene. She had gotten into the rear with them, and had sat out of the way as the Brother Rhage arrived to drive them off.

It had been whilst they had pulled away from the scene and turned around in the center of the lane that she had allowed Caldwell to resume its churn. A glimpse out of the pane of glass up in front had shown the clutch of humans reanimating out of their freeze. There would be confusion for them, but she didn't have the energy to manipulate their memories. They would just have to make peace with what they believed they saw—and when they went over to speak unto the man outside of the club, he would inform them that, yes, there had been a discharge of a firearm, and a stray dog had been shot, but the thing had run off.

And that would be that.

On the way unto this facility, she had been too scared to speak, especially as so many things were done to Nate, so many . . . tubes, patches, cuffs, and machines connected, implanted, stuck into him. The two males treating him had spoken in a volley of words, the syllables outside her understanding, a language foreign.

It had been a lifetime, the traveling, yet a clock with red, glowing numbers, mounted atop a glass-fronted casing of supplies, had informed her that only seventeen minutes passed. When their destination had been reached, the lumbering, rumbling vehicle of healing had come to a stop. As the double doors had been opened a woodland landscape was revealed and the scent of pine and earth had flooded in, replacing the blood smell and the heat. Rahvyn had followed behind as Nate had been removed upon a rolling table along with a host of beeping, flashing equipment and those wires, those tubes.

From what had appeared to be an earthen mound, a male with tortoiseshell glasses and a white coat had thrown open a well-disguised door, exposing a brightly lit interior. Females in white uniforms had accompanied him. Brothers had come forward.

And so had Sahvage.

Her cousin had rushed to embrace her and she had collapsed into him, babbling details about what had occurred that were not terribly relevant. The one bullet was all that mattered. Well, that and whatever happened next.

Nate and the various uniformed attendants had gone down in a steel box first. Then she and Sahvage and the Brothers had followed, a mechanized contraption lowering them into the earth.

They had been so kind to her, the fighters. And in the face of their gentle compassion, so at odds with their weapons and their protective leather clothing, she had finally cried, tucking her face into Sahvage's chest, just as she had when they had been youngs . . .

When her pony had died from eating that weed. And her cat had wandered off.

And her parents had been killed.

Now she was here, sitting on this tiled floor, in a maze of lemon-scented hallways and closed white doors, wishing she had not left the club when she had. If she had waited only a moment longer—either when Nate had suggested their departure or perhaps right before they had stepped out onto the street.

A moment was all it took to change the course of everything. The problem was . . . one never knew which moment was going to matter, and there were so many, so very many, even in the lives of mortals—

The muffled scream from inside the treatment room rippled out from behind the closed door like a shock wave, the bodies of the Brothers weaving as they put dagger hands unto their faces, the fronts of their throats. Their hearts.

There followed the weeping of the *mahmen.*

Horrible, ear-stinging weeping from her, behind that closed door.

He was gone. Rahvyn did not need to be told.

As tears welled in her eyes and slipped down her cheeks, she too placed her hands unto her cheeks in a vain attempt to hold herself together, contain the horror, understand how an evening on a whim had ended in a life-defining tragedy.

And then it happened.

From the forest of strong-backed Brothers, their sadness a stain upon the still air around them, her cousin Sahvage's head slowly turned unto her.

His eyes burned with emotion as he looked down the long bare corridor toward her.

Whate'er is he asking of me, she thought with heartbreak.

And yet . . . she knew.

CHAPTER TWENTY-TWO

T he solitude of the collector was almost never a burden.

Sometimes, you just wanted to be alone with your shit, you needed that special time.

Tonight was not it.

As Devina walked up and down the aisles created by her hanging racks, she was way too alone, and nothing, not her newest bouclé jacket from Chanel, not even her oldest acquisition, either, was filling the void. Which, of course, was not the way hoarding normally worked for her.

Worse? She didn't want to buy anything else. So her shopping addiction was failing her, too.

It was a while before she realized what was bothering her—or maybe it was more like it took a while before she could stand to acknowledge the problem: She was here again, dumped by a male. Dumped by a male who so completely couldn't stand her, he'd slit his own throat to get away from her—

No, wait, it was even worse. That Bastard Balthazar had killed himself to save the female he really wanted, and Devina had been part of the measure of how much he cared about his little chippie. He hated

Devina, but he'd been willing to get stuck with her in Hell for an eternity just to protect Little Miss Homicide Detective.

It was downright insulting, really.

Devina couldn't believe the whole damned thing. Okay, yeah, sure, she could be a thundercunt, but she wasn't all bad.

Okay, fine. Maybe she was all bad.

She was sex on a stick, though, and she could be good to a lover. If she felt like it. If it worked for her. So come *on*.

Stopping in front of her full-length gowns, she pulled out the white one she had put on to be inside Balthazar's mind when he'd been having his post-bleed-out nap. The satin was so virginal and smooth and cool over her hands and she loved how the red of her glossy fingernails looked against the sheen. Like blood on a wisping cloud.

Lifting her head, she stared across all her hangers, all her babies.

The Book was up against the far wall, suspended as if in an invisible sling. The damn thing was snoring, the front cover bubbling in a soft, rhythmic purr, the pages beneath shuffling quietly.

Exhaling, she felt her shoulders droop. She couldn't keep doing this, getting pushed aside for so-called "better options" by males. The rejections were giving her a complex. Fuck being someone's priority. She wasn't even an alternative.

"Please," she said with defeat. "Please help me find true love."

Fuck knew, if she were left to her own devices, it was never going to happen—

The Book's cover popped open and slapped down, as if it woke up. Then it sat itself up, so that it was facing her instead of lying flat on the thin air.

She wasn't getting her hopes up, though. For all she knew, it was going to Uber Eats some Thai food to the lair. Or maybe an office chair. Fuck if she could tell what was going through its head.

There was a series of coughs and then the pages seemed to lick themselves. After a final shake, as a bird might rearrange its feathers, that ugly, mottled cover blew wide open and stayed that way.

Those pages started flipping.

Devina blinked a couple of times. Then she dropped the dress's skirting and walked forward, called by the movement of the parchment, at first furiously fast, and now slowing. It was the strangest thing. More pages turned than were bound, but she had always believed there were an infinite number of folios confined within the tome—

The flipping stopped.

Just dead-on halted.

"Don't be cruel," she said before she took a look. And she meant it as a warning, but the words came out as a plaintive appeal to the thing's better nature. If the Book even had one.

When the tome didn't move at all, when it just stayed inanimate, she hitched her breath and leaned down.

The first thing she saw, in a graceful, handwritten script, was "Love Spell for a Beautiful Demon."

Her eyes flooded with tears. "I'm sorry I'm such a bitch."

One of the pages lifted up and brushed her cheek, catching her tear. Then the Book resettled as if it was done both with fighting with her, and any soppy emotion.

"Right." She sniffled and rubbed her nose. "What do we have here."

Like she was whipping up a pot roast and had to see whether all the ingredients were in her cupboard.

Her eyes watered again as she read out loud. "'If faithfully followed, this shall bring unto the caster a true love for the whole of her, all parts contained within her, evil or no.'"

She reached out and stroked the page. "Thank you, old friend."

There was a sniffle from the Book, the upper right corner of the folios whiffling.

"Now . . . what do I need," she murmured as she resumed reading.

◆   ◆   ◆

"What do you need, Erika?"

As Balz asked the question, it was one hell of a leading one. But here was the thing: Her body was already with him. He could scent her arousal, and even if his nose was wrong—which it wasn't—there was no mistaking where her eyes kept going.

He wanted her to look at him like that for the rest of both their lives.

It was as if she not only approved of his body . . . but wanted to touch him. Taste him.

And big frickin' surprise, he was incapable of not responding to the sexual need in her. Even though the Brotherhood's hidden garage was about as romantic as an AutoZone store, and he was beat to shit, and there was absolutely nothing comfortable to lie down on, he was still more than ready to . . .

"Tell me," he whispered. "What do you need."

Her eyes went back to his mouth, and it was like she was testing them out with her own already, taking from him, having a proverbial bite—and it was then he knew he was going to have her. The "yes" was in her hungry stare, the turn in her body, and that holy-shit scent.

As she took a deep breath, he wanted to keep talking, if it would put her at ease—

"I need you to let me go," she said hoarsely. "Please."

Balz dropped his lids. And prayed that he could hide his reaction. It wasn't anger; it was disappointment—and not just because he wasn't going to get the chance to mount her, and penetrate her, and give her the best orgasms of her life. The biggest regret was with himself. As usual.

"You know," he said as he shook his head, "I'm really getting tired of being a thief."

"There are other professions," she said dryly. "You could try accounting. Legal work. Probably not teaching, though, given where your expertise lies. Some things shouldn't be passed down to the next generation."

He smiled a little. Then went back to being serious. "I don't want to steal anymore. At least not when it comes to you. I'm done with it."

Staring into her eyes once again, he entered her mind and flipped all her memories free. All of the ones he'd hidden. Every single recollection he'd buried.

Immediately, she gasped and then focused on the middle ground between their faces, her eyes blinking. And when she finally looked at him properly again, she seemed to reassess all of his details—and there was no way what she saw worked in his favor.

"I was right," she said. "You took my memories—"

"Patched is more like it."

"How?"

He cleared his throat. "Just like flipping switches on a motherboard. The human brain is a conduit for electricity, so it's all about routing."

"But . . . how . . ."

As she stared off into space again like she was trying to solve *pi* to the tri-billionth decibel—*decimal*, he corrected—he couldn't bear anything about their whole situation. The whole goddamn thing was fucked.

Getting to his feet, he wrapped the sheet fully around his lower body—because flashing her was not going to be a value-add—and went over to a fireproof lockbox the size of a big-screen TV. Mounted on the interior wall of the garage, the arsenal safe had a conventional lock, not one made of copper, so all he had to do was will it open, and then it was a case of—

"Welcome to the gun show," Erika said haltingly.

"Holy crap, I was literally just thinking that." He glanced over his shoulder and saw that she'd gotten to her feet. "I want to make sure you're properly armed before you go."

As he turned back to the guns that were arranged on racks, his instincts told him she was closing in on him—and God, he wished they lived in a world where she didn't have a reason to be armed, and he didn't have a reason to make sure she had so many bullets on her. Taking stock of the autoloaders, the rifles, and the big-bore stuff down at the bottom, he chose two nine millimeters and grabbed a pair of backup magazines.

"Here," he said, holding out the load. "I don't have any holsters, but you have at least one on you, right?"

"I can't accept those weapons."

"You're going to. Toss 'em in the river tomorrow morning if you want, I don't care. But if you're leaving, you're not going out there without a way to take care of yourself."

When she just stared at him, he nodded. "You told me to let you go. So that's what I'm doing."

Pushing the guns into her hands and tucking the magazines into her pockets, he walked unsteadily across the garage to a side pedestrian door. Another lockbox was beside the exit. Opening it, he picked at random one of the sets of car fobs. Checking the tab, he noted the nothing-special make and model.

Incognito, he thought. It was perfect for not drawing attention to herself.

The reinforced exterior door was dead-bolted with a copper lock, but the key was hidden on the top of the jamb. After unlocking the industrial-strength mechanism, he opened the way out. As cold, river-mungy air rushed in, he looked over his shoulder.

Erika was standing where he'd left her, in front of an arsenal's worth of projectile delivery systems, a gun in each hand, the magazines jammed messily into her jacket. Looking at her from this distance, he noted the blood spots on her clothes, the dirt and dust, too. There were also wrinkles on her slacks and that scrape on the side of her face.

She looked like she had had a really long, hard night.

He wished they could stay together, even if there was no sex. He could have done with holding her.

"Did they check you out medically?" he demanded. "In the RV?"

"Yes." She glanced down at herself. Then she walked over. "I wasn't hurt. Not really. I don't know what happened to me."

Balz released a breath. Outside, a truck's Jake brake was engaged, the hissing a little too close for comfort. God, all he wanted to do was shut the damn door, lock it, strap ten rifles on his body, and stand guard over her while she got a little rest.

And then what, though.

"You're just going to let me walk out of here?" she asked.

"You're not a prisoner."

"What about my memories?" She lifted her arm as if to touch the side of her head—but then seemed to realize she had a gun in her hand. "I have all of them. From the moment . . . I first saw you. In the collections room where Herb Cambourg was killed. You and another man were fighting over one of the books. The really old one, that's still missing."

"Yup."

When that was all he said, she shook her head. "Why? Why are you leaving me with my memories."

"Because they're yours."

"Then why did you take them in the first place?"

"I thought it was the right thing to do. It wasn't. And I'm sorry."

Erika looked away. Looked back. "You've told me nothing really. You've explained nothing."

"Which is why you're free to go. The less you know, the more freedom you have and the less danger you're in."

Provided he could keep that demon away from her.

As they both fell silent, a siren flared somewhere down the street. And then there were a couple of shouts, but they were off in the distance.

He held out the car keys. "It's a ten-year-old Honda. Silver, black interior. Do you know how to drive a stick?"

"Yes," she answered absently.

"It's right out in front, just a block away. I'll watch you until you get into it." With a sense of profound regret, he looked over her face, well aware it would be the last time he saw her. "Goodbye, Erika—"

"I'm going to come after you, you realize." She cleared her throat and squared her shoulders. "I still have a job to do, and you're on the wrong side of the law. None of what happened tonight will change the reality of what I have to do."

"I know. And listen, not that this matters much, but you know those watches?"

"The ones from the Commodore?"

"Yeah. Well, I did steal them from that guy, and I did take them to that dealer's trailer. I left with five thousand seven hundred seventy-four dollars. I took the cash down to St. Roche's animal shelter. Call them and ask them about the bag that was left on the desk of their administrator, Wanda Trumain. She'd have seen it as soon as she walked into her office the morning after the theft. She'll remember it for a lot of reasons, but mostly because she'll swear that she locked her door the night before and she can't figure out how anybody could have gotten in there, especially as they have night staff roaming the halls."

"So you're saying you're Robin Hood?"

"No, I'm telling you that I stole from a rich asshole who cheated on his wife and treated her like a piece of art he could acquire and then hang up and forget about. And then I gave the cash that I would have gotten on the black market to an animal shelter that's trying to take care of mistreated or abandoned dogs and cats."

"Just like Robin Hood."

"I'm not ever going to feel bad about it."

Erika cleared her throat again. Like it was a nervous tic. "How many times have you done that?"

"Since I came to Caldwell? Or over the course of my life?"

"Either. Both." She pushed some flyaways out of her face. "I don't know."

"It's what I do. I've got a knack for getting into places that people try to keep others out of, and I have to do something with what I take. I don't need the shit."

"So it's a game to you?"

"It's just a way to keep up my skills. And not everybody can have six fucking watches that are worth, collectively, more than a lot of people's houses." He shook his head. "Like I said, I am never going to apologize for what I've done."

"And you're not going to stop, are you."

"Nope. The proceeds always go to places that need it more."

He met her right in the eye, but not aggressively. More so that it was clear he was telling his truth, and she was free to judge.

"You know," she said in a lowered voice, like all her CPD colleagues might be listening in on a wiretap, "I wouldn't feel bad if I were you, either."

Balz smiled a little. "Thanks for understanding."

Her boss-voice came back online. "It's still illegal. And assuming the things you take are insured, it's not a victimless crime even if the owners get reimbursed."

"Still not sorry."

"It's wrong."

"I don't care. It feeds people or animals who are hungry. It gives unfortunates a place to sleep when they have none. And it keeps those who are desperately afraid safe."

"True virtue doesn't come with an asterisk."

"And thieves can have morals—hey, is this our first fight?"

She blinked—and then seemed to be trying not to smile. "I'd call it more of an argument than a fight." Then her brows twitched into a frown. "And you're seriously just going to let me go? What about your buddies?"

"Don't worry about them. They won't come after you. And neither will I, Erika. You can trust me on that."

She opened her mouth, but he went back into her brain one final time. Leaving her memories alone, he instead gave her a gift: He inserted the very clear cognition that it was in her best interests to never, ever come near him or this garage, and never, ever do any further investigating into any part of what she had seen, heard, or done tonight . . .

Due to the trance he had to put her in, all she could do was stare up at him, her eyes fuzzy, her mouth slightly parted, her body poised.

It would have been the perfect time to kiss her.

But he'd already taken too much without her permission.

And everything ended between them right now.

Everything.

CHAPTER TWENTY-THREE

And still Sahvage stared down the long white corridor at Rahvyn.

Whilst the Brothers around him displayed a masculine pattern of grieving, strong faces drawn tightly, eyes watering, but no tears falling, he faced her and locked her stare with his own, the demand not a call to action but a shout.

Opening up a communication link between them, she said unto his mind, *You hated what I did to you.*

He shook his head from side to side. Whether it was a denial or he was saying that none of that mattered, she was not sure—and meanwhile, on the other side of the closed door behind him, that *mahmen's* weeping was a stain upon the air, seeping out and infecting all within its sorrowful earshot with a weighted sadness.

How could she not respond to such grieving?

Rahvyn's body moved first, before her brain consciously instructed her legs to push her feet into the floor and her arms to steady her balance upon the bare, clean wall as she rose. On the vertical, she had an absurd notion to smooth out her clothes, and thus she did so, trying to ignore the red stains from where she had cradled Nate on the concrete outside of that club.

She walked forward in a daze.

Focusing only on Sahvage, the hall disappeared in her peripheral vision, and so too did the fighters who surrounded him. All was gone except for her dearest first cousin, the remnant of her family, the living, breathing symbol of what she had once been.

Before she had emerged from violence in her full power.

As she stopped in front of him, he said in a low voice, "You have to save him."

Whether it was her arrival upon their midst or the intense words spoken by her cousin, one by one, the Brothers looked at her. Turned to her. Narrowed their eyes upon her.

"Save him," Sahvage repeated as that crying continued inside the room.

Rahvyn lowered her head. She would have avoided this revelation as to herself if she could have—and knew once again that she should have left the night after she and Sahvage had been reunited. Once she had reassured him she lived, her reason for being in this place and time had been served.

"There is no going back," she said quietly. "You know that yourself."

"I don't give a shit and neither will they. Just bring him back. If Nate is lost, we lose two others tonight."

When Rahvyn looked at the door, the Brothers asked no questions and put up no argument, as if they didn't need to understand to agree with what Sahvage was saying. But she knew without being told that she would be accountable unto them if things went badly.

And mayhap that was the point. This tragedy felt as though it was her fault, and she wanted to make amends. What she had to offer was not without strife, however, and she was not certain what would be harder to live with: Doing nothing . . . or doing what she could—

Once again, her body made the decision before her mind formed the thought to move. Her feet started forward, step, step, step. And as she passed through the throng of males, she was a willow tree to their towering pines, yet their deference was in the way they wordlessly parted for her.

Rahvyn watched her hand reach out and open the door.

The scene on the other side was a tableau of suffering around a dead body, the living leaning down, Nate lying prone and motionless and spotlit on the steel table. All of the tubes and wires from the transportation were still attached to him, but the machines had been silenced, no beeping, no flashing lights or patterns appearing on their screens. On the floor beneath where he lay, there were tufts of bloodstained gauze and plastic wrappers and puddles of blood.

The healers had tried valiantly to save him, she thought as she took in further details.

Nate's lower body was draped with blue sheeting. His chest was stained with something orange along with dried blood. His eyes were closed and his mouth open, and his hair . . . looked as it had when he'd been alive.

The male with the spectacles and the white coat was the first to look at her, and he cleared his throat in an officious manner. "I'm sorry, I'm going to have to ask you to leave."

Murhder, Nate's adoptive father, glanced over. Wiping his red eyes, he said hoarsely, "It's all right. She's a friend of his. Come here and say goodbye—"

His voice choked off at that point so he used his hands to motion her near, waving at her to close in.

The *mahmen* did not lift her head from her son. She just stood on the far side of Nate, her hands on his shoulder and upper arm, her tears falling onto his cooling skin.

"I am so sorry," Rahvyn whispered.

"You did everything you could," the sire said. "You called for help and gave him the best chance he had."

"Will you allow me to revive him?"

At that, the *mahmen* raised her head, her face a vision of despair. "What?"

"Whatever is going on here?" the healer demanded. "Shall I call for security—"

"Shh," Murhder cut in. "Sweetheart . . . he's gone. It's too late."

"No, it's not." The Brother's brows came down, but before he could argue and break the heart of his *shellan* even more, Rahvyn said quickly, "Will you allow me to help him."

Murhder cleared his throat. "I'm sorry. If you're not going to pay your respects to him, we'd like some privacy—"

The *mahmen* reached across the body of her dead son and grabbed at Rahvyn's arm. "Yes, yes . . . *yes.*"

Her eyes were wide, and her whole body trembled—and Rahvyn was aware that she herself had been in the same state when she had stood over Sahvage's arrow-strewn body.

"What can you do?" the female begged.

"I will bring him back for you," Rahvyn whispered.

"Please, oh, God . . . I just need him alive."

As the males started to raise protestations, she and the *mahmen* locked eyes—and then Rahvyn closed her lids.

Instantly, everything became so crystal clear to her senses that the smells of blood and fear and anguish were like shards of glass in her nose, and the glow of the ceiling lights and the chandelier over the table was a brilliant beam shining right in her face. She could hear the tense, shallow breathing of the *mahmen* as a scream, and the voices of the father and the healer as booming basses, and even a shuffle of clothing or shift of weight were loud as metal on metal.

There is no going back, she thought out at both of the parents.

"Please," the *mahmen* begged. "Save him."

With a heavy heart, Rahvyn called upon her—

The strobing of the room's lighting fixtures registered through her closed eyes, and she had a dim thought that the blinking had not trans-pired the last time she had done this. The first time she had done this, rather. To Sahvage.

Then again, that had been centuries ago when it came to linear time. No electricity back in that castle. Candles only. And moonlight.

As the flickering intensified, the pulsing began. She could feel the energy emanating from her body in all directions, not just toward Nate—

Thump. Thump.

Thump.

At the sounds, she opened her lids. The three people who had been around the bedding table had been propelled back against the walls of the room and they were pinned in place by waves of magic that dis-torted the air, turning the oxygen that should have been invisible into something that was like water's surface after a stone was thrown into a still pond.

Rahvyn moved without walking to the table, her body levitating and propelling itself upon her will unto Nate's side. When she focused on his face, shadows were thrown as if a brilliant light was trained upon him, though it was not. There was no illumination, and yet the contrast doubled and redoubled until even the softest contours of his chin and cheeks, his hair and ears, were as if drawn in jet-black ink.

And then all color leached out of him and that which was around him. No more was the sheeting blue, nor his abdomen stained with orange and red, nor the wires red and blue and yellow that ran off the pads affixed to his chest. All was black, white, and shades of gray. His skin, too, became without a tint, that which had been graying now fully there. Thereafter, the distortion intensified and took on further characteristics. He became a leaded pencil rendering of himself, not only black and white, but no longer three-dimensional, all aspects of him flattening out into two.

In Rahvyn's concentration and summoning of power, she lost track of that which surrounded her and him. Gone were the room, its equip-ment and its people, disappeared was that corridor and those males outside, null and void became the entirety of Caldwell . . . and then this New World . . . and finally the ocean she had crossed and the Old Country from whence they had all originated.

The rotation started slowly, she and Nate making a single turn. And another. And one more and one more after that. Speed began to gather next, the spinning increasing until they were a blur—and yet there was no breeze to riffle her hair or his. Faster, faster . . . faster still they went. Faster. Faster . . .

The momentum increased until the revolutions were at such a velocity that the center could not hold. As critical acceleration was reached, there was a great clapping, as if lightning struck a tree.

Upon the sound, they broke free of the spinning and floated in a void. The state of transcendence was an impossibility to describe, and yet an undeniable experience as all opposites became one: both static and spinning, one dimension and yet three, time stopping and also racing, the two of them weightless and more dense than the earth.

Life and death, together. Coexisting. The line that separated the two states of mortality no boundary at all, the distinction disappearing.

Such that Rahvyn could merge the incompatible through her will—

Upon the table that existed and was not existent, Nate's mouth opened wide and he drew in a tremendous breath that was loud as a yell, silent as a feather landing.

With a lurch, his torso bolted up, his eyes peeled wide, and his hands went to his stomach where he had been shot. As he breathed with desperate, hungry draws, his lungs inflated him out of his two dimensional state, the contours of him reemerging and pulling free of the flatness, the color coming back not just to his face and skin, but all that was around him.

Rahvyn watched, right by his side and from a vast distance away, as he struggled with the divide he now straddled.

And could never leave.

Both alive and dead.

Forevermore.

CHAPTER TWENTY-FOUR

As Erika tore off from the garage, she was running away, running as fast as she could, running for her life.

As her heart pounded and her throat burned, her shoes slapped against the pavement. With a set of car keys in one hand and a—

No, wait, she had guns in both her hands and a key fob hanging off her pinkie. Whatever, like it mattered. The only thing she cared about was getting to the silver Honda that she had to get to because if she didn't get to the silver Honda she was never, ever going to be safe, ever again. Silver Honda was base. Silver Honda was panic room. Silver Honda was savior—

She ran faster, even though she had less than a block to go, her goal so close as her jacket flapped and her hair stripped back from her face in her self-created windstorm. And still she ran. Until it felt like the silver Honda was just getting farther and farther away.

Finally. With heaving breath, she fumbled with the key fob, hitting every button there was on it as she juggled the guns—until the trunk popped at the same time the doors unlocked. She left the back open as she threw herself behind the wheel. Slamming the driver's door, she was more with the slapping and flapping while trying not to shoot the dashboard or herself—where was the lock button!

When there was a *thunck* of those latches engaging, she felt a split second of relief. It didn't last. As she glanced out the driver's side window, the sight of the grungy building she had come out of filled her with a terror so intense it was as if a dagger was at her throat—

Between one blink and the next, she saw Balthazar putting a sharp blade up to his neck. His mouth was moving, he was yelling, his eyes were vibrant with anger . . . as he confronted that brunette, the one from down under the bridge the night before, the one who had been the old man in the bookshop before she had been herself.

And then Balthazar was bleeding heavily. He was falling to his knees, and bleeding down the front of his chest . . .

Erika looked at the guns in her hands. Felt the weight of the clips in her pockets. Remembered the way a man she shouldn't know had looked into her eyes as if he saw all parts of her soul.

Please let me go.

At her request, he had set her free with her memories, but the liberation was only physical. Mentally, she was trapped by what she had seen tonight, what she knew now, what she could not believe. And meanwhile, he was still in the chaos with the brunette, with those shadows, with those other fighters.

"I gotta go," she said to the windshield. "I've *got* to leave."

When she went to punch her foot into the brake, she was too far back to reach the pedal. She put the guns on the passenger seat and reached between her legs to find the pull bar for the seat. Scooching up, she tried again with the footwork and was able to start the engine.

Gripping the wheel, she looked forward over the Honda's hood . . . but could not go forward.

Turned out she wasn't as free as she'd thought. Not as free as Balthazar had promised.

Stuck—

One look back over her shoulder at that garage, which was disguised as just another rundown, nothing-special in the rundown, nothing-special neighborhood, and a wave of terror mobilized her.

Freshly gripped with panic, she stomped on the clutch, threw the old-fashioned gearshift into drive, and punched the gas—

As she swung out of the parallel parking spot, she caught a glimpse of the door she'd come out of. It was just closing. Balthazar had kept his word and watched her to make sure she got to the car safely.

Just like he had protected her before.

Leaving him seemed wrong, but the fear inside her was so powerful, she had no choice but to give in to it and flee the garage, flee him and his world.

As she shot down Shore Avenue, she had no idea where she was going. Or where she was except for, well, down on the shores of the Hudson River, traveling deeper into downtown. Which was the wrong way. She should go home.

That was what she had to do. She needed an on-ramp to the Northway, so she could head in the opposite direction than she was going now.

She needed to go back to her apartment . . . which wasn't actually an apartment, but a townhouse that she had not properly claimed as her home because there had been no home for her, not since she was sixteen.

Her place. That was right. Even though she was no more safe there than anywhere else, she was like someone in the hospital with a dreaded disease, whose only thought was that if they could just get back to their own bed, everything would be okay.

It was a foolish belief.

But an undeniable one.

◆   ◆   ◆

Standing over the Book, Devina read the spell that had been created for her and her alone for the third time. Which was what the spell informed her she was supposed to do. Three times with the reading, like it was worried that she'd be so excited, she couldn't concentrate.

Which, of course, she couldn't. But she got the gist of things just fine.

Turning to her collection, she had to smile.

It was so fucking remarkable, and yet completely apt, how perfect the spell was for her. Then again, over the course of eons, she had come to understand the way the Book worked. Between those covers, in all those infinite parchment pages, was a portal that opened in a different way for whoever it chose to serve, as if each soul who approached it had a separate key for a specific unlocking. And as for the written words themselves? They were infinitely transmutable, all the languages ever spoken or read within its grasp, an endless horizon of power available, expressible in an incalculable number of ways.

Always on its terms, however.

"I shouldn't be surprised," she murmured as her eyes caressed her clothes, her accessories, her shoes. "But you really do know me, don't you."

Her spell was the absolute tailored fit for who and what she was, and what she had to do to follow its recipe struck her as magnificent. The second and third readings had been unnecessary. She had known immediately what she was going to use for what had been prescribed.

And for once in her immortal life, she was going to follow instructions.

As desperate as she was for the outcome, she was unhurried as well, the sense of anticipation like a delayed orgasm, something that was a delightful, burning frustration. So she was slow and easy on her wander, zeroing in on her destination in a roundabout way that took her on a review of all that was precious to her, all that she had chosen and curated with care . . . all that she loved.

Walking by the racks, she put her fingertips out and encountered all manner of fabrics, from blue jean and cotton to satin and silk. Sequins, too. She even paused to pull out a set of Stella McCartney velvet hip-huggers. They were from the Fall/Winter collection a couple of years before.

Annnnnnnnnd now Devina was finally in front of her Birkins, the Lucite stands making her think of that book room back at the Commodore, where the Book had been and been determined to stay. But as she thought about its obstinance, she wasn't going to get pissy with the thing. Hell, for what it was giving her tonight, she'd be kind and generous to it for the rest of eternity.

Maybe even get it a tufted pillow instead of that trash bin to rest on.

Her eyes lifted to the summit to her Mount Everest of Hermès. That pinnacle display position had remained barren, the stand empty as if a vital organ had been removed, but no transplant was available.

As she summoned back the little coffin, she thought it was so ironic. She'd been in this exact spot, laying to rest her most beloved, figuring it was gone forever and of no more use—and now she was back, finding a purpose for the thing even though it was ruined.

In fact, the ruination was key.

"Who'da thought," the demon murmured as she opened the casket's lid.

Reunions with the dead were always sloppy affairs, assuming they were your dead, and as her eyes teared up, she hated the weakness. The resurrection was stinky, too, the scent of the burned leather making her nose wrinkle. Yet she clasped the purse with gentle hands, as if it were pristine, as if it were alive.

Planting her stilettos, she held the Birkin out in front of her. The spell was so simple, so obvious, that she might have been able to guess it herself—or ignored it for being so uncomplicated. But she had seen firsthand the power of the Book's commands.

And she was choosing this totem wisely.

According to the words meant for her, she was to take a precious object, something that was personal to her, something that had great meaning, and behold it as if she were the lover she sought and the object was her. As she trained all of her adoration and her attention on what she picked, all her wants and desires, her hopes and dreams, her love was the summoning agent, and she would, in the words of the spell, get as she regarded.

The more she projected love, the more love she would receive.

So she decided that, among all her beautiful things, she needed to choose the one that was most like her . . . and that was the burned shell of the most expensive handbag in the world. Beautiful and ugly by turns, functional and broken at the same time, engendering sorrow for what had been lost and joy for what had once been, it was a contradiction that challenged standards and tested love and loyalty.

Yes, it was hard to admit that she was ugly, but goddamn it, she had value—and parts of her were fucking pristine.

Bottom line, she was done with males flaking off because they saw something in her they didn't like. Full disclosure was here in her palms, the stand-in for her exactly what she was—and yet she could, she *would*, love the ruined purse as she had never loved anything else.

And thereby be loved like she deserved.

See? She had made progress. That therapist had once told her she needed to be accurate in her "personal inventory." Fucking fine. She was being super accurate now—and she could fit a cell phone and a wallet into her fucking effigy to boot.

Oh, and who the hell would have thought that that idiot female who had burned the Birkin had done her a roundabout favor. She'd have kissed that Mae if she could have.

Taking a deep breath, Devina cradled the bag to her breasts. The smell of the singed hide was strong in her nose, but she told herself it was perfume, it was the very best fucking perfume she had ever smelled. Then she unfurled her arms and stared at the bag.

"You are beautiful," she said, "in every way. You are everything I've ever wanted or needed. I will never, ever leave you. Ever . . ."

As she repeated the words over and over again, a little audible she was adding to the spell, she traced the scales that were still in good condition with her fingertips, feeling the gentle undulations of the texture, noting the subtle changes in coloring. Moving up to the spangle, she turned the touret and pulled free the blackened diamond plates. Even through the soot, the fine gems gleamed, and she cleared some of the residue off with her thumb. It was a struggle to free the flap, one side of the twin handles especially compromised. But then the inside was exposed.

"Yes . . ."

The inside was positively immaculate. Fresh as the day it had left the workstation of its craftsman. Resplendent.

Just like her. Sure, there were some superficial issues, but under the bullshit, she was perfection.

Sheer fucking perfection.

Devina remembered everything about buying the Birkin, how she'd felt as it had come out of its herringboned bag in the private room at the store. How her whole body had tingled with orgasmic joy, how the rush at seeing it and knowing it was hers had made her head spin, how her heart had pounded and she'd let out a giddy sound. She was careful to recall how the S.A., who she'd worked with for a couple of years, had stood back and watched in total approval.

Devina had taken herself out to dinner at Astrance that night because she'd wanted others to see what she had—

It was as she pictured herself walking into the tiny, then three-star Michelin restaurant that it happened.

The bag became a window she could look through, the precise line of its form containing a bottom-out that revealed . . .

An unearthly landscape. Which was not gruesome or particularly unearthly. She just knew within her being that what she was shown was not upon the earth: White marble floors and white walls with candles on stanchions throwing yellow light that did not move in any drafts.

A sanctuary and yet . . . a place of evil.

Like a camera lens shifting focus, something was pulling out of the white landscape . . . a bed. A bedding platform—

She gasped.

There was a male lying on it. He was naked and sprawled on white sheets, his blond hair gleaming, his body absolutely magnificent.

Her thought was he was just like a Birkin, lying on its tufted, contoured tissue, inside the white interior of its orange box.

The camera-like angle changed again, swooping around to zero in on a patrician face with high cheekbones and sensual lips, his arched brows arrogant even in his repose, that pale hair so thick and gently curling. And then the visual altered once more, shifting to his shoulders, going across his well-developed pectorals, floating down over his abdominal muscles to his—

"Holy *fuck*."

Yeah, that'll do just fine. Yup. Juuuuuust fine.

And then she was back up at his face.

It was all perfect, what she would have asked for if she'd had to check off what she'd thought was attractive. And she had the strangest feeling that this was like a virtual shopping trip—and she got to choose whether or not to buy him.

Devina stared at that face. The masculine beauty of it was on a par with what she saw in the mirror any time she checked her makeup, and she liked that high standard. But could she look at this for an eternity?

"I want to see his eyes," she demanded.

There was a rustle, and at first she thought it was the sheets, as if a plane of sound had opened within the connection. But no, it was the Book.

She looked across at where the tome floated in the air. "His eyes. I need to see them."

The ruffle was a clear "nope," although she'd have been hard put to define exactly how she knew that.

"Please?" What the hell, she figured, the polite route had gotten her this far. "Pretty please with sprinkles on top?"

Wasn't that a human saying?

When the Book just repeated the same ruffle of pages, she cursed under her breath and stared back into the Birkin-window. The male was perfect—and he would adore her, just as she had adored the bag. What did she care about his eye color?

"Fine," she announced, "I'll take him."

Having made the pronouncement, she set the Birkin back on top of its stand and sent the little coffin away. For this service, she would keep the bag permanently in its place, ruined or not: Finally, after so much heartache, she was going to get what she had always wanted, what she deserved.

A male who loved all of her unconditionally.

And they were going to live happily ever after.

Or she was going to beat his ass.

CHAPTER TWENTY-FIVE

Talking.

Super-fast talking, right above Nate's face. Also . . . some beeping . . . electronic beeping that reminded him of the old-fashioned video game that one of the staff at the lab had taught him to play, the one where the black screen was cut in half by a straight vertical line and two slashes volleyed a dot back and forth. Except this beeping was rhythmic and even—

Oh, God. The smell. It was just like the lab, an antiseptic waft in the air, and layered on top of that the saltiness of tears and a copper tinge that suggested someone had been bleeding.

Yup, he was back in the lab. He was having one of his lab dreams where he . . .

No, wait. *He* had been bleeding. He was the one who'd had blood shed.

His brain was slow on the uptake, but then it all came back: Being at the club with Rahvyn and telling her they could go. Her pulling a yes-please. Them heading out the door.

Andthenacarhadscreechedaroundthecornerandsomeonehadshot—

Nate popped his eyes wide, jacked right up, and threw both hands out in front of himself.

Like that could stop the bullet from hitting him in the stomach.

Except . . . he instantly realized he wasn't out on the street, and there was no car, and he wasn't shot—

Arms were suddenly around him, hugging him, holding him close and comforting him. Two people. One on either side of him. Tears, now, lots of them.

His parents? What were they doing in the lab?

Wait, this wasn't the lab. This was a hospital room.

His awareness struggled to catch up with it all—until he breathed in deep and smelled his mom's shampoo, the Pantene kind that she liked and always used.

"Mom?" he said hoarsely, because he was still so confused.

His human mom, the one who had adopted him along with his new father, put her face in his. She looked—well, she looked awful, her cheeks blotchy and slick with tears, her breathing rough like she was about to pass out.

And then his father's visage was right next to his own, too. In contrast to his mom, his sire was paper white. Murhder had been crying, too, though. Was crying now—

"Am I okay?" Nate blurted. Then he looked down at his stomach.

Okay, so he had actually been shot: Beneath a staining of orange and some dried blood, there was a small round hole over to the left of his belly button. It didn't hurt. In fact, nothing in his body felt bad—other than a damp patch at the small of his back, which he instinctively took to be where he had bled out.

His mom put her hands on him, patting at his arms, his shoulders, now his cheeks, as if she couldn't believe she was touching him. And she was talking to him, his father, too. He could hear them pretty well, and he supposed their words made some sense. But he really couldn't track anything—

"Rahvyn!" he shouted abruptly. "Where is Rahvyn?"

What if she'd been hurt—

"She's . . ." His father couldn't seem to go on.

"Amazing," his mom finished.

For some reason, this brought out a fresh round of emotion from them both, their hands clasping his, their words rushing out faster.

"Where is she?" He glanced around and saw all kinds of clinical equipment, but nothing else. Not even a chair for someone to sit in. "Is she all right?"

Okay, yeah, sure, fine, they'd kind of answered that—he seriously doubted that anyone would use the word "amazing" if she'd had a bad injury. But he'd feel better if he could just see her.

"She saved you," Murhder choked out. "I don't know what she did . . . but you were . . . gone."

"Gone where," Nate asked. And then he licked his lips. "Can I have something to drink—"

He barely had the request out and his mom was lunging across to a stainless steel sink like if he didn't have a cup of water in the next two and a quarter seconds, his internal organs were going to fail on him and ooze out the back of his gunshot wound.

As she went to bring a white plastic cup to his mouth, she spilled some on the blue sheet that was draped over his lower body. His hands were steadier than hers, so he helped hold things, and after he finished what was in there, he stared down at his abdomen.

And half expected to see a little arc of H_2O coming out of his second belly button.

When he seemed to be water soluble—no, wait, that was the wrong word, and "water resistant" wasn't right, either—he held the cup out to his mom. He didn't even get to the first syllable of the request for a little more. She rushed back at the sink, and this time, her hands shook less during the handoff.

He drank three cupfuls, and the taste was magical. Cool and pure. No chemicals.

"Water retention," he announced. "Or maybe retentive, if that's a word."

His parents looked at him in a way that made him wonder if they'd be less surprised if his head spun around.

Patting his tummy, he said, "I'm holding water. No leaks."

His mom sniffled and wiped her nose with a paper towel. "That's right. No more leaking."

"We thought we'd lost you," Murhder whispered.

Meeting the stare of his father, Nate had a thought that he didn't really grasp or appreciate what had happened to him. It was as if his parents had been watching a different movie: His had been on cable, where there were commercial breaks that were kind of boring, and a storyline that had a little drama, but nothing that knocked your socks off or was all that revelatory or surprising.

Theirs had been a raw documentary on war atrocities that had won an Oscar for Worst Heartbreaking Thing on Film Ever.

"Are you okay?" he asked, looking back and forth between them.

"We are now," his father said. "Now . . . we're okay."

It was at this point that he could finally see them properly. His adoptive sire was still so menacing-looking in all that leather he always wore outside of the house, his red-and-black hair sticking straight up as if he'd been pulling his hands through the stuff and nearly ripping it out. His mom was smaller, but no less strong, even if her normally direct honey-colored eyes were watery and her I'm-a-scientist clothes were rumpled.

"I feel all right," he told them. Mostly because he was trying out the response in case, consciousness and lack of pain to the contrary, somehow he wasn't. "I really am."

On the floor, all around the table he was on, there was bloody gauze and discarded medical equipment. Clearly, someone had saved his life— and worked hard doing it.

"I really am okay."

Nate hugged both of them—and then wondered how long he had to wait before he could ask to speak with Rahvyn. He didn't want to be insensitive to his parents, but he had to see her. He just really wasn't going to believe anyone but himself when it came to making sure she was all right—and not just in a not-been-shot sort of way.

If he'd seen her almost die in front of him like that? Even if she wasn't that into him, it would be terrifying. Especially as he knew she'd had trauma in her previous life. Lots and lots of trauma.

"Thank God Rahvyn called for help," he said, by way of easing into a discussion that would involve leaving them and finding her. Or them breaking up this family moment by including her. "I mean, quick thinking, right? Did Dr. Manello operate on me out in the field? Because it happened outside of the club?"

As he glanced back and forth again, he saw their expressions change, subtle tension replacing the open love and powerful relief.

"What," he said. "Did someone else patch me up?"

When they still didn't respond, he cleared his throat. "Listen, I'm worried about Rahvyn, okay? She must be so freaked out. Can you just . . . can you bring her here?" He looked around. "Wherever 'here' is? I really need to make sure she's not in shock or something."

"You don't have to worry about her," Murhder murmured. "Ever."

Nate frowned, some instinct flaring, not that he could exactly decipher what it was trying to tell him.

"I need to see her," he demanded. "Right now."

◆   ◆   ◆

Back at the Brotherhood's garage downtown, all Balz was thinking was that he needed to see Erika again. Right now. He had to go after her, and jump in front of that silver Honda, and beg her to . . .

Beg her to do what, he thought. Forgive him for being exactly what he was? For living as he did, with people like him, in the middle of a metaphysical battlefield?

While a demon had thrown a pup tent up on his personal back lawn and moved in with her Coleman stove and her cast-iron frying pan?

The farther away Erika was from him, the safer she was going to be, and that was why he'd given her the implant of total terror if she tried to come back to this garage or look for him. And if for some reason she could override that, which she couldn't, it didn't matter if she attempted to find him. Even though he'd let her go home with her memory box full, and in spite of the fact that she had video footage on him from that trailer, he didn't legally exist in her world. He was a ghost who lived and breathed among humans like her, and there was no way she could drag him over onto her side of things.

At least he didn't feel like he had stolen something from her anymore.

He'd always been a thief with principles.

As he turned on his bare feet and looked across the expanse of the garage, the echoing, empty black space seemed like a good goddamn metaphor for his lonely life. Although of course, he still had one waaaay too loyal parasite he had to get rid of.

Across the bay, the two mismatched Archie Bunker armchairs he and Erika had been sitting in provided him with all kinds of misplaced heartache, proof that the mind-emotion conspiracy could elevate even a pair of uglies like that to a scene of tragic beauty.

The last place he would ever sit with her was like a Mount Rushmore *memento mori* to their never-could-be love.

Maybe he could steal the chairs.

Replace the chairs with something better, he amended.

Yeah, and where the fuck was he going to put them.

And yes, he'd used the term "love"—

Bang, bang, bang.

Not gunshots. Someone knocking on the side door with the heel of their fist.

Looking over his shoulder, he narrowed his eyes. He hadn't barricaded the thing, just set the copper lock back into place.

The demon Devina never knocked. The Brothers and others had the access code. No other vampires knew where this place was.

So this was a human who was way fucking lost.

Bang, bang, bang—

"Wrong address," he muttered.

Given that V had kitted out the place with all kinds of security, no doubt there were exterior cameras with feeds, but with no cell phone and no idea how to access them, he couldn't check and see exactly what had gotten misdirected and ended up on the garage's transom. And like he cared? No offense, but if some guy was willing to just stand out there in the cold—

Bang, bang.

"Mother*fucker.*"

Marching his half-naked ass over to the gun show, he took a forty millimeter off its mounting, and he was not surprised as he checked the clip to find things fully loaded. Naturally, it would be better to let the *Homo sapiens* on the doorstep do his or her own math on the no-answer door under those knuckles, but Balz had to get a game plan started on the shitty state of his life, and he sure as hell was not going to go through those depressing mental gymnastics to the tune of a bad amateur of "Boom Clap."

Yes, he'd watched *The Fault in Our Stars.* So sue him.

"Fucking rats without tails—"

As he did a simulcast of ripping open the garage's door and pointing the muzzle at the average face-height of a human male, he—

"Don't shoot!"

In some kind of reality-bending trick, it appeared as though Erika Saunders was the one who'd been imitating Charli XCX. And as she popped her hands high, she could barely take a breath.

Her body was shaking violently, her eyelids peeled back in fear, her face sheened with sweat from her absolute terror.

"P-p-p-please," she stammered. "L-l-let me in."

"How are you here," he said as he pulled her inside. "You're not supposed to be here."

She looked around the empty bay as if she expected to be pumped full of lead, stabbed, mauled, and decapitated all at once.

"Y-y-you're in d-danger." She swallowed compulsively and hugged herself. "C-c-can't leave you in d-d-danger."

For a split second, Balz could only stare at her in numb disbelief. Courtesy of that implant he'd put into her memory banks, she was literally overriding her own survival reflex . . . just to try to save him, a degenerate thief of a vampire.

He didn't even try to stop himself.

As he unlocked the manipulation in her mind, he pulled her against him and wrapped his arms around her, sharing the warmth of his body in hopes that he could calm the shivers that quaked her.

I love you, he thought at her. Even though it made no sense.

And as those three words permeated his awareness, he realized, with the way he'd hugged her, that the loaded forty millimeter in his dagger hand . . . was pointed right into his own face.

Fucking perfect.

CHAPTER TWENTY-SIX

Nothing happened.

Nothing *fucking* happened.

Devina was not the most patient of demons. Like, not at all. And as she stared through the portal of the ruined Birkin, and was able to see her dearly goddamn beloved, the male of her dreams lying there like a slab of very-high-grade meat on that bedding platform, she hated waiting. Especially as she waited some more. And . . . waited even longer.

Pinning a frozen smile on her face, she looked over at the Book with what she hoped was a patient expression. Even though she was thinking fondly of turning the old fart into a stake-mounted tiki torch.

"Sweetheart," she said in an aw-shucks tone. "Something is not working here."

The Book fluffled itself. Fluffled again.

Bringing the Birkin-window with her, she knew that she was leaving footprints that steamed in her wake, little curls of anger rising up from the floor. Nothing she could do about that, though. Maybe the Book wouldn't notice.

"Yes?" She forced her eyebrows to raise in pleasant inquiry. "You were about to say?"

More fluttering, while the Book remained open to the same place.

Devina tried not to roll her eyes. "But I already read it thrice, just as it said. Although of course, I would *love* to read the spell again."

Her eyes trained loosely on the words, the ink indelible on the page and yet capable of shimmering as the lettering registered: *Blah, blah, blah, regard as you would be regarded, blah, blah, the object of your desire, blah, eternity, blah, blah, blah, other lovers, world revolves around the perfect pair . . .*

She got to the end and wanted to scream, *Well, get on with it, then!* All she could think of, all she gave a shit about, was getting that male whatever-the-hell-he-was out of the viewing pane and into her lair. At which point, she was going to fuck him and then—

"What." Devina gritted her molars. "I mean, do you think I'm missing something here?"

In response, the text shined up at her so brightly she had to blink the glare away. And then, as her vision adjusted, she followed along a sequence of highlighted words. But if the Book thought this was helping her read, it was wrong. The exercise of focus was like hopscotching for her, her eyes jumping from one block of letters to the next, leaving what had just been looked at behind.

When she got to the end of the spell, she put her hands on her hips while the Birkin floated in thin air right next to her. "And?"

The text flared again.

"Look." She blew an exhale up at bangs that did not cover her forehead. "I did what you told me to do. I stared at what I love most in my collection, and I like what you showed me in return. He'll do just fine. So, I don't mean to be an impatient bitch"—no, she actually *was* an impatient bitch; there wasn't any oops-maybe-I'm-coming-across-wrong about it—"but let's move this along."

The pages in the Book stood straight out of the binding, like it had been called to attention. Then they flopped back into place as if the thing had given up trying to talk to her.

"Thank you." Then she leaned in and put her hand on her heart. "And I mean that sincerely—"

There was an explosion of light out of the windowpane of the Birkin, the beam a column of pure energy expressed as illumination. It was so powerful, Devina even stumbled back, the purse now a portal between dimensions, not anything made by Hermès.

And from out of the tear in the fabric of space and time, came her true love.

The male she had seen on the bed emerged from the opening, squeezing through the confines that remained limited to the Birkin's profile. The constraint distorted his features, pulling his skin taut on his face, his neck straining as his shoulders got caught in the aperture until one popped out, then the other came free—after which his torso emerged, followed by his hips, his sex.

His legs and feet were last, and he landed on the hard floor in a flop.

Its job done, the energy retracted, the beam sucking back into the ruined Birkin.

Which then dropped down as well.

The male was facedown and he was breathing hard. And for what seemed like an eternity, he just lay there with his ribs pumping in and out. But then he planted his palms and pushed his pecs up off the floor.

The muscles in his shoulders and down his arms bunched under his smooth, hairless skin, and the display of his spine undulating was erotic as fuck. And he had a great . . . ass, wow what an ass he had.

Devina licked her lips. And ducked a hand inside her blouse to feel her own breast.

She couldn't wait to have his mouth on her—

With a sudden shift, the male looked around his bicep, his beautiful face turned upward as if he sensed her. His lids were still closed, but his mouth was parted, and oh, fuck, yeah, the muscles of his chest were corded with power.

And then his eyes opened.

Devina gasped.

His irises and pupils were reversed, the center a sapphire blue, the outer rim jet black, and what radiated out of them was straight-up malevolence. The contrast of those two pits of hell with his sunshine-blond-and-white-streaked hair was electric. Especially as he looked down her body, that cunning, aggressive stare taking its sweet time— and stopping altogether when he saw her hand inside her silk shirt.

And that was when it happened. Down at his hips, his cock, which was a very nice size all flaccid and shit, began to thicken and get longer.

Devina bit her lower lip as a wellspring of pure, unadulterated lust blasted in between her legs.

"And who are you," he demanded in an aristocratic, arrogant tone that was a surprise.

When she didn't immediately answer, one of his brows arched up— as if he were used to being the best and the brightest in any situation, a special gift to the world, and everybody around him needed to justify their existence. On his frickin' timeline.

Entitlement, thy name is Adonis, she thought.

Holy shit . . . he was exactly like her.

Devina smiled so wide her cheeks hurt. "Your one true love, that's who I am."

CHAPTER TWENTY-SEVEN

As Rahvyn regained consciousness, she wasn't exactly sure where she was.

She was lying down on something very soft, and as she opened her eyes, she saw blank, windowless walls, and supply cabinets that had glass fronts, and silent machines with cords. There were a sink and cupboards in the corner. A rolling chair with a black seat. A smooth, speckled floor the color of porridge. A door that was closed.

She had no memory of how she had come to be here. No clue as to who had transported her thusly.

She recalled what she had done, however.

"Dearest Virgin Scribe, forgive me," she whispered.

Overhead, there was a soft whistle of heat coming through venting, and out in what she presumed was the corridor she'd been waiting in, someone walked by on soft-soled shoes.

"You're awake."

At the sound of her dear cousin's voice, she lifted her head. Sahvage was sitting on a chair pulled up to her opposite bedside, his elbows on his knees, his weight leaning forward as if he'd wanted to jump into her unconsciousness and pull her out of it.

His face was drawn in tight lines.

"He's okay," he said. "Nate."

"I know." Her voice was rough and she cleared her throat. "May I have something to—"

Her cousin jumped up, as if he'd been desperate to help, and he immediately produced a white cup like he'd been waiting to perform the rehydration function. He had to help her get the straw in between her lips, and he held everything in place. After a couple of sips, she settled back against the pillows.

Sahvage put the water aside on a tray that was as tall as the bed was high. Then he sat down again and stared at her.

"Yes," she whispered, "that is what I did to you."

"There was a lot of wind in that room. We tried to get in, but the door was barricaded."

"It takes a lot of energy to get to the junction of creation."

Sahvage stared down at his hands. "How did you know you could do that? I mean, I was aware that you had . . . power. But I had no idea . . ."

As he trailed off, she knew he was not solely considering her rejuvenation of him. He was thinking about what she had done at that castle. To the guards who had sought to keep her therein, and especially to the aristocrat who had so violently abused her body.

She had killed a dozen or more males that night.

And brutalized the one who had taken her virginity with force.

"Where did you go after you left that castle?" he asked absently, as if it was another inquiry he had pondered many times by himself over the centuries that had separated them.

"I was in time," she murmured. "I told you."

"I don't even know what that means. I don't understand any of this."

Rahvyn sat up upon the bed. As she looked down at herself, she found that a blanket had been pulled over her. She was still in the same clothes—the black sweater, the jeans—and she brushed at the dried blood.

Even after she washed them, she was never going to put on this outfit again.

"I am sorry," she said. Because it was easier than telling him she had to leave.

"I used to think this . . . immortality thing you gave me . . . was a curse." He shook his head and spoke slowly. "But if you hadn't given me this . . . new life, whatever it is, I wouldn't have my Mae. I couldn't have protected my Mae."

Rahvyn wasn't sure what to say to that.

"Anyway, thank you," he said roughly. "I can't . . . thank you enough."

He took her hand, holding it gently in between his much larger palms. And then he lowered his forehead down and placed it on the clasp that joined them.

Reaching over, she stroked her cousin's hair. Again, she found that she had nothing to say. Whether it was because of the amount of effort she had had to apply unto the saving of Nate or because—

The knocking was quiet. As if whoever were on the far side of the door was concerned about interrupting something. And then she caught a scent she recognized.

"Nate?" she said.

The door into the room swung wide, and there he was, up on his feet, his color bright and healthy, his balance buttressed on a rolling stand on which was suspended a deflating transparent bag full of some kind of liquid. Behind him, both his parents were shaken, but no longer crying, the twin sentries of his well-being having clearly had one hell of a night.

As she met Nate's eyes, her own filled with tears, and he rushed forward—even as his parents tried to keep him from bolting. But he didn't need any aid to walk. He didn't need whatever was being transfused into his arm vein. He was not going to require help with his physicality in any fashion, ever again.

Rahvyn sat all the way up at the same time he came upon her, and then they were embraced, his arms around her shoulders, her own tucked around his waist. As she ducked her head into his neck, she was dimly aware that the others in the room were speaking softly . . . and then retreating out into the hallway.

After a long moment, Nate eased back and sat on the side of the bed more properly. "So were you shot, too? Are you okay?"

"Yes."

He paled. "Yes, you were shot or—"

"No, I mean, I was not injured, therefore I am okay."

"Thank God."

There was a silence, their eyes clocking the details of survival in the other. And then he looked down, and she braced herself for what he was going to ask. What he had every right to know. What she could not explain.

Dearest Virgin Scribe, who was she to wield this power.

"What happened, Rahvyn. No one really wants to tell me."

"I am so sorry." When he went to respond, she stopped him from speaking. "I wish I could have asked you whether you wanted to come back."

"Of course I want to be alive—"

"Yes, but there is a price, and you deserved to choose. I just did not know what else to do—"

He put his hand out. "We're not talking about CPR, are we."

"What is that?"

"Cardiopulmonary resus—" He shook his head. "Never mind."

There was a pause because she did not know where to begin. And that was when his expression changed. She had seen as such many times before, back in the Old Country, back even when she had been a young and not understood herself any more than anybody else did: Wariness and a little awe.

Meanwhile, she had lost her voice. This was perhaps good. There was a truth she refused to share with anyone, even herself, and she worried over what would come out of her mouth.

"The night that the meteor landed behind Luchas House," he said slowly. "And I saw you there, by the impact site . . ."

She watched his mind work through the subtle shifts in his facial muscles, his lips tightening, his brows dropping and raising, his jaw working as if he were grinding his back teeth. Indeed, he was stitching together things he had overlooked, pulling the truth out of a series of previously unconnected details. And that was life, was it not. One went about, not aware that the superficial details were but a screen for a revelation yet to materialize.

"What exactly did you do to me?" he demanded.

◆   ◆   ◆

Sitting on Rahvyn's hospital bed, his legs dangling off the side, one hand braced on the mattress, Nate was aware of feeling different in his own skin. It was hard to put a bead on exactly what was so off. The closest he could come to defining the sensation was what he'd experienced in the nights immediately after his transition.

He was supercharged. Vibrating with energy. Not just alive, but . . . awakened.

And his brain was crackling with thoughts and memories—although that could be a result of his confusion over this whole thing with her. He kept thinking back to going out into the field behind the house with Shuli to investigate that celestial show and impact. Rahvyn—or Elyn, as he'd known her at first—had been back there in the forest, standing apart from the others who had likewise come to check things out.

Then he could remember when he'd spoken to her the following evening, and fireflies had circled her, the little sparks of light casting a beautiful illumination on her delicate face.

At the time, he hadn't questioned where the insects had come from.

But he'd never seen them before out there in the cold and hadn't seen them since.

If he was honest . . . he wasn't sure what the pinpoints of lights had actually been.

And then he recalled that moment in her bedroom when she'd looked into his eyes and he'd felt a strange draining feeling, as if she had been reading his mind. The horror that had come into her face had sure as hell made it seem like she knew all the details of his past, everything from his time in that lab, and all the pain and the fear he'd suffered as he'd been experimented on by those humans, to the death of his *mahmen* there and his impossible rescue.

"I was at the door unto the Fade," he heard himself say. "And I didn't just stand in front of it, I opened it and I stepped through. I was on the other side . . ."

Hazy memories, of a white landscape and then something so beautiful he didn't have the words to describe it, flooded his mind, blinding him to the hospital room, even to her. But he came back from the vision of eternal glory.

Just as he had come back from what had been his death.

"I was dead." He focused on her. "And you did something to me, didn't you."

The female he had been thinking about nonstop—ever since he'd seen her at the meteor strike—whose presence he'd sought out and tried to be cool about at Luchas House, whose face he had fantasized being close to his own as they'd shared a first kiss . . . was suddenly a stranger.

"Who are you."

As she lowered her head, her white hair fell forward, her features obscured by the waves. When she finally spoke, it was with sadness.

"You shall ne'er worry for death's cold hand coming to land upon your shoulder. You are free of the mortal burden of the grave. You are . . . immortal, Nate."

The impact of the words was delayed, his brain reexamining the syllables like they were an archaeology site, sure that on the first pass he'd misinterpreted a few. Most.

Try all.

"I'm not hearing you right," he said numbly.

"You are released from death's leash, ne'er shall it come to claim you."

"How . . ." He rubbed his face. "I don't understand."

"I could not let you die." The dewy, salty scent of tears wafted up and she brushed her eyes with hands that trembled. "Your parents were weeping over your body, the Brothers were outside your door . . . and it was my fault. I was the reason you were hit—"

Nate recoiled. "How was it your fault?"

"I halted by the human and thus so did you. Or mayhap I set it all in motion even before that." She sniffled. "If I had been able to withstand more of the chaotic interior of the club Dandelion, we would not have departed then. You would not have been shot. You would not . . . have died."

"None of that makes it your fault."

Rahvyn tucked her hair behind her ears and her eyes were luminous as they looked at him. "Nate, I am sorry. I have given you no gift. It is a complication with heartbreaking implications."

Like someone who was lost in an unfamiliar territory, one that might or might not be threatening, his senses came alive and he glanced around the room on reflex. Oh, they'd had this conversation in front of an audience: His parents and Sahvage were in the room with them. And unsurprisingly, the adults all looked grave and serious. Then again, this was pretty unparalleled.

If what she said was true, no matter how unbelievable it sounded, then he had been reborn in a way that went against the natural order of things.

And she was something altogether different than just a civilian female of unknown origins who was related to a member of the Black Dagger Brotherhood.

She was powerful in a way that dwarfed even the Great Blind King.

She was powerful like the Scribe Virgin.

"And now I'm here," he murmured absently.

"I could not let you go." Her voice cracked. "I could not . . . bear to lose you, Nate."

The white noise in his head instantly calmed down, the fire of his spinning, vaguely panicking thoughts doused.

Of all the things she'd said to him, the simple words struck the biggest chord.

Which, considering a female he was in love with had told him she'd turned him into an immortal, was really saying something about the way males work.

The idea Rahvyn might feel something in return for him was . . . like being immortal. Nothing could touch him.

"But I don't understand who you are," he said softly.

"I am what I am."

"Popeye."

"Pardon me, I know not pop-eyed?"

"It was a cartoon character. When I was in the lab, sometimes they let me have a TV and I watched both the animated show and the movie. 'I yam what I yam.'"

"Oh."

As she fell into another silence, there was such a somberness to her, her eyes downcast, her shoulders tucked into herself. He had a thought that he was going to remember this hospital room, with its hospital bed and its single padded chair and its medical equipment so discreetly tucked away, for the rest of his . . .

Life.

"I'm going to live forever?" he asked as uneasiness threaded through his chest again.

"You are not going to have death."

"So I can't die?" He imagined the earth hit by an even bigger meteor and him floating out in space, spinning slowly in the cosmic void, for infinity and beyond. Permanently Buzz Lightyear.

"You do not die."

"How did you do it?"

"I took you to the plane of creation. And now you are both different and the same. There is no going back and there was no way to ask you what you wanted. I believe you will find there are benefits and tragedies to this state. Then again, perhaps that is just like a normal life, the good and the bad intertwined. The difference for you being, now, that there shall be no end."

He stared at her, rememorizing her features, trying to catalog all the changes he now saw in what had been so familiar to him. Then he thought of his parents, and the way they had looked as he had come to, the confusion, the tears . . . the grief that had shattered their souls.

"You did the right thing," he said abruptly. "I don't . . . understand a lot of this, but I wouldn't trade being here for anything."

There was no relief in her as he spoke. Just that grim cast to her eyes.

"I hope you continue to feel that way," she whispered. "I truly do."

CHAPTER TWENTY-EIGHT

"Y ou sure you're okay with this?"

As Balz put the question out there, he realized he was being a little duplicitous. His eyes were staring out the front windshield of the old silver Honda, locked on the front door of a nice little townhouse—and unless Erika had pulled them up at the garage door of someone else's pad, this was where she lived.

In his mind, he was already inside, taking a shower in one of her bathrooms.

After which, he was getting in between the cool sheets of her bed and pulling her into his naked-ass body—

No, I'm not doing that.

She turned and looked across the front seats. "I'm sorry? What?"

Shit, he'd spoken that out loud. "Oh, nothing." He glanced at her. "I just want to make sure this is really what you want to do."

"You have nowhere to stay, right?" She shrugged. "And the more I thought about those shadows . . . I'm not sure I can defend myself against them without you. Besides, I was safe with you before. You've never been aggressive toward me, and I also don't have to worry about your buddies coming after me."

"Like I said, they won't harm you."

"Because I'm your female, right?" She narrowed her eyes. "I heard one of them say that."

"It's a term of art." Whatever the fuck that meant—and who the hell had been throwing around the *f* word? "And you're right. If I'm with you . . . those shadows have a big goddamn problem."

His female, huh. He wasn't sure he could argue with that, but there had been plenty of revelations already for one night—ah, crap. Had he really bonded with her? Then again, the rule of thumb with that for male vampires was, if you were even entertaining the question, the answer was probably *yes*.

Great. Another layer to this shit cake—

"Hold on, is that . . ." She frowned and leaned into her window. "Is that my bag?"

Balz looked across the dashboard again. Sure enough, right on the front stoop, just outside of the light thrown by the lantern over the mailbox, was the purse he had seen her carrying.

"How did it get here?" she asked as she popped her door open.

Well, at least he knew the answer to that one, and it wasn't a bad surprise.

Thank you, V, he thought as he jumped out himself.

Balz stayed tight on her heels as she hit a little walkway with a long stride, and about halfway to her front door, he realized how ridiculous he looked: He was still nakie with a sheet wrapped around his hey-nannies, and he had a gun down at one thigh and a duffle bag full of click-click-bang-bang hanging off his other shoulder.

Too bad this wasn't Halloween for the humans. He could have called himself a flasher-assassin and maybe gotten away with it.

Plus, hey, guy shows up on your trick-or-treat doorstep with a forty caliber in his palm, you were likely to dump your bowl of candy wherever he told you to put the stuff. So he'd clean up and Rhage would be psyched.

As for the duffle's contents, Erika knew what was in his little carry-on. She had watched as he had taken the autoloaders and the snub-nosed shotgun from the safe back at the garage—and he'd been sure to pack up plenty of ammunition, too. The way she hadn't reacted to that amount of metal had made him sad: She had to have seen a lot to be that calm. Then again, she dealt with death every day in her job, didn't she.

Three stone steps up, and she was picking up the purse. He braced himself for her to rifle through it out here in the open. She didn't. She linked her arm into the straps, and lickety-split, unlocked the dead bolt and cranked the knob. They were inside in the blink of an eye and she locked up just as quick.

Although honestly, how safe were they anywhere? From the shadows, that was. From Devina, as well.

While Erika put the bag down on the coffee table and started to go through it, he glanced around. The layout was as he expected, this living area opening to a kitchen in the back that had an alcove you could eat in. A staircase ran up the solid common wall behind him, and he could see two open doorways on the second floor.

The furnishings were not fancy, but looked really comfortable, even though nothing particularly matched. It was as if Erika had collected the couch and chairs and the side tables piece by piece, to plug holes in function, rather than to coordinate colors.

Oddly, there were no pictures or photographs anywhere, not on the walls, not on the mantelpiece over the electric fireplace, not on the built-in shelves on either side of that hearth.

If you looked past the lack of harmony in the decor, it was like the showcase model of the development, an anonymous, clean stage set occupied by no one but a salesperson.

He tilted into the bow front window behind the couch and parted the closed drapes. Outside, there were ten other buildings along the dead-ended road, each one bifurcated, the scale of things modest, the couple of cars parked outside of the garages sedans or trucks that were less than five years old. If he had to guess, the structures had been built in the eighties, so that things were old, but kept up well.

"It's all here." She looked over her shoulder at him. "My gun, my cell phone, even my badge. But how did it get back here—"

He let the curtains fall back into place. "My friends took care of things."

"What do you mean, 'took care of things.'"

"You know, made sure there was nothing left behind before they called in the scene at the bookshop."

"Called in to who? Nine-one-one?"

When he nodded, she shook her head, but not like she was disagreeing with him. More like she felt as though her thoughts were fuzzy or she'd missed something.

"Why would they do that?" she mumbled.

"Why wouldn't they? It's human business."

"Human . . . business." Closing her eyes, she said to herself, "I need a beer."

Balz followed her into the kitchen that took up the rear of the townhouse. The color scheme was cream and yellow, the wallpaper all sunflowers with green leaves, the linoleum a speckled saffron color, everything faded but in good condition. Likewise, the appliances were older but clean, and the countertops were Formica, not the granite you saw so much of in newer places.

Dated. All of it was dated, probably even the original stuff. But it was also a place where he instantly relaxed, although that probably had to do with Erika rather than anything in the environment itself.

On that note, he went over to the little circular table in the alcove and sat on a chair that he was mostly sure would hold his weight. A wicker light fixture on a chain hung down low, and centered under it was a napkin holder that was empty.

"I don't keep a lot of food around," she announced as she headed for the fridge. "Fortunately, I have four bottles of Miller Lite."

She got two of them out and came over to him. After she handed him his, she twisted the top off the other one and took a long sip. Then another. As she sat down, he just wanted to stare at her, but considering he'd looked at her for most of the trip over here in that old Honda, it was probably better to play it cool.

Cool-er.

Cool . . . ish.

"So you're telling me," she said after she took another draw off the glass bottle, "that if I call dispatch, they're going to report that a body at that address has been phoned in already."

"Yup."

"Do you people do that a lot around here?"

He shrugged and opened his beer. "It's not the first time."

"I'm just going to text my partner and ask. No offense."

"None taken," he murmured as she got out her phone.

The instant she looked at the screen, her brows went together. Then she went into what seemed like her texts or her emails, and started reading something.

Balz looked out to the living room. As he measured the couch, he totally pictured himself sleeping on it, his head on one end propped up by that throw cushion, feet dangling off the far—

Shit. Windows.

Or did he really think that he'd magically outgrown a vampire's sensitivity to sunlight in the last, oh, twelve hours?

"I may not be able to stay here during the day," he said.

She glanced up. "You're right. A call came in from nine-one-one. My partner's on the case. Man, what a night."

"I'm glad. The old man's family has a right to be notified."

"Yes, they do." Erika stared at the little glowing screen. "And I should notify my department that I was there."

In the pause that followed, he knew she was thinking to herself: *But what the hell can I tell them that won't make me sound crazy.*

"We're going to figure this out," he volunteered.

Her eyes lifted to his. "If I knew what the 'this' was, I might feel more optimistic."

Actually, you'd probably feel worse, he thought.

"And honestly . . ." She released a long sigh. Took another sip from her beer. "I'm really glad you're here."

Balz blinked. And then felt himself go red in the face. Which was totally a flush from the alcohol. 'Cuz Miller Lite packed one helluva punch.

"You are?"

"Yes." She shrugged. "I really am."

◆   ◆   ◆

Erika had to look away from Balthazar. Like she was frickin' twelve and had just admitted to having a crush on Billy Wittenhauer in seventh grade.

Which was something that had actually happened, so the metaphor, simile, whatever, truly did apply.

Or maybe it was just a comparison, she conceded. Instead of anything grammar-glamorous.

"I'm glad I'm here, too," he said.

There was a period of silence, and she was aware that there was a big question she wanted to ask him, maybe "the" big question. She wasn't sure she could handle the answer, though. So she asked a less dire one on the dip-your-toes-in-cold-water theory.

"That brunette woman . . ." She took another swig from her beer. "What is she? Really."

Balthazar's brows went together over his eyes. "You sure you want to do this right now?"

"As opposed to when, next Christmas?"

He tipped his beer to her. Then he apparently gave up on the couching-terms thing. Like, entirely: "She's a demon."

Erika sat back. And yet wondered why she was even slightly surprised.

Well . . . because it wasn't every day you woke up and realized you were in a *Conjuring* sequel. And she really should have a response. A shocked face, at least. Maybe a curse or two breathed softly.

Instead, she felt absolutely nothing.

"A demon." More beer. She needed a loooooot more beer. "As in, pea soup, spinning heads, Linda-Blair-type demon?"

Like there was another kind?

"That's what you humans call them."

Annnnnnnnd that was a lead-in to the real question.

So she kept going with what they were on: "She's what you are fighting."

"Not by choice, but yes." He put his hand on his bare pecs. "She's in me, Erika. Do you understand what I'm saying."

As the little hairs on the back of her neck stood up, she thought about her dream of the shadow. Then she focused on him properly. Funny, how this man wasn't a stranger anymore. Then again, they had so much in frickin' common after tonight that things had changed. He was more like a friend now.

No, that wasn't the right word, was it. "Friend" was not how she thought of him.

Not when she looked at his lips.

But whatever, the not-a-stranger thing was why she had asked him to come to her "apartment" that wasn't really an apartment. If he'd been a straight suspect, a thief, a possible killer, she'd have taken that Honda right over to HQ and called for backup to go raid the garage and bring him in.

None of this was normal, however. Not one goddamn thing, not what he was able to do with her brain, not that brunette, certainly not the shadows. So yeah, Balthazar was a thief, but what would turning him in do for her or anybody else? He'd just manipulate the minds and memories of anyone who showed up with handcuffs. Work of a moment.

So instead of losing him into the night, and understanding nothing about what had happened to them, she'd rolled her own dice and taken a chance that he wouldn't hurt her. Which was no chance at all, really. He'd only ever tried to keep her safe—

Wow, she thought abruptly. He was still half naked.

And what a view at her kitchen table.

Funny what you noticed . . . and didn't, depending on how stressed you were.

She cleared her throat. And stammered anyway. "So you're . . . she's possessed you?"

He looked down at her empty napkin holder. When he nodded, that chill on her nape got worse.

"How can you get her out?"

"I need that Book," he replied. "The one that was at the triplex. That's why I was there the night I met you. And then tonight, I went to the bookshop because I Googled rare booksellers in Caldwell and it was the first that came up. I thought maybe I could get a lead or some background on the thing."

"I went there for the same reason." She tapped the side of the bottle with her fingernail—and then promptly irritated herself with the sound. "I have an idea about how we might be able to get some information on it. But it's going to have to wait until morning."

"What's your plan—"

"What are you."

There, she was out with it. The big question. The one that she was most worried about the answer to.

And when he didn't immediately respond, she shrugged. "You might as well tell me. You said that the less I know, the more free I am, but that's not true when you're sitting in my kitchen in a sheet."

After a moment, he nodded. "I agree."

But then he didn't say anything else.

As the silence stretched out, she got up from her chair. Maybe it was the half of a Miller Lite. Maybe it was just how much she had seen in the course of the night.

Maybe it was because of all the places life had taken her—most of them being really fucking god-awful—the idea that something other-worldly was in her house seemed more *meh* than emergency.

When she went around her table and stood in front of him, he looked at her, the heavy cords of muscle that ran up the sides of his neck flexing as he tilted his head back.

Don't touch him, she told herself. *You touch him right now and there's no going back.*

"There isn't one anyway."

"What?" he murmured.

"It doesn't matter."

She got so close that his knees had to part to accommodate her. And then she brushed at his hair, thinking of how she'd stroked it when he'd been lying there on the floor of that storeroom, in a pool of his own blood.

"Show me," she demanded. "If you can't tell me, show me."

There was a heavy pause that seemed to have the same density as the aftermath of a bomb blast. Instead, it just turned out to be the pre-amble for what really knocked her over.

His upper lip rolled back off his front teeth.

And as she noticed that he had really, really long canines . . .

. . . they dropped down from the roof of his mouth, right in front of her very eyes.

Erika started to breathe hard, and even that didn't do anything to relieve the crushing suffocation in her chest.

"Vampire," she whispered.

"You have nothing to fear from me. You need to know that—"

"Oh . . . God."

With an expression of exhaustion, he put up his hand as if trying to stop the conclusions running through her mind. "Hold on, you humans have it all wrong. There's no biting and turning people, and a stake through the heart is no different than a dagger. And to hell with the de-filer of virgins bullshit—and no, garlic and crosses don't do anything." He shook his head. "We are a separate species from you and we just want to live our lives in peace, something that's really hard to do when there are so many of you around—and when we have other things un-related to humans that want to kill us. It's a battle, all the time. Good thing we're really good at fighting."

On that note, he linked his arms over his naked chest and sat back in the chair. Going by the jut of his jaw, she had a feeling he was of-fended by a lot of her kind.

Join the club, she thought to herself. Sometimes she wasn't all that impressed with humans, either.

"Why are you smiling?" he said.

She reached up and touched her mouth, unaware that there was a wry lift to her lips. "Um . . . I guess I'm just surprised I'm not scared. And shocked that I don't feel as though we're all that different."

"You shouldn't be frightened of me."

"I'm not. Instead, I find you . . ."

As she let the words drift, she focused on his mouth. And wondered what it would feel like to kiss him. Just bend down and press her lips to his.

But are you ready for what would happen next, she asked herself.

"You can finish that thought," he said in a husky way.

"Hmm?"

"Finish your thought about what you think of what I am. Because you're totally free to share any opinion when you're looking at me like that."

"How am I looking at you." Her voice lowered, and not because there was anybody around to hear her. "Tell me."

"Like you want to kiss me."

Erika opened her mouth. Closed it.

He put both his hands up. "And honestly, even if you're just curious, that's okay with me."

Erika frowned. "As if I'd use you as some kind of experiment?"

"It's all right." His lids lowered. "Because if you try me, only to see if I'm the same as a man, it gives me a chance to prove to you I'm better than anything you've ever had."

"You're pretty confident."

"Not at all. Facts."

As her body heated up, she could have sworn he purred in the back of his throat—and she became very aware, as she stood so close to him, that this . . . electric moment . . . was where things had been heading all along. Probably from the first time she set eyes on him.

"Do you believe in fate," she murmured.

"Kiss me right now and I'd say yes, absolutely, I do."

Erika waited for some kind of self-protective instinct to steer her into such neutral conversational territory as: *So how long have you been possessed by a demon? How many times have you fought a shadow? Are all of your buddies, including the one with the tats on the temple and the goatee, vampires as well?*

Any plans for the summer?

Yankees vs. Mets?

But nope. Her warning system stayed silent.

So she did the only thing she could think of.

She leaned down and took his face into her hands. As he tilted his head even farther back, the way he acquiesced to her touch made her feel even more in control. And wow, that cologne of his . . . it was as if he'd just put more on.

Right before her lips brushed his, he sighed. Like he had been waiting for this for as long as she had.

"Me, too," she whispered.

And then there was the first contact, her mouth pressing into his, the sizzle of pure lust going all the way through her body as that purring sound rose from him once again.

Turning her head to the side, she gently explored what he so willingly offered. And what do you know, he was right.

He was one hell of a kisser.

When she finally eased back, his eyes glittered up at her. "So what do you think?"

"I think . . ." She brushed his hair away from his forehead. "It's a good start."

"My turn?"

She had to smile a little. "Like I was doing that wrong?"

Balthazar sat forward, his hands going to her hips. "Oh, no. You're perfect."

"But you can do better?" She raised an eyebrow. "Fine. Show me what you got, vampire—"

He was up and out of that chair in the blink of an eye. And the next thing she knew, she was in his arms and being bent backward—so that the only thing keeping her off the floor was his strong arms. As she gasped and grabbed on to his bare shoulders, she was aware of the power in his body—and how much smooth skin and hard muscle there was on him. Staring up into his heated eyes, she'd never been so turned on in her life. And it wasn't about some Dracula myth, either. It was about *him*. This man—male, whatever. It was about . . . Balthazar.

"Now I'm going to show you the way a vampire kisses a female he wants."

The mouth that claimed hers was not gentle. It was demanding and a little rough, and when his tongue entered her, she gave up any pretense of trying to hold herself up. She gave in fully to the sexual wave, letting herself go.

And he was right.

He was the best she'd ever had. Her whole body came alive, her breasts tingling, her sex aching, her legs going straight to jelly. God . . . she just wanted more. No, she *needed* more.

When he finally lifted his head, they were both breathing hard—and he seemed surprised. Like he'd thought it would be good, but he hadn't thought it would be *that* good.

"Your scent is beautiful," he growled.

"I'm not wearing perfume."

"You are." His eyes went down her body. "The very best kind. The kind that's going to make it impossible for me to sleep during the day. It's your arousal. I can scent how much you want what I can give you."

Erika was panting—and didn't bother to hide it. Especially as his words sunk in. Wait, what? He wasn't going further with this?

"Or maybe . . ." She slid one of her hands up to the nape of his neck. "Maybe we can do something more about this?"

The smile on his face was dark. Erotic. As hungry as she felt.

"I thought you'd never ask," he purred.

And then he kissed her again.

CHAPTER TWENTY-NINE

Back at Devina's lair, the demon watched as her long-awaited happily ever after rose from the floor like he was a mountain range birthed by the earth itself, growing more powerful with each inch of height he unfurled for her very approving eyes. And when he was at his full vertical, his magnificence was too much for her, and she covered her face with her hands.

Beneath her palms, she was smiling as her eyes flooded with tears.

The sense of a long journey coming to an end, a home reached, a family finally established, struck her with such force, she swayed on her stilettos.

And that was when he touched her for the first time. It was just a fingertip, pressing into her sternum, between the swells of her hypersensitive breasts.

As Devina's breath caught, that pinpoint of contact moved to the side slowly, and it took the fragile silk of her blouse for a little ride . . . until her taut nipple felt a rasp and then the cooler air.

"I'm going to fuck you," the male said in a low voice.

Yes, you are, she thought as she lowered her hands—

Oh, God. He was aroused, fully aroused, his cock jutting out from his hips, clearly capable of doing the job she wanted it to, deep inside her core—

Her one true love clapped a hold on the base of her throat, right at her collarbones, and the smile he gave her was the kind that she imagined a serial killer wore when he was just about to go to work.

Between her legs, her clit throbbed.

Those strange, all-wrong eyes bored into her as he started to push her back, and she had no choice but to walk with him if she wanted to keep on her feet.

It was a dance between their bodies, a to-and-fro of balance and steps, all of it directed by him—and when the wall came up behind her and there was no farther she could go, he stopped, too. His upper lip curled back, and that was when she saw the fangs. Clearly, they'd been there all along, but she'd had too much eye candy to gorge on to notice them.

Devina moaned. She had a thing for vampires. She really did.

"You like these," he murmured as he bared his canines at her.

She liked all of him. "Yes."

"I plan on using them on you." He pressed into the base of her throat with his grip. "For a while."

Her breath came hard, *pump pump.* "You think you're going to kill me, don't you."

"You look surprised. But you didn't summon a Tinder date."

Devina shook her head. "You can't kill me."

"Who's going to stop me." He glanced around at the clothes, the shoes, the bags. "Nobody's going to save you. Especially after I put a gag in your mouth so no one will hear you scream."

"I don't need saving, lover."

With that, she cast him off her with a burst of energy, sending him flying back through the air, all the way across to the very far side of her lair. As she slammed him into the solid concrete, the expression on his face was so fucking priceless, she wished she had a cell phone and could take a picture.

Now Devina was the one coming forward, and she deliberately left her blouse wide open, her exposed, tight-nippled breast bobbing with her stride. As his eyes locked on what she wanted him to see, she undid another couple of buttons and unveiled the other one.

She hoped he enjoyed the view. She was certainly approving of the way that enormous cock stood out at her, thick as her forearm, the potent sac beneath promising her all kinds of ejaculations—

Babies.

She faltered as the thought ricocheted through her.

A male like this . . . could get her pregnant, couldn't he. If she wanted him to.

When she halted a good ten feet away from him, the male she was easily holding in place frowned. Then he strained, pulling against her hold. Which of course would get him nowhere. She was more powerful than that—

As his right arm broke free, he glared at his left like he was pissed it wasn't following directions—and at the show of strength, Devina dropped the baby bullshit and narrowed her eyes. How was he that strong?

"What's your name," she blurted.

Those black-and-blue eyes narrowed on her. And when he didn't answer her but just continued to pull against his confinement, she realized . . . he was not going to ask her to let him go. He was also not going to tell her anything simply because she wanted the information. He was not going to follow any order or even a request.

Goddamn . . . she wanted him.

Devina's Louboutins started moving again, and she stopped when she was right in front of him, watching as he continued to strain and jerk against that stuck left arm of his, his erection thrusting forward, retreating, swinging to the left, to the right. The struggle, coupled with his arousal's slapping movement, was the most erotic thing she'd ever seen, his growing anger at her making him glow with nasty intent.

Her hand went to one of her exposed breasts and she played with her nipple, tweaking the flesh between her fingers. Pulling it out and letting it snap back into place. Rubbing it.

Those fangs made another spectacular appearance and he hissed—like in his mind, he was biting the tip off and swallowing it.

"What's your name . . ." Even though she knew he wasn't going to answer. "Tell me."

There was a delicious thrill to his denying her, and later, she would recognize that this was when it all started. The addiction to him.

Turned out, her version of true love had a compulsive element to it. Made sense. Happiness had always bored her. A cycle of aching need, followed by ecstatic acquisition or fulfillment, culminating with a glow of satisfaction? That was her fucking jam.

Devina smiled. "I'm not letting you go, unless you tell me your name—"

His left arm popped loose, and she lifted an eyebrow. Then he began to bend forward, his chest and abs flexing, his teeth with those fangs gritting, sweat breaking out across his skin—until his torso somehow peeled free of that wall. He should not have been able to do any of this—and that was when her second realization hit.

"You're like me." And she wasn't talking about character traits. "You're something else, aren't you."

No ordinary vampire could do any of this shit.

And of course, her true love didn't say a damn thing. He just continued to pull, pull, pull against the hold on him. He trembled, his shoulders flexing, the veins that ran down his arms popping, his abdominals standing out in stark relief—and he was still aroused, whether it was from fury at her or sexual attraction, she wasn't sure, didn't care. She'd take the former, because it was fun, and the spell should have ensured the latter.

So maybe it was both.

She glanced at the Book. It was still open to her page, the wording dark on the parchment.

The male's right leg came off the floor, the thigh muscles bunching as his bare foot lifted. He put his arch and sole back down . . . and yanked the other one up. His ass was the last thing that was liberated, and though he had to grind his perfect jaw to do it, he managed to get himself totally free of the lockup.

"Impressive," she said in what she hoped was a cool tone.

Inside, she was jelly, no more bones, not even cartilage. She had melted—and the fact that her instincts told her she better not let him know just how much he affected her was a huge part of the excitement.

They stared at each other, and she knew he was measuring her just as she was doing the same to him. Opponents? Yes, but it was going to be so much more than that.

"I'm not kissing you until you tell me your name," she said. In a pretty fucking good stab at being prim.

By way of response, he turned away from her and headed for the door.

"Wait—what?" Devina demanded.

As a ringing set off in her skull, like she'd been sucker-punched in the side of the head, she hurried after him. "Where do you think you're going?"

As he came up to the lair's exit, the male looked over his shoulder. "I don't have to tell you anything."

"You're not leaving—"

"I'm absolutely leaving."

Devina jabbed a forefinger at the steel panel in front of him. "There's nothing on the other side of that for you."

"*Au contraire.* There's all of Caldwell."

"No, there's not." She was getting bitchy and she felt no need to hide it. "You're not on the same plane of existence as the building you think you're in—wait, how do you know you're in Caldwell?"

"There is only one place I want to be."

"Yeah, and it's with me. Fuck Caldwell."

One of his brows arched. "You know, I've never cared for females who swear. It's unladylike."

Devina closed her eyes—and pictured herself stabbing him. About a hundred and fifty times.

Then she popped her lids back open. "You want to know what I *hate* in males? Dickheads who say things like that."

"Guess we're not a match made in heaven then, are we." He paused. And seemed to be memorizing what she looked like. "Pity. You're fucking hot."

"Well, I don't like males who curse," she parroted.

"Good thing I'm out of here, then."

Andjustlikethat, he was gone.

The rat bastard literally stepped through the door as if he knew exactly how to manipulate the space/time continuum.

"Wha . . . what just happened here?" She spun around to the Book. "*What the hell just happened here?*"

As flames sprouted off her fingertips and the tops of her shoulders, and she felt the heat rise to engulf her head, she marched over to the Book, intending to rip it up with her bare-fucking-hands.

"Was this all some kind of joke? What the fuck is wrong with you—"

A burst of gale-force wind blasted up from the open pages, and kept her from taking hold of the Book, kept her from getting too close. As her hair peeled back from her face and she threw out her arms to maintain balance, the gust instantly resolved itself.

And the ink on the parchment glowed again, so vividly, it was like getting hit in the face with the sun itself.

Devina frowned and tilted in so she could read the page once more. None of the text was a news flash—

One part had an iridescent, rainbow sheen to it, the words standing apart from the rest as if highlighted with all the colors on the color wheel.

Devina read the passage yet again, her eyes bouncing around even with the glowing—or maybe because of it. Rubbing her face, she wondered why this all had to be so hard, and with an exhausted exhale, she thought about walking away from this bullshit.

Then she pictured that erection. He'd still had it as he'd left. And he better not be using it on anyone else—

The words of the spell glowed even more brightly. Then they started to blink as if they were a sign in a bar window.

"I don't know what the hell you want me to do," she muttered.

The illumination faded, the text returning to the matte brown cursive of the rest of the letters. Then the page curled up—and unfurled.

Like the Book was washing its hands of the whole thing, having met its responsibility.

Devina glanced at the door. Then she walked over and put her hand on the solid steel. She could feel a vibration in the metal, remnants of the power the male had used to walk away.

Narrowing her eyes, she glanced back at the Book. "Who is he really?"

She didn't expect a response. But she got one.

On the white walling above where the Book had perched itself in thin air, a pattern appeared, the glow of it not that different from what had just highlighted parts of the spell. As her eyes adjusted, she tried to figure out what the vertical line with the three horizontal ones coming off of it was—

"Do we have to play games," she muttered. "Just come out with . . ."

Her voice drifted off as a second symbol manifested by its side on the left: Four angled lines that formed two points—and now, a third image, a little farther out from the two that were together . . . a tent shape—

Letters.

The Book was spelling something for her—and it wasn't until the final symbol in the sequence, all the way to the left . . . the first one, actually, in the word . . . that she saw . . .

The name.

OMEGA.

"Holy . . . fuck," she breathed.

CHAPTER THIRTY

Whereupon things took an unexpected turn.

As Erika sat on her bed and listened to the sound of the shower in the guest room across the hall, that was the thought that kept cruising around the track in her head, an omniscient narrator with a British accent. Balthazar had been in there under the water for a while now, more than long enough for her to have had her own shower. Then again, she was efficient with the shampoo and soap routine. Always had been.

And God knew, he had more surface area to cover. That body of his was—

Behind the guest room door, the spray was cut off and she heard the shower curtain get pulled back. Then there was dripping. Followed by the sounds of a towel flapping around.

OMG, she was stalking him with her ears. And wow, that was a mental picture, him all naked and damp, his body gleaming from—

The image was just too damned hot, so she busied herself plumping pillows. Then she got to her feet and fussed with the duvet. On or off with the overhead light? Glancing at herself, she pulled her t-shirt down farther over the flannel boxers she had on.

Definitely off. The bedside lamp with its low glow was more than enough. In fact, pitch black was preferable, except for the fact that she wouldn't be able to see him that way.

Tiptoeing across the area rug to the light switch, she was nervous, but not because she was thinking of turning back from this. No, she was nervous because she knew she *wasn't* going to stop things, and one-night stands had never been something she'd done before. She was all for sexual expression; she just had had trouble opening up . . . given all her baggage.

Click.

As she hit the switch and things got dimmer, she looked through her open door to the stairwell. In an instant, she was back in that dream, hearing noises, going downstairs . . . seeing that shadow behind her in the mirror—

A huge shape stepped into her field of vision, and she started to yell. But Balthazar's voice cut through the panic.

"Erika! What's wrong?"

She was so relieved it was him that she reached out and grabbed his forearms. Then, before she looked like a fool, she pulled herself together.

"Sorry. Sorry—I'm sorry . . ." *Babble, babble.* "I don't know what my problem is."

"Oh really?" he said softly. "Then I've got a helluva list to show you."

She laughed a little. And then she wasn't smiling, although not because her mind was trying to scare itself.

Balthazar had traded his sheet for one of her towels, which considering his size made it seem like she'd hung her rods with handkerchiefs. He smelled like Dial soap and her own shampoo . . . and he was so beautiful, his body all cuts and hard angles, veins and muscle.

"Kiss me," she said.

She didn't have to ask twice. His mouth was on hers and oh, God, it was even better than it had been downstairs. He was raw hunger and urgency—and he was right. He was the best she'd ever had and they hadn't even gone horizontal yet.

She could fix that.

Wrapping her arms around his neck, she pulled him back into her bedroom, to her bed.

"Erika . . ." he said. "I want you."

"Me, too." She shook her head to clear it. "I mean, I want—well, you—you know what, I'm not very good at this."

He cupped her face in his broad hands. "You could have fooled me. I think you're perfect."

Lowering his head again, they went back to the kissing, and the next thing she knew they were lying down and he was on top of her. His body was so heavy, but the mattress was soft—not that she would have cared if she'd been on a brick walkway. Splitting her legs, he settled right between them—and flannel boxers were no real barrier to his stiff erection.

Every time those hips of his moved, he stroked her with that hot, thick length. And she couldn't wait for more, for all of him.

As they kissed more deeply, she ran her hands down his ribs to the top of the towel. Her brazenness surprised her. But in a way, she wanted this right here and now because then it meant he was real, this was *all* real—

He broke off the kiss and eased back.

"Don't stop." She rolled her own pelvis into him, as if to remind him what they were doing. "I know you don't want to end this."

Balthazar's eyes traveled around her face and then a hand smoothed her hair back. When he hesitated, she had a thought that he was maybe going to turn away from her.

Even though she could feel exactly how much he wanted this—

From out of nowhere, she thought of the brunette from back in the bookshop. Talk about buzzkills. That . . . demon . . . was the last thing she wanted to welcome into this sacred space. But the exchange she'd witnessed between the two of them begged all kinds of conclusions that made Erika sick to her stomach—and she had a feeling that was where he'd gone in his own head.

"I'm not her," she heard herself say. "She's not here."

"Isn't she, though," he answered in a hoarse voice.

"No." Erika stroked his shoulder. "This is just you and me."

After a moment, the tension that had come into him eased some. "I've wanted this since the moment I first saw you."

"You did?" A flush hit her face. "Was that before or after I put a gun on you?"

"During." He smiled a little. Then smiled a lot. "You're hot when you're all ordering me around and grrrrrrr."

"You like that?"

"Mm-hm."

"Well, then kiss me again. Right now."

She didn't have to ask twice. Even though Balthazar clearly had other things in the back of his mind, he returned to the mouth-to-mouth, and it was so good for them both, the way he dominated her, penetrating her with his tongue, pushing those hips against her. Under his body, she was alive in ways she hadn't ever been—alive in a good sense, as opposed to the twitchy, paranoid awareness she usually operated out of.

When his lips eventually left hers once more, it was not because he was rethinking anything anymore. It was so he could go down to her throat with soft brushes that made her feet arch into points and her thighs tremble—and she could have sworn she felt a sharp point dragging over her skin. The idea it might be his fang—and come on, did she think he'd packed a pocketknife in between his eyeteeth or something?—made her arch into him, and as her breasts came up against his hard pecs, he groaned.

What a sound. The kind of thing she felt inside her own body.

Before she was fully aware of what she was doing, her hands slipped back down to the towel, and man, that thing came off like it had been hanging by a thread. Balthazar took care of tossing it to the floor—and oh, God, the heat in that erection of his.

He was so damned big.

Things got hotter and hotter, their bodies moving together in a wave pattern, surging and retreating, a preamble to what was going to come. And it was so good. So *good*—

Until she felt one of his hands go to the bottom of her t-shirt.

The sweep of that palm to her waist and then the warmth of his skin on her own was not a record-scratch, stop-everything kind of thing because she'd been expecting it. But it pulled her out of the sex.

She didn't want him to see her scars.

Not because she was embarrassed or ashamed of them. But because she didn't want the spell to be broken with all that shit from her past: He would inevitably ask about them, and she would feel compelled to explain, and then he would get that look on his face that people did, that sorrow that was on the knife-edge of pity.

And suddenly, once again, as always, it would become about what had happened to her and her family, that single, defining night, taking this single, electric night away from her.

She was tired of being cheated of normal things like a sex life that was about pleasure and nothing more. A work life that was uncomplicated. A leisure life that wasn't tainted by the chance a documentary was going to be made about her tragedy.

"Can I keep that on?" she asked roughly as she put her hand on his to stop him.

His head lifted from her neck. There was a passing shift in his expression, like he didn't understand why she wouldn't want him to see her breasts or touch them or kiss them. But then he nodded.

"Of course. Do you want the light off?"

He was so concerned as he asked the question, as if he would have done anything to make her feel comfortable.

Funny, how the simplest things could make someone feel cherished.

She stroked his face and had to blink a couple of times. "No, because then I can't watch you."

That smile of his came back, that naughty, sexy smile. "Good. I want your eyes on me."

On that note, he eased back, his weight lifting from her. As his enormous chest retreated, she did what he approved of and looked down his ribbed abdomen. His erect sex hung from the front of his pelvis and the sight of it made her moan and shift her knees up so she was even more open for him.

Except he eased her legs back together.

Just so he could take off her boxers, though.

Lifting her hips to help, she brought her arms over her head, one of her hands finding her mouth, her fingertips brushing against her lips. Arching again, she felt uninhibited and free thanks to keeping the top half of her covered—and she had a thought that she was glad he hadn't made a big deal out of the request.

Compatibility had a lot to do with mutual respect.

And holy crap were they in lockstep with each other.

✦   ✦   ✦

As Balz let Erika's boxers drop to the floor, he was totally into the sex—and yet aware that his heart was breaking.

It was a strange duality, being stretched between the extremes of wanting to fuck his woman so good she cried from the release . . . to wanting to hold her so she could tell him herself exactly what was under that shirt she wanted to keep on.

He had accessed her memories before. He knew that her skin carried the legacy of all that physical and emotional pain. And he wanted to know her origin story firsthand because she chose to tell him.

Now was not the time, however. She had made that clear.

"You're beautiful," he murmured as he resettled on top of her.

Her legs accommodated his larger body, stretching wide to give him a place, and he loved the way she penetrated her mouth with her fingers, probing the interior like in her mind, she was playing out how it would feel to have his cock buried deep in her body.

"So are you," she said. "Beautiful."

"Really?" He winked at her. "You can tell me more if you want."

Her laugh was the best sound in all the world. "Fishing for compliments?"

"A male wants to know he pleases his female."

As she got serious, he wanted to kick himself. But then she whispered, "I wouldn't mind being yours, you know. If the world were different. If . . . we were different."

He studied her face, memorizing, for the hundredth time, what the curve of her cheek was like, and the arch of her brows, and the lashes around her deep-set hazel eyes.

"I'm going to make you mine tonight," he told her. "And then we'll see about tomorrow."

It was the best he could do. And as she just closed her eyes and nodded, he knew she was equally aware that there would be very few tomorrows for them.

Better make the dark hours count, then.

And what do you know, his erection was right where it needed to be—almost. As he rolled his hips, he reached down between their bodies, grabbed his shaft, and stroked himself on her core. In response, she moaned and arched once again. Her arousal scented the air even more thickly with that perfume that got into his brain and altered his chrome-dome's chemistry, yet even as his blood pounded through his veins, he wasn't worried about hurting her. He would never—

Balz jerked his head up and looked over his shoulder.

"What is it?" she asked.

As his instincts prickled, he lifted himself away from her, got to his feet, and yanked the duvet across his female.

"What do you hear?" she said while he grabbed the towel and wrapped it around his hips.

From out of the corner of his eye, he watched her stretch out to a little table, open a drawer, and palm a nine millimeter.

Balz looked around the room. The two windows across from the door out into the hall both had privacy curtains drawn. Closet was in the corner with louvers closed. Bathroom was open and dark.

Shit, why hadn't he brought that duffle in with him?

Because guns weren't romantic, that was why.

"You got an extra gun?" he asked as he looked at that open doorway.

"Right here."

There was the sound of the drawer opening for a second time and then a rustling of sheets. When the butt of something cool and heavy hit his palm, he closed his grip on it. There was no reason to look down and see what kind of weapon it was. He didn't care as long as it pumped out bullets.

"Safety's off," she said. "Fully loaded."

More rustling now, like she was putting her boxers back on.

Double-palming the gun, he pointed it straight out in front of his chest, at the darkened stairwell.

"Stay here," he said under his breath.

"Not a damn chance."

"You're a distraction," he snapped as he started to walk forward.

"No, I'm another highly trained asset."

He glanced over his shoulder. She had her back to him and was covering the windows, to make sure that he was defended.

Okay, that was hot. And she was right, she was goddamned useful.

They moved together toward the doorway, and he didn't have to ask to know that she was also making sure the bathroom was going to have no surprises for him.

He hated that they'd been interrupted. But he wasn't surprised. Just his fucking luck. He'd had four months of uninterrupted hell with that demon in his sleep—and only what felt like four minutes with the human he wanted like nothing else he'd ever come across. In all his years of sex—in his years of thieving, too—there'd been no female or object more precious than the one . . .

. . . who at this very moment was making sure he didn't get a bullet through the back of his head.

Tiny waists and big tits were all fine and good. But sexy to him was so much more than that. And what do you know, Erika Saunders ticked all his boxes. If they lived through whatever the fuck this was? He was going to swallow the orgasms he gave her like they were wine and fill her up between her legs until he was dry as bone.

But first? Living through this next threat.

Fuck.

CHAPTER THIRTY-ONE

T he King's Audience House was located in a part of town where the population density was about two humans an acre, tops. Which according to V's sense of proportion was two humans too much—but it wasn't like the Caldwell zoning committee was calling him and asking for his opinion. With grand houses that were set back behind gates, and yards that were mowed by private gardeners in warmer months, this was where the rich lived and entitled themselves to their hearts' desires.

As V drove his R8 up the hill, he was late. He'd taken the long way into town from the Brotherhood's mountain, but the first drive of the year was always a good thing for his mood. When you lived in a place where snowbanks could get as tall as small trees, and sometimes Prince was right and it snowed in April, you waited with the bated-breath shit to drive your car properly. Granted, his Audi had that Quattro stuff going on, which helped with traction, and given that he'd gotten the performance engine, some front-wheel drive added to the rear-wheel vroom-vroom was handy no matter the weather conditions. But the supercar was still not an all-four-seasons kind of ride.

He'd learned that firsthand.

He'd taken it out in snow once, with Butch on shotgun. Things had gone pretty well in terms of traction, but the rate limiter had been the air dam in front. With ground clearance that could cover at most ten sheets of paper in a stack—okay, fine, twenty-five—it had been no time at all until they'd gotten stuck.

That had been a fun time.

This was not a fun time.

But the car ride helped.

When he got within range of Darius's old place, he laid off the accelerator and coasted for a good fifty feet. The driveway was something he had to take real slow and at an angle, the R8 shifting to the side as he eased into the up-and-over. After that, it was a straight shot to the detached garage at the back of the property, and as he parked, for no particular reason, he looked up to the little building's second story and recalled what Saxton had done to the male who had fucked with his mate there.

Talk about needing a wet vac.

And you had to respect a solicitor who could use both the pen and the sword. There might've also been a power tool involved, he couldn't remember.

Getting out of the car, his back cracked, and the involuntary and unhelpful readjustment made him grimace. A side stretch got whatever vertebra was being a little bitch back in line, and as he started for the rear entrance to the Federal mansion, he lit up a hand-rolled. He never smoked in his R8, even when the top was down.

Just as he came up to the door into the mansion's kitchen, he glanced back at his car. He'd murdered it, everything from the body color to the rims to the four overlapping circles that formed the Audi logo, black.

It was a missile with a gas tank and a pair of airbags.

A disquieting thought challenged him that he didn't drive it much. But as if he would ever sell the thing? Audi, like most car makers, was going electric for their next bomb on wheels, and although he was all for taking care of the environment, there was nothing like the sound of that naturally aspirated V-10 engine sucking fossil fuel like it was going out of style.

Which he supposed it was—

The back door swung open and Fritz leaned out, the butler's old face falling forward like a basset hound looking over the lip of a step.

"Sire? Would you care for me to wash your automobile?"

V shook his head. It went without saying that when this *doggen* offered something like that, there was no royal "we." The ancient male would get a bucket and a clean cloth and some appropriate soap, and he would stand out here in the forty-five-degree weather playing Mr. Miyagi until the R8 gleamed like onyx.

"I'm good, but thanks."

Fritz stepped aside as V entered. "A Grey Goose for you then, Sire?"

"On duty."

The butler bowed low. "But of course. May I mention that the others have already arrived? I do believe they're waiting for you and Master Lassiter."

"Great," V murmured.

Man, he wished he could have yes sir'd that vodka offer.

As he walked through the kitchen, with its cooking staff in uniforms and its homey smells that he'd never grown up with and only knew as a grown-up because Fritz was in his life, the sense that there was something on his heels dogged him.

That paranoia was the real reason he'd taken the car instead of just dematerializing here. He'd been hoping to lose the nagging awareness somewhere along the winding roads around the mountain, or on the Northway going a hundred miles an hour, or maybe even in the suburban sprawl of strip malls and apartment complexes and nebbish neighborhoods that eventually thinned out to this wealthy zip code.

Nope.

Stopping in the tall hall that connected the servant part of the house with the public rooms, he stared out to the front entrance where the civilians came in to meet with their King, and receive blessings, and advice, and rulings on disputes.

V glanced behind himself.

Then he closed his eyes. Sending his instincts on a recon mission, he searched the house without moving from where he stood, tracking the sounds of the brothers talking in the converted dining room where Wrath took his audiences . . . hearing the receptionist accept an appointment in the waiting room across the foyer . . . noting the genial pitter-pat of chat from the *doggen* in the kitchen. Up above, the second floor was silent, and for some reason he thought of the first time he'd ever slept next to Butch in that guest room there, those twin beds regressing them back to being kids.

Re-leveling his head, he narrowed his eyes. No vision had come to him during the day, and that should have made him feel better. When a person only saw previews of the future that were of the maim, flame, and war game variety, you were kind of relieved to have a blank screen in that part of your brain.

The problem was . . . he never saw things that directly affected himself. And that was what was worrying him. With all the shit swirling around, he had a feeling another shoe was dropping. He just couldn't see the where. Yet.

Taking out his phone, he put through a call. And after things were answered on the second ring, his heart rate quadrupled—

"Well, hello there," his *shellan*, Jane, said.

Thank fuck, he thought.

Immediately, her voice got tense. "Wait, you're on rotation. What's wrong—"

"I want you to do something for me."

"Anything. What do you need."

Goddamn, he loved her. "I want you to stay in at the training center for the rest of tonight."

"Oh." Pause. "Well, I was going to go to Havers's and see about Nate. Manny's been updating me, but I just want to check the kid out for myself."

"You're at your clinic now though, right?"

"Yes. Ehlena and I are catching up on medical charts."

"Jane, you gotta stay there. You can teleconference for Nate, okay? And I don't want you to go to the Pit, either. Stay inside the compound."

"Vishous. What the hell is going on?"

"I don't know, and that's what scares the piss out of me. But as long as you're safe, I can concentrate on everything else."

There was the briefest of hesitations. "All right. Should I tell Ehlena and the others to stay in?"

"Yes, all of them. All the *shellans*, all the young."

"Okay. I'll make sure of it."

He closed his eyes. "Thank you."

"Be careful," she said.

"Always."

As they ended the call with ILYs, he started walking again. The dining room was on the left and its double doors were closed. Before he went inside, he leaned into the waiting area and hi-how're-ya'd the receptionist. She gave him a little wave with her pen and didn't break stride with her rescheduling.

Made sense. She had at least eight appointments to cancel. Maybe more depending on whether the rest of the night was in the shit show or the floor show category.

One was just drama that took care of itself. The other required intervention to get right.

Over at those floor-to-ceiling doors, he grabbed the matching brass knobs and gave a pull. Instantly, the conversation on the far side dried up—and then when the group saw it was just him, the volume boomeranged to prior decibels. He re-shut things not because the real discussion was going down, but to spare the staff the noise.

At least the Brotherhood, the Bastards, and the fighters could fit in the cavernous space. With the long mahogany table moved out, and the chair contingency cut to two padded ones in front of the fireplace and only a couple by Saxton's desk over in the corner, there was plenty of room. Searching through the bodies, V spotted his roommate over by the sideboard and he shouldered his way through the congestion to Butch.

As he came up to the brother, the cop put both his palms in the air. "Jesus, Mary, and Joseph, I take one night off and all this shit happens."

"Add a couple trays of pigs-in-a-blanket and this is one helluva cocktail party, true?"

"What the hell happened at the clinic?" Butch asked.

"Did someone say Hormel?" Rhage piped up.

Butch frowned. "Wait, don't they do chili?" Then he refocused on V. "I heard something about Nate being brought back to life by some kind of magic?"

V exhaled and snagged an ashtray off the mantel. "No, not Nate. It was Balz, by some human woman, after he had a neck wound—"

"No, it was Nate, who was shot in the stomach outside Dandelion—"

"Yeah, I was there when we took him to Havers's. But he died—"

"Actually, they do so much more than chili. But their dogs are first-rate."

Both V and Butch focused on Hollywood:

"What?"

"Huh?"

As they played echo chamber with the inquiries, Rhage stepped up and turned their little group into a circle. "They own Dinty Moore beef stew also. But yes, I like both Hormel's chili and their hot dogs."

Vishous closed his eyes and rubbed his temple with his gloved hand. "Do you ever lose the food filter?"

"You were the one who brought up pigs-in-a-blanket—"

"Do we have an angel in this room or are we just fangs?" Wrath's voice cut through the talking. "Lassiter? Where the fuck are you."

The King was over by the fireplace, sitting in the armchair to the left, all black leather against the red brocade. With an expression of barely restrained hate-the-world, he was sweeping the room with his blind eyes, those wraparound sunglasses scanning left to right. Meanwhile, there was no angel, and nobody was volunteering to make that report. Then again, Wrath already knew that there was a copious absence of a Lassiter in the crowd, and this growling interruption was more along the lines of voicing his dissatisfaction at being made to wait.

Tohr, ever the peacemaker, cleared his throat and took the heat. "Ah, no. He's not here. I'll text him again."

"Well, where the fuck is he," Wrath demanded. "I want to know how two females, one of whom is supposedly a civilian and the other of which is a goddamn human, managed to magically drag two males back from the Fade tonight."

V glanced at his roommate, and as he met those hazel eyes, Butch's brows gave him a see-I-told-you-so.

Guess Nate had been saved somehow. V had had to go back to that bookshop to clear the scene as soon as they'd dropped him off at—

All at once, everyone in the room froze.

No more shifting of weight back and forth. No movements of hands or heads. No talking, no blinking, no breathing—and he wouldn't have been surprised if all the hearts stopped, too.

His had certainly turned solid in his chest.

Something was wrong. Something . . . terrible was wrong.

As if every male in the room had the same instinct, the same feeling of dread he had, out came the guns, all kinds of palms finding all kinds of grips.

V was the only one who didn't go for his forty. He went for his Samsung, and with a quick sequence, he initialized the defense protocol for both the Audience House and the mansion. Then he went into his monitoring feeds and played firsthand witness to the daytime shutters coming down all around the exterior of the two structures. Finally, he sent out a group text that he had only ever tested before.

It was the all-points-bulletin duck-and-cover, shelter-in-place alert to every single person in the First Family's community, from *doggen* to *shellan* and everybody in between.

And within the dining room, there was an instant repositioning of fighters: Xcor and Tohrment flanked Wrath while Rhage and Qhuinn slipped out the double doors to cover the front entrance. Other brothers and Bastards paired off with fighters, the teams predetermined and practiced as they surrounded the house and sent everybody who didn't have a gun underground for safety.

V just wished he knew what the hell they'd all picked up on.

But something was off in Caldwell, on a nuclear scale.

"Where the *fuck* is that angel," Wrath gritted out.

CHAPTER THIRTY-TWO

Lassiter had to wait until everyone left Rahvyn's hospital room. It was a while. And when Nate finally walked out and took his worried father, who had been loitering outside in the corridor, with him, the angel did a double check before becoming corporeal.

Approaching the closed door, he pulled up the waistband on his leggings. Then he looked at them—and changed their color from pink and black to just black. Then he changed them altogether from spandex to a nice pair of slacks.

With pleats. And a razor sharp press down both legs.

No. Too formal.

He changed his bottom half to a set of Adidas sweatpants in black. Nice, normal, tight-legged on the lower part so that his thighs looked bigger and stronger. There, good. Oh, crap. Shoes. He needed shoes. Flip-flops with Disney princesses on them were probably not going to strike the right note.

And P.S., the fact that he'd had to enlarge them to fit his twelve-

and-a-half flappers had offended him. As if real men couldn't like Tiana and Ariel.

It was a somber night, though. He also wanted Rahvyn to take him seriously.

Especially after what she had wrought this evening. God, he'd had no idea what she was capable of, but he had sensed within her something unique, something . . . powerful. He'd just thought it was the effect she had on him.

It was so much more than that, though, wasn't it.

Knocking on the door, he waited. When there was no response, he knocked again.

After pulling another look-both-ways-before-you-cross in the corridor, he pushed things open a little—and just in case she was changing or something, he was careful to keep his eyes on the floor.

"Hello?" he said.

When there was no response, for a split second, he thought she was dead—as if she had traded her own life for Nate's. But then he leaned around the jamb and looked at the bed.

The female who had delivered a miracle upon a deserving young soul was lying back against two white pillows, the adjustable bedframe tilted up at a forty-five-degree angle. Her white hair, which was like fine, spun silk, was splayed out around her shoulders, and her civilian clothes, which were loose and contemporary, seemed ill-fitting, and not because they were the wrong size.

She should have been in silks and satins . . . a gown of old-fashioned sensibilities and cut, something handmade specifically for her with reverence.

Spring green. Yes, that color would be the perfect complement to her.

He moved himself over to the base of the bed, but he did so on a float over the flooring so as not to risk waking her up with any footfalls. Her body was so slight under the blanket that had been pulled up over her, and she was utterly still, in a way that made him think she didn't sleep much and was catching up on all that she'd missed. He didn't think she had been given a sedative—there was no IV in her arm.

Yeah, going by the dark circles under her eyes, she was just exhausted, and he wondered if maybe she finally felt safe enough to sleep here. They were underground, after all, in a secured location.

Maybe she needed to live somewhere other than Luchas House. Someplace where nobody could make her scared again.

Someplace on a mountaintop where humans didn't go.

Someplace that didn't exist on any maps and that, if somebody happened to set foot on the property, had an extra layer of magic security around it that would confuse any interlopers and blur their eyes and ruin their sense of direction.

Someplace with soft beds and good, wholesome food . . .

And an all-powerful angel who could spirit her away to the Other Side in the blink of an eye if she were ever threatened.

He still wasn't sure why she didn't live with Sahvage and Mae. He'd heard that they'd asked her to move in, but she'd maintained the new couple needed their privacy.

"Oh, I'm sorry, I didn't know anybody was in here—"

Lassiter wrenched around and threw out an energy buffer before he got a visual on the uniformed nurse who'd entered the room. As the female was frozen where she stood and then levitated about a foot off the ground, her eyes went wide and so did her mouth.

"Shit," he said under his breath as he quickly lowered her back to her feet and released the hold.

She stumbled to the side and caught herself on the wall. "Oh . . . dear."

"Sorry about that."

"I, ah . . ." Her blond hair was pinned up under her cap and she patted at it. "I did not know this was a restricted patient. I am just here to make sure she doesn't need anything."

The words were mumbled, and he was fairly certain she had no clue what she was saying.

"Worry not." He smiled at her. "And is she okay?"

"Ah, she fainted. Back in the room of . . ." The nurse stopped herself. "I'm sorry, who are you to her?"

Lassiter lifted his hand and calmed the female's mind. Then he sent her back out of the room—although not before he searched her memories and reassured himself that, yup, as far as the medical staff were concerned, Rahvyn had nothing physically wrong with her.

They all just thought she'd fainted at the bedside of the young male who had made an absolutely miraculous recovery.

None of the rank and file staff had any idea what she had done.

Just as well.

The fewer who knew, the better.

Lassiter reached out a hand—but retracted his arm. It didn't seem right to touch her without her knowledge. And also, he was in awe of her.

He should go.

Over on the wall, there was a plain clock, with a white face and black numbers. The little and the big hands were black, the second hand was thin as a line and red as blood as it raced around. He watched the measure of time do its work and told himself he really did need to take off.

But God, it was going to be hard to leave her. Now . . . or at any time.

◆　◆　◆

In the kitchen at Erika's townhouse, Balz came in from the garage. He'd gone through all the rooms and found nothing, but a pervasive sense of unease made him wonder whether they should stay at her place or try to find something that was a better defensible position. Then again, the threat he was most worried about was metaphysical, so like any zip code, set of walls, or even fucking bunker was going to make a difference?

The good news was he wasn't tired. At. All.

"There's nothing here," she said softly.

"Not that I can tell," he said as he glanced at her.

She'd pulled on a pair of jeans and shoved her feet into some boots. Her hair was tied back as well. Meanwhile, he was still in a towel and barefoot—but he could dematerialize out if he had to. Not that he would leave her.

"You have the keys to the Honda," he said, even though he already knew the answer.

"Yes."

He had a brief idea that he could bunk her in at the Black Dagger Brotherhood mansion. He wasn't using his bedroom, for fuck's sake. But how would that work? They drive there and he'd just throw her out the car door and tell her to ask for Fritz to take her upstairs to his crib?

Besides, he had no idea what he was picking up on. He felt as though there were a thousand of some enemy outside the townhouse, but—

The subtle noise was so soft, it was almost impossible to hear over the aggression roaring in his ears, in his blood, in his body. When it repeated, though, it gave him something to track, and he turned around and looked through into the living room. He had to wait an interval before it recurred, and this time, he went over to where Erika's purse was.

"I think it's your phone," he said gruffly. "On vibrate."

Erika hustled past him and glanced around before putting her weapon down on the coffee table. "I don't have mine on silent, though."

Opening the bag, she went in with her hands, taking out a practical brown wallet, a packet of Kleenex, a roll of Certs. A notepad. Couple of pens. Receipts. Lipstick. And was that—

"Is that a parking ticket?" he asked.

"I had no choice. I had to get some coffee."

"Isn't there a professional courtesy thing?"

"No, and there shouldn't be. If you park wrong, you should get ticketed."

As more crap emerged out of the purse, he decided it was like a clown car for debris, and in spite of his on-alert routine, he found the mess endearing. She was so damned put together, her house so neat, her opinions so direct, her professionalism so obvious, the idea that there was some chaos under the facade made him feel like he didn't have to be so perfect.

And good job on that, as he was far from an A+ on anyone's grading scale.

"No, it's not mine." She held up an iPhone. "And I only have one—oh, wait."

She seemed to unzip something. And then she took out a Samsung phone he recognized.

As it vibrated in her hand, she frowned. "I don't know whose this—"

"It's mine." So V knew where he was. Then again, was it really that hard to guess Balz wouldn't leave her? "That's my phone."

"How did it get in my purse?"

She turned the thing over to him—and the second he went in and read the text, he was glad he'd taken all those guns from the garage with them.

"What is it?" she asked.

"We need to stay here." Shelter in place . . . which was V's formal way of saying hang-wherever-the-fuck-you-were. "And I have to find out what's going on—is there somewhere you can lock yourself in? A bathroom with no windows?"

Although like that was really going to help if there were shadows popping up all over Caldwell, particularly around vampires?

Erika stepped right up into his face. "You've got the wrong woman if you think I'm going to damsel-in-distress in some tub while you stomp around and get shot in the back because you're undefended."

Balz blinked. And then one and only one thing went through his mind.

Do not tell her you love her right now.

Even though it was his God's honest truth—

Oh, shit, he really didn't want that coming out of his mouth right now.

"What," she demanded. "You might as well tell me because somehow, I don't think tonight could get any worse."

His eyes traced her face and he shook his head ruefully. What the hell was he going to do with her?

What the hell was he going to do *without* her?

"Don't bet on it," he muttered. "Worse is always a possibility."

"Well, all I know is, where you go, I'm going." She crossed her arms over her chest. "And if you have a problem with that, I'm not really interested in hearing about it."

He cursed. Then he thought of her upstairs, guarding his six.

With another round of swearing, he went to the living room and came back with the duffle bag full of weapons. "Fine. I want to go clear your basement."

Erika nodded once. "The door's right behind you. And I'll go first."

CHAPTER THIRTY-THREE

How had the Omega changed its mind?

As the male walked down the city street, he was naked and impervious to the cold. He was also invisible to the few humans who were passing in cars. But he was *alive*.

With the wind blowing through his blond hair and across his bare skin, the sensations were distant and also foreign—and he wondered how long he had been in the miasma, the torturous void, the black oily Hell where he had known pain to the point where he had *become* pain.

No form, no function, just an agony that was somehow self-aware . . .

In spite of who he'd been sired by, he'd never thought much about *Dhunhd*. Now that he'd died, he knew firsthand that it existed—and not in terms of his father's private quarters, but rather the eternal damnation that humans waxed poetic about and that vampires, too, sought to avoid.

He wasn't sure why he was back here.

Striding by a parked car, he backtracked to check out the license plate. The sticker in the corner had a date that made sense to him. It was just over two years past when he had "died."

No, not died. Not in the conventional sense. Rotted out, was more like it, on that mattress, unable to fight the tide of putrefaction that had seeped through and out of his body: Forsaken by his sire. Stabbed and left to degrade and decay in Hell. Abandoned like an experiment gone wrong—or worse, forgotten like a toy that had been explored, mastered, and discarded.

He'd wanted to think his sire had played a long game with his "birth" and the embedding of him in his infant state into the rarefied bosom of that aristocratic family. It had been a very strategic move on the Omega's part, allowing him to infiltrate the enemy from the very moment of his first awareness, setting his son on a course not only to be trained by the Black Dagger Brotherhood, but to fight with them.

He had been the chosen one, not a *lesser* initiated into the Lessening Society, but the blooded son, the heir to power, the special gift to the earth.

When the son had been ready, he had assumed control of the coordinated vengeance against all vampires, and the first thing he had done was kill the family who had raised him. And then, because he had been in the mansions of all the aristocracy, he had taken the army of slayers out to do what they did best. He himself had led the slaughter, and nearly all of the *glymera* had been wiped out. The resulting societal chaos had been almost enough to topple the Blind King, and that auspicious beginning had been as he'd intended to go on. He'd been determined to eradicate all of that species he'd been reared among.

But somewhere along the line . . .

His father had become the enemy. The son just hadn't known it until far too late.

When he had arrived down in *Dhunhd*, he'd been shocked, and he'd suffered, and he was now a hundred thousand years older than he had been before. Forged in the fire of the agony, he was harder. Stronger. And he couldn't begin to guess about the motivation for him being renewed.

From a tactical point of view, it was stupid. The Omega was powerful and terrifying, and all of that was in the son—who was now disaffected and pissed off at having had to perpetually stew in the kind of pain that came when you were hit by a car and every bone in your body was broken. Why would anyone volunteer for an enemy that knew so much about—

The male stopped. Looked up to the sky. Looked down to his feet.

Then he turned in a circle. All the way around.

"Father?" he said quietly.

Closing his eyes, he reached out with his instincts, searching for . . .

His lids raised. And then he frowned when what was in front of him came into focus. It was the exit to a multi-level parking garage, the "Do Not Enter" sign glowing red above an arch in the concrete walling.

He couldn't sense the Omega. Anywhere.

Back before his death, he'd known his sire's presence sure as he recognized his own reflection, the dogged awareness of the evil who had spawned him like the sky above him, the ground beneath his feet, the air around him.

A law of nature.

And now . . . all he sensed was an absence of that particular chord within the musical arrangement of his reality. A bass note that was gone.

Had the Brotherhood finally done it? Had they eliminated that which had hunted them?

Twisting about, he glanced behind himself and tried to pick up on the echoes of any *lessers* . . .

Unless his resurrection had wiped out his ability to recognize the footprints of evil in Caldwell . . . it seemed like he was all alone. The sole survivor of some kind of Armageddon that had wiped out not only the Lessening Society, but its very origins, its creator and master.

Putting his hands on his stomach, he ran his palms down the ribbing of muscle and briefly clasped his sex. Then he touched his face. His throat. His pecs.

He had a substance. He had form. He had thoughts and free will.

Was it possible that the Omega had somehow known he wouldn't survive whatever had happened? And in a last-ditch effort to have a part of him live on, carry on . . . he had brought back that which he had forsaken?

As the male considered where he'd woken up, he realized the bedding platform had been the Omega's. The private quarters . . . had been the Omega's. He knew this because he had been summoned there from time to time.

He wasn't forsaken, he realized. He was the evil's goddamn lifeboat.

Was it conceivable that he had not been discarded, but that his rotting had been tied to the Omega's accelerating decline?

He would never know.

He was here now. That he did know.

And he knew one other thing.

That smoking hot brunette had helped bring him back to the earth. He had no clue who the hell she was or why she'd been going on about true love and other fantasies of a romantic variety. He didn't care. Down in his father's private quarters, the male had been aware, but going nowhere until she had summoned him—and she had some tricks up her own sleeve, apparently.

If their paths crossed again, he was going to enjoy submitting her.

But right now, he needed a plan. He needed resources. He needed . . .

The male let his head fall back. There was no seeing any stars, assuming they were not covered by clouds. Too much ambient light. He was sure they were up there, though, and in any event, their presence did not depend on his eyes for validation. They just were.

Like destiny.

And fate.

He was back in Caldwell. He didn't know how much time he had, what his life span was, what kinds of powers he could marshal.

He was his father's son, however.

Picturing Wrath, son of Wrath's face, the male started to smile.

His purpose couldn't be any clearer—although it would not be to honor the entity who'd brought him into existence, failed him, and then resurrected him. Finishing what he had started before things had gotten off course would be for his own satisfaction.

"Thank you, father mine," Lash growled into the night, "I'll take it from here."

CHAPTER THIRTY-FOUR

A s Erika led Balthazar down into her basement, she held her breath. She'd turned the light on before she'd started the descent and the good news was that there were no interior walls in her cellar. Just steel supports that were four inches in diameter.

Easy to look around.

And there was nothing behind the open staircase or through the doorway into the utility bath.

"It's clear," she said. Not that that was necessary.

While he cased the place for himself, she saw the subterranean square footage with fresh eyes and was glad she'd finished it—well, sort of finished things with carpeting and some furniture and a fresh coat of paint. When she'd done the renovation, about two years ago, it had seemed like an unnecessary extravagance considering the only thing she did on the lower level was her laundry. But back then she'd been recently promoted to homicide, she'd had a little extra money, and she'd figured as long as she didn't get precious about her choices, it was affordable. And maybe she'd been trying to turn the townhouse into a proper home. Which had seemed like a healthy thing to do.

Yeah, total failure on that one. No amount of Benjamin Moore was going to morph the three levels and a roof into a "home." It was still her apartment, her camp-out, her tent. Her temporary, rather than her permanent.

He checked out her laundry machines, and looked behind the couch even though there was only an inch between it and the concrete wall. Inspected the furnace and the water heater. Even opened the electrical panel.

"My contractor really wanted me to throw some Sheetrock over the mechanicals and put in a proper dropped ceiling." She shrugged even though his eyes weren't on her. "But I'm cheap by nature."

She'd also known about halfway through the painting and flooring that the real goal of the reno was not going to be reached, no matter how many pipes and electrical wires were covered.

"So what's the plan," she said.

When he just shook his head, she wasn't surprised. They'd gone through all the rooms, checked all the closets, and made sure all windows and doors were locked. But his grim expression hadn't improved and that duffle bag of weapons he'd brought with him suggested he was no more comfortable than he'd been before they'd started clearing each level.

"We're going to stay down here." He went over and put the cache of guns by the couch. "Until I get word back from the Brotherhood."

"The Brotherhood?"

"My buddies."

She had an image of that goateed male with the tattoos at his temple, and the other stockier one. Then she remembered the shadow from the bookshop.

"Okay. We'll stay down here."

He nodded. And then paced over to the washer.

As he turned around, for some reason she realized he still had that towel wrapped around his waist. With the gun in his hand, he looked like a fitness model who had decided to embrace his inner *Sons of Anarchy.*

And what do you know, now that they were relatively safe, her eyes cased his body and she thought about how it had felt to be under him—which she supposed was proof that procreation was part of the survival instinct: Given the danger they were in, sex should be the last thing on her mind. But humans hadn't made it five million years as a species because their libidos were shy about attraction, regardless of the circumstance.

Plus . . . he was a vampire.

Somehow, that little revelation had gotten lost with the threat that had yet to materialize. And shouldn't that whole different species stuff bother her? Shouldn't the existence of them make her rethink everything? Shouldn't the fact that the pair of them had almost had sex shock her?

Nope, she thought as she measured the smooth, hairless expanse of his chest. *That would be a big fat nope, at least for the sex part.*

Hell, with abs like that, he could have been a Chevy Tahoe and she'd want to jump him.

"Ordinarily," he said as he turned to the stairs, "I'm not much for rule following. But when it's a direct order from someone I respect, I'm in."

"Do you think it's shadows? Like what was in that bookshop?"

"Can't say." He seemed to bite down on his molars, the hollows in his cheeks becoming more pronounced. "Don't know. And it's making me mental. I can feel something, I just can't see it."

Then he looked at her. Tilted his head. Smiled a little. "You know, you're handling this really well."

"Am I?" she murmured, not sure of that at all.

"Absolutely." He smiled more widely. "Come on, when was the last time you had a vampire in your basement?"

God . . . he was incredible. He was a strange, mystical presence that was overwhelming and yet not scary. And it was bizarre . . . she hadn't known him—*consciously* known him—for more than a week . . . but she could not imagine not having him in her life. In contrast to all the people she worked with on her job, the folks she knew in Caldwell, the friends she'd made in college, this man, male, whatever he was, was irreplaceable.

She couldn't fathom not seeing him. Not having him here in her home—

Erika gasped.

"What is it?" he asked.

When she couldn't respond, he strode over and took her free hand. "Are you all right."

She glanced around her pathetically "finished" cellar. Thought of the floor above them with her mismatched furniture. Pictured her bedroom up on the second floor.

Shifting her eyes to him, she had to blink away tears. How could she explain to him that ever since she was sixteen, she had lived in places that she refused to claim? And yet he'd been under this roof for how long?

And he'd turned it into a home.

"Come here," he said as he drew her in against his bare chest.

Erika closed her eyes and leaned into his strength. She had been falsely composed for so long, she'd forgotten she was fronting, what had once been a survival skill now an ingrained habit that went so deep, it had become a defining characteristic of hers.

His broad palm stroked up and down her back and he murmured against the top of her head. In return, she held him tightly, and in doing so, tried to communicate through touch that which she couldn't possibly say out loud.

Because it was lame. And crazy—

A quiet vibrating sound stiffened them both, and he gave her a quick squeeze and then went over to the duffle to take out his cell phone. Whatever the text was, he seemed to read it twice. Either that or it was a long one.

"It's an all-clear." He shook his head as he typed out something, his blunt fingers flying over the little screen. Almost immediately, there was another vibration as a response came in. "V says everyone's okay and there's no engagement, but Wrath's calling all the fighters on rotation in from the field tonight."

"Wrath . . . ?"

"Our King."

Erika could only stare across in wonder as he continued to communicate with whoever was on the other end of the texting. A *king*? As in . . . a whole society, living under the radar in Caldwell, with their own political hierarchy, their own problems, their own world? And this had been going on for how long? And "engagement," "fighter," and "field"— those were military words.

Like they were at war.

But come on, as if she hadn't seen that up close and personal?

And it was at this moment that she realized why she was so calm. As shocking as all of the revelations of tonight had been, they actually explained everything that hadn't sat right with her and so many others for so many years: From her headaches to the completely clear brain scans of her homicide colleagues, from those ritualistic murder scenes that had happened with some regularity to the bodies found in inexplicable conditions, from the confusing fact patterns reported by witnesses to everything that had been simmering under the surface that she— and all the other detectives charged with investigating violent crime in Caldwell—had struggled to reconcile within the context of the world that appeared to be true . . . all of it was suddenly making sense.

And she would take a shocking reality over an irreconcilable fiction-quilt of crime scenes that made no sense and gaps in the memories of so many otherwise reasonable people.

Erika went over and sat on the couch.

A moment later, Balthazar came across and settled in beside her, laying the phone facedown on his thigh. When his heel bounced, and he rubbed his jaw, she got the impression that if she'd had a cigarette, he'd have taken one. Or twelve.

As a previous smoker, having quit in her early twenties, she could remember being twitchy like that when the cravings hit.

"So did we humans get the no-sunshine part right?" she asked. "That you can't go out in the daylight, I mean?"

He seemed to have to refocus. "Ah, yes, that's correct. And we do live longer than you. We also do tricks."

"Mind control." She touched her temple. "I'm aware of that one."

She wanted to ask more questions, about the enemies of his kind, and his history, and how long he had been in—

"Are you married?" she asked sharply.

"No, I'm not mated."

"That's what you call it?" And she was so relieved, she got a little dizzy. "Mated."

"Wives are known as *shellans*. But as I said, I don't have one."

"Well, I clearly don't have a husband or a boyfriend. You've been through my closets, after all."

The side of his mouth lifted. "They were really nice closets. So neat."

"I like to know where things are."

As their no-BFD conversation petered out and they fell silent, her awareness of him expanded to fill the basement, her attention so rapt, she forgot to track the sounds inside the townhouse or look out for threats. He was just that . . . captivating. He was like an animal, she realized—and she didn't mean that in a pejorative sense. Sitting here on her yeah-whatevers blue-and-white couch, with his eyes trained across her little cellar and his limbs relaxed . . . he was anything but casual. He was like a tiger, poised to attack, even at rest.

She pictured him fighting that shadow in the bookshop, all vicious moves and power.

Then she remembered the pair of them going through her house just now, him out in front, leading the way with that big body of his, everything from the cut of his jawline to the set of his broad shoulders promising one hell of a beatdown if anything got in his way.

Or threatened her in any fashion.

Funny, she'd never found protective, he-man types attractive before. Then again, he wasn't some posturing roid-junkie with gym-honed muscles and a chest-thumping attitude toward people who cut in line at Starbucks or tollbooths.

He was the real deal.

He was . . . unlike anything she had ever met before in her life.

Well, duh, he was her one and only vampire.

Feeling like she was getting way too deep, she glanced over at her washer and got back to her feet. "You need some clothes."

"You mean this towel makes my ass look big? Is that what you're trying to say?"

Over at her dryer, she popped the Maytag's door. "Your ass is perfect."

"Oh, my God, you're making me blush—but keep going." His voice deepened. "What else do you like about my body."

As she flushed, she fished out the load she'd put in there three days ago. No *Peanuts*-happiness-is-warm-laundry going on. The stuff was cold as a corpse.

"I like that you know how to use it in a fight, how's that," she answered.

"I can do other things with it." When she lifted an eyebrow in his direction, he put up his palm. "Not the time. I totally agree."

Sifting through all kinds of sweatpants and hoodies and leggings, her classic dark load, she tried to find the biggest sizes. Good job she liked things loose.

"Here, try these."

As she walked back over to him, she considered the long list of never-before's that had rolled out tonight. Never-would-believe's. Never-would-forget's.

He was the latter, she thought. She was going to indelibly remember him whenever he left to go back into his world.

Assuming he let her.

"Thanks," he said as he took the clothes.

"I'll avert my eyes to give you privacy."

"What if I'd rather put on a show for you?" He closed his lids and shook his head. "Sorry. I'm trying to stay on my side of the bed—line. Boundary. Fuck."

Erika felt herself smile, and didn't bother hiding it. "You're funny."

"Any chance you find funny males attractive? Will it work in my favor—" He pursed his lips. "I'ma just shut up and get my naughty bits covered."

Turning away, she put her head in her hands and laughed. Then told herself to lose the modesty routine. They were grown adults, who, P.S., had been *very* horizontal right up until he'd had that weird feeling—

"How did they know to put your cell in my bag?" she asked into her palms.

"V's a smart guy. He knew I wasn't going to leave you."

"So I guess he found my driver's license and that's how he knew my address."

"No offense, but he doesn't need your government ID to find you. What do you think?"

"I think he's good with a computer then—"

"I mean about my change in wardrobe."

Erika turned back around—"Oh. My."

Balthazar looked like he'd been shrink-wrapped in sweatshirt material—and not only was everything tight, it was way too short. There was a four-inch band of bareness around his waist and big gaps at his wrists and his ankles. On her body, everything was all kinds of room-to-grow. On him, the Nike-wear turned him into a birthday present.

And what a present he would be to rip open—

Clearing her throat, Erika tried to get back on track. "I'm sorry I don't have anything larger—God, you're huge."

He clasped his hands to the center of his chest. "You say the sweetest things—oh, wait, were you just talking about how tall I am?"

As her face flushed, she smiled again—and God, she loved this back-and-forth. It was a reminder of how long it had been since anything had made her . . . happy.

"You know," she murmured, "this is not supposed to be fun. Hiding in my basement from whatever the hell we're hiding from is just *not* supposed to be fun."

Balthazar came forward, that body of his moving lithely. And when he stopped right in front of her, his eyes traveled from the crown of her head to the shoes on her feet.

"You don't want fun?" he said as he brushed her face with his hand. "Well, then, we can change up the mood anytime you want."

"To what?" she breathed.

His response was spoken in a low, erotic tone. "You decide."

+   +   +

As Balz stood in front of Erika, here was what he knew to be true: There was no one and nothing in her house.

His hair-trigger senses were quiet and he trusted them more than he did his eyes and ears.

Added to that, the shelter in place alert had been lifted, even if everyone had been called out of the field—and V, who clearly knew where the hell Balz was, who also had a direct line to Lassiter, hadn't issued a direct warning about the demon.

Bottom line, they were as safe as they were going to be.

Which was still only safe-ish if he was awake. He really wished Devina hadn't pulled a Billy Ocean and jumped out of his dreams and into his proverbial car.

"I'm not going to let anything happen to you," he said.

"And I'm suddenly worried about you spending the day down here. What happens if there's a fire and we have to get out—or something? What does no sun mean, exactly."

"You ever seen a brisket?"

"As in the cut of beef?"

"Yeah, barbecued." As her face paled, he cursed. "Sorry, bad joke."

"The sun is that dangerous for you?"

"Commercially available sunscreen isn't going to help, how 'bout we leave it at that." He glanced around. "Not unless they develop an SPF one million. And as for being down in your cellar? If this is where you're going to be, this is where I'm going to be."

She shook her head. "Why are you being so loyal to a stranger?"

"Because you're not a stranger and it's my fucking fault you're in this mess. It's my duty to do right by you. I told you, I'm a thief with principles."

There was a long pause as they stared into each other's eyes. Then she said, "Kiss me again, will you?"

Dearest Virgin Scribe—or Lassiter, as the case was—she didn't have to ask him twice. Wrapping his left arm around her waist, he pulled her against him, and given how much of her he wanted to touch, the fact that he had to keep his other hand, the one with the gun in it, down by his side really teed him off. Fortunately, there were at least six feet six inches of other ways to connect.

As their hips met, his erection returned in full force, and he didn't bother trying to hide it.

Especially as she arched into him and splayed her hands out on his chest.

Dropping his head, he whispered against her lips, "Like I said, I'm not going to let anything happen to you."

"Right back at you."

And then they weren't talking anymore. They were kissing deeply, swaying together, melding as close as her clothes would let them. His body was in a roar to take her, his need to mark what was his so great, he wanted to yank down her jeans and get into her in any way he could: Bent over the sofa. Up against the wall. On the floor.

Right where they were standing, her legs around his hips, her sex open to his—

The next thing he knew he was backing her up to the couch, and she let herself fall off her feet, landing on the cushions in a bounce.

"Take your hair out of that tie for me," he said in a husky voice.

As she pulled whatever was holding it out, he sank down onto his knees. Setting the gun on the floor within reach, he curled his hands around the backs of her calves and stroked them.

"What do you like," he growled.

Her heavy-lidded eyes flowed from his chest to his hips. "I like . . ."

While her voice trailed off, she stared at the ridge of his cock, the contour of it under her too-tight sweatpants throwing a shadow thanks to the ceiling light.

"You like this?" He stroked himself until he had to grit his teeth. "Tell me."

"I like . . . that." Her tongue made a slow circle of her lips. "Yeah."

"You can have it."

With an abrupt surge, Balz leaned over and took her mouth again, and he was rough about it, kissing her hard, penetrating her with his tongue. She took what he had to give her and clearly wanted more, her short nails biting into his back through the sweatshirt in a delicious series of pinpricks, her breasts tantalizing him as they came up against his pecs once more, her legs splaying wide to accommodate his lower body.

But their angle was all wrong for where he needed to be, so he took hold behind her knees and pulled her down on the cushions. Even though he had to break it off with the kissing, as her core came up against his arousal, they both groaned. Locking a grip on her hips, he rolled his cock against her, stroking her, stroking himself.

And he got to watch as she closed her eyes and strained, the pleasure making her moan.

"Balthazar . . ."

Well, if that wasn't the best sound in the world.

He continued to work himself against her, the sweatpants offering no resistance, her jeans more the problem. When he finally had to pause, because he was about to come, damn it, he loved the way her hair had tangled around her flushed face.

Fucking hell, the scent of her arousal was in his brain, in his blood.

"How far do you want this to go," he asked roughly.

Because he was very close to the point of no return. And he needed to be sure.

She murmured something like *this is crazy*. Or it could have been *I want you like crazy*.

Shit, he thought. Maybe she was going to be the voice of reason and put a stop to this.

Which would be proof positive that she was as smart as she was beautiful—

Instead Erika's hands went to the fly on her jeans. "I don't want to stop. And I don't care that this is crazy."

Guess he could almost read lips correctly, he thought. Something else to put on his résumé.

"I'm not going to hurt you," he said as he caressed her face.

"Yes, you are." When he frowned, she talked over the protest he was going to make. "Your world's stayed hidden for how long? You're going to have to go back there."

"You could come with me. I could keep you safe—"

"I have my own life."

"You could bring it with you."

"A homicide detective's job? Really? How's that going to work."

Balthazar opened his mouth. Closed it.

"It's okay." She smiled in a sad way. "I have only one thing to ask."

"Anything. Whatever you want."

Her eyes traveled all around his face, and then went lower, to his chest, to his straining arousal.

"Before you leave me," she said, "let me know you. Let me know . . . all of you."

CHAPTER THIRTY-FIVE

B ack in Devina's lair, the demon refocused on the door her supposed true love had just waltzed out of, and her first instinct
was to shrew her way after him and demand an accounting for
exactly why he wasn't falling in line like the good little love soldier he
was supposed to be. Fuck the Omega shit. She didn't care who he was.
Civilian vampire, dumbass human, seat of all evil in the universe? His
lineage wasn't her slowdown.

She was *owed* him. It was like a transaction where she'd ponied up
the money, but the merchandise hadn't arrived.

Unable to curb her anger, determined to go out into Caldwell and
drag him back here by all that Cali-surfer hair of his, she extended her
Louboutin forward through the door . . .

Something in her snapped and she stopped.

It was such a defining moment, such an abrupt shift, that she could
have sworn she heard the sound of a tree limb cracking off its trunk.
And in the immediate aftermath, her vengeance instantly rebounded,
her impulse to take what was hers resurging—

Except it happened again. As she put her foot out for a second time, she heard that weird noise and couldn't proceed.

Looking over her shoulder, she glared at the Book. It remained open, although for once, it wasn't acting up. It was just mounted on its invisi-stand, floating at the wall, still and silent.

Devina ran her fingers through her hair and pulled the two halves of her blouse back together. When that didn't feel like enough of a glow-up, she went over to her three-sided, floor-to-ceiling mirror and pulled an all-angle pivot, checking herself out.

All she saw was perfection: Perfect body, perfect face, perfect hair, perfect smile.

"Have some dignity," she told her reflection. "Enough with the chasing."

When she finally turned away from the gorgeous brunette in all the glass, she was calmer, her pot off the boil, even if it was still next to the stove. With a calm, deliberate stride, she headed back over to the Book.

Her therapist had always preached, *Breathe and relax.* Just *breathe and relax* when things got dramatic. The woman had maintained it was because emotion changed, but reality didn't, and to the extent to which one could frame emotions, both positive and negative, one could remain in control even when the world was spinning in ways that screwed you.

Back during Devina's fifty-minutes-once-a-week era, she'd disregarded the advice. Now? After Jim Heron, the man she'd been obsessed with, had picked a goddamn virgin over her ... after a string of losers had passed on her ... after she'd pity-fucked countless humans ... it was time to find her spine. No more fury surges, no more stamping around and begging for attention.

"I've started this," she said to the open pages of the Book. "And I'm going to finish it. What am I missing."

For the first time, her eyes focused properly on the wording that had been created for her and her alone. No more skipping over and catching bits and pieces, no more skimming. She read each and every word, and let them sink in:

Love is perfect, but does not require perfection.
Read this three times in a row without ceasing.
That which you project shall come back unto you.
Regard a cherished object as you wish to be regarded. Cradle
upon the palm as you wish to be held. Embrace to your bosom that
which is inanimate and feel for it as you wish to be felt for.
The choice of object is critical. The more meaningful, the better outcome.
When the connection is made, the window will open and your desire shall
appear. Grasp he who shall be revealed, pull him forth, and be united.
A moment of love is free to you as a sentient being.
All who exist are deserving of love.
But if you seek an eternity, you must sacrifice that which you seek.
A true love must die for yours to survive.
Balance in all things.

Balance in all things, she thought. That was some Scribe Virgin shit.

Just for good measure, she ran through the lines two more times in the same fashion, setting each of the words to memory. It was strange. She'd missed a lot of them, even though she'd assumed she'd read every letter of every syllable.

Then she put her hand on the page, splaying out her fingers. A sudden warmth suffused her palm, and as you would a dog, she petted the parchment. Old Devina—the Devina who had existed two and a half minutes ago—would have stomped and yelled and then run off into chaos. New Devina was not going to do that.

A true love must die for yours to survive.

How had she missed that part before? Especially when the shit had gone disco and all the lines had lit up like a rainbow? Why hadn't she seen this?

But like that mattered. What was important was that she needed to follow directions—sure, she'd done the first part just fine, but there was a second step here.

And if the Book's spell required her to ruin true love to get the job done with her lover? Fine. She was going to enjoy the moment that that blond Adonis with the Omega in his DNA came crawling back to her, brought to heel by the prescription laid out by the spell.

Retracting her hand, she considered her options.

Then she started to smile.

Well, she knew just where to go with this, didn't she.

✦   ✦   ✦

As Balz stared down into the glowing eyes of a human female who he'd give anything and everything to if he could, he wanted to deny what she'd said. He wanted to tell her that, actually, there already was a homicide detective in his world—and other humans, too. Manny Manello, for example. And Doc Jane. And Sarah. And Mary.

But as soon as he generated the list, the primary fault in the argument became readily apparent: Each one of those people had given up their human identity and existence. So it wasn't so much that humans couldn't be in his world. It was that they had to pick.

Butch O'Neal had left homicide even before he'd learned who he really was.

The others had given up their lives on the human side when they chose to be with their vampire mates. Doc Jane was dead as far as the humans in her life knew. Sarah had pulled out of her scientific work. Mary and Manny had functionally disappeared.

"I'm not going to want to leave you," he said roughly.

"And I'm not going to want you to go." She ran her hand up his arm. "You make me feel alive and I didn't know how much I needed that until I met you."

He lowered himself back to her lips. "It's the same for me."

This time, when he kissed her, it was gently, reverently. And even when he deepened things, he took his time, savoring her lips against his own and the slickness of her tongue.

Easing back, he said, "Can I touch you? I don't have to . . . see you."

There was a pause. And then she whispered, "I'm sorry—"

"No, you don't apologize. Ever. But I would like to . . . touch you."

"I'll explain, later. I just don't want to ruin things. If they haven't already been—"

"Not ruined. Not at all."

She nodded, but he could sense the tension in her.

"Can I kiss you some more?" he asked.

"Oh, God, yes."

Dropping his head down once again, he stroked her mouth with his own. And licked his way inside. And waited until her arousal was back . . . before he put his palm onto her shoulder . . . and moved it down to her arm . . . and over to her waist.

When he hesitated, she shifted and he felt her hand on top of his own. She was the one who brought him to her breast—

The groan she let out was hot as hell, but he reined in his lust. Which was easy to do as he learned her contours, the t-shirt so thin, the soft fabric a second skin. As he cupped her, he circled her nipple with his thumb, and she was both tender and taut under his touch, the weight of her tantalizing, that arousal of hers ramping up as he caressed her . . . and then he couldn't wait anymore. He had to explore with his mouth. Moving down onto her neck, he gritted his molars to keep from raking his fangs across her jugular on his way to where he wanted to be.

When he was in between her breasts, he trailed kisses up one of the rises. Her nipple was tight and made for his mouth, and even though he wanted to tease her, tease himself, he failed on that. Sucking her in through the shirt, he nursed at her, tugging, pulling, as he continued to stroke the other side with his dagger hand.

She was writhing beneath him now, restless, starved. And he was so there with her, his cock pounding between his legs, so desperate to get into her that he started to shake with need. He told himself he was going to be able to make it good for her and last longer than the first penetration—but he wasn't sure about that. The good news? He was going to be ready for another round immediately. Another three or four. A dozen.

He had never been like this for any other female or woman.

Ever.

"I need you . . ." she groaned as she arched against him.

The sight of her breasts, so peaked under that thin shirt, undulating up to his mouth, was almost enough to make him come, and he forgot any kind of take-his-time as her hands left his shoulders and went in between their bodies, to the waistband of her jeans.

"I can do that." He brushed her fingers away. "Let me."

He was fast with the button, faster with the zipper, and then he was hooking his thumbs and drawing the Levi's down, down, down. Her panties were simple and blue—and ridiculously, he noted that they matched the color of the sofa. He left them in place.

He had plans for them.

She kicked off her shoes and he took her socks off along with the jeans in a coordinated move that, in his mind, he gave himself a gold medal for. Then he wasn't thinking much. Except for his hair-trigger instincts, which continued to monitor the house above them and the cellar around them, he was all about his female.

He felt like the only thing a piece of shit like him could do for a woman like her was give her pleasure.

And that was one thing he would not fail.

His lips drifted down onto her stomach, and when he got to the top edge of her underwear, he took his tongue and licked under them. Then he moved over to the side of her hip. The panties were kept in place by banding that had "Calvin Klein" on it, and he looked up at her. On the far side of her breasts, she was watching him, her eyes blazing, her mouth open. With every hard, panting breath she took, her nipples shifted under the shirt, under the wet spot where his mouth had been on her.

Fucking hell. He was so sexed up.

Baring his fangs, he snagged the elastic and snapped it in half. Then he did the same with the other side.

Her knees tightened on him, her thighs flexing.

Taking the free flap that covered her core between his teeth, he drew it off . . . and there she was. Glistening, swollen, begging for him.

He wanted to go down on her, but he was on the verge of ejaculating as it was—and call him sentimental, but he wanted to come inside of her first. Not into her sweatpants.

Rising up from her, he put his hands to the bulge at the front of his hips. Then he lowered the waistband. His cock broke out of confinement, all but exploding free, and when she saw his length and his girth, her fingernails bit into her own thighs.

The sight of her spreading herself even farther was what did it.

Palming his erection, he lunged forward and ran his head up and down her hot, slick flesh. As she cried out and squeezed her eyes shut, she jerked back on the cushions and her neck strained. Then she pulled her knees up.

Balz drove into her with one thrust of his hips, and as much as he wanted to watch her, his lids slammed down. Good thing. He was liable to pop his eyeballs out of their sockets if he watched himself go in and out of her.

She was tight and she was fire and she was wet.

His body took over, one hand locking on her hip, the other grabbing on to the arm of the couch. He started to pump, forward and back, and he had to see her, he had to look—

Erika was sprawled under him, her head rocking to the beat of his thrusts, her torso straining, her mouth open as she hauled air in like she was on a sprint. With a flush on her cheeks and the blood pulsing in her jugular vein, he knew she was getting close, so close.

Slipping his hand between his body and hers, he thumbed the top of her sex, brushing it just once.

His name exploded out of her mouth and she went rigid. As her core rhythmically tightened against his cock, her orgasm teed off his own.

Just as he started to come, at the moment his ejaculations began to fill her up and mark her as his own, he caught one last sight of her face. Her lids had partially opened and only the whites of her eyes were showing.

And then he lost all sense of time and place and self as well.

It was a perfect little death for them both.

CHAPTER THIRTY-SIX

L assiter had always refused to carry a cell phone.

Okay, fine. Sometimes he took one with him, but it was only really when he was in the mood to share TikToks or YouTube shorts. Some of the shit on the Internet was funny or instructional or cute as fuck, and he knew that the brothers needed a pick-me-up from time to time. Tonight, when he'd left the Brotherhood mansion to come to Havers's clinic, he'd deliberately not taken his with him because he hadn't wanted to be interrupted.

As he stepped out of Rahvyn's hospital room, however, he still managed to get a text from the Brotherhood. A group text, as it were: Even though he was invisible, and no one else knew he was on-site, somehow a cadre of brothers had formed a lineup on the wall outside. Like they knew he was in there.

Rhage was over on the left, a Tootsie Pop stick locked between clenched teeth like he'd just finished getting to the center without much licking. Next to him was Zsadist, the brother's skull trim especially tight, his scarred face as always a thing of nightmares. And then there was Butch, in his fancy threads, and V, who was not smoking, for once. Phury was at the far end.

Lassiter didn't need to ask where Tohr was. With Wrath, of course, as no doubt were the Band of Bastards. The King was not going to be left unguarded, especially not on a night like tonight.

"I know you're there," V muttered.

As Lassiter revealed himself, he put his palms forward, all halt-and-desist. "I wasn't hiding myself."

Not from them, at any rate.

"You missed our meeting."

As V put the condemnation out there, the other brothers were silent, but they were looking like a firing squad, all that black leather hiding bulges so the medical staff and the civilians weren't alarmed. But come on, as if anybody could look at them and not know that they killed things for a living?

"I'm sorry," he said to V. "I had to take care of something."

"Who the hell is she." Vishous pointed at the closed door to the hospital room. "And what did she do to Nate."

Lassiter glanced over his shoulder. To his eyes, the panel fell away and he could see Rahvyn as clearly as when he'd been by her side. She was still asleep, but not peacefully so. Her brows were tight over the bridge of her nose and she twitched in her hands and her feet, like she was running in her dreams.

"What did she do to that kid," V snapped.

"The same thing that she did to your brother Sahvage," Lassiter murmured. Then he refocused on the group. "It's not dissimilar to what your *shellan* enjoys, Rhage. Nate's outside the scope of mortality now. Nothing can kill him, which is a blessing and a curse that he will have to balance out for himself."

V stepped up close, those diamond eyes of his narrowing. "My *mahmen* saved his Mary."

"She did. Yup."

The brother jabbed his finger at the door again. "You're saying that female is as powerful as my *mahmen*."

"No, I'm not."

"So she just pulled that kind of hat trick out of nowhere? Twice."

Lassiter leaned forward. "She's no comparison to your mom."

"So what is she—"

"She's more powerful." As all kinds of you're-shitting-me hit that harsh, goateed face, Lassiter shrugged. "She is the Gift of Light. And if you want the vampire species to survive with Devina on the planet, you're going to need her."

"Why have we not heard of her before," Phury asked. "The Chosen have never spoke of such a—"

"This is bullshit," V announced. "I don't know what you're talking about."

Lassiter had to smile at the brother. "Get your panties in a wad if you want, V, but I've got news for you. Your sign-off is not required when it comes to the universe. The Creator does what he wants, not what you approve of."

Phury spoke up again. "Maybe it's somewhere in the Sanctuary's library. Or maybe the Chosen who didn't survive the raid all those years ago knew about it."

"Or maybe the Scribe Virgin didn't want anybody to know," Lassiter countered. "No offense to her, but she wasn't much for challenges to her power. And the female who brought back Nate tonight is unlike anything else in the universe."

"Motherfucker," V muttered.

"What are you pissed about. She saved that young male. Brought him back and healed the pain of your brother and his *shellan*. You should be thanking her."

"Yeah, that curse was about my *mahmen*, not that female." V patted around his pockets like he was looking for a smoke. "I swear, the more you know . . ."

Rahvyn saved me, too, Lassiter thought. But she'd done that way before now.

And it was strange. He hadn't known she was coming into his life, or what she would do now that she was here. Though he'd been able to see that gunshot going into the bouncer at Dandelion so clearly—he hadn't seen Nate being killed and what Rahvyn had done in response.

"Well, she wasn't the only one saving people tonight," V said in a quieter voice. "Xcor and I know what you did for Balz at that bookshop. There's no way that human woman plugged up an arterial bleed with just the life line on her palm."

Lassiter shook his head. "I don't know what you're talking about."

"Fine. But Xcor wants to talk to you."

"Then Xcor can come and find me whenever he wants."

There was a moment of awkwardness, and Lassiter frankly enjoyed the way V squirmed under the surface of all his intellectual, better-than, BDSM-hard-ass. The brother couldn't handle the fact that he felt indebted to a fallen angel who was perpetually on his last nerve, but he also couldn't ignore the devastation that would have happened if Balthazar, valued member of the Band of Bastards, had bled out on the floor of that messy storage room in the back of that bookstore.

Everyone at the mansion would have been affected, and some of them permanently.

V was sooo stuck.

"You know," Lassiter murmured, "I really wish I had brought my cell phone right now. Your face is *such* a picture. It's the kind of thing I'd like to have as my lock screen."

◆   ◆   ◆

Rahvyn did not know what woke her up. Nor did she know that she had fallen asleep.

But then she recognized that there were voices. Just outside the door to her healing room.

As she sat up in the bed, she pushed her hair out of her face.

You're saying that female is as powerful as my mahmen?

Now another male: *No, I'm not.*

Now murmuring.

The second voice stuck with her, and gave her a surge of awareness: That male with the strange, beautiful eyes and the blond-and-black hair had come to see her . . . and it was his absence, rather than his arrival or the voices, that had disturbed her unexpected repose.

His presence had eased her. His departure had roused her—

She is the Gift of Light.

As the next words he uttered registered, Rahvyn felt a cold rush hit her head, and when the chill permeated her body, she wrapped her arms around herself.

Those words . . . spoken in that tone of awe. She recognized the latter, even as she dreaded it. She had caught a similar tilting of emotions in all kinds of different syllables, uttered by different males, different females. Ever since she had been a young, and "oddities," as her parents had called them, had occurred in her presence, there had been hushed conversation, and darting eyes that had returned to her quickly, and wonderment and reverence among the villages back in the past, in the Old Country.

And now she was here, in what was the present for those brave males outside in that white corridor, an ocean's distance, as well as several centuries, away from where she had been birthed and lived for a time . . . and the same thing was happening.

The male who had come to see her was wrong, however.

He was very dangerously wrong.

She was not the Gift of Light.

Perhaps she had once been. But the night of her cousin's brutal death, when the loss of her innocence had been so violently imparted, had changed that.

Closing her eyes, she eavesdropped upon the rest of what was said. When the fighters dispersed, she thought perhaps the one with those arresting eyes would come in once again. He did not.

And that was just as well.

She needed to leave this place and time, and the fewer ties she had, the easier that would be. She did not belong here, with these people, in this year.

She feared that she did not belong anywhere.

But at least she could not hurt anyone if she departed. These kind souls here, of which there were many, would be so much safer without her.

Though she had a feeling it would break her heart to be without them.

Especially the one they called fallen angel.

CHAPTER THIRTY-SEVEN

A dawn of pinks and yellows rose in Caldwell's eastern sky, the rays spearing through the dark gray petticoat of cloud cover that was departing along with the night's black velvet skirt.

As Erika stood on the shallow front porch of her townhouse, she had a steaming coffee cup in her palms, and an ache between her legs that was the kind of thing that pulled a secret smile out of her mouth. And while the other people in her neighborhood headed off to work, she stayed where she was.

Enjoying the sunrise. Which was the most beautiful one she had ever seen.

Yes, the colors were especially arresting, so vibrant and bright, the hard edge of the weather front providing a unique set of atmospheric conditions resulting in the brilliant display of chromatics. But it could have only been a smudge of yellow at the sole of the sky and the sunrise would have made her breathless.

She hadn't expected to see the sun again. There had been too many opportunities to die the night before—and it turned out that a couple of stiff reminders of a person's mortality was like being hungry when you sat down to dinner. Everything was more vital, more special, more extraordinary, afterward.

She felt positively reborn.

Then again, she'd had sex for the last six hours straight with a man—a male—who not only knew how to use his spectacular body . . . but had taken allllll kinds of care to make sure she knew how beautiful hers was to him.

Lifting her hand, she slipped it inside her bathrobe and ran her fingertips over the uneven scars below her collarbone. The t-shirt had stayed on the whole time. He'd more than figured out how to work around it, however.

When she dropped her arm, she exhaled long and slow, and watched a neighbor from the pair of units next door back down his shallow drive. The curl of steam coming out of his tailpipe made her wonder how cold it was. Sure, she was in her bathrobe, but her hair was wet from the shower she'd just taken—and given the way the man looked at her like she was nuts as he passed by, she had a feeling she really should be in a parka with dry goldilocks.

The next sip of her coffee reminded her of the dead-soldier cups on her desk in the Bull Pen, and sure enough, as she peered into the mug, there was barely an inch left in the bottom. Turning away from the show in the sky, she went back inside—and in a rare moment of optimism, she decided those dark clouds leaving to the north were a sign that things were going to get better.

How? She hadn't a goddamn clue.

On that note, she threw the dead bolt and tiptoed through the living room. Out in the kitchen, she was equally quiet as she went over to her coffee machine. A filter full of Dunkin' later, she was sitting at her table with her laptop propped open and a fresh steaming mug at her elbow.

It felt utterly bizarre to check email, like she had hacked into someone else's account, someone else's life. So much had happened, and she supposed it was like coming home from a months' long vacation and feeling like you were lost among the familiar.

Yeah, except her night had been about as far from R&R as sunbath-ing in a hurricane.

As she went through her in-box, there was the usual spam and then a couple of work things. It dawned on her that she didn't have a personal email, just this CPD-issued one. Then again, who was she emailing out-side of her job?

Sitting back and cradling the warmth of the mug in her hands, she frowned as she looked around the counters and cabinets of her anti-quated kitchen. Nothing was out of order and there was no clutter. The same was true for the rest of the townhouse. But there were also no per-sonal items anywhere. No photographs of friends, families, or pets, no mementos from vacations to warm places or cold places, dry places or high places. No knickknacks. No art. Just bare walls, clean floors, and windows that had the drapes pulled.

And not just because there was a vampire sleeping in her basement.

Funny, how she kept using that word. She found herself wanting to get used to it.

Then again, she wasn't sure why she bothered. She didn't believe that Balthazar was going to leave her with her memories.

She believed he wanted to, but there was no way the others were going to let him.

Picturing that guy with the goatee and then the blond-and-black-haired whatever-he'd-been who'd helped her save Balthazar, she considered, from their point of view, the happy idea that there was a human woman, who worked for the CPD—in homicide, no less—out in the world with the knowledge that there were vampires in Caldwell.

Not going to happen.

They were not the Mafia, it was true, but the same rules had to apply for them to continue their fight against those shadows, against that demon.

Refocusing on her laptop, she knew it was just a matter of time before she was wiped clean, so she went into Microsoft Word and opened a new document. She hadn't been an English major, not even close, so as she put her fingers on the keys, she was not going to try to write Shakespeare.

But she didn't have to.

She was rusty, struggling to find the right words, but at least a rough chronology of the last week or so kept her on track. As she went along, not even adding paragraphs, the periods like tent poles holding the narrative up, she didn't know whether this would help her later or hurt. Back when her memories had been tampered with, anytime she got too close to what had been covered up, the headaches had been one hell of a punishment.

But at least she would know it happened, she told herself.

Oh, who was she kidding.

She was trying to make sure she had a record of the male who was in her basement, and it was ironic that someone as unforgettable as him was in danger of being lost to her mind. At the end of the day, she just wanted some permanence to the fact that she had known, in the midst of the cold, cruel world . . .

Well, what love felt like.

✦   ✦   ✦

Balthazar came awake in a violent surge, and as he sat upright, he brought his gun with him, the grab-and-point as reflexive as opening his eyes—

"It's me! Don't shoot!"

The instant he heard Erika's voice at the base of the cellar stairs, he diverted the weapon so it was pointed at the washing machine and dryer. "Oh, my God, I'm so sorry—"

She lifted a pair of coffee mugs over her head like it was a stickup. And then she laughed a little. "Don't feel bad. I did the same thing the other night at the Bull Pen."

"Bull Pen?" he said as he tucked the gun back under the lip of the sofa.

"It's what we call the area I work in when I'm at headquarters." She came over and gave him one of the mugs. "And it was the night before last. A cleaning person came in after hours and startled me—God, it feels like a month ago. I still have to file a report on the incident."

As he took a sip, he studied her carefully, but she seemed okay as she sat with him. Actually, better than okay. She was radiantly beautiful, her lips swollen from his mouth, her hair drying around the shoulders of a blue bathrobe, her feet in slippers.

"I think I know what your favorite color is," he murmured as he pulled the duvet she'd brought down earlier up a little higher on his stomach.

In spite of how many times he'd made love to her, he was hard again. Ready to take her again. He'd marked her inside and out, but he wanted his fresh scent to be on her. In her.

"Oh, really? So what color is it?"

"Blue." He patted the couch, then reached out for the hem of the robe as she sat with him. "Definitely blue."

Their eyes met, and he felt a sorrowful yearning that made no sense. It wasn't as if she were on the other side of the globe—she was right in front of him. And yet all he could sense was a distance so great he would never be able to close it.

"Hi," he said softly.

The smile that hit her face was small, a secret for only him to know, and he loved that. "Hi."

When they fell silent again, she cleared her throat. "How's the coffee?"

"Perfect."

"I didn't know whether you liked sugar or cream."

"I like it any way you make it for me—"

As he stopped talking and looked around the cellar, she said, "What's wrong?"

Like an idiot, he twisted to the side and checked out the cushions he'd been on. "I . . . was asleep."

"You sure were. When I woke up, I was careful not to disturb you."

"No, I mean I was *asleep*." He patted his bare chest with his hand. "I didn't dream."

"Well, that can sometimes be a good thing—"

"The demon didn't come to me. She left me alone." He pegged her with his eyes. "Did you dream of anything?"

"No, not that I can recall." Erika sat forward. "Wait, does this mean . . . the demon is gone from you?"

"I don't know. But every day that I slept, she's shown up." He shied away from any details concerning what the female had done to him in his dreams. "Not just now though."

"Maybe she's fallen off the edge of the world," Erika offered.

"Maybe."

Except they weren't that lucky. Still, it was the first time he hadn't been hounded since that December night and what a frickin' relief.

"Clearly, you're my lucky charm," he said with a smile.

"I wouldn't put too much faith in me. But I'm happy to be of service."

As she ducked her head in a mock bow, he thought about the situation she was in with him in her house, in her life. Making love to her. Warming the couch in her basement and tucking a comforter that smelled like her around his naked, well-used body.

Before you leave me, let me know all of you.

He was fooling himself, wasn't he. To think that there was any kind of future for them, full of countless hours like this, sitting together in her cellar. The fantasy had seemed so real when they'd been pleasuring each other. Now, it was back to being just figments in his mind. In his heart.

"You're looking really serious all of a sudden," she murmured. "Penny for your thoughts—or will I need a dollar?"

Taking another draw off the rim of her mug, he tasted the very best coffee he had ever had.

"I grew up in the Old Country," he said. "Which is England, Wales, and Scotland for you. It was my cousins, Syn and Syphon, and me for the longest time, and then with another male, Zypher. After a while, we crossed paths with a fighter who was . . . well, he was a force of nature. He still is."

"Who did you fight then?"

As they drank the coffee she'd made, he told her all about the Scribe Virgin and the Omega, the Lessening Society, the innocent civilians, the aristocracy, the King who would not lead. While the words tumbled out of his mouth, he was aware of rushing through the story, and yes, he edited things out. The Band of Bastards had been no one's heroes. They'd survived in the woods with no permanent home, fighting because they liked to, feeding because they had to, fucking when they wanted to. Back then, he'd thought it was the only existence he needed, but then they'd come to Caldwell and things had changed.

"So there are vampires still in Europe?" she asked, her expression riveted.

"Not many."

"And the *lessers* are those shadows?"

"No, they're de-souled humans. The Omega used to induct them into his society, and they served him." He shook his head. "You want to talk about nasty. They smelled like baby powder and roadkill—"

"The farmhouse, the other sites!" She motioned in the air. "The blood everywhere, the oil stains—that's what it smelled like. Homicide's been called to a number of these scenes over the years, and I never knew what they were. No one knew."

"That's the Omega. Or was. He's no more. He was eradicated recently, thank fuck. Although"—he lifted his mug in toast—"naturally we have someone new we're dealing with."

"The brunette."

"Yup." He took a deep breath. "So that's my story. I serve my King and my leader—he's the one who was with us in the surgical RV, the one with the lip? I live with them and their families—well, I did until Devina got her hooks into me and I moved out. Anyway, that's that. Oh, and yes, I've stolen some things along the way."

"And given the money to charity."

"That's right."

"For which you don't feel bad."

"Nope."

Instead of getting on him, she smiled a little. "I can't condone that."

"I know. Just as long as you don't expect me to turn over a new leaf."

They both laughed, but it didn't last, and that was when he knew she was thinking the same thing he was: That their future was limited.

"Now you know everything about me." He paused. When she didn't say anything, he tensed a little. "Yup. Everything."

In the quiet that followed, she seemed to age before his very eyes, her face growing drawn, her eyes getting grim.

He stayed silent, hoping she would open up to him and tell him what he already knew because he'd been inside her mind. He wanted to offer comfort in the face of her tragedy, but unless she chose to welcome him into her sacred suffering and loss, he couldn't do that.

Her privacy needed to be respected, even after he'd unintentionally breached it. All she'd willingly shared was a date.

"Quid pro quo, huh," she said tightly.

"You don't have to tell me anything you don't want to."

Her head nodded slowly, in a way that he wasn't sure he could interpret. "So what do you want to know."

There was no beating around that bush—and if their circumstances had been different, he might have eased into the subject. Like, started out by asking her about her job. Or how long she'd lived in the townhouse.

Instead, he set them both upon a cliff. And jumped off first.

"I want to know what happened June twenty-fourth, fourteen years ago."

CHAPTER THIRTY-EIGHT

There had only ever been one part of Erika's past, it seemed. And that was not merely true from an outsider's perspective, whether the questions from other people were generated out of pity, compassion, or morbid curiosity. For her, too, there was only one thing.

A single night, on June twenty-fourth, fourteen years ago, had wiped out all her birthdays and holidays. Her summer vacations. Good grades, bad grades. Best friends and frenemies.

Afterward? Nothing else had particularly mattered. Or would.

She'd been eliminated with the rest of them.

"You don't have to tell me," Balthazar repeated.

"It's okay. I've run through the story a hundred times."

Yet she struggled with where to start, which was a new one—and that was when she realized that she had a down-pat speech she gave people. The recitation was a rote A-to-B-to-C of it all, and she was prepared for the peaks and valleys of emotions that inevitably arose in her audience. She knew the places she had to steel herself against the reflexive, unsolicited empathy that would always come back at her.

And she braced herself not because such displays of human connection would make her get teary or something. It was because she really wanted to tell whoever was pulling the soppy bit to fuck off. If she could suck up the pain of going through it, they could leave their stupid compassion at the door when they merely heard the story.

"I shouldn't have pressed. I'm sorry—"

"Dispatch called me the night before last." He immediately stopped speaking when she interrupted him. "Dispatch is how detectives find out about cases and get assigned them. In the homicide division, we have a rotating schedule and whoever is covering a given night gets whatever comes in. You ever heard of that TV show *Forty-eight Hours?* Every second counts in the beginning, if you want to find out who the killer is, so you have to be quick about getting to the scene, finding witnesses, gathering evidence."

She took another draw from the mug and didn't taste a thing. "My partner, Trey, he starts lighting up my phone. He doesn't want me to go over to Primrose. He tells me to stay away, he'll handle it. I refuse to listen to him, and that was my first mistake. See, when dispatch rings, they'll let you know basic details. Number of victims, status of victims, location, any preliminary suspects who may have been apprehended. There were four victims at the house. A man, a woman, and two teenagers. So I knew . . ."

As her voice trailed off, she had to clear her throat. "I knew why Trey was calling me and why he was probably right. That I shouldn't go to that scene. That I wasn't going to be an asset."

A slideshow of images flickered through her mind's eye, and with them came a hopelessness that fit her like a hand-tailored suit of clothes, covering the contours of her body as a second skin.

"I threw up in their bathroom. After I went upstairs to the girl's bedroom. It was pink. She was sixteen. Her boyfriend raped her before she shot him. He'd murdered both her parents before he went upstairs to get her. She shot herself after she put two bullets in his chest, while she was on with nine-one-one." Erika felt her brows lift. "Their bathroom was blue, now that I think about it."

"I'm so sorry—"

"If the parallel is not obvious to you, the same thing happened to me. Except I survived." As her heart rate sped up, she felt as though she were living through the actual events, for some reason. And she let her mouth go. "I'd forgotten it was my mother's birthday and I was late for dinner. I stopped at a CVS and grabbed the first card that had the word 'mother' on it. I didn't even bother to look at the message inside." She shook her head. "That's among the things that hurt the worst, by the way. Her last card, which she never read—and I didn't even give a shit when I picked it out."

Horrible, too-clear images assaulted her. "I parked outside the garage and walked to the front door. It was open, which was weird. As soon as I stepped inside, I smelled the blood. I ran back to the kitchen— and I slipped in the pool that was under my father." She frowned. "I'm pretty sure I started screaming then."

It was a while before she could continue. "Just as I was going to go for the phone, he dragged my mother in from the garage. I think . . . I think she'd been trying to run out. He had a knife to her throat."

"Who was he," Balthazar asked tightly.

"My boyfriend. Ex . . . I mean." A lump in her throat made it difficult to speak. "He killed her in front of me. Disemboweled . . . her. He said he wanted to destroy any place I had ever lived and that meant he had to cut out her stomach. My mother . . . screamed and fought and . . . the next thing I knew . . . he was on me. With the knife."

As her hands went to her collarbones, and then drifted down in between her breasts, she felt the white hot spears, the sting, the sudden sense of gurgling suffocation that had come when the stabbing had started.

"He told me my brother was dead upstairs in his bed. Johnny was nine."

"How old were you?" Balthazar said in a rough voice.

"Sixteen. It was . . . right after school got out for the summer. I was going to camp out of state to be a counselor. He didn't want me to go. He didn't want me to leave him. He thought—well, in the end, it didn't matter what he thought. He was crazy."

"What happened to him."

"He slit his wrists with the knife he'd used on me and my family. And when that didn't go far enough, he took out what turned out to be his father's gun and shot himself in the head." She touched her eyelid as it started to twitch. Then rubbed the thing to try to get it to stop flickering. "He thought he'd killed me, and I played like I was dead. He was . . . utterly distraught. He didn't want me to live, but he didn't want me dead, either."

"Here," Balthazar said.

Erika glanced at him, and found that he was holding out the sweatshirt she'd given him from her dryer. When she just stared at the thing in confusion, he leaned in and blotted at her face with it.

"Am I crying?" As he nodded, she was surprised. "I don't cry over this, you know. Ever."

Well, if that wasn't a stupid statement, given the tears he was mopping up.

"Can I tell you something I've never told anybody before?" she whispered.

"It would be my honor to hold your secret here." He touched over his heart. "And keep it within me."

She took her sweatshirt from him and moved up a little higher to a drier place on the sleeve.

"I just stood there." Erika began to cry openly, the tears streaming down her face and dropping onto the blue bathrobe. "While he killed my mother. I just . . . fucking stood there as he cut into her and she screamed. She held her arms out to me, her eyes . . . they locked on me . . . she called my name . . ."

And that was when the snap happened.

She just broke in half. It was as if the composure she had maintained was a hard shell, and with enough force exerted on it, it lost its structural integrity—and what was inside, all the horror and regret, the poisonous self-hatred, everything so pressurized, just exploded.

Strong arms wrapped around her, and she went with them as they brought her against a broad chest.

Erika cried so hard, she made no sound, could draw no air, lost track of everything.

Even herself.

But she knew who was holding her. That, she remained clear on.

◆   ◆   ◆

All Balthazar could do was hold on to his female. As she released her pain, he reflected that the secrets buried by shame were always the most poisonous ones, and the destruction they wrought was the insidious kind, under the surface and mostly hidden.

And he was honored that he was the one she'd chosen to reveal herself to.

"I'm so sorry," he whispered against her hair as he stroked her back. "Oh, God . . . I'm so sorry."

To be that young, that innocent . . . and to have your childhood ripped away from you by that sort of violence. He had been through a lot in his life, but nothing that came close to what Erika had endured.

That she had gone into homicide made sense. She was trying to do right by others like her family. But he also knew that she never got away from death; it no doubt haunted her at night as well as stalked her during the daylight hours at her job. She had not healed over the last fourteen years; she was stewing in tragedy.

Although could anyone really heal from something like that?

With a push against his pecs, she moved away from him. "Will you excuse me for a minute?"

She was steady on her feet as she walked over to the utility bathroom, and when she closed the door, he rubbed his face with his hands.

There was the sound of water rushing—for a while. Then a toilet flushing. Then more with the water. When she emerged, she carried a pleasant scent with her as she wiped her hands on a paper towel, which she pushed into her robe's pocket.

He expected her to make a pronouncement that that was done. She wasn't talking about it ever again. But she didn't.

She came directly over to him, standing tall and much more composed, even though her face was red and her eyes bloodshot.

Her hands were steady as she went to the tie around her waist, and when she removed the robe from her shoulders, she just let it drop to the floor. The t-shirt underneath was a fresh one of the same kind she'd had on throughout the night, plain, white and loose, the creases from it having been folded while warm from the laundry making a pattern down the front.

She lifted it slowly, the hem going up over her belly, her ribs . . .

Her breasts were beautiful to him, her nipples peaked from the chill—

And there were the scars.

He closed his eyes briefly. Then focused on the healed wounds.

She had been stabbed repeatedly by a right-handed assailant, the wrinkled and knobby pattern located under her left collarbone. He was well familiar with those kinds of injuries and he knew she had to have been penetrated by a blade at least ten times, because there were satellite punctures around the main impact zone.

Her hand lifted, and as she ran her fingertips over the uneven texture, he had a feeling she did that a lot.

"I can't fix it, you know," she said in an absent way. "I mean, plastic surgery won't really make it go away."

"Why would you?" When she recoiled, as if he'd shocked her, he shook his head. "The scars are not ugly. They don't detract from how beautiful you are. And what happened is always on your mind anyway. Besides, you probably needed surgery afterward. A couple of times. You're done with operations, aren't you."

She nodded, as if in a daze. "I can't make it go away just by . . . you know, trying to get rid of this."

"We can't run from our pasts. We shouldn't even try."

There was a long silence, and he worried that he'd said the wrong thing. Maybe he needed to—

"Thank you," she said softly.

Now it was his time to be surprised. "For what?"

"You're so . . . accepting."

I love you, he thought to himself.

"But you've been in war, haven't you," she said. "This is . . . what you've seen before."

"It's true. It's a part of life. I don't want you to have gone through what you did. I hate it. I fucking *hate* it—and if that asshole weren't under the ground already, I would hunt him down and bring him back to you in pieces. I would *ahvenge* you and your dead to honor you and your parents. I would see that it was done in the proper way, in the painful way. I would have him suffer under my bare hands and breathe in the smell of his blood and the stink of his cowardly fear."

He had to stop himself before he got too far into all that. And then he bowed to her from his sitting position on her blue couch.

"Verily, it would be my honor to *ahvenge* you and your bloodline."

When he looked back up, she had put both her hands over her mouth and her eyes were shining.

He couldn't tell whether he had offended her or scared her or—

Erika came forward, came to him. And as she dropped her hands, she whispered, "No one's ever said that to me before."

"Is that . . . good? Or—"

She settled on top of his lap, one knee on each side of him. As her eyes roamed around his face, she ran her fingers through his hair.

"It's hard to talk about my past," she murmured. "Because people are interested for reasons of their own and they get emotional for reasons of their own. I lived through it. I don't want to help others manage my tragedy."

He ran his hands up her arms to her shoulders. "Makes sense."

"You've been through war," she repeated. "You're different."

Balz focused on her breasts. "May I touch you?"

"Yes."

Just as she had during the night, she took his hand and moved it onto her tender flesh. And as the weight of her breast filled his palm, he moved his thumb back and forth over her nipple. In response, her hips rolled against his, her back arching, her chest rising up.

Slipping his hands around her waist, his mouth brushed over her sternum, her heart. Then he kissed her scars, gently, reverently.

"You're so beautiful to me," he said.

He glanced up. Her eyes were luminous as they watched him—and the fact that she was so open, so vulnerable . . . told him she believed him. She knew what he was telling her was true.

Balz took his lips farther down onto her breast. It was hard for him not to think of all her pain, but she was right. He wasn't going to ruin this moment with her with his own emotional response to what she had had to endure.

Instead, he was going to show her how desirable she was. How absolutely perfect. How sexy and alive she was.

He worshipped her, sucking at her, stroking her, nipping and licking. And she felt exactly how he wanted her to. She was liquid on top of him, fluid in her hunger, aroused in her anticipation of what he was going to give her—and then her hand was in between their bodies, encircling his erection, standing him straight up.

Erika positioned him, holding him in place, and then her core took over the job, encapsulating him with a tight, hot hold that he knew he was never, ever going to get enough of: They could spend an eternity together, and still, entering her was going to be a revelation.

As she sat all the way down on him, their sexes joined, she pulled back a little.

Their eyes met, and neither of them moved.

And that was when it happened. Somehow, her thoughts and memories became his own. He didn't mean to get into her like that, but he did, the connection between their bodies so seamless that it melded their minds as well.

What he saw consumed him, and he opened his mouth to speak.

But then she started moving, her hips riding his pelvis, his cock going in and out of her to the motion she set.

That was all it took. He tightened his hold on her ass, cupping her, squeezing her, moving her up and down on his shaft. There was so much to see where they were joined: His erection glistened every time she lifted herself up, and each time she sat back down, the visual of him disappearing inside her body made him crazy with lust.

He started coming. He couldn't help it, didn't want to.

Things got a whole lot more slick.

And then he couldn't see anything anymore because his eyes closed on their own. That was okay. He could hear her moan and then feel her go tight. After that, the rhythmic, milking grip of her sex on his cock teed off another round of orgasms for him.

It was all so perfect.

Just like her.

CHAPTER THIRTY-NINE

By the time Erika left her townhouse, it was past eleven a.m. She knew that Balthazar was not a fan of the departure, but she had to get her unmarked back and she wanted to check in at headquarters: The former was because the sedan was municipal property and she'd left it by that bookshop in an iffy part of town. The latter was because, as much as she had loved the time she'd had down in that cellar, as close as she'd become to the man—male, she meant—she felt the need to keep a foot in her own reality.

The silver Honda was where she'd parked it, grill-in to her closed garage, and as she got in behind the wheel and drove off, she was on autopilot. The traffic wasn't bad, except for getting on the Northway, and as soon as she was cruising at a smooth sixty-one m.p.h., her thoughts returned to Balthazar.

She told herself she wasn't falling in love with him.

"You're just not," she said as she hit the directional signal and changed lanes to get around a slowpoke eighteen-wheeler. "I mean, you can't be."

Yes, they'd been through all kinds of crazy stuff together, and yes, they'd had some incredible sex.

Reaaaaally incredible sex.

And yes, she had revealed the deepest part of herself, a part that she didn't even visit, and he'd handled it in a way that she hadn't known she'd needed.

But that wasn't "love." That was sexual attraction fulfilled. A sensitive moment shared. A surprising compatibility.

It wasn't *love*. People like her didn't fall in love—unless she thought that shrink she'd gone to her senior year in college had been lying about the attachment disorder diagnosis? And to think she'd gone to the guy herself, not because a roommate or school administrator or professor had made her go. She'd known that she was out of sequence compared to her peers and she'd wanted to know why and he'd told her.

She still was out of sequence.

For chrissakes, the fact that she was sleeping with a vampire was actually right up her outlier alley, wasn't it. Everybody else was engaged, married, married with babies, or married with children. She was seeing Dracula.

"Stop it," she muttered as she got back into the middle lane.

Balthazar was so much more than that. He had accepted her scars. He hadn't judged her darkest secret, the thing that stung her right to her soul. He had cherished her and held her, and when they'd fallen asleep together for a half hour, he had kept a gun right under their sofa in case he had to protect her.

She'd never felt like all parts of her were accepted before. Right as they were. And the irony was real.

All it had taken . . . was a member of another species.

As her downtown exit arrived, she cut in front of a Mustang and descended the ramp that dumped her out on the edge of the business district. The route she had to take to get to the Bloody Bookshoppe was inefficient, but that was the way of one-ways. Pulling up in front of the little store, she stared at the door and remembered stepping through it . . . into another world.

Police tape, as familiar to her as her own face, crisscrossed the inset stoop, and there was a seal on the jamb.

The sight of it made her wonder what they did when they "cleaned up a scene," as Balthazar had put it. Did they lift evidence if it linked them or suggested their presence? Or just get rid of the metaphysical stuff? They'd certainly removed anything that proved she'd been there.

The temptation to go in was nearly overwhelming. Instead, she continued on. She'd agreed to leave the silver Honda in the area and bring the key back to Balthazar. He'd told her they'd handle getting the vehicle back to that garage—

Erika braked and checked her rearview mirror. Glanced around. Then twisted in her seat so she could get a second look at the lineup of cars that were parallel parked on both sides of the one-way. Crap, she'd gone by her unmarked.

As she set about making another box formation with the one-ways, she made herself concentrate. Maybe she was mistaken about where she'd left her car.

A second trip around got her the same result.

Absolutely no unmarked.

Where the hell was her car?

◆   ◆   ◆

Back at Erika's townhouse, Balz was taking a shower in her bedroom upstairs. As he stood under the warm spray and ran her bar of Dove soap over his body, he really didn't like the idea that she was out in the brilliant light of day, traveling over roads that were chock-full of distracted, idiot drivers, heading back to where Devina had killed an old man and pretended to be him.

He particularly hated that last part.

On that note, where the hell was the demon, he wondered as he reached for her shampoo. He'd fallen asleep after they'd made love again, and still no demon in his dreams. That was twice that that bitch hadn't shown up—

Balz froze with his hands on his head and something made by Paul Mitchell palmed in his hair. As the water continued to wash over him and the shampoo dripped into his eyes, he heard a voice in his head. Lassiter's voice.

True love is going to save you.

Like an absolute piker, Balz's hands dropped to his sides and he stared at the tile of Erika's shower stall.

"I love her. I really do."

When the sting from the shampoo got irritating, he turned around and faced the spray. Rinsing his hair, he felt a cosmic shift inside himself. The Book didn't matter. That was why Lassiter had told him to let it go when he and Sahvage had been playing tug-o'-war with the ugly, nasty-ass thing.

Erika was his savior. Not anything in that old tome.

She was his solution.

Hanging his head, he thought about all the don't-know-why's of destiny. He hadn't had a clue about why the demon had chosen him or exactly how she'd gotten into his soul at the moment he'd been electro-cuted in that snowstorm. And now, he didn't know why he was so lucky to have crossed paths with a human who'd changed the course of his life.

He should have felt empowered and lucky.

Instead, he felt just as out of control as before; he only happened to like the current outcome better.

That was life, though. For all the choices consciously made, there were forces at work under the ground of daily and nightly existence, deep aquifers of fate that drove an existence that fluctuated in and out of happiness, sorrow, boredom, fear, up above.

Yet he was grateful.

How could he not be? Except maybe he had more Syphon in him than he wanted to admit. He'd rather be in control.

Cutting the water, he stepped out and used the still-damp towel

Erika had run over her body on his own. As her scent rose up to his nose, his libido raised the hand it had. He wasn't going to do anything about his perma-rection right now, though. He scrubbed his hair dry, smoothed it down with his hands, and threw the sweat suit, as he'd come to think of it, back on.

Out in the shallow hall, he peeked through the open door of the guest bedroom. Erika had pulled all of the shades on the first and second floor, but the ones in there weren't blackouts and he reared back as if slapped. Closing the space up, even though he was going downstairs, he descended to the kitchen and hit the fridge looking for food.

Condiments. Lots of condiments.

Like she never cooked and only ordered in.

He could relate to that. Back when he'd been living at the Brotherhood's mansion, the only reason he'd had homemade meals had been the *doggen* there.

In Erika's cupboards, he found a box of pasta and a jar of spaghetti sauce. Getting out a pot and setting it to boil, he noticed her laptop was on her table. He didn't open it. Even if it wasn't password protected, whatever was in there was her business.

He took out his phone. On the screen, there were all kinds of messages, sent in response to his I-am-alive missive that had gone out just before he'd taken his shower.

An odd thought went through his mind: *This is what I am leaving behind.*

"What?" he muttered. He wasn't going anywhere.

When the pasta was ready to be drained, he couldn't find a strainer so he used a fork to keep the linguine from slipping out down the sink. Dumping the load of carbs in a bowl big enough to toss a salad in, he opened the jar of plain Ragú and doused the tangle like it was on fire.

Just as he was about to sit across from the laptop, he reminded himself that he wasn't in a structure that had true daytime shutters. Erika had been great about tacking up a wool blanket over the venetian blinds and the drapes she'd pulled in this room, but it was safer underground.

When he was back down in the cellar, he used his thigh as a TV tray and twirled his little heart out, throwing a good thousand calories into the gaping hole of his stomach.

When there was nothing but a Jackson Pollock of red streaks around the inside of the bowl, he set it on the floor and took his phone out again. The text he composed took a couple of tries, and even then he wasn't satisfied—

A creak upstairs brought his head up. And also the gun he'd tucked into the front pocket of the sweatshirt.

Well. This could be a problem.

Depending on who or what it was.

CHAPTER FORTY

Rahvyn recognized the dreamscape. It was where she traveled when she was asleep, a neutral ground within the Creator's master plan. She had started to come here when she began living at Luchas House, as if, with her body safe, the part of her that was connected to the energy in the universe was free to go where it wanted to.

Where it needed to.

She had learned that she could manipulate the landscape at will, adding trees to the flat plane. A meadow full of flowers. A sun in the sky, a cottage in the corner. She could tile it in lavender or yellow, red or pink.

Those were the parlor tricks she had mastered when she had first arrived.

The efforts had been trivial, however. She had the sense, deep within her, that this was an important place, of graver significance than merely a backdrop on which she could play with colors and arboreal fixtures—

A wind she did not create blew across her face, and as her hair was swept along with it, she saw that the waves were back to being what they had once been, no longer white but a rich black. Tucking the locks behind her ears and over her shoulders, she felt an arrival of some sort.

She turned to face whatever it was—

A table.

An unadorned table had materialized upon the deep blue grass, and she took a step back. Looking up at the "sky," such as it was, she saw nothing above her other than the baby blue clouds she had conjured up to shield herself from her bright red sun. There was naught behind her or coming at her from the sides, either—

An image appeared upon the tabletop, and whatever it was was flickering as if some signal were being interrupted by distance or weather.

She did not go closer.

Until she recognized the shape.

It was square and flat, a box, but one that was not very deep. No, that was not correct. It was not a box, but rather a . . . book.

Now Rahvyn moved forward. When she was before the object, she noted the way the image of it continued to come and go, a mirage of the actual thing.

The book had a mottled, uneven cover, and the curl of something that smelled bad reached her nose. In all . . . it was revolting.

And yet she was drawn to the ancient tome. Sure as the thing was calling her name, and had an urgent need that only she could fulfill, she could not look away.

Her hand raised of its own volition and her arm extended on its own.

Just as she was about to make contact, as the image was solidifying into a three-dimensional actuality, as opposed to a twinkling, two-dimensional representation—

Something flashed overhead.

Jerking her head up, she looked to the sky. It was not blue and red any longer. In fact, all the colors were gone from the plane of existence, nothing but grays and blacks and gloom above and all around her.

When she glanced back at the table, the book was real.

And it was demanding that she—

◆   ◆   ◆

Rahvyn woke up in a rush, and she put her hand to the center of her chest to hold in her thundering heart. Glancing about at her environs, she saw only the healing room she had been given, the one where the angel with the blond-and-black hair had come to see her, and where the Brothers had cloistered around outside in the hall to speak of what she had done to Nate.

Dearest Virgin Scribe. She still had regrets, fearing that she had saved him only to create another set of problems for her friend.

Perhaps death would have been kinder to him, even as it shattered those who loved him.

And as for the dream just the now? She did not know what that had been about, why that book had come to find her, what it had wanted from her.

Struck by a restlessness that suffused her with twitches, she was compelled into some kind of action, any kind. Slipping her feet out from under the blanket that covered her, she padded over to the bathroom. After a series of refreshments, which included a toothbrushing courtesy of supplies that were set upon the counter, she returned unto the larger space.

Whereupon she looked at the door out.

Driven unto motion, she stepped through into the corridor. And then she walked along the long, white, unadorned hall. Her senses were such that the walls of the clinic, as well as its various underground floors, disappeared, everything becoming transparent and revealing the dramas that were playing out around her: She could see them all, the males and females within the facility, whether they were patients or healers or people who were with machines or computers. She knew their stories instantaneously, drowning in their secrets as they received treatment, rendered treatment, recorded treatment, waited for treatment.

This transparency had happened before, and as the input swamped her, she attempted to put up her psychic boundaries to shut it out.

Something about that dream had disturbed her fundamentally, however, and she struggled to marshal defenses so that she could form her own and separate purpose, the segregation necessary for her to—

"Are you all right?"

At the sound of the female voice, Rahvyn snapped out of her tail-spin. A nurse in uniform was standing before her, eyes of brown looking concerned, a caring hand reaching forward. She recognized who it was. This was the one who had been checking in from time to time, who had been so nice. And in response to the present inquiry, Rahvyn took a steadying breath—and for a split second, entertained the option of telling the female that in fact, no, she was not all right. She was submerged in the lives of other people.

And wondering why she did not save the ones who were dying.

Just as she had Nate.

Rahvyn remained silent, however. She knew the kind of aid she sought was outside the scope of care offered by the female. By anyone.

"I am rather hungry," she said roughly, such that she could justify her presence outside of her room. "Is there a kitchen herein, perhaps?"

"Oh, yes." Relief marked the nurse's pleasant face. "If you'd like, you can go back to your room and I'll have someone bring you whatever you want?"

The idea of being cooped up made sweat bead along Rahvyn's forehead. "I'd prefer to sort it myself? If that is possible."

"Well, there is a cafeteria." Directions were provided. "Just follow the signs, then. It is not fully open, but there are choices for you there."

"Thank you very much indeed."

There was a little more conversation that Rahvyn did not attempt to follow, and as they stepped apart, she realized she had retained nothing of the instructions for the location. The last statement proved enough, however.

She followed the signs.

After going around many turns and down a couple of straight-aways, she caught the scent of food. It was not of the First Meal variety, however—and that, coupled with her sense that daylight had indeed arrived aboveground, informed her that it was not yet dark again.

She could not leave.

A set of double doors soon presented themselves, and proved a portal into a broad space fronted by stainless-steel countering and many glass-fronted units. Therein the equipment was an endless supply of available sustenance, as well as a long stretch of serving buffets, all of which were shut down, likely due to the hour. Walking over to a display of fruit, she took a tray and helped herself to an orange. An apple. A cookie wrapped in cellophane. A bottle of water. A premade sandwich—

Rahvyn stopped, the sense that she was being watched calling her to look over her shoulder.

Past all of the food offerings, there was an open area fitted with tables and chairs, the well-lit consumption gallery capable of accommodating a hundred diners or more.

It was empty. Except for one person.

There, far, far in the back, facing the wall, but turned to look at her . . .

. . . was Nate.

CHAPTER FORTY-ONE

As Balz tracked the footfalls overhead, he did a quick dive into the firepower duffle and took out two clips and another autoloader. Up on the first floor, someone was definitely moving around and it was not Erika. She wasn't due back yet, for one thing, and more to the point, he knew what she sounded like as she went around her home.

Going over to the base of the stairs, he willed off the lights and plunged the cellar into darkness. Then, being careful to stay out of the area where the illumination from the kitchen would stream down the stairwell, he trained both guns up at the closed door.

And waited. Sooner or later, they would come down to the basement.

The footfalls were heavy, and sure enough, they got closer to the cellar door. Balz remained as rock solid as the carpet-covered concrete he was standing on, certain that whoever it was, *whatever* it was . . . wasn't a shadow. They didn't weigh anything to make that kind of sound—

"I'm not the target you're looking for," came a dry voice on the far side of that closed door.

"Lassiter?" He lowered the guns. "What are you—"

The angel opened things up. "Well, you texted me—"

"—doing here?"

"—to come over, like I'm going to ignore that?"

"I didn't actually hit send."

"Oh, I smell spaghetti. Do you have any left?"

As the Scribe Virgin's replacement came down the wooden steps, Balz had a moment of what-if-it's-not-really-him, but then the subtle glimmer of the male's halo registered—and that demon had a lot of things floating around her, but not anything that was like sunshine.

"You know, Balz, you didn't have to choose your wording so carefully." The angel marched right over to the chair next to the couch and sat down. "I mean, come on, my English skills top sitcom level at best. I'm not even on one-hour dramas when it comes to vocabulary."

Balz blinked. Then he willed the lights back on and went over to the couch. "Okay. And ah, no, I ate all the pasta."

"Bummer. But that's cool, I'll hit a Domino's on the way home. Pizza Hut is too rough on the stomach."

As Balz sat down, too, he tucked the guns behind one of the cushions. Then he eased forward and plugged his elbows into his knees.

"What do you have on your mind," Lassiter asked gently.

"If you knew I was texting you without me hitting send, you know what I'm thinking about."

"Humor me anyway. Besides, it's nice to hear ourselves talk, isn't it? I mean, I've always found that to be true, especially if the 'ourselves' in a question happens to be me." The angel pointed to himself. "But I'll give you the stage and mic right now."

As Lassiter settled back and got comfortable, crossing his legs knee to knee, as opposed to assuming the more classic air-your-junk lap triangle that most males did, the guy looked like he couldn't decide whether to be a member of a hair band or a gentleman's club. The blond-and-black locks on his head and the Steven Tyler–ribboned layers of black and red on his body voted the former. His elegant hands and composure suggested the latter.

"I need to know . . ." Balz cleared his throat and glanced around Erika's cellar. Then he laughed in a short, hard burst as he thought about that phone call he'd tried to have with V. "I'm not sure you're going to even hear what I'm saying."

"We're four feet away from each other. But if you want to go the charades route, that's fine with me. It'll slow us down, but the element of guesswork could be fun. Plus exercise. Word."

"What are you . . ." Balz tried to stay on track. "I'm sorry, but I'm not following you."

There was a brief pause. Then Lassiter lost the jokey-jokey. "You want to know if the demon's still in you."

"Is she? I-I've been keeping myself awake for the last week, but I fell asleep today. Twice. And she didn't come for me in my dreams."

Lassiter focused on his fingernails, inspecting the cuticles as if he were a manicurist who didn't approve of the job someone else had done on them, his brows all tight, his mouth a line.

"I know what she's been doing to you," the angel murmured.

Balz looked away. "It's fine—"

"No, it's not. It's a violation."

"I don't want to talk about that. It's all just in dreams, anyway. There's no reason to get hysterical over a nightmare, right? It's not really happening."

"It's totally wrong of her. But I'm not going to force you to go into it. I think you might want to see Mary, though."

"Ah, Rhage's *shellan*, the source of all personal realignment, the chiropractor to the conscience." But he wasn't bitching, more just exhausted. "Besides, maybe she's out of me. The demon, I mean. So it's a nonissue."

It was then that he looked pointedly at the other male. And as he met the strange, silvery eyes of the angel, he was aware he was projecting both hope and desperation, which were not the kinds of things a fighter ever let anybody see—except maybe his female.

But he was beyond caring about pride.

Lassiter took a deep breath and slowly closed his lids. Then everything went quiet, no more whistling from the furnace or blowing through the vents or ambient noises from outside like a passing car or a dog barking. It was as if the volume had been turned down on the whole world.

As Balz waited for the verdict, he almost would have preferred to stay in the unknown. That way, at least there was a chance he was alone in his own skin—

Lassiter's eyes popped open, and his frown was not a good sign.

"Oh, shit," Balz muttered as he—

"I can't sense her. At all."

Balz jerked in surprise. "What?"

"I can't . . ." The angel's eyes pulled a head-to-toe on Balz, and still, he didn't look happy. "I'm not picking up anything."

"Nothing? Wait, that's good, right? That's what we want?" Balz patted himself, feeling like he was knocking on doors and hoping nobody answered. "What's wrong? I don't get why you're not psyched."

He had so many questions, but the lilt to his voice was more the unexpected good news giving his mood a hot-air balloon ride.

Fuck, he'd end everything with a question mark for the rest of his life if Devina was gone.

"And you're saying she didn't come to you?" Lassiter asked.

"No, and I really was asleep. Erika and I had—well, anyway, we were sleeping." Balz sat even farther forward on the sofa, so far he was almost off the cushions. "But listen, you were right. You told me that true love would save me. You told me the Book was not the answer. Erika is . . . *she's* the savior I needed."

He was talking faster and faster, and he had to pull back a little before he Tom Cruise'd on the couch and turned the angel into Oprah. But the pieces were fitting together. Everything was becoming clear, and it was good.

It was right.

"I know she's human." He splayed out his hands, all whoa-Nelly-I-know. "And I realize I haven't known her for long. But when true love shows up on your doorstep, you don't make it wait a calendar year just to be sure it doesn't belong to somebody else."

Lassiter smiled a little. "I'm glad I was right."

"Me, too. I know there are things to be worked out." He left the integration between worlds part deliberately vague. "But I'm just . . . well, I'm really grateful to you."

"I didn't do anything." The angel put his palms up in impotence. "The Creator is as the Creator does."

"But you gave Erika the power to keep me alive."

Lassiter got to his feet in a sharp surge. "I don't know what you're talking about. Like I said, I'm glad everything is working out for you— and for her. She's a fine female. Worthy of all the good things, especially with what she's been through."

"I couldn't agree more."

In the pause that followed, Balz prepared his see-ya-laters. But instead of leaving, the angel stalled out. And just stood there.

"What," Balz demanded.

The angel opened his mouth. Closed it. "Nothing. You enjoy your female, 'kay?"

And then justlikethat, Lassiter was gone, ghosting himself into thin air in the blink of an eye.

Left to his little lonesome, Balz sat back on the cushions—and wondered what exactly that male was keeping to himself.

◆   ◆   ◆

As Erika reached across the Honda's parking brake for her bag, the irony that she was a homicide detective about to call in a missing, possibly stolen, unmarked police car was not lost on her. But as soon as she checked her cell's screen, the issue of where her service vehicle was became a second-in-line candidate on her problem list.

Her phone had blown up. Per usual, she'd had the thing silenced—with no vibrating—so she'd missed calls from Trey. A lot of calls. As well as at least ten texts from him.

Hitting him back, she put the phone to her ear and waited for him to—

Her call was answered after the first ring. "Erika?"

"Hey, Trey. What's going on—"

"Jesus Christ, where have you been!"

"At home—"

"No, not at home. I checked on your house twice last night and then again just—"

"Wait, when—" Her partner was talking so fast and so loudly, she had to raise her voice to cut in. "When did you come by my house?"

"Around ten last night. And then at just past midnight. And finally about ten minutes ago, I used the key you gave me and walked around—"

"You did *what?*"

"You gave me a key, remember? 'In case something happens,' to quote you—"

"Oh, God. I forgot that. And Trey, you shouldn't have gone in there."

"—as well as 'in the event you went radio silent'—"

"Being out of touch for twelve hours is not radio silent—"

"Are you kidding me?" Trey cursed. "Erika, what am I supposed to think after you'd been to that scene on Primrose, and looked like holy hell in the Bull Pen yesterday—and then I find your car down by the river when I was working a scene that came in overnight—"

"Excuse me?"

Her partner took a deep breath. "All that's not really important. What I care about—"

"You found my car?"

"Yeah, down two streets in from the bridge where people go to jump off because the fencing is low and still hasn't been replaced by the city." Trey's voice broke. "I know the kind of stress you're under. You take your job really seriously and we're understaffed. I'm down to the bone, too. But you add on top of that stress what you saw at Primrose. I just . . . maybe I overreacted, and I'm sorry I went through your house. But I didn't know what the hell else to do. You're always available. I've never not been able to get a call or a text back. I was shitting myself that something really bad happened to you."

Fuck. "Look, I'm really sorry I worried you."

"It's okay. As long as *you're* okay."

"Ah, listen, Trey." As a car got blocked in behind her on the one-way street, she had to move up. "When you went to my house—"

"Your security system wasn't on. And yes, I was sure I locked everything back up behind me."

The memory thing, Erika thought. Of course, Balthazar had stripped his memories.

She relaxed. "Well, like I said, I'm sorry I worried you. I just crashed last night. I turned my phone off and just passed out."

"So where are you now?"

"Looking for my car, actually."

"I've got it. I brought it in to headquarters because I thought . . . well, anyway—"

"You thought I wasn't coming back."

"I thought you weren't coming back, ever," he conceded. "You and I both know the burnout for homicide detectives is high. You're one of the best that the department has ever had because you take everything so seriously. Except you're overworked and you're getting ragged, and I know my wife is going to get on me for saying this, but you really shouldn't have gone to that Primrose scene. You should have listened to me."

Erika closed her eyes and remembered her and Balthazar sitting on her my-favorite-color-is-blue sofa, her blubbering like an idiot, him holding her, even after she'd told him what she had. Then she recalled showing him her scars.

"You're right, Trey. I shouldn't have gone there. It was more than I could handle. Sometimes I feel like I have to push through, though. Otherwise, I'm going to be hamstrung by what happened to me and my family."

As her fingertips crept up to her collarbone and probed her uneven skin, Trey said, "You just take a couple of days off, okay? Don't worry about everything here. Kip and I are on it, and yes, we'll update you. And then I want you to come back—I want my partner back. We need you. Caldwell's victims need you. And it's so much better to take some time and recenter now, than to flame out and not be able to do the job at all. That's reality, not weakness."

Erika focused out the Honda's front windshield and wasn't surprised that her vision got wavy as tears came to her eyes. She didn't feel anything, though.

No . . . that wasn't quite right. She felt something, it was just very deep, and really painful so she was shutting it out.

"You know," she said hoarsely, "I've always done this job for myself. To make peace with my personal demons. It never occurred to me that . . ."

"That you were helping people? That your partner and your division depended on you? Come on, Erika, get real. You didn't think we were just enjoying your charming personality, did you?"

She laughed in a rush and brushed under her eyes. "Fine. I'll take a little time off—but I want to be kept in the loop. Everything is still cc'd with me, and if there are any problems, I want you to call me."

"Fine. It's a deal. Talk to you soon, partner."

As Trey hung up the phone, she took her cell away from her ear and just stared at the thing. Then she looked out the side window. Trey was right. She was down close to the river. Just two blocks over and she could have gotten herself up on a bridge where there was a big drop and a lot of cold water.

Instantly, she was back in the bookshop's storage room, and Balthazar had that knife to his own throat—

She covered her eyes, even though what she did not want to see was not in front of her, but in her mind.

And then she saw the pink bedroom at the Primrose scene, that young hand with its carefully polished pink fingernails still around the butt of that gun.

Finally, she remembered the first suicide attempt she herself had made in college. Then the other two. It was after the third stomach pumping that she'd called the psychiatrist. As helpful as the guy had tried to be, it wasn't those sessions that had changed things—and it certainly hadn't been the antidepressants she'd been prescribed but hadn't taken.

In the end, she had stopped with trying to kill herself because she hadn't wanted to get out of the punishment of staying alive. Her living and breathing, and suffering, seemed like the penance she deserved for having stood there and watched as her mother had begged her for help.

And she'd done nothing but watch the killing.

Dying was easy. The living was the much harder option.

With the decision made, she'd never thought again about taking pills with vodka. She'd just stopped with the suicidal ideation. But it was weird. Sitting here in this old silver Honda, which had been provided to her by vampires, with her lover in her basement hiding from the sunlight, and a dear friend and colleague having been worried she'd jumped off a bridge . . . she found herself very grateful to be alive.

Even if suffering was the only reason for her survival.

CHAPTER FORTY-TWO

In the subterranean healing place's cafeteria, Rahvyn walked with her tray through a maze of empty tables and chairs as Nate got to his feet. He seemed taller than she remembered somehow, although maybe that was just because they were truly alone for the first time. Previously, there had always been others around, at Luchas House, at the club of Dandelion, here in this facility.

"I'm glad you came to eat," he said as he pulled out the chair across from where he sat.

"I just woke up."

"Me, too."

As she lowered herself, he helped her move the chair in, even though such action would not have been a hard thing for her to do. And then he was across from her and she was peeling her orange and he was picking up a half-eaten sandwich.

They ate in silence for a while, and it was the kind of silence that seemed to permeate everything. Here at the far-back of the eating area, with those doors shut and nobody else getting or making food, they were insulated not only from immediate noise, but from the sounds of the larger enterprise.

"You have questions," she said eventually.

"Well, yeah."

"I am not surprised. It is a lot to comprehend—"

"I'm always waiting for you to leave," he blurted. And then he clapped his mouth shut as if he'd surprised himself by speaking thus.

"I am sorry." And in those words, was she not apologizing for so much more than his worry? "Truly."

"You know, I come to Luchas House and I always expect you to be gone." He wiped his mouth with a paper napkin. "And I mean, that's your right. Totally. Except I feel like we're . . . friends. So I don't want you to go, and if you do, I want a chance to say goodbye to you."

She went quiet for a bit. Then whispered, "I am not sure how to respond."

He shrugged and finished his bread and meats. "At least you're not lying to me and saying you're staying. But where are you going? And when?"

"That I do not know."

Nate stared into his empty plate, and she wondered what exactly he was seeing in the plain white china. "Do you have to go?"

"When one does not belong, one is always leaving even whilst staying put."

"You could belong, though." His eyes flashed up to hers. "There are people who care about you, who support you. Who want you to stay."

Ah, but she had been exposed, hadn't she. With what she had done to him, she had tipped her hand in ways that were going to complicate things. The Black Dagger Brotherhood and their fighting comrades were devoted unto the survival of the species, and though they were males of worth, her power was something they would want in their hands. And beyond them, there were always others who would seek to capture and control her and the magic she possessed.

"Nate, I am always going to be grateful for your friendship—"

He held up his forefinger to stop her. "You know, when I said I'd like to say goodbye, I was kind of hoping it wouldn't be today."

She thought back to the Old Country and being hunted by that aristocrat. "My presence is not always welcome."

"How can you say that? You're super nice. And you're . . . well, really nice."

His expression tightened as if he wished he had chosen other words. She wanted to tell him it was fine, it was all okay. If there was awkwardness, it was on her side of the table.

"Rahvyn, I don't want to put anything on you, but I really hope you hang here a little longer because I don't understand what I am now. And I kind of feel I might learn best from you what this all means." He put up his hand. "Not that I'm not grateful. I just—so here's a question . . . if I jump in front of a speeding train, I don't die? Is that what this is? If I get shot in the head, do I walk around bleeding for the rest of eternity or do I heal? Do I age? What if I turn into a rotting old guy, you know? I mean, what . . . happens to me?"

Rahvyn could only shake her head. "You will be as you are now, no matter what is done to you, no matter the passage of time."

He fidgeted in his chair, as if the enormity of it all was occurring to him and the stress was nearly too much to contain. Thus he shifted the conversation—and she could not blame him. "I talked to Shuli, by the way. He FaceTimed me."

"He heard then you were hurt, yes."

"Yeah. He was . . . I don't know, maybe he was just drunk still, but he was really emotional." Nate shrugged. "I was kind of amazed. He's totally about himself most of the time, you know?"

"He is much bluster—but that can be fun. In his heart, he is pure."

"He says he's never going to Dandelion again."

"It was nice inside. I liked the flowers." She frowned. "That was one of the last things I said to you, wasn't it."

"I just remember stepping outside the club and seeing that man on the ground, the bouncer. You were really nice to him. You knelt down and then came the pops." Nate shook his head. "It didn't hurt very much. I thought if you died . . . it was supposed to hurt."

"I would not know."

There was another period of silence. "Rahvyn?"

"Yes?"

"Are you like me? Or, I mean, am I like you?"

She focused on him properly, seeing him for the handsome young male he was—and yet recalling all that had been done to him in that lab. Indeed, she had been inside his brain, not because she had sought to take something from him, but because he had welcomed her with his emotions. In offering empathy to her, he had created a connection that had given his past over.

She had been horrified by all that he had endured.

"In some ways," she said softly, "I am very much like you."

He nodded a little. Then looked her straight in the eye. "Promise me you won't leave without telling me."

As she considered what she had burdened him with, there was one and only one reply to give him. Reaching across the table, she put her hand on his.

"I promise," she vowed.

CHAPTER FORTY-THREE

Erika ended up leaving the silver Honda a couple of blocks over from CPD headquarters. Locking things, she took the key, and as she started walking away, she was struck by the fine spring air. Downtown could be nasty as a proverbial armpit—particularly in August, down by the restaurants, when the dumpsters became stews of decaying food—but not today. Even with the trucks rumbling by, and the cars, and the pedestrians who smoked, there was only the smell of earth and growing things.

As she walked up to the place where she worked, she paused and stared at the building. It was modern, but not in a contemporary architecture sense. Modern for the Caldwell Police Department building was rows of windows you couldn't open, no adornments or design work anywhere, and six entrances with metal detectors in them. Basically every municipal structure erected in the sixties.

And yet it meant a lot to her.

Trey's conversation had opened her eyes. Or maybe her new perspective was from Balthazar this morning when he'd accepted her brokenness so easily. Either way, she was seeing everything from a fresh viewpoint.

The idea that she was making a difference for people who had been through what she had? That was a balm of sorts to her pain—and one she hadn't recognized she'd been applying to the scars she carried on the inside.

A solace she had instinctively identified and self-medicated with.

Funny, how you could take care of yourself without even knowing.

Heading down to the back of the building, she entered the parking lot. Trey had put her car at the far end, right in front of the impound dock. When she came up to it, the backup key fob was in the cup holders in the center console between the seats, just like he'd said. As she got in and started the engine, she felt like she should be checking in with someone. She supposed she had.

Leaving the lot, she glanced in her rear view and watched the gate arm fall back into place behind her. For a panicked moment, she worried whether she was going to have some instinct hit that told her these two or three days off were going to turn into forever. When nothing like that came, she was relieved, even though she'd never been psychic or anything.

The Northway was not that far, but courtesy of a broken water main, she got rerouted and then missed a turn. The next thing she knew, she was in a different part of downtown, less skyscraper, more upscale-ish retail. Passing by some of the shops, she saw things in the windows like dresses and pants and blouses—

The parking spot appeared from out of nowhere, the lineup of perma-parked, grille-to-tailpipe cars broken by a perfectly beautiful metered space.

Why she backed into the vacancy, she had no clue. And when she got out, she was still confused.

But then she looked at the facade of the Ann Taylor store and saw a dress . . . that also did not make a lot of sense. It was red. A bright red, with a deep V for the bodice and a skirt that was way too short—which for Erika meant it was just slightly above the knee.

"I don't have any change to put in the meter."

As she spoke, a guy walked by her and looked at her like he was wondering why he was being informed of this.

"Well, it's true," she muttered at his back.

Turning to her car, she told herself she did not need a dress, and most certainly not a dress like *that*—

The meter had thirty minutes left on it.

Glancing over her shoulder, she pictured herself wearing it in front of Balthazar. Except that was crazy. They weren't going on any dates.

She needed to be practical and just let it go. God, one good night of sex and she was reimagining her whole life. How ridiculous—

Erika froze. At first, she wasn't sure whether she was seeing things right. But a blink later, and nothing had changed: That guy with the blond-and-black hair, the one who had helped her save Balthazar's life, was standing right next to the front entrance of the Ann Taylor store. He was unmistakable, really, and not just because of his size.

There was a glow about him, a shimmer that seemed to emanate from him.

He was staring at her . . . and then his eyes made a slow scan of her body, traveling from her head to her feet. When they returned to her face, his expression changed, shifting from a reserved mask to someone completely brokenhearted.

As if somebody close to him had just died.

Or he'd figured out she had terminal cancer.

Forgetting all about both parking and dresses she had no business buying, Erika pulled her coat closer to herself and started forward toward him. An uneven lip on the sidewalk caught the toe of her shoe, though, and she pitched forward, nearly pulling a pratfall on the concrete.

When she recovered her balance, the man—or whatever he was—was gone.

Dear God, what did he know about her that she didn't?

◆   ◆   ◆

Ten minutes later, Erika had thrown off that weird exchange she'd had out on the street, and she was in an Ann Taylor dressing room with not just the red dress, but two skirts, a set of leggings, three shirts that did not have a "t" in front of them, and a "kicky, fun wrap" that Kelley, her "sales associate," had told her was just perfect for the transitional weather of April and May.

Transitional weather for Erika was rain before it turned to snow.

Apparently here in this store, however, it meant something altogether different—and further, all of the "transitional" clothes had to be color-coordinated to her "palette." Which was not what you tasted dinner with. Oh, and she was a winter? What the hell did that mean?

She was a cold fish?

Ha! Balthazar had proven that one wrong. And then some.

Feeling like an idiot for trying anything on, she dumped her jacket, stripped off her pants and her fleece and shirt, and then shivered as she took the red dress off its hanger. It took a little more effort than she'd thought to square it on her shoulders and her waist, but then the thing was on her right. At least, she thought it was on right. Bending over to give the skirt another pull, she—

"What the hell?"

With a frown, she put her right foot up on the little chair in the corner of the changing room. On the inside of her ankle, there was a dark bruise that ran up to the base of her calf. Lifting the skirt higher, she found another on her knee.

Well, if that was the price she had to pay for the best sex she'd ever had? She'd wear the contusions with pride, damn it.

And hey . . . check her out. For once, she wasn't running to Dr. Google to find out what dreaded disease she had. Ordinarily, she'd be convinced it was a sign she was—

She thought of the way that man had looked at her outside on the sidewalk. As a shiver of unease returned to her, she tried to push all the hypochondria away.

"What do we think?" Kelley asked on the other side of the privacy curtain.

Dropping her foot as well as the bottom of the dress, Erika smoothed things and refocused on her reflection. Of course this was going to be a no. Why would she think otherwise?

"It's really low-cut." She ran her fingers over her scars. They might as well have been a set of pearls she was trying to show off. "I don't think it's for me."

"May I see?"

"Ah . . ."

After a moment, Erika pulled the curtain back mostly because the girl had been cheerfully pushy and she had a feeling that if she didn't show the problem, there was going to be a lot of long, hypothetical discussions involving necklines.

Kelley smiled. "Oh, it's—"

And then it happened, as of course, it always did. The drop of the eyes. The frozen expression. After which would come the symphony of sympathy that grated in the ears.

She should never have come here—

"The size is perfect for you," Kelley said. "The waist is amazing and I wish I had your legs. Would it be okay to suggest something?"

If it's plastic surgery, Erika thought dryly, *I had them looked at a long time ago and the surgeon said there wasn't much he could do about it all.*

"I'll be right back," Kelley declared. "I hope you stay in the dress."

The curtain was pulled into place, and oddly, that was the moment Erika realized that she hadn't really noticed the woman. Not what hair color she had, what she was wearing, her height or weight. Erika was so incredibly out of her element that her mind was a sieve. All she could remember was the name.

Two minutes later, Kelley pulled the curtain back again—oh, interesting. The woman was in her early twenties and a redhead. Who knew.

"I think this will be perfect."

When she held something out, Erika wasn't sure what the object was: Shiny. Gold. A drape of . . . links.

"That's a necklace," she said stupidly.

"Yes."

For some reason, Erika reached out and took it from the woman. As her hands were shaking, and Kelley stepped in behind her and helped her put it on.

And then Erika looked at herself in the mirror.

The dress was the same. The necklace made everything different: The links formed a loose pattern all the way down the V of the bodice.

If you knew there were scars, you could kind of see them. If you didn't? You wouldn't really notice them. All you'd see was a woman in a really kick-ass red dress.

Erika touched the links. Tilted her head at her reflection.

Then she turned around.

And hugged a stranger.

CHAPTER FORTY-FOUR

Down in Erika's cellar, Balz was pacing back and forth in front of the washer-dryer units. With his cell phone up to his ear, he was ready for an argument, and on so many levels, he hated being at the mercy of another person.

But something hadn't been right as Lassiter had left, and the angel was not answering texts or calls. So he was back at square one, with his instincts telling him that he needed to go back to basics. Devina wasn't in him, but if he wanted to find out where she was . . . he felt like he probably could use the—

"Hello?"

Balz stopped walking. "Hey, sorry to wake you."

"No, it's cool." Sahvage's voice was quiet. "Let me get out of bed, though."

There was some rustling, a couple of words spoken to the Brother's *shellan*, then the sound of a kiss. After which, footfalls and a door closing.

"What's up?" the Brother asked in a more normal volume. "Helluva night you had."

"Guess you've heard, huh."

"Yeah. Look, I know we have our differences of opinion, but God's honest, I'm glad you're okay."

"Thanks, man. And on that note . . . I gotta talk to you and I'm not trying to piss you off. Honest."

There was a pause. "Let me get something first."

There was more rustling. Then the *shhhhscht* of a beer getting opened. "Talk to me."

"I don't mean any disrespect."

"Whatever it is, I believe that."

"And I am not trying to shit on your parade."

"Didn't know I had one, but generally speaking, the less poop, the better in any situation, so thank you."

"You know I don't think the Book's been destroyed." Balz started up with the pacing again. "And before you tell me to fuck off, yes, I realize I wasn't there when you and Mae were going rounds with Devina in that fire. But I've been to the site. There's no way that thing was destroyed. No way—"

"You really need to talk to someone else about this," the Brother cut in with exhaustion. "I've given my honest opinion, and I'm not interested in arguing with you—"

"Devina's still alive as of a night ago. I saw her."

Cue the pause. "Wait, what?"

"She stood right in front of me."

Sahvage cursed and there was another beat of silence. "So I guess this is why we got a meeting scheduled before First Meal today, huh."

"If she's still around, so is the Book."

The sounds of big gulps of beer were like a heart rhythm. And then a deep exhale came over the connection. "I guess I'm not really surprised. I'd had some hope, you know. But . . . whatever. I'll fight her again. I don't give a fuck—"

"Well, see, that's why I called. I need your help."

Upstairs, the sound of a door opening and closing was followed by footsteps he instantly recognized.

Balz spoke quickly, but he didn't scramble his words. He made sure they were clear. And as the door to the cellar opened, he ended the call and looked up. Erika was standing at the top of the staircase, her body a dark silhouette.

"Hey," she said. "Sorry that took so long, but I did some shopping. I've got no food in this house."

"Hi," he murmured. "You need help unpacking the car?"

"It's too light out. It's just after four, so give me a minute? I don't want you to get hurt."

He frowned as he wanted to bring *all* the groceries in. Like, for the rest of the woman's life, he didn't want a single bag in her hand. Ever.

"Okay," he said with frustration. "I'll wait here."

The door shut again, and he paced like a caged tiger as he heard her go back and forth and back and forth across the kitchen. When there was a final door closing, over at the garage, he had some idea she'd come back down immediately, but she didn't.

She was using the ladies room.

Finally, the cellar door opened once again. "So," she said as she started to come down the steps, "I found my car and took a couple days off of work—"

He met her halfway and swept her into his arms. Bending her back, so that she relied on his strength to keep her steady, he put his lips on hers.

And kissed the ever-living shit out of his female.

When he paused to take a breath, she was panting. "You sure do know how to make a girl feel missed."

All he could do was growl a little. Then he scooped her up in his arms and backed down to the floor.

"I did miss you." He sat her on the armchair, knelt down in front of her, and started off'ing her shoes. "Here, let me help you out of these. You look really uncomfortable."

"Do I?" Her smile was lazy. And hot. "You're a mind reader, aren't you."

"I sure am." He tossed one shoe over his shoulder. "And you know what you're thinking right now?"

"Tell me."

Balz tossed the other shoe over his other shoulder. "You're thinking you wanted me to go down on you all afternoon, every second we were apart."

As she gasped, he went to work on her pants, popping the button and then lowering the zipper. "Am I wrong?"

"Well, I'd be lying if I said I didn't like it when you—"

"Guess what?" He stripped off her pants—and took her panties with them.

"What?" she said breathlessly.

"I can also see into the future." Balz lowered his chin and stared out from under his brows at her. "You're about to have seven orgasms, right under my tongue."

◆   ◆   ◆

Erika went from hassled to desperately, sexually starved in the fifteen-foot distance between when Balthazar started kissing her on the stairs and when he put her into the chair. Or was she on the sofa?

Who the hell cared. She wasn't on the floor, that was all she knew for sure.

And she was also half undressed.

And fully aroused.

"I think you're right," she moaned as he grabbed the backs of her knees and yanked her forward to him.

He hissed through his front teeth as he spread her legs by running his hands up the insides of her thighs. And then he lowered his head, curling that huge back of his forward. She felt the first brush of his lips on her knee. After that, they were where his palms had been.

Taking his time, he nipped and licked his way to her core.

She expected him to tease her.

Nope.

As she speared her fingers through his hair, in anticipation of having to pull his face right into her, he went for it himself.

She got a full-on seal of his lips, and the sucking sent her right over the edge.

Calling out his name, Erika threw her head back and yanked at his hair. Not that he seemed to notice or care. He just made love to her with his mouth, his nose, his face, and the harder she orgasmed, the more he made her come.

Which didn't make any sense.

But it just proved that he was correct. He could see into the future.

She loved it so much that she was starting to come again already.

On his side, Balthazar was raw and unhinged, and he just kept at it, urging her to release more and more. And God, the sight of him between her legs, at her core, staring up at her as if he were drinking in her pleasure with his eyes? It was almost too much to bear.

It went on for what felt like hours. And when he finally lifted himself up from her, she was boneless and lying wide open, her sex throbbing and hypersensitive. But she wanted him to come, too.

Before she could tell him to take those sweatpants down, he yanked off the sweatshirt and then pulled the bottoms off, and she was treated to a spectacular show of muscle—that only got even better as he propped himself up with one hand and palmed his erection with the other.

"I want to fuck you," he growled as he started to pump himself. "I want to fuck you so hard . . ."

He ejaculated all over her, the hot jets streaming down the folds of her sex, coating the insides of her thighs, hitting her lower belly. And then, when he should have been more than sated, he plunged into her core and pumped into her.

As he rode her hard, and she hung on to his sweat-slicked shoulders, she had a thought that this was not a man she was with.

This was another thing entirely—and what was happening between them was something so much more than just sex.

She felt as though he was staking some kind of claim to her.

And damn it, she wanted everyone to know she was his.

CHAPTER FORTY-FIVE

After the fall of night, Rahvyn returned unto Luchas House. Or perhaps, more properly, "was returned." As if she were a satchel mislaid.

The van that took her back was driven by one of the social workers, and there was another male with her, one who had had a foot broken whilst playing a game called "basketball" and had had to have the bone set within a case. During the travel, Rahvyn said not much a'tall. The male and the social worker, on the other hand, chatted about all manner of trivialities, a relief really.

When there seemed not much relief to be found anywhere.

Upon arrival at the house, Rahvyn made her excuses and said that she required air. What she had intended was a return to the destination that had been pulling at her ever since that dream of the book. What she was granted was a reprieve of some short amount of time, after which the social worker was going to "come check on her."

An anger, deep and sour, curled in Rahvyn's gut at the kind shepherding—and she was well aware of where that emotion led.

Therefore, she nodded and walked away from the house, into the barren field. Out under a cloudy sky that offered no moon and no stars for illumination, she was struck both by the calling that refused to relent and a conviction that she would not hurt the compassionate female.

She could have, though. If she'd been so inclined.

And therein was another inner conflict she did not enjoy.

"Oh . . . whatever shall I do," she whispered into the night.

The question was not *wherever shall I go*. She knew the answer to the inquiry of destination. Knew also that she was setting into motion monstrous things, the implications of which should have shocked her into inactivity. But sure as if she had been marked, there was no way of stopping any of what was about to transpire.

That book, the one from her dreamscape, was not only calling her, it was demanding that she come unto its location. And she knew what it was asking of her, knew as well why she was the one it had chosen—

"I had to see you."

Rahvyn spun around. When she saw the angel with the long blond-and-black hair, her first instinct was to smile. But then she remembered who she truly was—and who he mistakenly thought she was.

"Hello," she whispered.

He took a step toward her, and in the darkness, she could see a tightness in his face, in his body. Had he somehow divined what she intended? she thought with a sudden shame. Could he read her mind?

"I just want you to know something," he said, his face grim. "It's not going to make a lot of sense to you. Or maybe it will. I don't know."

"What is wrong? What ails you?"

"I have to save two people tonight. I have to . . . sacrifice something to save them. And after this, it's all going to be different. For me. For . . . you."

In the silence that followed, Rahvyn was so struck by the magnificence he carried within him that she momentarily forgot her own troubles.

"May I help you?" she inquired.

"No, I have to go alone." He seemed so full of sorrow, she wanted to embrace him. "I just want you to know something, before I leave."

As he stared down into her eyes, she had a feeling that she knew what he was going to tell her.

His revelation had been foretold during his visit unto her healing bed, when he had hovered o'er her slumbering body and yearned for her. Verily, if he had known she was aware of him, he would have hidden his true intentions.

"From the first moment I saw you," he said in a hoarse voice, "that night when Sahvage and Mae came here . . . there was just something about you. I couldn't look away."

Flushing, she glanced down at her hands. "I could feel you staring upon me."

"I didn't mean to freak you out."

"You did not." And then, maybe due to the fact that she herself was departing, she added, "I rather liked your eyes upon me. Not just then, but later. And now, in this moment."

There was a pause. As if she had surprised him.

"You came to see me at the healing place," she said as she looked back up at him. "I sensed your presence o'er my bedding platform."

"I needed to make sure you were okay."

"And if I had not been . . . ?"

"I would have done what was required to save you."

Tears entered her eyes, putting a gloss over her vision that blurred him and the meadow. "Why," she breathed.

An eternity of silence stretched out between them. And then he reached out and brushed her cheek.

When he dropped his hand, she smelled the scent—and could not understand it. Why would the perfume of fresh flowers be out—

Rahvyn gasped.

Looking down at their feet, she saw violets spring up from the scruffy ground, the fragile purple blooms unfurling, little flags upon green nests. And among them sprouted also daisies and dandelions, then other colorful blooms, all of the heads lifting free of the soil, maturing as if it were July, not April, as if the air were warm, not chilled.

The rush of wild flowers swirled around them both, encompassing their vicinity in the meadow, bringing daylight unto the night—and Rahvyn was so o'ercome, she let out a sound of delight and swept her hands to the sky. In a twirl, she imagined that she could gather them up in her arms, a sight for sore eyes, a lift for a heavy heart, a sniff into a grateful, astounded nose.

And then she stilled.

Lowering her arms, she saw that he remained grim. "Are you leaving right the now?"

He took a step back. "I just wanted to give you something beautiful, so you can feel even a little of the wonder I have whenever I look into your eyes."

"Where are you going," she asked in a desperation that she did not understand. "Lassiter, where do you go?"

He stopped. "You know my name."

"I . . . yes, I do. Of course, I do." She wrung her hands, an anxiety striking her. "Oh, Lassiter."

Riding a sudden surge of emotion, she jumped into the space between them, and the instant she did, he caught her, his arms wrapping around her and drawing her flush against his strong body. With his great strength, he lifted her easily from the wild flowers he had created for her, holding her so tight that they nearly became one. And in response, she attempted to encircle his shoulders. They were far too large, so she settled for his neck to hold him back.

She had the sense this was a beginning for them.

But also an end.

And in the poignancy of the moment, so consumed was she . . . that she missed the young male who stood at the edge of the meadow, a bouquet of flowers dropping from his hand, his heart as shattered as hers, from an altogether different cause.

She was still embracing the angel as Nate turned back to Luchas House.

Walked around the far side.

And took off into the dark, cold night.

Alone.

CHAPTER FORTY-SIX

I need you to know something."

Erika and Balthazar were upstairs in her bed when he spoke up, the blankets on the floor, the sheets tangled around their still cooling bodies, only one pillow still within reach. Not that she was interested in moving at all in the dim room.

"That sounds ominous." She was so relaxed that lifting her head was a struggle—so she just turned herself over and laid its heavy weight on her upper arm. "What's wrong?"

"That night you found me by that human woman who had been killed. In the trap house."

Between one blink and the next, she caught a vivid, hard-to-see image of Connie's body on that dirty mattress. "Yes?"

"I went to find her because I tried to buy some cocaine off her boyfriend down by the river." He put a hand up. "I don't do drugs recreationally. I was trying to stay awake because every time I fell asleep, the demon . . . well, you know what she did."

Oh, God, Erika thought. He'd been down there ... with Christopher Ernest Olyn. That dealer who'd shot himself in the head.

Supposedly.

"What did you do to him," she said tightly.

"Look, I was desperate. I just needed to stay awake because I couldn't take Devina anymore. I even went to Vishous—the Brother with the goatee—and told him ... well, I'm going to have to apologize to him for what I asked him to do to me."

"What did you ask him." Even though, going by the expression on his face, she knew. She knew. "Did you ask him to kill you?"

There was a long pause.

"I figured—better him than my bloodline, my leader." He shook his head. "But I don't feel like that anymore. And as for Devina, after I met you properly, I couldn't get it up anymore with her. This all happened before you were in my—I was with you. Here, with you."

Erika nodded slowly as her heart dropped. Yet somehow, she wasn't surprised by any of it.

How could she abide a murderer? The stealing, maybe she could get over. But taking a life—

"I just went down there to get the coke," he said quietly. "The guy pulled a gun on me. I didn't want to deal with the shit, so I was only going into his mind to replace the memory of me. I swear, that was it. But once I got in there—I saw from his memories what he'd done to her. What he'd been doing to her. I knew he'd beaten that woman senseless. And fuck that, you know."

Erika sat up and pushed her hair out of her face. "You made him shoot himself, didn't you."

He didn't even pause. "Yeah, I did. The fucker had been abusing that poor woman—and I knew she was in trouble. I also knew, if I could get to her and she was still alive—and I saved her? He'd just go after her again. So yeah, I had him point the gun at himself and pull the trigger." There was another pause and then he shook his head. "I know you've heard it before, but I'm not sorry. Not at all. He took a life he had no right to take, and he ruined that woman before he murdered her."

Lowering her head, Erika closed her eyes for a second time. And all she saw on the backs of them was that fetid apartment and all that blood. And Connie, a woman she herself had tried to help.

"If that changes your opinion of me," he said, "I totally understand. I guess I just want you to know all the parts that matter about me. And killing one of your species two nights ago is pretty material."

Turning her head, she looked at him. The light in the bathroom had been left on, but the door was mostly shut, so there was only a soft glow. In the near-darkness, he was a sprawl of muscle beside her, his chin and hard jawline cutting an angle up from his throat, one of his arms lying on his stomach.

She thought of the damage a male like him could do to a female.

Then thought of that drug dealer.

And after that? An image of Connie in intensive care, a machine breathing for her, homicide already summoned to the bedside, ramping up because it was clear that she was not going to make it.

Then Erika recalled the last time she saw the woman alive, when she'd gone to that apartment to try to get Connie to leave her abuser. Connie had been so terrified, she'd been shaking as she'd begged Erika to leave.

Just leave. Please leave, oh God, if he finds you here, he's going to kill me.

"I'm not sorry, either," Erika said after a long silence.

◆   ◆   ◆

Balz had not been aware of holding his breath, but as Erika's words hit the tense air between them, the relief was tremendous. It hadn't occurred to him that he'd been keeping anything from her, but when he'd thought about what he was going to do tonight, and where he was going to go, he was worried he might not be back.

And that made a male extra scrupulous with things like conscience.

"I just wanted you to know," he said. "And also, I don't go around doing that, just so we're clear. I'm not a vigilante killer who's pulling a Dexter on all kinds of people, even if they deserve it. What happened down by that river was a one-off that started because the asshole put a gun in my face."

Erika released a deep breath. Then nodded. "If I had your powers with the mind, who knows what I would have done to the guy. I'd worked with her before, you see. When he'd nearly killed her a while ago. And though I understand what you did in this particular case ... I'm glad you're not walking over that line all the time. Let's keep it that way, okay?"

"Yes, ma'am."

As he went quiet, she said, "Okay, spill the second one."

"What?"

"What else do you have to get off your chest?"

"There isn't—"

"Yup, there is. Tell me." She looked him square in the face. "G'head. Let's hear it."

Balz frowned. And then wondered if humans could read minds. Because ... there was something else, but he certainly hadn't thought of bringing it up now.

Then again, if not now, when? "Erika. You may not want to talk about it."

"Too late. And God, just say it. My mind is torturing me with all kinds of things—"

"It's about the night your family was killed." With the way she went so still, he regretted giving in. But if he honestly thought he might not come out of where he was going alive, he had to tell her now. "And I'm sorry, I didn't mean to—"

"What."

He closed his eyes briefly. "Look, sometimes we read minds when we don't mean to. It can happen when there's a connection that's deep. Things open up, things are seen."

"What did you see."

Balz rubbed his face. "Your mother, the night she was killed . . . when you came into the kitchen and your boyfriend had her and the knife. When he . . . did what he did to her—your mother wasn't yelling at you to save her. She was screaming at you to go. Erika, you've had it wrong all these years. What you saw, that fucking horrible night, and what you've convinced yourself she said, are two different things. Your memory recorded the facts. Your emotions have turned what transpired into an experience." The rain-scent of tears bloomed up in the space between them and he took her hands urgently. "Listen to me. Your mom wanted you to save yourself, not her, and you stood there because you were trapped between what you heard her yelling and what your good heart wanted you to do, which was to fight to save her. This blame you've carried around with you? It's a false burden. Let it go. Really hear, in your conscious mind, what your mother wanted you to do, and stop blaming yourself by letting that lie you've turned into a cudgel go."

Erika covered her face with her hands. "You're not making this up, are you?"

"No, that would be beyond cruel. I'm just telling you what your memory is—the foundational memory, not the one you edited because you felt responsible for it all. Because you were the one who brought him into that house, into your family, as your boyfriend."

"Oh . . . God . . ."

He wanted to hug her to him, but he had the sense she needed the space. Finding a middle ground, he stroked her back in slow circles as she held herself and rocked. It was so hard to learn the truth sometimes, even if it did set you free. It was also so hard not to take false responsibility for things.

Sometimes, what we feared most about ourselves defined our lives. Even if it was a total falsity.

After the longest time, she turned her head toward him. "How could I have gotten it all wrong."

"She was your mother. She loved you and you loved her, and survivor's guilt is a powerful editor. It's that simple."

There was a longer silence, but it was less tense, more reflective. And he gave her the time she needed . . . even though it was time for him to go.

"Thank you," she said in a voice that cracked. "Thank you for that."

"I didn't really do anything."

"Yes, you did. In a way no one else I know could have."

"You'd do the same for me."

"In a heartbeat."

Speaking of hearts, he thought. *You've stolen mine—*

"I need to know how this is going to work." Her words, as she interrupted his thought, were spoken fast. "Like, what are we doing here. Like, what is this—and I'm asking this now because I have this weird sense you're leaving me. Is that true? Are you? Because the first thing you just told me seems like a confession. And the second is like something you had to get out before . . . I don't know, you don't come back."

Jesus, she read him like a book.

Balz pushed himself up against the headboard. "Do you want me to be honest or try to play it cool?"

"Honest. Always."

He shrugged. "I want to move in here. Stay with you in this house. In the basement. Until I croak seven hundred years from now."

"Seven . . . hundred years?" she breathed.

"Give or take. And no, I don't care if you age faster. I'm going to love you any way you are—" He clapped his molars shut. "I mean. Ah."

Oh, shit. Did he just—

"Did you . . . just . . ."

"Yeah," he said on a sigh. "I think I did. I did. It's too soon, I know. I've wanted to keep it from you for at least a week or at least another night. I think I would have looked really so much more reasonable—"

She was on him before he knew it, her mouth finding his, her arms around him. After she kissed him, she said, "I love you, too."

His breath caught. And then he exhaled for what felt like a century.

With a sense of reverent gratitude, he gathered her close to him and kissed her back.

The next thing he knew, he had rolled her over and was inside of her. They had made love with all kinds of heat and desperate yearning/ desire/need before. For all those hours. But this was different. This was just a gentle rock that was about communion. And as she found her release, he let himself go as well.

So they were once again flying together.

After lovemaking was over, he settled her on top of his chest so he didn't crush her—and he really wished he didn't have to go. It was too important for them, however.

"Except I can't give up my job," she said roughly. "You told me the worlds don't mesh, and I know that there is a lot at stake, but I can't desert my colleagues. My purpose. I need it to help myself. Help others—"

"I'll make it work. Somehow, I'll figure out a way to make it work. You won't have to give up your job. There have been exceptions made before, and there'll be one for you. We might have to live somewhere that's safer for me—"

"Not a problem. I'll move anywhere around Caldwell. Anywhere we need to."

Balz started smiling, the idea there was a future for them a fantasy that he wanted to believe would come true. "Are we moving in together, then?"

"Yes, we are."

They laughed together, giddy as lovebirds. And then she had to go to the loo.

As she hopped off the bed and her naked body danced across the dim room, he was looking forward to her return. Surely they had time for one more quickie?

In the doorway of the bathroom, her breasts and hips cut a hell of a silhouette as she turned the overhead light on and looked across at him. "I'll be right back."

"Take your time," he murmured while she closed the door.

Except don't, he thought to himself as he glanced at her alarm clock.

He'd told Sahvage, Syphon, Xcor, and Tohr to meet him an hour after sunset. So actually, he probably didn't have—

"Balthazar . . ."

At the weird tone in her voice, his head snapped away from the glowing display next to her bed. "Erika? What's wrong?"

When she didn't respond, Balz flew from that bed, his feet not even touching the floor as he launched himself toward the bathroom. And as he pushed open the door, at first he couldn't figure out what he was looking at. His female was standing at the sink, one leg braced on the counter, the inside of her calf and thigh facing him.

That was when he saw the bruising.

Her skin was marked with black splotches, the pattern running from the base of her foot all the way up to—

"What is this?" she asked weakly. "What's wrong with me?"

And then she turned to him. Her entire body was mottled with discoloration, the skin like that of a corpse, gray and white and black.

"Help me . . ." she said as she collapsed.

CHAPTER FORTY-SEVEN

ime was relative. Yes. It was.

And what that meant, in the emotive sense, was that something could take an eternity and also be of a duration shorter than the blink of an eye.

For example, when the love of your life, who you'd just decided to move in with, whose bed you'd been in all afternoon and into the evening, all of a sudden turned into a contusion, the diagnosis part of things was longer than the ice age, quicker than a gasp.

As Balz stood over the bed of his female, and watched as others tended her, he replayed each and every thing that had happened since he had caught Erika in his arms as she'd passed out. After he'd brought her back out here, his first call had been to Manny, and the guy had been right on it, firing up the mobile surgical unit that was downtown in the garage and rushing for Erika's neighborhood. On the way, Manny had called in his fellow healer, Doc Jane, to dematerialize over to the townhouse STAT. And she had brought with her her medically trained mate, Vishous.

It was all such a blur, but too acute as well. While Jane performed an exam and took vitals, Balz had told V everything he knew. Which was next to nothing: Perfectly fine. Went to the bathroom. Bruises all over her.

Balz would never forget the way Doc Jane had looked up at her mate . . . and shook her head. Like she didn't understand what was going on.

After that? V had taken his glove off. Balz had held his breath as the Brother stood over Erika's body and put that glowing weapon so close to her mottled skin that a flush of blood rose to the surface, cutting through the horrible bruising. He'd swept that thing up and down a third time as the next arrival came up the townhouse's stairs.

The Brother Butch. And as soon as Balz saw the male, he'd known . . . that they were not dealing with a medical emergency.

This was a metaphysical one. This was . . . about evil. Evil that had claimed his beloved.

Balz knew what Butch did out in the field, absorbing the essence of the Omega out of slayers who had been taken down. And it was with a feeling of absolute disbelief that Balz had said yes, yes of course, Butch could lie down next to Erika.

Proof positive that even bonded males could have a level head if the stakes were high enough.

And so Butch had lain down, chaste as could be, and taken Erika in his arms. By that time, it was clear that whatever process was occurring was speeding up. Her body was failing, her vitals slipping, her—

As reality snapped back into place, Balz transitioned from remembering things to experiencing them, his awareness shifting from the list of first-this, then-that, which he had been numbly detached from, to an achingly vivid this-is-really-happening.

It was the groan that did it.

The groan from the bed was agony. And it was not coming from Erika.

Butch, the former cop, jerked back from her and began to dry heave—

and Doc Jane was on it, producing a wastepaper basket from somewhere and holding it off the edge of the bed so he could roll over and vomit into it.

As the retching echoed through the too-quiet room, Balz's eyes traveled over his female. He'd pulled a sheet up to provide her with some dignity, and he'd appreciated that Doc Jane and the two males had been so respectful of her nakedness.

One of her arms was outside of the covers, and he recoiled at the deterioration of her skin.

"Manny's bringing the oxygen concentrator," Doc Jane said as Butch flopped over on his back. "And I'm going to run some saline into her."

Balz had never felt so helpless in his life. He didn't know—

A hard grip on his arm drew him away from the bed, and he looked over at V. "What—"

"Go," the Brother ordered. When Balz stared at him in confusion, V lowered his voice. "Sahvage told me where you were heading tonight. Go now and get the fucking Book. She doesn't have much time."

"But I have to—"

"Butch is the best shot at keeping her alive you have, even above us medical types. There's nothing you can do here. But you can bring that Book back. There has to be something in it that can help get whatever this is out of her."

"Get whatever . . ." Balz blinked. "You think this is a possession?"

And yet he knew that was the truth of it.

"I'm not sure what the fuck it is. But it's evil, that much I know—"

All of a sudden, Balz thought about the first time he and Erika had had sex. He could remember her orgasming . . . and her eyes rolling back. It had been right after that that Devina had stopped visiting him in his sleep.

What if the demon had merely relocated into Erika?

And she was killing the female out of spite, rotting her from the inside.

"*Fuck*," he barked. "Fuck!"

So this was why, when he'd asked Lassiter to come to see if the demon was gone, the angel hadn't sensed anything in him—but also hadn't looked right when he'd left. Lassiter had known that Devina was still—

"I'm going," Balz growled. "And I'll bring that Book back even if I have to kill that bitch."

Before he left, he went to the bed and dropped his head to Erika's ear. She was breathing in a wheeze, the rise and fall of her chest so shallow, it was almost not happening.

"I love you," he whispered. "I'm going to get you what you need. Just hang on. Erika, you've got to *hang on*."

◆   ◆   ◆

As Devina arrived back at her lair's building, her frame of mind had seriously improved.

Then again, a good fuck had always been a mood elevator for her, a clear sign that even though she was a non-temporal force of nature, the dopamine receptors in the body she projected herself into worked just fine.

And holy fuck, Lassiter was a good lay. Ohhhhh, man, if she'd thought Balthazar hated being with her, that was nothing compared to the angel's regrets. So obviously, she had stretched the fucking out for a good long time—and she wanted more of him. To make sure they weren't a one-night stand, she had big plans to do shit all about keeping her side of the bargain.

She'd leave that female of Balthazar's only when the woman was good and dead, something Devina could control by keeping the detective alive and suffering for quite some time.

God, Balz and that stupid human woman he loved so much. The demon had thought she'd use them for her spell, a great way to have revenge on him and get what she needed. And it was fun being inside the bitch and torturing them both: In the work of a heartbeat, she'd jumped from one to the other during a *le petit mort* moment in one of their sex sessions, her possession triggering an infection that had kindled for a day or two, before it had taken a firm toehold.

But as it turned out, the demon had found an even better candidate for her true love spell.

"You had a secret, angel, didn't you," she said out loud.

In spite of all the reasons she didn't deserve it, fate had given her one hell of a present tonight: Lassiter was in love.

And Devina had ruined everything. The instant she had taken that angel's virginity, which had been beyond enriching on an existential level, she had soiled him in his own mind, making him no longer worthy of the female he'd gotten soppy over.

What a surprise! And her spell's last stricture was met.

So it had been a great night—and even greater because thanks to that angel's sappy heart, she could now await the proper return of her blond Adonis.

Gliding through the building's front door—literally, because hello, it was way after hours so the thing was locked—she resumed her striding in the lobby, her stilletos clipping out a snare drum roll as she strode over the marble floor. Heading for the back stairs to go down into the basement, she would normally have played around with the nightshift humans on security detail. It was always a kick to fuck with the guards, sneak up behind them, play a little spook game.

Not tonight.

She had to get ready for her male.

"Talk about Christmas," she murmured as she descended and then hit the hall that took her to her lair. "Kwanzaa. Hanukkah."

The demon was whistling a little tune as she came up to her door and stepped through the reinforced panel, piercing into the other plane of existence—

The instant she entered her lair, she could feel that something wasn't right. Her eyes went immediately across to the Birkin display, but everything was where it was supposed to be, with the burned star on the top of her proverbial tree.

In the rest of the open space, her clothes were the same, the racks all orderly, nothing hanging cockeyed or anything.

The bedding platform was made.

The kitchen was neat. The furniture arranged as it had always been. Likewise, the tub and the towels and her sink were gleaming and static, just as she had left them.

But someone had been here, someone who shouldn't have been. She could scent them . . . and they smelled like a meadow of wild flowers—

"Nooooooo!"

Devina whirled around to where the Book had been suspended in thin air. It was gone . . . and no trace of it was left behind, not the rancid stench, not a fragment of parchment, not a shadow of where it had once been. The whole lair was empty of the ugly, stinking thing.

It could not escape on its own, though. It needed a proxy to become mobile.

Who the fuck had been in her space—

At that moment, as if the universe were answering her demand, she sensed arrivals outside in the corridor. Many of them. A cadre's worth of them.

Pivoting on her heel toward the door, she peered through the panel and what she saw got her attention, even though she was an immortal.

The Black Dagger Brotherhood and the Band of Bastards were just outside her lair, and they were fully armed and ready to fight.

"What the fuck," she muttered. "I have to get dressed and do my goddamn hair."

CHAPTER FORTY-EIGHT

This is where she was," Sahvage announced. "That last door."

Even though the Brother had been their guide into the building, he stepped aside so that Balz could now lead the way down the long basement corridor. As the other males flanked in behind him, they paid honor to a bonded male's right to *ahvenge* his female.

Protect his female.

To that end, a dozen more fighters than he expected had shown up in Erika's living room—and they had come with supplies. He had been given a new pair of guns. And fresh leathers. And steel daggers in a holster. And the best backup any warrior could have asked for.

Except for his Erika, of course.

As they went along now, Sahvage said in his ear, "To get inside, my Mae had to open up some kind of access to the other dimension the demon keeps her shit in. I don't think just busting down the door is gonna do it."

"We'll get in," Balz countered in a grim voice. "She wants me, so if I'm here, she'll come to me—if only because she'll have to lord her possession of Erika over me—"

From out of the corner of his eye, he saw a flash go by. It was so quick, so camouflaged, that if he hadn't been expecting it, he might have ignored the visual disturbance or written it off as something that was immaterial—

The shadow popped up right in front of him, the ghostly, evil apparition taking substance and falling into a fighting stance.

Partytime.

Balz let out a battle cry and raised a dagger as well as one of his autoloaders. He would rather have gone hand to hand with the thing, but there was no time. So he aimed that fucking muzzle, and just as an "arm" extension of the entity snapped out and caught him in the chest, he started pumping off bullets.

The screeching was so loud, his ears rang, but like he gave a fuck—

As he heard a shout right behind him, he glanced over his shoulder.

It was an ambush.

Shadows were everywhere, an entire army of them, materializing in the corridor, pulling free of inset doorways, and the contours of pipes in the ceiling, and from the deep well of darkness that suddenly enveloped the stairwell they had descended—

The strike came to the side of his face, like a slap made up of a thousand bee stings. Blinded by pain, he jammed the muzzle of his forty forward, and as he felt resistance, he discharged more rounds, just let the autoloader autoload the fuck out of everything that was in the magazine.

The shadow in front of him was driven back, tripping, falling, in a way that allowed Balz to get closer to his goal, to that doorway Sahvage had pointed out. As his eyesight improved, he switched his dagger for his other gun and just kept forcing the retreat, the popping sounds of the bullets and the horrible screaming noise one hell of a concert.

And what do you know, it was in surround sound.

It was too dangerous to check behind himself again, but he knew that the Brothers and his fellow bastards were engaging as well. Except they were doing it with one hand tied behind their proverbial backs: They couldn't use their guns because he would be downstream of any misses, and given how fluid the shadows were, there were a lot of lead slugs that didn't hit their targets—

A second shadow jumped him, and the weight of the damn thing plus the stinging sensation that went all the way through him were so great an overload that he went down on his knees.

And that was when shit went GOAT fuck on him.

He had to lose his guns. As he was rolled and pummeled, he didn't know which way was up, much less where his fellow fighters were. Unable to keep things straight, he couldn't risk killing anyone on his side.

Dropping the autoloaders, he switched to daggers, jabbing his hands into his jacket and outing his silver-bladed slicers. With practiced skill, he swiped at anything he came in contact with, and the defense was good enough to earn him some space. Except it never lasted. The entities were relentless. They were winning.

His energy was flagging.

An image of Erika on her bed dying gave him a brief second wind, turning those daggers into an extension of his arms, of his body, of his will. But as the punches and kicks kept coming at him, the rally didn't last.

Just as his head rang like a bell from him being thrown into the ground like a toy they wanted to break, at the very moment his consciousness started to ebb, as hope departed him and strength went along with it—

A wraith-like apparition appeared before him.

Dressed in black leather.

With a hand-rolled Turkish cigarette clenched between bright white teeth.

"V?" Balz mumbled as he stared up in confusion.

What was he doing here? Was this was a figment of his imagination—

The Brother didn't get out a gun. No daggers either. As he exhaled a plume of smoke, he ripped off that lead-lined glove of his.

Annnnnd that, folks, was all she wrote.

Vishous took that nuclear-bright hand of his and he wielded it like a motherfucker, slapping the two shadows that had taken Balz to the ground like the entities misbehaved and it was the Middle Ages.

As the tables were turned and Balz's attackers had to go on the defensive, he scrambled to his feet. Located his guns. Reloaded—

Poppppp! Poppppp!

Andjustlikethat the pair of shadows were gone.

Balz jumped up to the Brother, and grabbed the male's leather jacket. "What are you doing here!"

"She's still alive," V said as they both panted. "But Sahvage triggered the emergency code so I had to come."

Balz dragged the Brother in for a quick, hard embrace. And as he hugged back, V muttered, "You're welcome."

They pulled apart, and Balz said, "I have to go—"

"I'll join the fray." V cracked his knuckles. "But we might need a miracle. This is bad."

They both glanced down at the hall. It was a melee of hand to hand, the Brothers and the bastards engaging with the—

All at once, the shadows disappeared.

Sure as if they had been called off by their maker, the vampire warriors went from fighting tangible foes to kicking, punching, and stabbing at thin air. As they tripped, fell, slammed into the floor and the walls, the battle was over as quickly as it had started.

"What the fuck?" someone said.

"Where the hell—"

"—did they all—"

"—fucking go?"

It was the same snippets of conversation from each one of them, the males remaining braced with their daggers and their fists, their fighting stances unchallenged by any enemy.

Hard breathing was the only sound. No more screeching.

Until a door opened.

Balz pivoted toward the portal. And he knew who was coming out before he even saw her.

"Devina," he growled.

The demon walked out into the corridor, a red dress hugging her curves, a string of pearls around her neck, her heels so high that she was as tall as he was. With her hair swept up on top of her head and diamonds sparkling on her earlobes, she was Julia Roberts, *Pretty Woman*'ing it off to the opera, so classy, so elegant.

The fucking cunt.

"Give me the Book," Balz demanded as he pointed a gun at her. "Give me the fucking Book!"

She didn't seem to hear him. And that was when he realized she was translucent, like a hologram. Even if he'd tried to shoot her, the bullets were going to go right through.

She did pause as she came up to him. "It's gone." Her voice was distracted and her dazed eyes stared past him. "I don't know who took the Book, but it can't leave on its own. So someone got in there and walked out with it."

And then she just kept going.

Balz lunged for her, but when he tried to grab her arm, he just snatched at air. There was no substance to the demon at all.

"What about Erika!" he yelled. "You get the fuck out of her—"

Devina glanced over her shoulder. "It's too late. Sorry. Oops."

As she resumed walking, he started to go after her—but V locked a grip on him and hauled him back. "No, you let her go. *Let. Her. Go.* We'll find Lassiter. Lassiter will help us—"

That was when the lights came back on in the stairwell. And as the demon easily walked through the the crowd of Brothers and bastards, even while they stabbed at her and tried to catch her, someone emerged down at the base of the steps.

Someone else . . . arrived.

On the far side of her see-through body, a blond-haired male in a black suit stepped into the hall.

Were those roses in his hands? Like . . . a dozen red *roses?*

And it was like he didn't see what else was in the basement: The guy only had eyes for the demon, the transfixion so complete, it was as if he were under her spell.

V hissed to the group: "Retreat. We need to get out of here. That motherfucker in the suit is the son of the Omega and we're all wounded. Retreat, *now.*"

Balz wanted to argue. He wanted to fight. He wanted the fucking Book and to hell with Lassiter. But as the warriors began to dematerialize out one by one, their broken bodies bearing the toll of the shadows' impacts, he knew he was out of gas, too.

The angel was his only hope.

As he admitted defeat, the last thing Balz saw before he closed his eyes was the blond male grabbing the demon and pushing her up against the wall. Their heads came together as their bodies fused into one . . . and then, with those red roses still in his hand, the male tilted his head and kissed Devina like he had been waiting his entire life for her. As if she were his one true love.

Balz intended to dematerialize out. But his body wobbled on his feet, his vision got wonky, and he couldn't seem to remember what he was doing or why. Out of hope, without a plan, and knowing his mate was dying . . .

What was all that copper he was suddenly smelling?

"Oh, shit," he heard V say. "Jesus, Balz, you've been stabbed."

Oh. Well. That explained the smell—

His last thought was of Erika.

Maybe he'd see her in the Fade.

Right . . .

. . . about . . .

. . . *now.*

CHAPTER FORTY-NINE

Exactly nine minutes before Devina arrived at the building down-town, at precisely thirteen minutes before Sahvage led Baltha-zar down into the basement there, Rahvyn returned to Luchas House one last time. She was careful to hide what she had with her in her jacket, and after checking in with the social worker, she went up-stairs. On her made bed, with its smoothed duvet cover and precisely stacked pillows, she took out that which had called to her.

The Book was warm to the touch, and as she put her palm upon it, it seemed to get even warmer, as if her body heat compounded its own.

The temptation to open the tome was overwhelming, and she felt as though the thing wanted her to lift its cover, the pages ruffling them-selves between its hard, leathered confines.

It was alive, she realized. Living though it did not have breath or heart rate.

"You have caused much trouble," she said.

A shudder registered under her hand, contrition made manifest.

"I know you did not mean to. But you are responsible for what you have wrought. You must know that." She petted the bumpy cover to soothe its feelings. "In that, you and I are much the same. We are neither one nor the other, neither good nor evil, and that means we are by definition bad. We are agents of chaos, we are not right for this world."

She passed her hand down its spine. "And that is why you called me to you, is it not. You know you have done wrong and you are tired of being used. You assess the balance of your deeds and recognize more ill has been done with you than you can bear. You need to just get away."

The Book seemed to let out a sigh, air leaving the bottoms of its pages. "All right, then."

Rahvyn looked around the tidy little room, and recalled setting up the furniture with Nate. All had had to be built of pieces and hardware provided, from the bed to the bureau to the bedside table. It had taken them quite a while, and as they had worked together, there had been such hope in his face. Distracted by her own troubles, she had been ignorant of his affection at the time. But she had recognized thereafter certain looks that he imparted upon her and tried to hide, a special warmth entering his voice and his eyes, whenever he was in her presence.

She had cursed him twice, hadn't she.

Once with eternal life. The second with unrequited love.

Putting her hand in her pocket, she took out the cell phone she had been given, one of so many new instruments and mechanicals that existed in this era. She was not sure she would miss any of them.

She would miss Nate, however.

Calling up his number, she dialed and listened to the ringing. She kept her hand on the Book as she awaited him to answer. He did not.

Voice mail was a strange concept to her, but then again so much was.

For her next destination, she would go back in time, to a simpler era. Verily, this one did not suit her at all.

When it was time for her to record her words, she cleared her throat and became nervous, as it was only the second such message she had ever left, the first being to her dear cousin, right before she had gone to retrieve the Book. "Ah . . . Nate. I am calling to let you know that . . . I am sorry I have to go. And to thank you for being such a good friend to me. I wish I could stay, I do. But I must be moving on. I left a voice mail with Sahvage, too. I told him to mentor you. He has lived in your state for centuries. He will guide you in ways I cannot."

She was not sure how to end things.

"Goodbye, Nate."

Ending the call, she placed the cell phone on the bedside table and picked up the Book. Then she went over to the window, cracked it, and closed her eyes.

When she was calm enough, she dematerialized out to the field. The flowers Lassiter had given her were still alive, the springy bounce of their petals and greenery providing a lift to both her steps and her spirits, one that stayed with her as she walked the Book into the forest, to the great wound in the earth that marked her arrival.

Dropping herself down into the hole, she held the Book to her chest.

She had said goodbye to the only two people who would miss her.

Well, and then there was her angel. But they had already parted after their one and only embrace. She had so wanted to ease his suffering, but he had been willing to share none of it with her. In the end, she had had to let him go because he had demanded it of her.

And because she had to for her own reasons.

They might have had a future, if they had been other souls. Their destinies could not intersect in any permanent way, however.

Star-crossed lovers, she thought as she called upon the energy of the universe.

The light that came for her was so brilliant it did not just blind Rahvyn, it blew her molecules apart, scattering her off the earth, to an infinite number of planes of existence.

And with her the ancient tome, which she would find a safe place for, far, far, far from the contact of mortals.

At least in this, she felt as though she was doing a service unto her species and humanity at large.

Like her, it was only safe for the Book to remain . . . untouchable forevermore.

CHAPTER FIFTY

Y ou need to wake the fuck up and save him."

The words were spoken to Erika in a flat tone. Like the mouth they came out of was a ticker tape sharing an update on stocks or something.

"If you want him to live," the voice persisted, "then you need to get your ass up and go to him. Without you, he's going to fucking die."

Maybe this is a dream, she thought. Which would explain so much— Erika's eyes popped open. And she wrenched her head to the side.

It was the goateed fighter, the one who had stood next to her a lifetime ago by the mobile surgical unit—and somehow, she was not surprised. What shocked her . . . was that she was still alive.

With a full-body jerk, she looked down at herself. She was in a hospital bed, and as the covers over her lower body registered, she was terrified at what was underneath.

"You're going to be fine," the goateed vampire muttered. "He's the one we're worried about now—"

"You were there," she said in a rough voice. "After Balthazar carried me back to bed . . . you were there—where am I?"

"We don't have time for this—"

"What day is it?"

Her mind refused to move very fast, even as some instinct told her that she needed to hurry the hell up—

"You're in the Brotherhood's training facility. You were brought in last night. I've been treating you with this." He held up a gloved hand. "And with the help of my roommate, we were able to get the infection out of you. It was touch and go—"

"Balthazar!" She sat up. Then threw out a hand for help as the world spun. "Where is he—"

"Annnnd now we're really awake. Fucking finally."

There were other males in the room, and she recognized some of them. They were injured, too, wraps on their hands, arms in slings, one of them had an eye patch. The instant she looked at them, they bowed to her, lowering their heads in respect.

She was surrounded by vampires. And she'd never felt safer.

"Where is Balthazar?" she demanded.

"In the next room—"

Erika threw the covers off herself and put her feet over the edge of the bed. The mattress seemed seven feet off the ground. She didn't care. She launched herself right—

As her legs collapsed, the goateed one caught her weight. Except then, when she went to head for the door, he held her back.

"Wait, IV. You've got an IV."

Lifting her arm, she had a moment of relief that her skin was a normal color again. Then she ripped out the cannula in her arm and started walking.

"Don't you dare stop me again," she muttered to Goatee as he jumped forward to catch up. "I've got to get to him."

His chuckle was one of respect. "I'm not going to keep you two apart. Don't worry about that, female."

The fighter with the scarred upper lip held the door open, and there were two others who helped her along. When the door to another room was opened for her, she looked in—

"Oh . . . *God.*"

Somebody took her arm. Goatee? Yes, that was the one.

"I know he looks bad," the vampire said. "But he's a bonded male. As soon as he hears your voice, it's his best shot at coming back. When he was fighting a shadow, we think the entity somehow got ahold of one of his daggers—and did some serious damage. He lost a lot of blood, and he's sustained a stroke. It was a minor one, but he needs a reason to fight. You're it."

Lying back against the pillows, plugged into all kinds of machines, Balthazar looked already dead. And holy hell from the injuries. His face so swollen, his features were nearly unrecognizable, and his breathing was nothing but a wheeze.

Erika rushed to his bedside, using Goatee like a walker, pushing him in front of her at the same time she hung on to the waistband of his leather pants.

"Balthazar. It's me. I'm here."

As she leaned over him, a Kleenex was put in her hand and she impatiently swiped at her eyes. "I need you, please come back to me."

Dropping her head next to his on the pillow, she was aware she was getting really weak, and Goatee must have recognized this. She felt her body get lifted up and settled on the bed next to Balthazar's.

She wanted to touch him, but his skin was covered in welts. And as the world went on another ride around her, she couldn't believe they were both in such rough shape. But that didn't matter.

They had each other to live for—and that was more than enough.

Steeling her resolve, calling on every ounce of will she had in her soul, she turned his face to her.

And spoke in a loud, clear demand, the three most important words she knew: "I love you."

✦　　✦　　✦

It was what Balz had been waiting for.

In the midst of his stasis, trapped between death and life, in a prison of pain, he had prayed that his Erika would come to him. He had refused to believe she was dead, that the demon had won, that the Book was lost. If he just held on, if he fought the lure of the Fade, surely she would come for him, and he would follow her scent and the sound of her voice out of—

Balthazar, come back to me. I need you. Please . . . after everything, don't let this be our end. Remember my basement, be with me down there again, hold me . . . don't leave me . . .

He thought he would have to fight to return.

Instead, he just floated his way up to her. As his female whispered to him, he orientated himself to her syllables and they became his map, showing him the way to go home.

Rising, rising . . . rising . . .

Opening his eyes, his vision was blurry. But he didn't need clarity to know her features because he saw them with his heart.

"Balthazar?" she said with wonder. "Balthazar?"

"I . . ."

"Oh, my God, he's alive, he's back!"

"Love . . ."

There were all kinds of conversations at that point, other people in the room with them talking with excitement, the voices ones that he recognized. Meanwhile, he didn't understand how Erika was still alive.

How was his female still alive? They hadn't brought the Book back. They hadn't . . .

Vishous?

The Brother Vishous was right at his bedside, and Balz focused on that gloved hand. Then he remembered the power in that palm, and what it had done to those shadows. He thought also of Butch who— there he was. The former homicide cop was by the bed, too, looking like he had food poisoning, his face sallow, a little green line around his mouth. As the pair of roommates met each other's eyes, they nodded, as if they'd worked hard together. As if they'd toiled on a project . . . and finally gotten it past a finish line.

No, Balz thought. They may have helped keep Erika alive, but something else had had to have intervened to cure the infection.

And he'd been saying something to her, hadn't he?

Oh. Right.

"You . . ."

As he finished that last word, Erika moved her face even closer to his own, and that was when he finally saw her properly.

"Beautiful . . . female . . . mine . . ." he croaked.

"Yes, yes—"

When she tried to kiss him, he hissed because he hurt all over—and he didn't care about the pain. "Kiss me anyway . . ."

Her lips were soft against his own, and then he was exhausted—but stayed where he was, a balloon tethered to life by her presence. As long as she was with him, he knew where he was supposed to be; wherever she was, was his place.

"I love you, too," she whispered.

At the end of the day, even though he had so many questions still, and so many blank spaces that needed filling in . . . that was all he needed to know, wasn't it.

The rest was history.

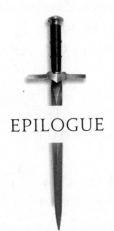

EPILOGUE

Three nights later . . .

Not all spring nights were warm. Some of them were down-right cold, and as Balz stepped out of the Brotherhood mansion's vestibule, the difference in temperature from the balmy foyer and the chilly great outdoors was enough to make him zip his leather jacket up over his steel daggers.

As he looked across the courtyard to the glowing lights of the Pit, his sight of the smaller caretakers' house was partially obstructed by the fountain. The great basin, with its central marble statue that spit water all over the place, was still winterized. Good thing. It was below freezing tonight.

Before he took off, he glanced back at the great manse. All of the diamond-paned windows were glowing, and with his keen ears, he could hear both the laughter of Last Meal as families lingered over dessert as well as the talk that was starting up in the billiards room as Brothers and fighters gathered around the pool tables.

It was all still home to him, this raucous, imposing life here, everything revolving around the First Family.

He was going to miss living with them, he thought as he walked down the steps.

He did not look back again.

Taking out his phone, he checked to see if the text he'd sent had been answered. When he saw that it hadn't, he put his cell back in an outside pocket.

Everyone was looking for Lassiter.

But Balz had a feeling he knew where the angel was. Closing his eyes, he took a deep, steadying breath . . . and dematerialized off the mountain. When he re-formed, the terrain was the same, though he was a good ten miles away, on the slope of a different Adirondack peak.

The hidden den he had squatted in, and which Fritz, butler extraordinaire, had more properly kitted out, was tucked behind a waterfall of boulders, the kind of thing that unless you were a bear looking to hibernate, you wouldn't know was there.

Not that anybody, even a bear, was out and about on this north-facing elevation—and fucking hell, if he'd thought that things were icy in front of the mansion, here he was in Siberia.

"It's me," he called out as he went around to a juncture between a rock the size of an SUV and another hunk of granite that would have given a king-sized mattress a run for the money for surface area. "And I know you're in here."

The wind pushed his words into the cave as he ducked down, bending his body in half to fight through a crevice. On the far side of the squeeze, candlelight, buttery yellow and very still, called him forward to an open area nearly big enough to be considered a living room.

He found the angel everyone was looking for sitting back on the pallet bed that had been kitted out with monogrammed duvets and feather pillows. Next to the male was a sterling silver candelabra on an inlaid French bombé chest, a propane stove, and enough camping supplies and nonperishable food to keep anybody going for a year.

It was like Versailles meets Bear Grylls.

"Seventy-two hours," Balz said gruffly. "They've been searching for you for three nights now."

The angel didn't look up; he just sat where he was, poised as if he were on the verge of getting to his feet, his elbows on his knees, his shoulders tilted forward, his long blond-and-black hair hanging in his face.

A sense of foreboding shimmied down Balz's spine. Or maybe it was more like clawed its descent.

"What did you do," Balz whispered.

When there was no response, he approached the angel, easing down onto his haunches, both his ankles cracking.

More loudly, he repeated, "I know the demon left Erika, but I don't know why."

Lassiter took a deep breath. "How are you feeling now?"

"Fine. It's just me in my skin."

"And what about Erika?"

Balz frowned. "She's fine, too."

"Good."

"V and Butch think they saved her, but they didn't, did they. You did."

It was hard to say exactly when Balz had made the connection. Difficult, too, to ascertain the precise combination of clues that led him to the truth that the male in front of him was not currently speaking of. But he knew he was right. And he knew he was looking at someone who had been where he himself had been, that frozen face and too-still body something he had seen in the mirror.

"You fucked her, didn't you," he breathed as he let himself fall back onto his ass. "Devina."

As the packed earth provided him with a seat that was about as comfy as a paddle, he passed a hand over his eyes.

With a grim voice, he continued, "She took herself out of Erika because you fucked her. You didn't want to, but you did anyway, and now you feel dirty and used and stained on the inside—"

"I didn't say that."

"You don't have to."

After a long moment, Lassiter shook his head. "You've got it wrong, actually. Well, part of it."

"Tell me." Then Balz added, "I won't tell anyone else."

There was another long silence. Then the angel said, "Devina had to ruin true love to get what she ultimately wanted. It was part of a spell she took from the Book. She'd intended the couple to be you and Erika. And you're right . . . I did what I did to get her out of you both. She refused to hold up her side of the bargain, however. When the Creator found out, He made her keep her promise to leave you two in peace."

"Well . . . shit." But then Balz frowned. "Wait a minute. She didn't ruin our love, though. You said she needed that for this spell thing, right?"

"It all worked out, didn't it? You and Erika are fine. You have your happily ever after."

Balz closed his eyes. The stroke he'd suffered still caused moments of confusion, and something wasn't adding up—but the angel was right. He loved his Erika and was so grateful that they had both survived the possessions.

He re-focused on the angel. There was something . . . still not adding up. Devina did not quit anything until she got what she wanted.

"How did you know I was here?" Lassiter asked.

"Just a lucky guess. You haven't been home and you aren't answering your phone. V went up to the Sanctuary to find you and you weren't there. None of the Chosen have seen you. I thought to myself, where would he go for some privacy? I figured you'd know about this place and use it."

"I could have been somewhere outside of Caldwell, you know."

"But you weren't. You aren't"

There was a long silence. And then Balz said hoarsely, "Thank you for saving us."

"I told you. It was the Creator, not me." Lassiter smiled in a dead way. "At least if I had been the one who rescued you both it would have been a little easier to live with."

This was still not making sense. But one thing was clear.

Balz narrowed his eyes. "I'm going to kill that bitch—"

Now the angel's head whipped up and his stare focused in a hard way. "No. You don't go anywhere near that demon. Are we clear? You fucking leave this right where it is. I gave up my own shot at love for nothing, as it turned out, but you've got yours as long as you don't wake up dead from being a fucking hero."

A wash of cold emotion hit Balz's head and ran down his entire body. "What did you say . . ."

Lassiter slashed a hand through the air, like he regretted saying too much. "Nothing. I didn't say a goddamn thing. Just know that when it comes to that demon, I don't have anything else I can trade with. I'm out of sacrifices, not that mine helped anyone but her. So stay the *fuck* away from her."

Balz put his palms forward. "Okay. Okay, I'll leave it alone."

"Tell the brothers and the bastards, too."

"Now that I can't do. You know that. For one, they'll know I found you. For another, like they listen to anybody? Except maybe Wrath, and even that's iffy from time to time."

"Goddamn hotheads. They'll fight with anything."

"They'll defend the race against anything, you mean."

Lassiter shook his head. "Well, whatever, they'll have to fight her without my interference going forward. I'm not supposed to help. It's against the Creator's rules. And I've done all I can."

With that, Lassiter retreated into himself once again, his head lowering, his back curving so he could hunch over his legs, his body stilling into statue-land again.

When Balz eventually got up, he felt a little dizzy, but it was from emotion, not because of anything medical. And he wasn't sure what the angel was going to do as he sat down on the bedding platform.

Lassiter didn't respond. Didn't seem to even notice.

Wrapping an arm around a set of big shoulders, Balz pulled the angel into him. That the male capitulated with the urging was a surprise—and then Balz was holding the savior of the race and staring off into the candle-lit interior of the hideaway. When his vision blurred, he closed his eyes.

How do you reconcile both gratitude and grief, he wondered.

"Thank you," he said softly. "I'm going to love her with everything I'm worth, for the rest of my life, and I owe it all to you."

"My sacrifice didn't mean shit, remember?" the angel returned. "Just enjoy true love enough for the both of us, okay?"

"I promise," Balz vowed through a tight throat. "I swear on the life of my *shellan.*"

◆   ◆   ◆

Back at her townhouse, Erika was in her bathroom, trying to get a look at herself—and not as in her face, but her whole body. With only the front of the medicine cabinet over the sink to work with, she was bending and stretching into all kinds of positions that were getting her little in the way of additional view angles, but closer to a herniated disk.

Screw Pilates. Just live in a house without a full-length mirror.

Well, that and care what you look like for once.

Giving up, she smoothed the red dress over her hips and tugged at the low neckline. Then she fiddled with the gold links that filled the space between her collarbones and her cleavage. In the Ann Taylor store, when she'd had the outfit on and been standing in front of the three-way, she had felt so beautiful. Now? In her bathroom? It was like she was wearing an imposter's clothes.

"What the hell possessed me to buy this," she muttered.

Besides, Balthazar had been talking about going to that 24-hour diner. Not some fancy place with tablecloths and a maître d'—

Down below, the door opened and two big feet registered on the floorboards, the creaking carrying up the staircase.

"It's me," Balthazar called out as he closed things.

There was no jangle of keys. She was getting used to that, the kind of thing she hadn't noticed until the love of her life had moved in with her—and didn't need them to get past dead bolts.

Not because he was a really good thief, either.

"How did it go?" She shut the medicine cabinet. "Did it . . . are we okay?"

She was coming out of the bath as he took the steps two at a time, an enormous figure dressed in black leather emerging at the head of the stairwell.

"Please tell me we're okay—"

He didn't speak as he entered her bedroom, and when she got a load of the tension in his face, she wanted to curse. And cry. Especially as he gathered her up in his arms and just held on to her like he was afraid she was going to disappear on him.

Like maybe he'd found out this was all a dream and his alarm clock was about to go off.

Like what had felt like destiny was the curse of star-crossed love.

"Shit," she whispered as she stroked his broad back. "Just . . . *shit.*"

When he'd left to see his King, whoever that was, it had been to iron out how much he could stay in his world and what he could do there if he was living in hers. Although some human mates had been allowed in his community, they'd all given up their human existences, and though she hated putting him in a predicament, she couldn't abandon her job. Balthazar, to his immense credit, hadn't given her an ultimatum to quit homicide. Instead, he'd been resolved to let his side go if things came to that.

And it looked like they had.

"Come here," she said as she drew him over to the bed. Their bed. "And you might as well just spit it out. I'd rather deal with reality, even if it sucks."

He sat beside her on the mattress, his weight such that she was tilted into his body. Not that she minded.

His scent, the dark spices she'd once thought were cologne, was as much a thrill in her nose as always, and as she studied his profile, he was even more mysterious and beautiful than he'd been when she'd first seen him.

After he'd allowed her to remember him, that was.

"Tell me," she murmured. Even though she knew—

He pulled himself together. "We're fine. And I can still fight and pull shifts at the Audience House. They've asked me to move out of the mansion, but I get that. It's the First Family's crib. The security risks are too great." He took a deep breath. "My cousins can't wait to spend some proper time with you. The Brothers and fighters as well—and their *shellans*, too. Wives, I mean."

Erika blinked. "Wait . . . what—"

"Vishous, you know him—well, he does all the security, and he's going to insist on coming here to upgrade your alarm system for the time being. And they are requiring us to move into a house that's better equipped for my safety. You know, daytime shutters. A tunnel escape. A little more rural, to get away from a congestion of your kind. But you'd said you were open to relocating?"

She shook her head. "No. I mean, yes, of course. But I don't understand. What went wrong then?"

Balthazar stared into space for a moment. "I love you with all that I am, all that I will ever be. And I don't care what I have to give up to be with you and keep you happy and safe. It's going to be my life's work."

Erika flushed, her heart warming inside the cage of her chest. Funny, she had waited a lifetime to hear those words, without being aware that they were what she'd wanted to hear. And now, sitting in a bedroom she had slept in for years . . . she was really and truly home.

But that was about him, wasn't it. Not any street address.

"I love you, too." She reached up and smoothed his hair. "I know this still must be hard for you. Moving out of—"

"Nah, that's not the tough part." His eyes searched her face. "I'd give up anything for you."

When he leaned in a little farther, she lifted her lips for his kiss and they lingered in that suspended moment forever. Then again, love made everything an eternity, whether it was a gasp or a heartbeat . . . or decades of life together.

As he eased back, he looked down her body—and his eyebrows popped. "Um . . ."

"Oh, yeah." She pulled at the bodice again. "It's a little much."

"Can I have a twirl? Just so I can see you properly."

Standing up, she struck a pose in front of him and then spun on the ball of one foot, as close to a ballerina as a homicide detective with no dance training or innate talent could get.

Which was to say, she'd have had better luck pretending to be a linebacker.

Balthazar stroked his jaw. "Damn, woman. You are . . . a frickin' smoke show in that dress."

"I am? Really?" Okay, enough with the "pick-me girl" stuff. "I mean, of course I am."

"I can ask Fritz to get me a suit? A proper one, with a tie and shoes that don't have steel toes? And then I can take you out properly."

Erika looked down at herself once again. Then she shook her head. "Actually, I think I'd like to just change into jeans? This is nice and all, and I guess I'll keep it. But it doesn't feel like me."

Her man reached out and snagged her waist. Pulling her close, he lowered his lids and murmured, "So you want to take it off?"

"Yeah. Is that okay?"

Biting his lower lip with his fangs, he purred deep in his throat. "A-okay. And allow me to help you. Call me Mister Zipper, m'lady."

When he stretched his arms up her back to the fastening, his face went right in between her breasts—and sure enough, the nuzzling and the licking left her liquid inside her skin.

"You've made all my wishes come true," she whispered as the red dress fell to the floor.

"Just wait until I lay you down," he vowed as he swept her off her feet.

Like only the man of her dreams could do.

As the male she loved did indeed lay her down and settle on top of her body, she smiled even though she wasn't fooled. There was something else under his shift to a happier mood. But he'd tell her when he was ready, and whatever it was, they'd get through it.

Together, they could get through anything.

True love was like that.

ACKNOWLEDGMENTS

With so many thanks to the readers of the Black Dagger Brotherhood books! This has been a long, marvelous, exciting journey, and I can't wait to see what happens next in this world we all love. I'd also like to thank Meg Ruley, Rebecca Scherer and everyone at JRA, and Hannah Braaten, Andrew Nguyên, Jennifer Bergstrom, Jennifer Long, and the entire family at Gallery Books and Simon & Schuster.

To Team Waud, I love you all. Truly. And as always, everything I do is with love to and adoration for both my family of origin and of adoption.

Oh, and thank you to Naamah, my Writer Dog II, and Obie, Writer Dog-in-Training, who both work as hard as I do on my books!

In Memoriam to Our Beloved Archieball.